Life in Spades

FRANCES FROST

Tony. Atteyne -
May you always
playa winning
hand.

Frances Frost -

For information, contact
InvisionBooks, LLC
P.O. Box 6102
Silver Spring MD 20916
www.invisionbooks.com

ISBN: 0989113906
ISBN-13: 978-0-9891139-0-8

DEDICATION

To D, L, B, J, N

Thank you to my family for allowing me the time and providing the

encouragement for this work. All I do is dedicated to you.

Gina

If she had ever bothered to think about dying, Gina would have imagined being an old woman, sitting in bed wearing a floral, lace-trimmed zipped-up robe with her salt-and-pepper hair neatly curled, surrounded by children and grandchildren. She would whisper a prophetic, wise bit of advice then gracefully close her eyes. That's how women should die. Not like this. Not wearing sneakers and sweaty running clothes in a playground on the Washington, D.C. side of Rock Creek Park. She wasn't even forty yet.

Gina should have learned from her great-grandmother's and grandmother's and mother's warnings:

Don't mess with white men. They're nothing but trouble.

Of course, she never listened because she knew everything. She was determined to show her mother this white guy was different. But if she died, Gina would never get to prove her mother wrong.

She leaned back on the green slide, her hips fitting neatly in the space designed for a child. She closed her eyes, listening to the echo of her heartbeat thumping against the warm plastic.

Gina regretted having told Alex her mother didn't like her dating a white man. If she had kept quiet, she wouldn't be running through the park, sweating and light-headed, on the verge of passing out. One night at happy hour, a few weeks before Gina found herself on a green children's slide, Alex had suggested that if they did something together, it would prove they were compatible, and her mother would realize he was a respectable, upstanding guy, albeit white. Gina should've known not to make any life plans while sitting at a bar facing shot glasses.

Alex first suggested doing charity work, perhaps volunteering for an NAACP event. Before Gina could comment, he admitted that was stupid, her mother would see right through it. A children's organization would make him seem sensitive, but maybe too fatherly and they weren't anywhere near that phase. He thought Habitat for Humanity was a good option since no one could argue with building houses for low-income families. Gina had glanced at her well-manicured nails and rolled her eyes up in the direction of her regularly coifed hair. By the time they were on their third round of tequila shots, he struck upon the idea that they should run the DC Parks Marathon together. Despite her customary wardrobe accessory of 3-inch heels and an aversion to sweat, Gina agreed. She said yes to the 26-mile run for a myriad of reasons: she wanted to make him happy, she thought there might be the slight chance her mother would come around, and most importantly, she thought Alex would discard the plan once they were sober.

As Gina recovered her breath, she realized that, like dying, she had also never considered what would become of her things when she died. She thought about her mother and friends inheriting her possessions. Cookie, her oldest and best friend, should get her collection of purses so she wouldn't have to carry that same red tote bag all the time. Laura would like the too-large easy chair, the one she always flopped into when she came down the hall to visit. All the houseplants, the live ones and the almost dead ones, too, could go home with Sherry who was much better than Gina at nurturing little things. Sherry hadn't lost much in the divorce, not financially, anyway, so she didn't need anything important.

Gina was the smallest in their group of four, so none of the others could fit her clothes; her mother would probably donate it all. She cringed at the thought of her collection of heels and boots in a picked over pile at the local clothes closet. She promised herself that if she did indeed survive, she would write a will.

Footsteps crunched behind her through the mulch and shuffled to a stop next to her. Although Gina knew it was Alex, she kept her eyes closed and didn't move, even when he touched her shoulder.

"Gina. You okay?"

She lay still. "I think I'm dying."

"You're not dying," Alex said, laughing. "You can't really be that tired."

Gina lifted her hand to shield her eyes from the sunlight sifting through the treetops. Alex stood there, a sweaty version of his handsome self, his gray-blue eyes smiling from underneath the shadow of his baseball cap. Her co-worker, friend, and lover.

"Are you trying to kill me? Was this part of your plan?"

He laughed again and reached to pull her up from the slide. Gina raised her eyebrows at him as if still contemplating a possible ulterior motive.

"What are you talking about? You've run one mile. One. I can almost see the car from here."

"Good. Go get it so we can go home." Gina let him pull her out of the green molded plastic.

With his arm around her shoulder, Alex walked back to the car. "We've got a lot of work to do if we're going to make it for the long run."

Sherry

Sherry heard the house phone ringing as she opened the door of her tudor-style cottage.

"Goodman Vivian," the caller ID announced.

Sherry dropped her gym bag and water bottle on the bench inside the door and rushed into the kitchen to reach the phone before Vivian hung up. Three missed calls while she was at Pilates class, all from her sister.

Why didn't she leave a message, Sherry thought, pulling off her blue athletic jacket. She filled a kettle and put it on the stove to boil then dialed Vivian's number.

The phone rang one and a half times before her sister's voice filled the airwaves. "Sherry! I've been tryin' to call you all morning! Where have you been? Why haven't you called me back?"

"Calm down. I was at the gym. Why didn't you leave a message?" Sherry heard her sister huffing as if she were trying to stop crying enough to talk. "Viv, what's the matter?"

"I don't know where I went wrong. It's so hard, you know, it's only me and I can't be with her all the time, but I thought I raised her good, taught her right. I took her to church. I put her in a good school. Hasn't she been watchin' me all these years, strugglin' to try to raise her all by myself? Maybe I made it look too easy, actin' like I didn't need nobody to help me, she didn't really understand all that I was doing to keep my head above water."

Apparently, Sherry's niece, Jordan, had done something to upset Vivian. Again. Last year, it was not studying hard enough and barely making it out of the eleventh grade.

"What has my dear Jordan done now?" Sherry opened the cupboard to retrieve a china teacup, one of the four remaining from her wedding set. She had dropped the first cup the day her then-husband appeared on the news, being escorted by police out of his Capitol Hill office. His trial and conviction on several counts of financial wrong, including misuse of campaign funds, embezzlement, and bribery, explained how they had been able to afford their vacations, his fishing yacht, and his Mercedes. She had thrown the second cup across the kitchen after the divorce was final. At least she had an even set again.

She leaned against the counter, waiting to hear about her niece's most recent exploits.

"I don't even know how to say this, I can't even believe it myself."

Sherry heard Vivian blow her nose, still crying.

"Jordan is pregnant."

"What!" Sherry fumbled, trying to keep hold of her teacup and the phone. "Oh, Viv. Are you sure? How do you know? Who's the father?" Sherry sat on one of her brushed-iron bar stools, placing her teacup on the kitchen counter. She kicked off her sneakers without untying them and pushed them to the side.

"I shoulda known somethin' was wrong with her, I mean, I'm her mother right? She's been lookin' a little sickly, even thrown up a few times. I thought maybe she was stressed, maybe had the flu. Maybe she had become lactose intolerant." Vivian took a deep breath and blew her nose again.

"Never even crossed my mind that she could be pregnant. For God's sake, Sherry, I'm a nurse! How could I not know my own daughter was pregnant? I should turn in my nursing license, good gracious. If she had been a patient and I missed these big ol' clues, I'd be fired. But as a mom, I can go bumblin' along totally clueless."

"Well, unless she tells you what's going on, how're you supposed to know?" Sherry said.

"Because I'm her mother. I'm supposed to know these things. That's what mothers do -- know the stuff kids don't want them to know. Good mothers, anyway."

"Oh, please, don't do that, don't blame yourself."

Over the years, Sherry had had to reassure Vivian countless times that she was doing a good job as a single mother. Vivian had become pregnant her sophomore year of college. Sherry was in her junior year of high school when Jordan was born. Until she left for college herself, Sherry helped their mother raise Jordan while Vivian stayed in school in Atlanta. When Vivian finished school and established herself with a nursing job at the Raleigh Durham Hospital, she took Jordan back to live with her. Sherry knew Vivian's biggest life regret was that Jordan didn't have a father in her life. Before Jordan was even born, the father told Vivian he didn't want anything to do with either of them, and hadn't changed his mind in the past seventeen years. Vivian had always hoped Jordan would follow a different path to motherhood. Sherry could imagine her sister was now broken-hearted that she evidently wouldn't.

"How many times have I told her – 'no one in the house when I'm not home'? And we've talked about safe sex. Well, I tried to talk about abstinence and she looked at me like I was growin' a horn."

"I told you that you needed to tell her more about protection…"

"Don't start with what you told me, Sherry. I know, I know." Vivian sighed. "Still, I didn't really think she was having sex with that boy."

"What boy?" Sherry asked.

"You know she's been going out with that boy, Brandon. She sent you the picture from the winter dance. He seemed like a nice guy, comes from good folks, I guess." Vivian paused a moment.

Sherry was sure that her sister had resorted to one of her nervous tics, either pulling on a dreadlock or biting a nail. On her end, Sherry was biting her lip. She used to bite her nails, too, until she started getting manicures and decided maintaining chewed up nails was too expensive.

"Okay, so I was in denial, but I couldn't wrap my head around the idea that she was actually, already, having sex," Vivian continued. "Dang! How many pregnant teenagers have I seen wander into the emergency room in labor? How could I not know? How could I bury my head this much? My child is three months pregnant!"

The whistle from the tea kettle startled Sherry as she tried to figure out what to say next. She reached over to turn off the stove and poured boiling water into the cup. She swished an herbal mint tea bag back and forth, calming herself with the routine.

"So, how is Jordan takin' all of this? What's she thinkin'?"

Under stress, both Vivian and Sherry's perfect grammar gave way to the "lazy English", as their mother called it, of their North Carolina upbringing.

"She's a bit scared, nervous. I see it now that I know what's going on with her, but that's to be expected, right? She hasn't told anyone, other than Brandon. Not even her girlfriends know yet. She took the test by herself, then told him about it. She's still getting used to the idea and nervous about what her friends are going to say."

"Yeah, I guess she would be," Sherry said.

"I should've known, the way she was sneaking around the house, tryin' to avoid me." Vivian paused. "I'm such a bad mom. How could I ignore all that?"

"Viv, you're not a bad mom. You've done the best that you can for her. This is..." Sherry stopped before saying 'her fault'. "This is a situation she has gotten herself into and we're going to help her, like we always do."

Sherry winced as she asked the next question. "Is she gonna keep it, the baby?"

"Oh, yeah, of course, she's gonna keep the baby," Vivian answered quickly as if any alternative would never be a consideration.

Sherry sighed in relief while her sister continued talking.

"Jordan thinks they're gonna be a family. He said he'd take care of her. She thinks he and his parents are going to support their baby. Has she not looked around, taken a look at her own life? Has she seen any daddy around here? I mean, does she really think this boy is going to stay with her?"

"He might, Viv. Maybe his parents will help out. Have you talked to the boy or his parents?"

"No. She just told me last night before I came to work." Vivian blew her nose again. "I gotta calm down and pull myself together before I talk to his parents. I want to go today but I'm heading into a second shift and I don't want them to think their son's baby-mama's mama is a tired-looking, raving lunatic running around in her pajamas."

Despite the situation, Sherry laughed picturing her two-hundred pound sister in purple nurse's scrubs, "her pajamas" as Jordan had called them when she was a kid, and rubber shoes, dreads piled on top of her head, standing on the boy's family's doorstep, crying about being their grandchild's other grandmother.

"Maybe in a few days I can make it over there. I should have a plan when I go talk to them, don't you think? I can't show up crying, have a cup of coffee, and go home. What I'm supposed to say? 'Sorry, my daughter's having your son's baby? I know you planned for him to go to some fancy college, but you better figure out a way to take care of your grandchild?' Oh, gracious, I'm not ready for this. I need a cigarette."

Sherry heard a rustling and then crunching. This was the signal her sister was starting to calm down: Vivian was eating potato chips. The verbal request for a cigarette was a vestige of Vivian's old habit of going through several cigarettes when trying to think through a situation. She blamed her weight gain on the school's stop smoking campaign that had convinced Jordan her mother would one day drop dead on the floor. To stop her daughter from tiptoeing into her room each night and prying her eyes open to make sure she wasn't dead, Vivian promised to stop smoking. She then promptly replaced the Virginia Slims with Lays.

"So Jordan, she's okay? I mean, you know, as 'okay' as she can be, right now?"

"Jordan's going to be all right, I guess." More crunching came from Vivian's end. "She made up this crazy reason why she wasn't playin' lacrosse this spring. She didn't like it anymore, she didn't think she'd get playing time. That should've been a clue, too, right? All these years playin', all the money I've spent on sticks and pads and camps, and in her senior year she's not gonna play?"

Vivian had worked hard to keep her daughter in private school. She was sure a private education would give her a step up in the world, a comfortable level of protection from all the evils of public school and the downfalls of having a single mother. But all the modern technology, small classes, and nationally recognized faculty obviously didn't keep her from the same temptations haunting public schools. Hormonal boys seemed to lurk on high-priced, well-tended school grounds as well as county maintained ones. And apparently hormonal girls' emotions weren't suppressed in buildings covered in ivy.

Vivian continued telling Sherry about her daughter's symptoms and the drastic turnaround of the life she had planned for her daughter. Vivian flip-flopped between being optimistic that she'd be able to support Jordan and crying over her daughter being a single teen-age mother, despite the boy's promise of being there for her. Upset she hadn't been a better role model, Vivian seemed as confused as Jordan surely was.

Knowing her sister could talk for hours, Sherry caught Vivian on a good note, just as she was talking about being able to provide a safety net for her daughter.

"Hey, Viv. I've got to go," Sherry said. "I've got to show a house and I'm not even dressed yet. Are you gonna be okay? Can you take a break for a few more minutes and I'll check on you this afternoon?"

"Sure, I'll be fine. Call after four o'clock. Jordan should be home by then and she wants to talk to you, anyway."

"I'll call you guys later. Don't cry anymore, okay? We're gonna take care of this, we're gonna take care of the baby. Okay?"

Vivian promised not to cry anymore for the day and blew her sister a kiss through the phone before hanging up.

Sherry quickly showered and blow-dried her short natural hair. While in college, going through a period of realizing their black-ness, Vivian, then Sherry, shunned hair processing chemicals and decided to grow their hair out in dreads. Sherry's lasted until the divorce, when she found she needed to redefine herself. She cut off the dreads and dyed her black hair to brownish red, a pretty contrast against her caramel skin. She started going to the gym, finally learned to swim, and lost a few pounds. She even took guitar lessons for a while.

At the same time, realizing she was going to have to take care of herself, Sherry took on additional desk hours at the real estate office to get more sales calls. She made enough money and contacts to finally open her own real estate office last year. Sherry now had four agents, an office assistant who had followed her from her first broker's office, and her own portfolio of investment properties. She was going out this morning to find a home rental suitable for a diplomat who would be moving soon with his family.

Dressed in a navy blue pencil skirt, white blouse, and burgundy cardigan, Sherry grabbed her black leather briefcase and purse. On her way out the door, she realized that she never did finish her tea while talking to her sister. Sherry checked her watch and decided she had enough time to stop by Cookie's bakery to pick up a quick breakfast and cup of tea.

Cookie

Cookie switched the pink and brown apron covered with floured handprints for another identical, clean one and pushed through the swinging half-doors separating the kitchen and front bakery.

The bakery filled with the scent of coffee, layered with the sweetness of sugar and cinnamon and speckled with chocolate. A keen nose could pick out the vanilla and almond extracts swirling through the batters, the surprising smell of vinegar poking through the red velvet.

She pulled up the shades on the windows and tied open the long, pink-rosebud floral print curtains framing the front window. As she unlocked the door, she saw Sarah, her sole employee, strolling leisurely along the sidewalk from the direction of the Metro stop, her orange afro bouncing on top of her head as she nodded rhythmically. The ever-present white headphone cords hung from her ears. Sarah was great with customers and really good at cleaning up the kitchen, but the matter of getting to work on time still evaded her.

"Morning," Sarah called. She shook the cowbell hanging on the door as she stepped into the bakery. "I'm here!"

"Glad you could make it this morning," Cookie said, picking dried leaves from the miniature rose plant sitting on the old white Agar oven at the end of the display counter. Cookie had bought the non-working model because it reminded her of her grandmother's kitchen.

"Me, too! I was shooting a video for this group over in Southeast and we didn't finish 'til like four o'clock and I barely got home and got to sleep before it was time to get up and get over here. Man, I need some coffee." Sarah continued her monologue, peeling off her hooded sweatshirt, as she wandered back into the kitchen.

Cookie unlocked the cash register. The bills and coins she had left the night before for change were in the designated slots.

Sarah was still talking when she came back to the display counter carrying a tray of creamers and milk. "I tried to tell the girl that the dress was all wrong and wouldn't look good on camera, but she didn't want to listen. I mean, just because I was the cameraman, she thought I didn't know what I was talking about."

Cookie glanced at Sarah's outfit: red and black plaid leggings, a pink lacy shirt, white socks and black low boots. "I can't imagine why she didn't take your advice." She handed the register key to Sarah, who stuffed it into her apron pocket.

"Right? But hey, it's her video. What can I do? I can only work with what they bring me." Sarah poured herself a cup of coffee. After a few gulps to wake herself up, she turned back towards the kitchen. "Now, let's see what we've got today."

They circled back and forth through the kitchen and the front counter all morning. Sarah replenished trays for the front counter and waited on customers. Cookie brought her new trays, finished the baking, and boxed up orders to be delivered all over the city.

Sherry rushed in the door as Cookie brought a fresh tray of muffins out. She pulled her wallet from her purse and handed Sarah her bankcard. "One of those green teas and a muffin, apple cinnamon is fine, please. Good morning, ladies."

"Morning," Cookie said to her friend. "You look nice. Where you going today?"

In contrast to Cookie's everyday white button-down shirt, jeans, and gray Converse sneakers, Sherry was dressed in a skirt and blouse with high heels. Cookie's friends encouraged her to change her outfit some days, wear a different colored shirt or a skirt, but she stayed true to her uniform. She even carried the same red leather tote bag, unlike her friends who changed purses on a regular basis, sometimes daily. But their jobs required them to look more professional. Cookie baked cupcakes and pastries all day. The jeans and shirt kept her morning routine simple; the pink and brown apron was one of the half-dozen she'd go through by the time the day was done.

"I'm showing houses to clients looking for a nice rental." Sherry paused, then sighed. "I just got off the phone with my sister. My niece is pregnant." Tears were on the edges of her eyes and she blinked quickly before they could fall.

Cookie gasped and her eyes widened.

"Yeah, I know. I'll have to fill you all in on the details, later. Talking to her, I'm running late now."

Sarah handed Sherry her order and her bankcard.

"Thanks. Let's get drinks after you close, okay?" Sherry said on her way out the door.

Drew Archer, the manager from the liquor store down the street opened the door and held it open as Sherry rushed past him.

"Hey, Drew," Sarah said. "What d'you know good?" She poured a medium cup of coffee without him having to ask.

"Nothing exciting. Beer coming in, that's all," he said, picking up the morning paper from the counter. "What about you?"

"You know me, always looking for my next job, another hustle, especially if I can get some more film work. That would be good."

"You aren't going to leave the bakery, are you?"

"Nah, what would she do without me?" Sarah pointed her thumb at Cookie and grinned. "Whatever I find, I'm sure I can work it around being here."

"That's good," he said. He took his coffee and newspaper and sat at one of the round tables by the window. "Cookie, you still have the Metro section?" He asked, flipping through the paper. "And Food, too?"

Cookie retreated to the kitchen and returned waving both of the missing sections. "Here you go. Forgive me for reading my paper."

Drew laughed as he retrieved the newspaper and returned to his window seat.

Cookie leaned on the counter, sipping coffee and watching the people out on the sidewalk rushing to work. She felt her heart involuntarily quicken when she saw the familiar blue uniform and rasta-hat step into the frame of the shop window.

The cowbells clanged as David walked in whistling. Cookie smiled and wondered what his hair looked like under the striped, poofy hat.

Sarah waved at the delivery man, then raised her eyebrows and grinned wildly at Cookie, as she continued to take her customer's order.

"Hey, Sarah. Morning, Cookie. Are you ready for this new day?"

Cookie loved the song in his voice. "Morning, David. I do believe I am ready for the day, now that I've gotten my fill of caffeine. I've got your favorite today. Blueberry muffins. Want one?" The offer was a part of their daily morning pick-up ritual.

"Well if it's blueberry, of course." He stepped around the counter and followed Cookie back to the kitchen to pick up the deliveries and the muffin.

"So what have we got today? To what far reaches of farm and dale are you sending me?" Both Cookie and David admitted neither actually had any idea what a dale was, but it didn't matter. Early on in the months he had been delivering for her, Cookie said the phrase and it stuck with them ever since. He looked at the label on the top box.

"Suburban Pediatric?"

Cookie nodded.

"You get a lot of cupcake orders for the hospital."

Without answering, Cookie shifted the boxes around, pretending to re-check the labels.

"You know, those nurses sure do give me a hard time every time I bring cupcakes for those children."

"Really?" Cookie looked up from the boxes, only partly surprised.

"Yeah. Some people, nurses and doctors, especially, don't think sugary sweet cupcakes should be a part of sick kids' diets."

Cookie thought about his comment. "You think I should send muffins, instead?"

David grinned. "I knew they were from you." Then he laughed as she realized her admission. "I take quite a beating from those nurses. I tell them they have to keep them, that I could lose my job if I don't make all my deliveries. They fuss and scold me, but I eventually convince them to keep them."

"The kids who aren't on a restricted diet could enjoy them. I mean, if you have a broken leg, why can't you eat a cupcake?"

"I don't think kids with broken legs stay in the hospital."

"Okay, bad example. But, every child in the hospital can't be on a sugar-restricted diet, right?"

"True. At least it's easier getting them to the kids than getting them into Walter Reed. I couldn't get through there, not even for you." A smile peeked from the corner of David's lips.

"Then the hospital's the most interesting place I've got for you today. A few businesses, team meetings, a baby shower. There are two churches, First Baptist up the street off Georgia Avenue and People's Congregation over in Northwest." Cookie handed the boxes to David one by one so he could plan where they fit in to his route. After he noted each address, she placed the box carefully in the bakery's soft-sided carrier.

"That'll do it, then. I'm all set."

Cookie signed the space for her electronic signature on his handheld route planner. "Thank you. Take good care of my cupcakes."

"Without a doubt," he said, picking up the two cooler bags.

"Bye, David," Sarah called as her boss and the delivery man rounded the counter on their way to the front door.

"See you tomorrow, ladies," David said.

Cookie leaned in the kitchen doorway after he was gone.

"He sure does ring your bell, doesn't he?" Sarah said.

Cookie hoped she wasn't blushing as she clicked her tongue and waved her dish towel at Sarah.

"I don't get why you don't just ask him out or why he hasn't asked you out. It's so obvious y'all like each other."

"Please," Cookie said dismissively.

"For real, why don't you ask him out?"

The door bells clanged, giving Cookie an excuse not to answer her.

The fifty-ish woman with short silver and black hair and her gray-haired gentleman companion always ordered two red velvet cupcakes. Cookie remembered them by their rhyming names: Mary and Harry.

"Hello, Mary. Red velvet for you today?" Cookie asked.

The couple didn't hold hands and giggle like newlyweds and they didn't scold each other for eating too much sugar like an old married couple, either. They would sit at one of the small round tables by the window while they enjoyed their dessert and coffee. Harry dressed as if he was on his way to a golf game, in slacks and a polo shirt, a sports jacket if it was cool. Mary looked like she was headed to lunch at the country club or a sorority meeting, in her straight skirt and sweater set, with a delicate circle of pearls around her neck.

Each time they came, Cookie watched them, longing for someone to grow old with. Someone to hold her hand and walk through downtown, without a care.

"I'm not sure, Cookie. What else do you have today?" Mary walked up to the counter and glanced over the selection in the display case as if she wasn't quite sure she liked cupcakes.

Cookie checked the window, looking for Harry. Seeing no one, she asked, "You alone today?"

Mary nodded and stood silent.

"Do you think red velvet is appropriate for a funeral?" Mary finally asked.

"Umm, excuse me?"

"You know, red. It's kind of jarring for a funeral. No one wears red or brings red things to a funeral. They only bring bland colored things — fried chicken, macaroni and cheese, rolls, string beans, greens. You ever noticed that? Lemon pound cake. Nothing too bright, nothing to stand out. Nobody brings watermelon. Or lasagna." Mary took a deep breath and stared at the sweets. She spoke as if to no one in particular. "Or red velvet cupcakes."

"M-may I ask whose funeral it is?" Cookie asked, afraid she already knew the answer.

Mary's half-smile faded and she blinked a few times. She answered with another question.

"Have you ever been in love? Not, 'oh, he's so cute' love. But real, lifelong love?"

Cookie's eyes widened as she thought how to answer without tearing up. She wasn't sure if the question was a query about Cookie's own love life or a reflective personal thought.

"Yes, once," Cookie answered simply. She had thought it would be lifelong.

"Well, then you're lucky." Mary stood a moment without saying anything, still staring blankly at the cupcakes.

Cookie waited patiently, chewing on her lip and hoping that her guess was wrong and that the cupcakes weren't for Harry.

"Harrison and I met in college. We were a terrible couple. He was jealous, I was catty. We bickered, we ignored each other at parties, then got mad if the other danced with anyone else." Mary chuckled lightly.

Cookie laughed along with her. She had heard pieces of the story of their romance before, but usually in tandem, with Mary and Harry trying to best each other with their own versions.

"Then the next day, he'd wait at the front steps of my dorm, waiting for me to come out. We'd both be hoping we could make up. This was back in the days of single-sex dorms, before wandering into the opposite sex dorms was allowed." Mary pursed her lips and shook her head.

"We'd get back together and be happy for a week or two, then something else would happen and we'd blow up again. Yes, we were a terrible couple." She chuckled again at her memories.

Cookie thought she saw a tear in the corner of Mary's eye.

"Over the summer, he would write me these wonderful letters about how he loved me and couldn't wait to see me. Real letters, in ink, that came in the mail. None of this email and texting nonsense. Then when we got back in the fall, the madness again. We finally broke up our senior year. But I still loved him like crazy." She stared across the counter, looking past Cookie and the cupcakes.

"At graduation, we planned to meet again in ten years and see if we were meant to be together or not. See if I was married, or if he was married, what we were doing with ourselves. You know, one of those *An Affair to Remember* type deals."

"I love that movie," Cookie said softly.

As Mary continued her story of their romance, Cookie thought about her and Dexter's own naïve belief that their love would last and they would live happily ever after. She wondered, as she had for years, if Tennyson was right when he said it was better to love and to have lost, then never to have loved at all. Cookie wanted to challenge his notion.

Cookie didn't cry much anymore when she thought about her college sweetheart. But not because she was over him. Reminders of him were everywhere. His name was on the motorcycle helmet she wore to ride the bike he had taught her to ride. His picture stood on her nightstand. Cookie thought about him at random times when something would trigger a memory, like this new widow or when she saw a guy who had his same haircut or build or walk.

Over the years, the pain of his absence had dulled to an ever-present comfort, rather than a sharp hurt. She imagined it was like the phantom pain amputees talked about in reference to their missing arm or leg.

A glimpse of Sarah's orange Afro next to her brought Cookie's mind back to the bakery. Mary, her voice full of tears, yet her face totally dry, was still talking.

"But to make an already long story a bit shorter, me and my first husband eventually got divorced."

Sarah quietly reached into the glass case and took out two slices of almond pound cake, Cookie's salve to make people feel better. Sarah put the plated cake and two cups of green tea on the counter in front of an empty barstool. Cookie noticed Sarah's quiet movements and slowly started walking towards the space and Mary followed her like a magnet. She took a seat on the barstool as Sarah took the tea bags out of the cups.

Mary held the mug in both hands and thanked Sarah before picking up where she left off.

"On the May date Harrison and I had chosen for our second ten-year meeting, I drove to campus and waited outside my old dorm. I wasn't sure if he was coming, but I was really hoping he would. On that day, I really needed him to come. Well, he did show up. Obviously or this wouldn't be much of a story, right?"

Cookie broke off a piece of pound cake and put it in her mouth, chewing thoughtfully. After Dexter died, Cookie punished herself with the "what-if" game. She still found herself asking those same questions. What if they hadn't gone on separate spring breaks? What if he didn't go jet-skiing? What if that boat hadn't come so close to him and his friends?

Cookie could barely hear the woman talking, noticing her on the very periphery of her attention. She wondered what their life would've been like now, as husband and wife.

"His daughter called me to the hospital and I rushed right over there. I was so surprised. I didn't think she really cared much for me. After her mother, his wife, passed, I guess she expected him to just be a widower and stay single forever." Mary blew across the tea cup, even though the drink had cooled.

"But when a loved one dies, you can't go on being lonely for your whole life. You're still here, you have to live your life. And if you're lucky enough, you'll find another person to share it with," Mary said. She reached out and patted Cookie's hand, looking straight into her eyes.

Cookie blinked, startled and confused by Mary's directness. How did she know? Cookie thought. She couldn't know; Cookie never mentioned Dexter to customers. She must be talking about herself.

"But I was glad she called me. She left me there to sit with him for a little while, just holding his hand. We had our moment to say good-bye," Mary said, smiling slightly.

Cookie held onto the little shred of memory of her and Dexter's last conversation. Of course, at the time, they didn't know it was their last. It had taken her a day or two to recall it after his parents called to tell her he was gone.

She had sat at his desk, doodling hearts on a pad of paper. He was throwing clothes into a duffle bag for his trip with his friends.

"I'll miss you. But after we're married, we'll have the rest of our lives together," Dexter had said. Or at least, that's the way Cookie remembered it.

"His funeral's tomorrow," Mary announced. "And I want to bring his favorite red velvet cupcakes. His sister and daughter will probably think it's so inappropriate. Red at a funeral." She shrugged, then sighed, as if deflating.

Dexter's parents had the memorial service in his hometown, at his home church. A framed photo collage stood where there should have been a coffin, with flowers all around it. It was an odd experience for Cookie. Although most people knew she was his fiancee, it was not an official, legal role and no one knew how to formally recognize their relationship. She was casually mentioned in the obituary as part of the

"Dexter leaves to mourn" list with his cousins and close friends. During the funeral service, she sat on the pew behind his family, leaving the reserved row for his parents, grandparents, and brothers. When his fraternity presented his mother with a bouquet of white roses, one of the members quietly gave her a single flower.

Cookie had wanted to scream out that she loved him, she was going to be his wife, he was going to be her husband, they were supposed to have children and grow old together, and now what was she supposed to do with the rest of her life? She had taken the one white rose gratefully and stuffed down all her feelings.

Mary took a bite of the pound cake then stared at her ring-less left hand.

"We thought there would be time to get married, eventually," Mary said, wiggling her fingers.

Cookie stared at her own empty left hand. She had kept the single rose on her desk for months. Now, all she had left of Dexter were the dried rose petals, his bike helmet, and a shirt he had forgotten in her room. And the irrational thought that he might show up, one day he might walk into her bakery.

"So, would I be able to get two dozen red velvet cupcakes for the morning?" Mary said smiling apologetically through her tears.

Cookie handed her a tissue from the shelf behind the counter.

"Sure, of course," Cookie said. She quickly wiped a few tears from her own face, then looked for an order pad. Sarah surprised her again by appearing next to her, handing her the pad of paper, along with a pencil she pulled out of Cookie's hair. By the end of the day, Cookie often had half a dozen pencils stuck in various directions in the French twist on top of her head.

"Name?" Cookie dutifully wrote out Mary's contact information and cupcake order.

"Okay. Twenty-four red velvet cupcakes. You're sure two dozen's enough?"

"It'll probably only be enough for his golf and poker buddies, but that's okay. It's just the point of having his favorite sweets."

Cookie nodded and wrote *24* on the order pad. "What time will they be picked up? Or, we could deliver them for you."

"That would be great, thank you. And let me take two home today, please."

Sarah boxed the two cupcakes while Cookie rang up the order, leaving off the pound cake. "The cake's on us. I'm glad you enjoyed it."

Mary rose from the barstool and picked up her bag.

"And I'm sorry about your — friend," Cookie said.

"Thank you. You take care of yourself, dear," Mary said as she left.

Cookie left Sarah at the counter and returned to the kitchen, thinking about Mary's statement about finding someone else. She caught her reflection in the mirror hanging by the doorway and paused to look at herself. Her hair was pinned up and covered with a barely noticeable hairnet. Her face was bare, without any make-up. She wore two small gold hoops in each ear. She turned and tilted her head, touched her face.

"Do I look lonely?" she asked herself.

♠ ♥ ♣ ♦

The following day, Cookie boxed up the two dozen red velvet cupcakes first. As she jotted down a short note in the sympathy card, she wondered how long Mary would mourn Harry and if she would ever find someone else. And Cookie wondered if now was the time for her to do so as well.

With Sarah working the front counter, Cookie kept herself busy in the kitchen, baking and decorating for the day. She frosted the strawberry cupcakes and glazed the carrot cake muffins, then arranged them on the trays ready to go out front. The chocolate hazelnut and peanut butter and jelly cupcakes were next to go in the oven. Cookie whisked a pot of heavy cream on the stove to mix with the chopped chocolate to make a ganache for the next batch of red velvet cupcakes.

Cookie heard Sarah greet David, followed by his whistling as he made his way to the back of the bakery.

"Smells good in here. What do we have this morning?"

Cookie smiled and waved her hand over the worktables like a hostess for a game show displaying the prizes. "Today, we are serving red velvet, strawberry, carrot cake muffins, chocolate and peanut butter and jelly."

"Chocolate and peanut butter and jelly what, cupcakes?" David raised his eyebrows in confusion.

"No, two different things. Chocolate cupcakes. Peanut butter and jelly cupcakes."

"Really, peanut butter and jelly? What do they taste like?"

"Tastes like the sandwiches your momma used to make for lunch." They were one of Cookie's favorite flavors. She used to donate them to the daycare down the street, but so many parents complained about peanut allergies, she stopped sending them.

"With real peanut butter?"

Cookie nodded.

"With real jelly?"

Cookie nodded again.

"What flavor?"

"Half are strawberry, half grape. But, they're still in the oven. This should hold you 'til they're ready." Cookie handed David a carrot cake muffin.

"Thanks. So, what've you got for deliveries this morning?" David munched on the muffin while looking at the boxes stacked on the table.

"I have one for a funeral -- two dozen red velvet cupcakes. The woman wondered if it was an odd choice for a funeral, but they were her, umm, friend's favorite." Cookie drummed her fingers on the table. "What do you call a grown woman's male friend? 'Boyfriend' sounds so juvenile. 'Beau' is kinda southern, huh?"

"People say 'significant other'," David said in between bites.

"I don't know. That sounds so legal. Kinda non-emotionally attached."

"Partner? Lover?" He offered.

"'Partner' sounds, well, it sounds like a gay couple, not a woman's boyfriend. 'Lover?' Now that sounds romantic, but a little secretive, too, don't you think?" she wiggled her eyebrows and grinned.

"It has a nice ring to it," he agreed.

"It does, doesn't it? I think that's what I would call him."

"Your lover?"

"Mm-hmm. Well, if I had one."

Cookie wiped at a few crumbs on the table, embarrassed about the light flirting and admitting she, in fact, did not have a lover, or boyfriend, or whatever one called a grown woman's male friend.

"You don't, uhh, you don't have a, uhh, someone?" David asked.

Before she could start crying, as she was likely to do whenever asked this question, Cookie answered quickly. "No, I don't."

Cookie debated how much of an explanation to give, if any at all. On more than one occasion, Gina had scolded Cookie for offering too much information about Dexter. She said it intimidated guys to be competing with her fiancée's ghost.

"How about you?" Cookie asked instead.

"Nah, not…not right now. I'm not seeing anyone," David said.

"Oh."

They stood on opposite sides of the worktable, staring at each other, not knowing what to say next. David finished his muffin. Cookie wiped at the table again.

David cleared his throat and balled up the empty muffin wrapper. "So, you were saying? About the woman and the cupcakes?"

"Oh, yeah. The cupcakes. The couple came in regularly, real nice folks. The man died a week or so ago. Out playing golf, had a heart attack and died. Isn't that terrible?"

David whistled and nodded his head in agreement.

"His friend, his lover, came in yesterday to order the cupcakes for the repast. She was going to come pick them up but I said we would deliver them. I knew you would take great care in getting them to her. Here's the church address, the funeral's at noon."

David took out his route planner and entered the church address. "It's on the other side of the city, but I'll make sure they get there in time. What else you got?"

His hand brushed hers as they packed the boxes. She felt a mixture of nervousness and excitement with their newly revealed information.

"That'll do it, I guess." Cookie wished there were more orders so she'd have an excuse to keep him longer.

"A'right. Then I'll be on my way," David said, picking up the insulated bags. "What about those peanut butter and jelly, when'd you say they'd be ready?"

"They'll be ready soon actually. I'll be sure to save you one if you want to come back for lunch." She wondered if her giddiness was evident in her voice.

"Great. I'll be back about one." He winked at her and headed toward the front door. "Save me a grape one."

Cookie knew she was grinning like the latest Powerball winner, but couldn't help herself. She whistled a tune without any melody and did a little dance while pouring the ganache into a pastry bag.

Laura

Laura walked quickly when she stepped off the train in order to be toward the front of the line on the escalator. She kept up with the fast-moving businessmen and maneuvered her wheeled carry-on around the tourists who were awed by the size and population of Penn Station. She wasn't in a particular hurry to get to her hotel; she just didn't like meandering slowly in a crush of people.

Outside, she pulled on a pair of over-sized sunglasses and scanned the curb for an available cab.

I should've told him to send a car for me, she thought, heading toward a cab driver waving at her.

"Marriott Marquis," she said, getting into the backseat.

Laura enjoyed visiting New York. Washington, D.C. was a different kind of city. It didn't have the honking cars, yelling street vendors, and smell of roasting peanuts and cashews and hot dogs rising from each street corner. In D.C., people moving from block to block and into the glass-topped Metro escalators didn't seem as exciting as New Yorkers, rushing down the street, disappearing into and appearing from mysterious stairways leading underground on every block. Laura watched the traffic and the people as she rode across town to Times Square.

She waited patiently in the lobby and let the cab driver pass off her luggage to the bellman, and the bellman to the doorman until they got to the check-in desk. On the elevator ride up, Laura held the room key and mentally gave herself a pat on the back for Rule Number 4: Separate rooms when traveling. Personally, she needed her own bathroom, bed, and place to sit and enjoy a cup of coffee in the morning. Professionally, it was a clear reminder of Rule Number 2: Sex is not part of the agreement.

The bellman asked Laura about the red, white, and blue conference registration packet she had picked up at the front desk.

"This?" Laura looked at the envelope with a mixture of disdain and disinterest. "I don't really know anything about comics. But my friend is a comic artist and he asked me to come with him," she explained.

After Laura gave her cursory approval of the accommodations, the bellman put her suitcases away in the bedroom closet. She hadn't noticed the other items on the luggage cart until he pointed them out.

"A guest, your friend, perhaps, left this for you at the front desk," he said, placing a silver bag on the sitting area desk, "and requested that this be delivered when you arrived." He set an ice bucket holding a chilled bottle of wine next to the gift bag. "Would you like me to pour it for you?"

"Sure, why not?" It wasn't as if she'd have someone to share it with later.

She pulled a black box out of the bag and shook it gently next to her ear. There was just a soft shushing sound, like paper. "What do you think it is?"

"I can only imagine," the bellman said, handing her a glass of wine. "Is there anything else I can do for you?"

Laura thought for a moment and tasted the wine. "Mm, this is good. Thank you." She played with the ribbon around the gift box. "No, I can't think of anything I need, right now. Unless you want to open this for me?"

The bellman smiled slyly and shook his head. "I probably should leave you to open that alone. Usually a gentleman's gift for a lady isn't meant to be shared with the bellman." He graciously accepted Laura's tip before leaving her alone in the room.

Laura called her client before returning to the gift box. "Hi, Samuel. This is Stacey. I've just arrived in New York. Please give me a call at your convenience."

Rule Number 1: Laura never used her real name because she didn't want anyone to be able to find her without her knowledge.

Next, Laura called Gina to check in on Lady, her white terrier, but she only got her voicemail. "Hey, it's Laura. Hope Lady's not giving you any trouble or whining too much. I'm here in New York. My client left me a gift. Lord knows what's in this box. It better not be something crazy. But, what am I saying, it probably is. Talk to you later."

She untied the ribbon and hoped whatever was inside was not as risqué as the bellman had suggested. Wrapped carefully in tissue paper, Laura found a deep purple, leather-like catsuit with matching boot covers, and a platinum-blonde, almost silver, wig.

"And a cape, too. Of course," she said to the empty room.

Inside the accompanying envelope was a comic book with a shapely woman gracing the cover, dressed in an outfit identical to the one in Laura's box. Clipped to the front was a hand-written note which read, "I'll be looking for you."

Was she supposed to where this? She laughed, taking another sip of wine. Laura dropped the costume back into its box, but not because she doubted she would look good in it.

He is not paying me enough for that shit, she thought. She never imagined this situation would come up and added another rule to the list. New Rule Number 11: No costumes. Rule Number 11a: Especially no superhero costumes.

The costume did, however, pique her interest. An hour before she was supposed to meet Samuel, Laura changed into black tuxedo pants and a leopard print sheer blouse. She considered throwing on the blond wig, but decided against it, considering all the work it would take to pin up her own hair. Laura picked up her purse and convention badge with her alias neatly printed: *Stacey Tavares*.

As Laura waited for the elevator and laughed to herself about the femme-feline costume, she wondered what the hell they were doing downstairs. If it's really bad, I'll go to the bar until he calls me, she told herself.

When the elevator doors opened, she screamed, then quickly slapped her hand over her mouth. Inside, a muscular green man and a guy with wolf-like hair and razor sharp nails stepped aside, clearing an empty space between them. She thought she saw a smile from the green guy as she timidly stepped on the elevator, trying to convince herself they were going to the convention, too. They were not crazy men who were going to kill her on the ride down from the sixteenth floor, she told herself.

At the ballroom level, Laura stumbled in her haste to get out of the elevator, in case they had changed their mind and decided to throw her down the elevator shaft, after all. Walking toward the Jefferson Ballroom, she noticed a familiar looking guy coming down the hallway, although it was hard to tell with the huge silver wings floating behind him. Before she could get a good look at him, she was distracted by a woman slinking past her, dressed in a black leotard a couple sizes too small, purring and meowing, swinging a long black whip. By the time Laura stopped looking at her, the winged guy had disappeared. She decided that the green man, his wolf friend and the pudgy whip-bearing woman were enough comic characters. Laura made a U-turn and headed to the bar.

"A lime martini, please." Laura said to the bartender. At least he's not in a costume, she thought.

"I don't guess you're here for the comic convention?" The bartender slid a slice of lime around the rim of a martini glass and dipped it in sugar while appraising his new customer.

"Believe it or not, I am. I'm here with somebody." Even after years as an escort, Laura was still not certain how to succinctly explain her role without sounding like a call girl. When asked, she tried on different answers, but none really stuck.

"Lucky guy." He shook the vodka, simple syrup, and lime juice, then poured it into the glass and placed the drink in front of her. In between serving other bar customers, the bartender returned to Laura, continuing their bar small talk and replenishing her bowl of snacks and nuts.

As she finished her drink, a gray-haired man took the empty barstool next to her. "Can I buy your next drink?"

Laura was pleasantly surprised he didn't have a cape or claws. However, since she was, technically, with Samuel, although she hadn't seen him yet, she politely turned down his offer.

"Perhaps, there's something else I can pay for?"

Laura looked at him as if she was not certain what he meant. When he looked her up and down with squinty eyes and a smirk she gasped sharply.

"Oh, no. I'm sorry, you've got the wrong girl, the wrong idea," she said. What the hell? She thought. Who just sits down next to a woman and assumes she's a common street-walking prostitute?

The bartender overheard the brief exchange and walked back over to her end of the bar. "Is there a problem?" he asked, directing the question to Laura.

The gray-haired man nervously rubbed his finger on the bar space in front of him and shook his head. "No, not at all," he mumbled.

"I think he mistook me for something, someone else," Laura said. She wanted the bartender to understand the man's assumption about her was wrong.

The bartender nodded and asked the man if he needed help in leaving or if he wanted a table. The old man mumbled under his breath again, then got up from his seat and left the bar.

The bartender fixed another martini and offered it to Laura. "It's on the house."

As she took her first sip, her phone rang.

"Stacey? Hi, it's Samuel. I got your message. Where are you?"

"I'm in the bar, hanging out 'til I heard from you."

"You're down here already, great. The Comic Parade is starting in the ballroom in half an hour. Are you ready?"

"Sure. I'll meet you there in just a few minutes." She hung up and turned back to the bartender. "Thanks for the drink. Can I put a "reserved" sign on this seat? I might need another one when this is over." Laura laughed as she slid a ten-dollar bill across the bar with her check.

She found Samuel near the ballroom doors. He was easy to spot. He was one of the few people not in costume. Instead, he wore a pair of dark blue jeans with a blue and white striped, button down shirt.

"Did you get the gift I left for you?" He looked around as if maybe she was hiding the costume behind her back.

"Yes, I did. Thank you." Laura grinned and nodded enthusiastically.

"Did you open it?"

"Yes. What a surprise!"

"Why didn't you put it on? Didn't you notice everyone else around here is in costume?" He waved his hand at the people milling around the open area.

She wanted to point out that he wasn't in costume either unless "black man in stripes" was a new superhero.

Out loud she said, "Oh, I didn't realize it was for right now. I didn't get a chance to read the schedule." Laura snapped her fingers and grimaced as if she were truly disappointed at having missed the opportunity.

Samuel mumbled something about unveiling an amethyst queen, then shrugged and sighed, as he indicated for her to follow him into the ballroom. Instead of lining up for the parade and the costume contest, Samuel led Laura to the middle of the seating area, as the rows up front were already filled. She had to stretch her neck a little to get a good view of the line of animated people as they walked, jumped, crawled, flipped, and nearly flew across the stage.

These are grown-ass people up here looking like Halloween on steroids, Laura thought. She looked twice when she saw the same winged guy from the elevator again. He looked like Max but she thought it couldn't be him dressed up in a costume.

What the hell would he be doing here? She didn't remember him ever mentioning any interest in comic books and definitely not comic conventions. Maybe it's not him, she thought, as she watched the six-foot, very muscular, dark brown man walk out onto the stage, dressed only in silver-gray briefs and a chest-plate, red and white boots, and bird-like wings. He wore face paint around his eyes, but even through the silver-gray paint, she thought she recognized that face. She listened carefully to the announcer's introduction.

"Maxwell Hunter as the winged fighter, Hawk."

One reason Laura was successful in her business was that she billed herself as a unique date. She could almost guarantee a client wouldn't see her with a friend or associate at a conference, business event, or even a social event. She did this by diligently having each client complete a detailed questionnaire asking him about his employer and industry, professional organizations, fraternities, acquaintances, even church membership. The point of a man discreetly hiring an escort was to have a female companion he wouldn't run into with someone else. And nowhere on Max's questionnaire did he write, "I like to dress up as a big damn bird at comic conventions."

Max had been Laura's one exception to Rule Number 5.

She preferred to keep her relationships professional, not mixing in anything personal. She didn't ask about clients' family, other than if they were married. A wife was definitely reason enough for not taking on a client. She only met with clients for their scheduled public events. She did not go out with them for purely social engagements involving only the two of them. She did not talk about her own personal life. She rarely even mentioned her dog. She wanted to make sure Laura and Stacey had separate lives.

Max started out as a client and while attending his corporate functions and conventions together, Laura and Max found they genuinely enjoyed each other's company. After a business event, they would go dancing or walk along the Mall. A bar association gala ended with a late night at the bar and eventually breaking Rule Number 1. They acknowledged that the line between business and personal was getting blurry, but continued to cross it anyway. Laura was nervous at first, uncertain whether she was making a big mistake by allowing herself to actually feel any emotion for a client. A couple months of dating assuaged her fears.

Then Max shared his reservations about how her profession might reflect on his image and his job. All of a sudden, he was concerned about how it would look for a law firm partner to be dating a personal escort, though he didn't exactly have a solution. He didn't suggest they stop seeing each other on a personal level and he didn't want to return to paying her for her company. Laura wasn't clear where they stood and reaffirmed her rule against mixing business and pleasure. She made the decision to end their relationship altogether. She hadn't seen or heard from him in over a year.

Laura sighed and started tapping her foot.

"Is everything okay?" Samuel asked. "You seem bothered."

"No, I'm fine. I just realized I hadn't checked on my dog, that's all."

He patted her knee and went back to watching the parade. Laura planted her foot quietly on the floor and resolved not to think about Max. She watched the remainder of the parade, continually amazed by the costumes grown people dared to wear in public. Laura pretended to pay attention as Samuel pointed out the characters featured in his line of comic books. In between superheroes, Laura's thoughts periodically returned to how good Max looked in his costume, then she would scold herself and try not to think about him again.

At the post-parade reception, Samuel made his rounds to the characters while Laura wandered around, trying to look casually interested and not like she was looking for anyone in particular.

Yes, you did not belong in the parade, she thought as she noticed another overweight woman in a red and blue leotard, gold bracelets tight around her wrists, standing with a five-foot-tall, scrawny guy in a red caped outfit.

She looked back at Samuel, checking to see if he wanted her to come back. He was talking to some other heroes, nodding in her direction. It was obvious they were talking about her. She imagined him boasting that she was his date.

Laura waved at Samuel and smiled to confirm his story that she was, indeed, his date. The other heroes waved back and returned to their conversation. Laura noticed the tips of large silver wings coming across the room toward her and tried to turn in yet another direction.

"Laura?"

She opened her eyes wide and gasped, feigning surprise. She didn't want him to even suspect that she had already spotted him, or worse, was looking for him.

"Max! What a surprise to see you here. I didn't know you were into comics." She realized he was wearing a flesh-toned body suit; he wasn't actually bare-skinned. But he still looked good.

Max took her hands and kissed the air near her cheeks. She laughed to herself, thinking that she never imagined the situation in which the guy would be the one worried about messing up his make-up. However, she was relieved; she wasn't sure that if he kissed her, she wouldn't melt into a mass of confused tears.

"I guess there were still some things for you to find out about me," Max said.

Laura smiled, trying to force herself not to blush as she, again, thought of their short relationship. She played it safe by leading the conversation into the generic "how have you been" chit-chat. Max continued to hold her hands as they talked; Laura hoped they weren't sweating.

"What are you doing here? I know this isn't your crowd," Max said.

Max was in clear violation of Rule Number 6. She told her clients, in no uncertain terms, "Do not speak to me if I am with someone. Ever. Ever. Unless I speak to you first, which I won't." She added this violation to the breaking of Rules Number 1, 2 and 5.

In that moment, she was reminded of the uncomfortable feeling when he told her he didn't think she was good for his image. The feeling of not being good enough overcame the lust of seeing Max in tights. She pulled her hands away, pretending to have an itch she needed to scratch on her arm. She was preparing to answer when she saw Samuel walking toward them.

"Here's my reason for being here, right now." Laura beamed at Samuel, with more affection than necessary. She reached out her hand as he approached. "This is my date, Samuel. He's introducing me to the world of comics," she announced, looping her arm around his, pulling him close to her.

Samuel reached out to shake Max's hand. "Hey. Great costume. The Hawk is one of my favorites. I have the first book when he was pitted against the Captain," Samuel said.

As the two went on about their favorite characters and their adventures, Laura watched them, still shocked that she had two clients at the same convention. And not just any convention, but a comic convention. What were the odds of that? There must be a loophole in her screening process and these two had managed to find it.

"Well, Max, it was good to see you again. Samuel, why don't we get a drink," Laura waved at Max while pulling her client towards the punch bowl table.

"How do you know him? Is he a client, too or a friend?" Samuel asked when they had filled their cups with green punch.

"What a surprise that was; I haven't seen him in such a long time." Laura arranged a few meatballs on a plate and handed it to Samuel. "Don't these look delicious?"

They continued to walk around the ballroom, Samuel talking to masked crusaders, Laura stewing over Max. He introduced her to a blue-caped muscle man and a green-winged fighter, beaming at the costumes of characters he drew. Laura nodded and tried to look excited.

Do all female superheroes wear skin-tight catsuits? Obvious male fantasy, she thought as they passed what seemed like the hundredth woman wearing an outfit identical to the one upstairs in the gift box.

Finally, after Samuel let everyone know he had a date, he was ready to go upstairs. In the elevator, they were finally by themselves and he turned to Laura.

"There were some great costumes tonight, don't you think?"

"Nothing like I've ever seen before."

"Did you enjoy yourself? I mean, I know this isn't your thing, but considering, did you enjoy yourself?"

"Oh, sure. I like going to different events, peeking in on different worlds." Though this costume thing was a bit odd, Laura had to admit some of the people were impressive.

"Great. I was hoping you wouldn't be bored." Max almost sounded nervous.

"It seemed like I was the only date, at least the only one not in costume," Laura joked.

"Yeah, most people don't bring dates, but I thought you would be a much better choice than walking around with a bunch of guys all night."

"I sure hope I was," she laughed at what she took as a compliment.

"Been there and I can definitely say I was right. I enjoyed your company."

The elevator opened on their floor and he gestured for her to get off first. They stopped in front of her door.

"Well, I guess this is the end of our evening." Again, the nervousness rose in Samuel's voice.

Laura nodded. "Unless you want to go back downstairs to get a drink?"

"Nah. I think I'll just go to my room, check what all the blogs have to say about the convention. Sketch some ideas I've collected in my head. I'll see you in the morning for breakfast?"

"Umm. Sure, breakfast."

Samuel waited while Laura slid her key in the door before heading down the hall toward his room.

Laura dropped onto the couch and stared out of the dark window. She tried to envision how Samuel would draw "Escort Girl". She remembered the gift he left for her and laughed out loud. Of course she would wear a black catsuit and four-inch stiletto pumps.

She imagined fluffy thought bubbles appearing over her head: Was Max really my last real date? Why does it seem like years ago? How much longer can I do this?

She sighed deeply and poked the air above her head as if to pop the bubbles full of her questions. She didn't want to be in her room alone and pushed herself back off the couch and out the door.

When the elevator doors opened, Laura stepped aside just as a trio of webbed, caped, and muscled costumes stumbled out. On the lobby level, she headed back to the bar. She was relieved to see an open barstool far from the remaining costumed characters.

"You did come back. Good thing I put that invisible "Reserved" sign there. Only they can see it," the bartender joked, nodding his head at the guys at the other end of the bar. "Lime martini?"

Laura laughed and sat down. "Yes, thanks." She was impressed he remembered her drink.

"Enjoying yourself so far?" The bartender asked.

"It's bizarre! Now, don't get me wrong. Some of them look good in their little bikini costumes. But a lot of 'em! Shit! They're a mess."

"You should've stayed here. You missed all the action." He grabbed a martini shaker as he spoke.

"First, a woman in safari gear and another one dressed like some goddess got into a fight over a guy in purple boots and a bodysuit," he said, slicing a lime.

"Then, this fish-dude apparently couldn't hold his liquor as well as he could hold his breathe underwater and had to be carried out of here." He capped the shaker and mixed her drink.

"And, you just missed her, did you see the woman whose costume was painted on?"

"Painted? Painted how?" Laura asked.

The bartender chuckled as he answered. "Painted like with paint. A green flower vine, wrapped around her body." He raised his eyebrow and smiled slyly.

"And she was naked? Just paint?" Laura asked.

"I swear. I checked. The vine bloomed into flowers in the uh, let's say, in the most interesting places." He poured the martini into the sugar-rimmed glass and pushed it across the bar to her.

Laura laughed hysterically as they told stories about the characters they had seen. She finished off two more martinis and stayed at the bar until last call. To save herself the embarrassment of falling over while walking down the hall as several had already, Laura slipped her heels off as she stepped down from the barstool.

"You going to be all right?" The bartender asked.

"Sure. If not, I guess someone will save me," Laura waved her shoes at the last few heroes standing out in the lobby.

She left reluctantly. It had been a long time since she'd had a good time with a man who wasn't paying for her company.

The next morning, Samuel was at her door at 9 o'clock, just as he promised.

Laura sipped her coffee and took bites of her Western omelet while he chatted about the booths of booksellers, merchandisers, and artists he wanted to visit. Instead of listening, her mind wandered and she wondered where he got the money to pay her and whether cartoonists really made any money.

He allowed that she didn't really need to accompany him for a full day of business. She agreed while trying not to appear too eager to abandon him.

"How about splitting the day? You can tag along with me until you get bored." He laughed as he continued, "Hopefully, you'll make it through at least an hour, then you can go relax or do whatever you need to do."

Laura managed to make it to lunch. For the rest of the afternoon, she read by the pool before heading back to her room to get ready for the cocktail party.

As she stepped out of the shower, she noticed the gifted costume lying on the coffee table. Nah, can't do it, she thought. She picked up the wig and twirled it around on her hand. Well, maybe?

After she got dressed, Laura sat in front of the vanity mirror. She smoothed her hair back and pinned it up neatly, as flat as possible. She pulled the blond wig down on her head and carefully tucked her own brown hair under the edges. When she finished pulling, pinning, and brushing the wig into place, she decided that she needed to intensify her make-up to complete the look and pulled her cosmetic bag out again.

Laura was swiping on a coat of lip-gloss when she heard a knock on the door. She peeked out the peep-hole. It took her a second to recognize Samuel in his black and green skintight bodysuit. When she opened the door, she saw the black leather knee-high boots that completed the outfit.

He smiled as he looked at Laura's face. "Wow, you look great!"

Along with the blond wig, she had drawn out her eyes dramatically with black eyeliner and silvery-gray eye shadow and her lips shimmered in red lipstick and shiny lip-gloss. "Escort Girl" was complete with a red halter cocktail dress and heels.

He frowned as his eyes ran down the rest of her body.

"But, where's the costume?" he asked.

"It didn't fit," she lied and tried to look apologetic. She almost did feel sorry for not wearing the costume, but the wig and make-up, she thought, was a pretty good effort. "It was a little too big."

He glanced at his watch. "Don't worry about it. You look fine."

At the cocktail party, Samuel led her around the room and talked to different characters, introducing her to some, pointing her out to others when she wasn't standing right next to him. Laura ate and drank and appeared impressed by the good guys and intimidated by the bad guys. She played the role of "pretty date" perfectly. She also looked around for a Max sighting, but didn't see his wings all night long.

At the end of the party, they again parted ways at her door. This time, he kissed her lightly on the cheek, thanking her again for her services. They wouldn't see each other in the morning, as Samuel was scheduled for an earlier train. Like the night before, she dropped on the couch and stared out into the same darkness.

Instead of getting up and going back to the bar, she kicked off her shoes and poured the last of Samuel's gift wine into a glass. She turned on a movie, settling back onto the couch. She picked up her phone and looked at it. No messages. It was too late to call her girlfriends. She couldn't call Samuel; that would be ridiculous. She wanted to call Max, but couldn't think of what to say.

Instead, she imagined another square for her comic strip.

Kapow! The evil forces flood Escort Girl with emotions, her own kryptonite. Loneliness. Exhaustion. Uncertainty. She lies motionless on the couch, trying to recover with the elixir of Vino.

Spades Night

Gina poured the concoction of brandy and schnapps over orange, lemon, and apple slices in the pitcher. When the doorbell rang, she was relieved it was the deliveryman from the new Spanish restaurant, instead of her friends arriving early for their monthly game of Spades.

She randomly pulled out red and yellow platters, bowls, and serving trays from the kitchen cabinets. Being careful not to spill anything on her jeans or her casual tribal-print blouse, she arranged the delivered food on the plates.

It almost looks like I've really been cooking, Gina thought, surveying her dinner buffet of calamari, mussels, shrimp, sausages, fried potatoes, and yellow rice.

She blamed her lack of culinary skills on her mother, who never had to refer to a recipe or the back of a box. She cooked by instinct, the way her own mother had, and though she tried to teach Gina, Gina thought her mother's repertoire was a collection of incomprehensible, un-measured concoctions. Gina had tried making cornbread using her mother's recipe: a cup of corn-meal, half cup of flour, some butter, an egg, a little sugar, and a cup of buttermilk. Instead of the golden, soft bread she savored, Gina ended up with a hard, yellow disk she ended up setting out on the balcony for the birds who wouldn't even eat it. After another failed attempt, she figured out the called-for cup was not a measuring cup, but an old souvenir drinking glass from a trip to Atlanta her mother took before Gina was even born. She had no idea what her mother meant by "some", but guessed that it probably corresponded to some other decades-old dishware in her mother's cabinet. Gina also tried a few of her mother's other recipes to the same disastrous end: ribs (burnt), sweet potatoes (too hard), macaroni and cheese (crunchy), even scrambled eggs (stuck to the pan). Gina had considered taking a class but couldn't find "Cooking for Dummies" anywhere. The one thing she had mastered however, was mixing drinks.

She arranged the food on the counter, poured red wine over the fruit and liquor mixture, and placed a new deck of cards and a scorepad on the table. Finished with the set-up, she poured herself a glass of sangria.

Her phone beeped indicating a text message.

What time are your friends leaving? It was Alex.

Probably late. I made sangria.

Oh. Never leaving.

See you in the morning?

Early meeting at 8. C u there.

Gina laid the phone on the counter when she heard the doorbell ring. Laura leaned on the doorframe, pretending to be exhausted by the walk from her apartment down the hall.

"Whew! I need a drink. I might be dehydrated," Laura said. She fanned herself with her hand as she wandered into the apartment. "What're we eating? It smells good. Am I the first one here?"

"Tapas and sangria. Yes."

"Yummy. Where'd you get the food?" Laura fell into the cream upholstered wing chair. She moved the throw pillow to her lap as she folded one leg underneath her body. In contrast to the elegant dresses she wore when with clients, she was dressed comfortably in purple yoga pants and a fitted t-shirt, with her hair pulled back in a neat ponytail.

"How do you know I didn't make it myself?"

Laura rolled her eyes. "There's a lot of things you are, but a cook sure as hell is not one of them."

"I made the sangria." Gina handed Laura an iced glass of the red drink. "Any good clients lately? Any more superhero costumes?"

"See, it's craziness like that that made me have to develop my 'just in case I don't come back' plan." As her safety net, Laura left Gina an envelope with pertinent information whenever she went out of town with a client. City, hotel, event, and dates of travel were all printed on a form, attached to an envelope with the name and contact information for the client inside. Laura was very particular about her clients' privacy and instructed Gina not to open the envelope, unless necessary. The possibility of having to open the envelope made Gina nervous and she always hoped "just in case" never happened.

The doorbell rang and Cookie and Sherry walked in, continuing their conversation. "Maybe a cream cheese mixture, like a Black Bottom."

"*Hola*, ladies," Gina greeted them, handing each a glass of sangria.

"What's a Black Bottom?" Sherry asked.

"One of those reality show housewives is coming out with jeans called Black Bottoms. They're blue jeans with black designs on the butt," Laura offered.

"Are you kidding? That's tacky," Gina said.

"Well, I meant the cupcake, not jeans," Cookie said.

The women sipped their wine while munching on the selection of food, their conversation taking random, tangential paths, from celebrity gossip to work to an upcoming shoe sale. When they were finally ready to play cards, Gina unwrapped the plastic from the new deck.

"Starting fresh," Gina said as she turned the notepad to a clean scoresheet.

Each month, the women played with a new deck of cards, despite each having piles of old ones in their homes. The old decks were fine for the casual get together or the occasional game of Solitaire on a quiet Saturday afternoon, but for Spades night, it was always a new, fresh deck. It was the one aspect of their lives in which they could forget everything that happened last month and start anew.

Gina pulled out the jokers, then quickly shuffled the cards. She fanned them out and extended them to the others. Each woman in turn picked a card and turned it over, then they each took a seat around the table in the numerical order of her card. Holding a three, Cookie took the first seat, then Sherry, followed by Laura and Gina.

In this way, they paired off for their game. It was a random choosing of partners. No one's feelings were hurt because they were not chosen. No one felt extra pressure because they were. There were no pre-determined game plans. They were dependent on the partner chosen by the draw of the cards.

Gina handed the new deck of cards to her partner, Sherry, to shuffle and deal. As they checked their cards, each woman complained or celebrated, depending on her hand.

Cookie made a face at her cards as if the pursed lips and closed eye would magically make her hand better. There were no clear winners for the game that involved playing the highest card of a given suit: a few spades and a whole bunch of diamonds. Cookie and Laura made a cautious bid of five books.

"Five? That's it? We'll go six," Sherry said without asking her partner.

"Okay, there's two out there up for grabs," Gina said, scribbling the numbers on the score pad.

As the first player, Cookie contemplated her cards and how to begin. Normally, she was very cautious in making decisions, but in spades, she allowed herself to play with a little more risk and strategy.

Cookie threw out the queen of diamonds, holding onto the king. If either Gina or Sherry had the ace, they would play it. That would still leave her the king as the highest diamond, Cookie reasoned. Otherwise, her partner, Laura, had the ace and they would have both high cards. Gina threw out a four and looked at Sherry for a sign. Laura never showed emotion during the game, keeping her mouth positioned in a slightly downturned frown. She quietly laid the three on the pile of cards. Sherry threw in the two and rolled her eyes.

"I've got a feeling I'm going to win tonight," Cookie sang and pulled in the first book of cards.

"Oh, hush! Those aren't even the right words," Gina retorted while looking to Sherry for some indication of what she had in her hand.

Cookie threw out the king.

"You have any good open houses coming up so I can come be nosy?" Gina asked her partner.

"No talking across the table," Laura fussed.

"That's not talking across the table. It's a regular question," Gina said.

"Now, if I said 'why yes there is and I've been digging four rows in the garden' — *that* would be talking across the table," Sherry said as she threw out the four of spades.

"Go 'head partner!" Gina piled the book in front of her.

"Are you kidding me? Are you cuttin' shit already?" Laura asked. She furrowed her eyebrows, still frowning.

"You've got to be kidding!" Cookie agreed.

"Now, how you feeling?" Gina asked Cookie with a wide smirk.

As Sherry tossed the ace of hearts on the table and won the next book, Laura took a long swallow of sangria. Sherry led with the six of hearts. She nodded, satisfied, when her partner won the book with the queen.

"You might need to keep that pitcher nearby, tonight!" Gina teased Cookie and Laura. They had an ongoing drinking game in which the partners who lost a book had to take a drink. Leading with clubs, Sherry and Gina took the next two books.

"So, Cookie, how's the delivery dude?" Sherry asked.

"He's fine, still coming by to pick up deliveries," Cookie said, trying to sound nonchalant and hoping she wasn't blushing.

"Yeah, but he's coming for more than your boxes of cupcakes," Sherry said. "I've seen how you look at him when he walks in."

"Oh, I didn't realize there was a thing between you and the delivery guy," Gina said.

Cookie shook her head. "There isn't. He's nice, friendly, that's all."

Her feelings for David were like a school-girl crush. There was no better word for it and it felt silly to mention them out loud. She thought about him whenever there was quiet time during the day, but didn't imagine he gave her another thought once he walked back out the door with the carriers full of boxed up cupcakes.

"Well, I've got a friend. He's a really nice guy. I could hook you up," Laura offered.

"Could you hook up your cards and play?" Sherry teased.

Laura waved off Sherry's remark and turned back to Cookie. "For real. You want me to set you up with him?"

"What's wrong with him? Why aren't you going out with him?" Gina asked.

"There's nothing wrong with him. But we're friends, it would be weird for us to go out. I've known him for a long time; we were in Psych classes together in college."

"No, I don't need to be set up on any date. I'm fine." Cookie played her next card. She fidgeted and gulped her sangria, not really wanting to discuss her dating. Or not dating.

If she were honest, Cookie would have to admit she hadn't seen anyone seriously since after college. Her friends and family would gently, unnecessarily, remind her Dexter was gone. In her deep subconscious, Cookie knew it, of course, but in her heart, she wasn't ready yet to admit that reality, regardless of how many years it had been.

"You're not getting any younger," Laura said, scanning her cards.

"And you are?"

"I'm just saying, I don't know what the hell you're waiting for." Laura slapped the three of spades on the table and challenged Sherry. "Come on, what you got, girl?"

Reluctantly, Sherry threw out the three of clubs. Cookie threw in her last club and swept up her partner's book. Despite Laura's small victory, Sherry and Gina won the round with all three of the big spades. Sherry refilled everyone's glasses while Cookie shuffled the cards and Gina cut the deck. After the ladies looked at their cards, they made their bids and began the next round.

Gina glanced at Sherry then played the first card.

"What's Alex up to? Still trying to get you to a hockey game or a Nascar race?" Cookie asked, diverting the conversation away from her love life.

Gina smirked at Cookie's question and shook her head. "Oh, he will never get me to a car race. I don't even get it, watching a car go around a track a million times?"

Sherry picked up the first book and threw out the next card. "I don't know how you decided to date a white man anyway. That was kinda out of the blue."

"It's not like I was purposely trying to date a white guy. After Jason went and moved across the ocean, you know there were a couple knuckle-heads I went out with," Gina said, rolling her eyes and making a face like she was gagging. "Then, Alex asks me out. I always thought he was pretty cool, and, he is cute, so why not?" Gina swirled the red wine around her glass, then took another sip.

"Maybe I was ready for something a little different. But, if you had asked me last year would I go out with a white boy, I'd be like 'heck no'. So I can see why my mom's a little caught off guard, she didn't really see this coming."

"Plus, she loved Jason," Sherry said.

"Yes, she did. I don't think she's gotten over him being out of the picture," Gina agreed. Her mother seemed to be having a harder time getting over their break-up than Gina, who did, at times, miss her ex-boyfriend since his move to London.

"She would've died if you had moved with him," Cookie said.

"Exactly. She still mentions how we could've made a long-distance relationship work. I guess, every other weekend I could jump on the Concorde and fly over for dinner and a good shagging."

Sherry laughed. "Shagging?"

"It sounds so much more civilized doesn't it?" Gina replied.

"Do they still even fly the Concorde?" Laura asked.

"I don't know, whatever superfast thing they're flying," Gina said. "Anyway, Alex wanted to come by tonight, but, I guess I'll see him tomorrow at work."

"You should've told us to get out so your man could come over," Laura said.

"Like hell she should've. This is Spades night. She's not puttin' us out for a man," Sherry said. "Good thinking, Gina."

"What? You wouldn't give up Spades for a man?" Cookie asked.

"Shit no. I wouldn't give up a good game of Solitaire for a man. I've given up enough."

"You know, the real problem is, Alex doesn't get it -- the reason why she doesn't want me dating him. He thinks its as simple as 'she doesn't approve of inter-racial dating', but its more than that," Gina said.

"It's always more complicated," Sherry agreed.

"Because my way-long-time-ago-great-grandfather was white and my great-grandmother was black, and whatever happened between them that no one in the family wants to talk about, now I can't date a white guy."

"I get it," Sherry said with a light laugh. "In fact, my father used to tell me the same thing as your mom about the holiday dinners. His grandmother was a domestic for a white family, too. He would never eat the holiday leftovers from the white family, though. While his mother warmed up the slices of ham and potatoes, he'd eat a cold biscuit and a cup of milk. He said it would make his mother so mad." Sherry shrugged. "But what could you do? Folks had to work."

"Right. Isn't it time we got over some of that? But I don't think any of that that would make sense to him," Gina said.

Sherry watched Laura sweep up the next book. "Damn it. You know Gina can't concentrate when she's talking about Alex. Stop distracting my partner."

"You were running your mouth, too, Sherry," Laura said, laughing.

"Whatever. Stop talking about men," Sherry said.

"Then what else are we gonna talk about?" Laura asked.

Cookie laid the seven of hearts on the table. The other women looked at the card then around the table in confusion as Cookie scooped up the pile of cards.

"What the hell? A damn seven? Gina what do you have in your hand? You better not be messing up over there!" Sherry said, incredulous a seven had won.

Everyone, even Gina, laughed at Sherry, as Cookie threw down the jack of hearts.

"Damn it," Sherry said.

"So, you two think you can change your mom's mind. Convince her that she doesn't mind that he's white?" Laura asked, ignoring Sherry and turning to Gina.

"He does. Which is why he's still stuck on this bright idea of running in this marathon to prove to my mother he's the one for me."

"I still don't think that's going to work," Sherry said.

"Probably not. Running twenty-six miles and messing up my hair is going to prove nothing to my mother other than I've lost my freakin' mind. But he thinks if we do this together," Gina paused to make air quotes with her fingers, "the training and the running and all that, it'll show her how well we work together, support each other, think alike, blah blah blah. I'm like, let's go to Hawaii and prove it by making it through the ten hour flight."

"But y'all don't think alike, obviously. He thinks this is going to win your mother over and you don't," Sherry said.

"It does sound a bit crazy, maybe even more crazy the more we talk about it," Cookie said. "I mean, you've never run that far before. You've never run at all, have you?"

Everyone, except Gina, laughed at the idea of their friend running, joking about her running in her heels and her newly permed hair.

"Why don't you at least pick something you like to do? How about a bar crawl?" Cookie said.

"Ha! If you finish a bottle of tequila and vodka without fighting, you belong together," Sherry said.

"And if you finish without getting sick, you might as well go on and get married," Laura added.

"It's tequila that got me in this mess in the first place," Gina laughed.

"Obviously, this guy has never met Mrs. Morrison," Cookie said.

"And Gina must have forgotten her if she thinks this dumb-ass idea's going to work," Sherry said.

"True. He could run around the world and Gina's mother is not going to go for his white behind dating her daughter," Cookie said.

"Anyway," Gina said. She munched on a chip, ready to change the subject. She partly agreed with her friends, that this plan wasn't going to change her mother's mind. But she appreciated Alex's effort and wanted to be the type of girlfriend who was supportive and went along with her boyfriend's ideas. She turned to Sherry. "What's going on with Jordan?"

"Ugh. Don't want to talk about it."

"Has she decided what she's going to do about school?" Gina asked.

"It's still up in the air. She's been accepted to schools from Georgia to New York, but hasn't made a decision yet. I'm thinking she should stay close to home, but Viv doesn't want to restrict her," Sherry shook her head. "It's not like the North Carolina schools are bad choices."

"Staying in-state would be a good idea so she can have some help with that baby. She's got to consider that now," Cookie said.

"Who's going to take care of the baby if she goes away?" Gina asked.

"Exactly. My sister thinks she could handle it. Take care of the baby during the school year, then my niece can be mommy in the summer."

"That might work in the beginning, but someone -- grandmom, mom, baby — is going to start rebelling after a couple years," Laura said.

"How about you?" Gina asked.

"How about me what?" Sherry said.

"You taking care of the baby? You've said you still would like to have a child."

Sherry stared at her cards and shrugged. "I don't know. I mean, yeah, I've said that, but, I haven't really decided." Sherry waved Cookie on to play her next card, indicating she was through with the discussion.

Cookie cut diamonds with another spade, spurring Sherry's next cursing frenzy, and slid the pile of cards to Laura.

"Gina, I sure hope you've got another pitcher of sangria ready," Laura said, accepting the newly won cards. "And a spot for your partner to lie down after you all lose!"

"Don't you worry about where I'm going to lie down, Miss Laura. Pay attention to your cards, Gina." Sherry said, concentrating on her next move.

Gina

"Are you leaving with me or should I pick you up at home?" Alex asked, poking his head in Gina's cubicle.

"Pick me up at home. I've got to finish a few things for the music festival then I'm going to get my hair done."

Alex waved and blew Gina a kiss as he left.

The Potomac Music Festival, a weekend-long event of seafood and a music concert series on the D.C. waterfront, was one of Gina's favorite events in her portfolio. The coordination was routine now. She contracted the same companies for graphics, printing, and decorating every year and all the dockside restaurants participated with special menus. The part she didn't like was the fundraising. Each year, she had to get enough sponsors to help cover the costs of the entertainment and raise money for the Potomac River Clean-up Fund. She finished addressing another twenty-five sponsorship packages and dropped them in the administrative assistant's out-going mail basket, hurrying to make her hair appointment.

When she got home, Gina listened to her voicemail messages as she changed from her slacks and silk blouse into blue jeans and a casual tie-front top. One was from Laura asking about her dinner plans for the evening. The other was from her mother, calling to see how Gina was doing and whether she was seeing anyone new, meaning, had she broken up with the white boy, yet.

Gina thought back on their conversation a few months ago when she told her mother about Alex. Her mother was still recovering from the disappointment that Gina's previous relationship did not result in a son-in-law, so Gina had tenuously mentioned she was dating a new guy.

"Yeah, Mom. He's very nice."

"So how'd you two meet?" her mother asked.

"We work together. I've known him for awhile."

"He's from Washington or from somewhere else?"

"He's from Connecticut. He grew up there, then went to school in New York."

"Oh, really? I have a cousin in Bridgeport. Is he from around there?"

"No, he's not from Bridgeport." Gina paused a moment, then in the middle of the waiting silence added, "His family lives in Darien."

"Darien? I never heard of that. I thought most of the black folk lived in Bridgeport or Norwalk?"

"Uh, yeah, I guess there aren't a lot of black people there."

"Well, where's his folks from? How'd they end up in Connecticut?"

Her mother asked because, of course, black folk don't just live in Connecticut, they had to have a reason to be there. Gina's mother needed to know the family's northern migration pattern out of the south to fully evaluate what she thought of them. Were they industrious people who had moved up north for a job or were they running from the law?

She was asking all the wrong questions and Gina sat in silence trying to come up with answers to the ones she should have been asking.

"I was thinking. I've always dated black guys and I have a few friends who have dated other guys and that's worked out pretty well for them, so, maybe I should give something else a try," Gina ventured, her voice slightly above a whisper.

"What? I can hardly hear you. What do you mean 'other guys'? What 'something else' is there?" Gina could envision her mother's eyebrows scrunching together as she put on her serious, questioning face.

"It means Alex, my new boyfriend, is white." Gina's voice lifted a few notes at the end of her sentence, like the happy, annoying blondes on TV. She tried to sound cheerful, but at the same time she winced while she waited for her mother's reaction. And as she had expected, her mother said nothing.

Silence from Lucille Morrison was a bad sign. Gina's mother's silence meant she thought her daughter was so far gone and had done something so stupid or irresponsible words could no longer save her. She wouldn't yell or fuss, because that would be unladylike, but her disappointment was understood and punishment was inevitable.

In second grade, when her mother had to visit the school principal's office because Gina was blowing spitballs across the classroom in the middle of reading class, she squeezed Gina's hand quietly as they left the school. For a week, Gina was permitted to eat or drink only through a straw. When she was sixteen, Gina and her friends went to a Boys II Men concert and then decided to hang around the hotel where the group was allegedly staying. Between the cab ride to get to the hotel and a late night snack, they ran out of money for a cab or even a bus to get home and Mrs. Morrison had to come pick them up at 5 a.m. from the downtown hotel. The forty-five minute ride seemed to last hours in the quiet morning. Their short career as groupies resulted in Gina being grounded for two weeks and having to use her hard-earned babysitting money to repay her mother for the concert tickets and gas.

After a full two minutes of silence, Gina took the phone from her ear to check that the "on call" light was still on.

"Hello?" Gina asked softly.

Her mother responded with a deep sigh. "Well. This carpet is a mess, I guess I should go vacuum."

Gina quickly agreed, as if she believed her mother's excuse to end the conversation, and was relieved not to mention the new boyfriend at all.

Since then, Mrs. Morrison still hadn't progressed much further in accepting Alex.

Getting ready for her date, Gina wasn't in the mood to discuss her mother's steadfast disapproval of her relationship. Instead, she checked her new hair-do in the mirror then applied the dark berry wine lipstick the guy at the make-up store had convinced her would be perfect for her pecan shell skin tone, as if there weren't already half a dozen berry/wine/chocolate lipsticks on the bathroom counter. She heard the doorbell ring and the click of the key turning in the lock.

"Hey?" Alex called. "You ready or are you putting on more lipstick?"

"I'm ready. I'm coming," Gina called. She pouted to check her make-up once more. "You think you know me, huh?" A quick kiss hello and they were back out the door.

For work, Alex and Gina attended many of the museum exhibit premieres, restaurant openings, and hotel ribbon cuttings in the city. They had discovered that on their own, they enjoyed some of the same activities, such as going to the movies, but that they also had a number of differences in what they liked. They had agreed to take turns choosing places and activities for their dates. Even with the movies, they alternated between the chick flicks she liked and his choice of action/car-chase/shoot-em-up movies.

Tonight was his choice and he drove them to a sports bar. In the back of the restaurant, they found a couple of empty barstools at a long table. They ordered their food and watched a group of guys throw darts at the board closest to them.

"I didn't know you had to stand back so far. I don't think I could do that," Gina said.

"Come on, let's try." Alex scooped up the darts at an empty board. He gave three of them to Gina and kept the others. Standing on the line, he flung the darts, hitting the inner rings. "It's all in the wrist." He stepped aside to allow Gina to take her turn.

"Everybody says that about everything. You'd think wrist movement is the magic key to doing anything right." She placed the tips of her platform sandals on the line on the floor. "I have to stay back here?" Her first dart hit the board, then fell to the floor underneath. Her second hit the board outside of the ring, barely hanging on.

"One more. Throw it straight." Alex grinned behind his beer mug.

Gina's third dart hit the wall above the target.

The guys playing on the next board jokingly clapped after her last dart. Gina played along and curtsied, then returned to her seat.

"Okay, so that's not my game." She tasted her amber hard cider, her sports bar drink.

"Maybe you'll be better at skee-ball," he said biting into a buffalo wing.

"Are you kidding? When I was ten, I won a big pink dog at the county fair on skee-ball."

"Really? Who knew I was dating a skee-ball ringer?"

Gina brushed her knuckles across the opposite arm. "I haven't played in a while, but when I get warmed up, you watch out."

"Okay, champ," Alex teased.

"Hey, are you going to the Potomac Music Festival with me?" Gina asked, hoping he had changed his mind since she asked him last week.

"Don't think so." He ate a couple of onion rings, not even considering another option.

Gina grinned across the stack of wings, thinking that if she looked cute enough she could convince him to go. "But it's so much fun, great music, and so delicious -- steamed crabs, crabcakes, crab chips!"

"Yes, yes. How could I pass up R&B with a side of Benadryl? I think I'll pass." Alex washed down his onion rings with a swallow of beer. "Plus, you won't go with me to the hockey game."

"Uh, no. That's different. Have you ever seen a black woman at an ice hockey game?"

Alex's laughter confirmed Gina's assumption. "But you could be the first. You know you like to stand out in a crowd, be the first."

"I don't need to be that kind of pioneering woman. First in line for a shoe sale, yes. First black woman at an ice hockey game? Nah."

"You just don't want to be cold or watch guys get their teeth knocked out. Me, I could go into shock with all those crab germs in the air if I go to your thing." He continued to laugh as he took a bite out of another chicken wing.

"Alex. You are not that allergic to seafood."

"Okay, maybe I won't go into shock. Just my throat will close up and I'll pass out." Alex grabbed his throat as if gasping for air, then playfully kissed Gina on the cheek.

Gina realized they wouldn't always want to do the same things and wouldn't always be willing to compromise. Although this had been true with previous boyfriends, too, in a corner of her mind, she still wondered if it was a racial thing.

"So, has your mother said anything else about us?" Alex asked.

"No, not really." Gina turned her head to avoid eye contact. It wasn't really a lie since she hadn't spoken to her mother, she only listened to the voicemail. "She's an old woman, I told you. She's set in her ways and she doesn't really understand things are different now."

Long-held feelings of an old black woman, was the way Gina had tried to explain it to him before. It was the simplest way to summarize a family and personal history of racial experiences. A bad relationship between a black grandmother and a white grandfather several generations back. Bitterness over a mother who missed important family holiday dinners, like Thanksgiving and Christmas, because she had to make sure the home and meals of the white family she worked for were perfectly in order. The young white college grad that was hired as her husband's boss. Her daughter never being picked for the lead role in the school play; watching her daughter as a Munchkin or a field mouse while a curly blond-headed girl played Dorothy or Cinderella. Mrs. Morrison had a laundry list of reasons why her daughter shouldn't date a white man, but Gina didn't wish to relay her mother's life history.

When she told Alex her mother had misgivings about their relationship, he was quite puzzled by it. His feelings had been hurt a little bit. How would she feel if his mother reacted the same way, he had asked. Gina said she would be surprised if his family didn't feel the same, but for a different set of reasons.

"In that case, the marathon's a great idea, don't you think?" Alex said.

Thinking back on their training runs thus far, only up to five miles, Gina sighed at the thought of running a full twenty-six miles.

"*Great* idea? I'm not so sure. I'm still thinking we could've come up with a better plan."

"Maybe we can enter a skee-ball tournament. Come on, let's see what you've got."

"All right. And let's make it interesting. If I win, you go to the music festival."

"And if I win. You go to a hockey game."

"You better get your Benadryl, boy."

Sherry

Sherry stood behind her cherry wood desk, sorting through house contract offers. For the past hour, she and her office assistant, Corey, had been going back and forth between their offices, between the fax machine and email, receiving bids and making counter-offers for two houses she had listed. Hopefully, they would have two solid contracts by the end of the day. She was scribbling an offer to include a new oven in the older duplex when her office phone rang. She hit the speaker button on the console and greeted her sister.

"Has Jordan told her friends yet?" Sherry walked back over to Corey's desk and handed him the paper. She watched him read her note.

"I think she's told a few friends and that's really enough in her school. So, everyone knows now, but still pretending *not* to know if she didn't tell them. I don't think Brandon has told anyone that it's his, though."

Corey nodded and turned back to his computer to write up the counter-offer.

"You said you talked to his parents?" Sherry returned to her office.

"Yeah. They haven't come around and are, understandably, still upset. But I dare them to say it's not his baby when it comes out high yella."

"What do you mean 'high yella'? Is the boy white? Lord, don't tell me the baby's daddy's white." Sherry stopped in the middle of the floor waiting for her sister's response. She didn't have anything against interracial dating, but in this situation, it could make things more complicated.

"No, he ain't White. But he could pass if they wanted him to."

"Is he mixed?"

"Not that I know of. His folks are just light. I bet you could shake a white great-grandma or grand-daddy out of the branches of the family tree, though."

"That's everybody's family tree." She fell into the armchair in front of her desk and kicked off her heels.

"True. Anyway, I met his parents a while ago at a parents meeting or some school event. Then, well, since this whole thing, we've talked a couple times. But I don't think they've really, you know, fully accepted that their son is going to be a daddy."

"Hmm. It's got to be kinda hard. They're probably wondering how this is going to affect him going to college and what people are going to think about him getting some girl pregnant. How this is going to ruin *his* life and all," Sherry said with a slight hint of sarcasm. While talking, she found the ballerina flats she kept in her office laying under her desk.

"Sherry, don't be like that. They're nice people. And I think we're *all* a bit concerned about how this is going to affect their futures. I've been paying a lot of money to send her to that school so she could get into a good college. And for this to happen? I'm wondering if I've been wasting my money?"

"Well, if you thought tuition was a security fee to keep her out of temptation's way, then, yes, it apparently was a waste of money. But if you were writing those checks every month for Jordan to get a good education at a great school, I don't think having a baby is going to take any of that away from her." Sherry arranged the papers left on her desk into two neat piles, awaiting the next offer.

"But this is not the life I planned for her."

"Viv, you're not living the life you planned for yourself." Sherry paused a moment, looking at her desk. "Neither am I. Who is? Think about it. Who do we know actually doing what they said they would do when they grew up?"

After a few moments of silence, Vivian answered. "What about Cynthia?"

"Cynthia who? The chick with the hair salon?"

"Yeah. That's exactly what she said she was going to do when we were in high school. And now she's doing it."

"She's also been divorced three times and is almost a certified alcoholic. You think she planned that, too?"

"Well, I'm just sayin'."

"Like I said, no one is living the life they planned or at least hoped for. If so, I'd be home, playing with my beautiful baby and fixing dinner for my darling husband." It was like poking herself with a pin. She could see the pain coming, and though she was the one about to cause it, she didn't stop. She winced at her own mentioning of the dissolved marriage and the baby who would never be.

Sherry took a quick, deep breath. "Anyway, Jordan's going to be fine. Look at you. You're a single mom and she's grown into a functioning person. Its not like you're dragging her from gutter to gutter. You went to nursing school. You work a respectable job. Hell, you make enough to send her to private school! You're doing a fine job raising your daughter."

"With your help," Vivian said, considering her occasional request for financial aid from her sister.

"Whatever. Okay, *we're* doing a fine job raising your daughter. And *we're* going to do a fine job of getting her through school and raising your grandbaby, too. All of us." Sherry was making an important commitment to Vivian in offering to help with Jordan and her baby, but there was no doubt she would do whatever was needed to do to make sure her niece went to college.

"Speaking of what Jordan's going to do, what *is* she going to do? Has she replied to any acceptances yet?" Sherry asked.

"Not yet. She's got to do that soon, I guess."

"Maybe she should consider some of the ones close to you or me - North Carolina, Wake Forest, Maryland, Howard - so we could help with the baby."

Sherry could hear her sister tapping her nails on the other end of the line, a sign of nervousness.

"Yeah, I guess that would be a good idea." Vivian sighed on her end of the phone. "Or maybe she should go to whatever school she wants to and leave the baby here."

"And what, you gonna raise the baby?"

Sherry was surprised to hear a knock and turned to see Corey standing in the door frame. She waved to tell him to bring her the paper in his hand.

"Well, I have raised a kid before. There's a daycare in the hospital for staff, so that part would be taken care of."

"You don't think you're too old to be raisin' a baby?" Sherry said, reading over the latest offer. She wrinkled her nose as if she smelled sour milk, a face Corey had seen many times and knew meant, "What the hell kinda offer is this?"

"Please. I see women our age and older coming in everyday to have their baby. I ain't too old. And neither are you."

Sherry understood the implication in her sister's words. "We're not talking about me. We're talking about Jordan."

"Just sayin'. We looked at all that information about in-vitro and sperm banks and adoption agencies. You haven't said much about any of it lately."

"I'm still thinking. I'm not sure I can really handle being a single mother. Or if an adoption agency would actually consider me. I'm divorced because my ex is a convict. Who's going to give me a baby?"

"I doubt that matters. He's not in your life anymore. And anyway, it's not like he's a violent criminal," Vivian replied.

"I don't know. I have to admit, I'm kinda enjoying being single." She held up her index finger to Corey, indicating for him to wait at her desk until she got off the phone. "Look, I got to get back to these realtors about their offers. Tell Jordan to call me, we can talk about which of the colleges she likes closer to home, yours or mine."

Vivian promised to make the suggestion to Jordan before they said good-bye.

"You know if she comes up here, you're going to be the one raising that baby," Corey said after Sherry hung up the phone. "My sister came home with her baby, supposedly just for a little while, 'til she got herself back up on her feet. My nephew is three, still living with my mother, and we haven't seen my crazy sister in months."

"Well, Jordan's not crazy," Sherry said. She held her hand out for the note in his hand.

"They said they want a new refrigerator, too." Corey read from the counter-offer from the buyer's agent.

"Are you kidding me? The refrigerator is only a couple years old."

"They want cubed and shaved ice."

Sherry took the paper and read it over. "Some damn shaved ice. They're getting nothing. I'll get another offer, damn greedy people," she mumbled while scribbling a response across the offer and giving it back to Corey. He chuckled and left her office, returning to his desk.

Sherry went back to thinking about her conversation with her sister. Did she want Jordan to come to school near her so she could have a chance at raising a baby? Should she offer to keep the baby while Jordan went to one of her first choice schools? Sherry didn't really like either of those plans. In both scenarios, she would eventually have to return the baby to Jordan. There were too many players, too many rules, and too much shuffling.

Sherry wanted her own child, not a borrowed baby.

Laura

Laura checked her reflection then straightened her floor-length, black gown. This gown with a mermaid bottom and off-the-shoulder cap sleeves, bought specifically for the evening's black-tie dinner, was more modest than the dozen or more gowns hanging in her spare bedroom. She gave her lips a final swipe of lip-gloss before heading out of her apartment.

The doorman smiled as Laura stepped out of the elevator. "You look beautiful this evening. Your car is waiting."

At the curb in front of her building, a chauffeur stood next to a black town car. As she approached, she wondered whether he or his boss was taller, both appearing to be near six and half feet tall, if not taller. She noticed his brown eyes and the dimple in his left cheek as he greeted her and opened the back door.

"Good evening, Ms. Tavarez," Michael Stone said as she slid into the backseat next to him.

"Good evening, Mr. Stone."

Michael Stone, a local sports agent, was Laura's newest client. He was a handsome, affluent man who wouldn't seem to need to pay a woman to accompany him to public events. But, as she had learned over the years, these men often felt they could never be sure if women were truly interested in them or just the possible financial pay-off. For these types of clients, the maximum financial liability to her was the contracted fee.

Laura had caught a glimpse of him standing next to a basketball player on the news one evening. Seeing him again, she thought he was much more handsome in real life. He was the color of coffee with too much cream and had salt and pepper hair, cut short, with a very neatly trimmed mustache and goatee. Tonight, he wore a black tuxedo, without a cummerbund or tie, but with the appropriate black shiny dress shoes.

"Ma'am, there's a glass of wine there for you. I hope you enjoy it," the driver said over the back of his seat.

"Thank you," Laura said, accepting the glass from Michael and noticing the gold cufflink peeking out from under his jacket sleeve.

"I hope we won't remain so formal all evening and you'll call me Michael from now on."

"Okay, Michael. And you'll call me Stacey?" Laura replied, then nodded towards the driver. "And can you get him not to call me ma'am?"

"I think we can work that out. Sidney, her name's Stacey, not ma'am," he called to the driver. He leaned back in the seat and turned back to Laura. "Done. And your wine, you like it?"

"Mm hmm."

"Good. Now, did I tell you where we were going?"

"I don't believe you said specifically, only that we were going to a formal dinner, right?" Laura quickly glanced down at her dress. Generally she wasn't concerned about being overdressed, but a floor-length, black gown could easily be a bit too much.

"Don't worry, you're quite appropriate. In fact, you look absolutely fabulous. Well worth the price."

Laura blushed at this acknowledgement of their for-hire arrangement. She still felt a sliver of embarrassment or self-consciousness when it was addressed outright.

"Oh, sorry. I'm not supposed to say that, am I?" Michael apologized. "I'm used to dealing with my athletes and being blunt with them. I should be more considerate when I'm talking to a lady."

Laura giggled as a way to wave off his comment, as if it didn't bother her at all. While he explained that the local basketball team owner's wife was throwing a lavish dinner in honor of her husband's sixty-fifth birthday, Laura wondered for a moment what it would be like to be on a real date, to be a real girlfriend or wife, to be in a real relationship. If this were a real date, would she have spent the afternoon at the hairdresser, spending a week's grocery bill to have her hair put up in a loose, sexy chignon? Would this be an appropriate dress for a real girlfriend? She imagined a wife would be flattered if her husband thought she was worth all of that.

"It'll probably be mostly team members and their wives, other athletes, a few local politicians, business people. Do you like sports? Basketball, football, baseball, hockey?" Michael asked Laura.

She shook her head "no" as he listed each sport.

"Bowling?" He asked. "Okay, I can't imagine what else there is to watch other than sports." Michael had a laugh like tumbling water. It rolled over itself, bubbling and bursting.

"Ballet," she answered.

Michael furrowed his eyebrows and swallowed his wine. "Really?"

"Yes, really. The Capital Ballet here is great; it's one of the premiere companies in the country." When Michael looked amused, but unimpressed, Laura continued. "You know, Herschel Walker and Lyn Swann took ballet. I think Michael Jordan did, too."

"And I would much rather watch Jordan fly through the air with a basketball in his hand than in a tutu."

Laura laughed in response. "Well, if you ever find yourself with ballet tickets, feel free to pass them on."

"I'm more likely to get tickets on the space shuttle, but if I do, they're yours." Michael finished off his glass of wine. "Since you don't watch sports, let me fill you in on the guys who are going to be at the dinner."

Michael went on to list the various star players of the basketball team and other athletes who lived in the area. Laura vaguely recognized a few names from the local news and tried to at least keep track of what sport Michael said each played.

Laura now realized that maybe she should've done a little bit of background research on sports, maybe even a simple review of the local sports teams or the athletes Michael represented. But how was she to know he would actually want to engage in a conversation about his business?

Sidney pulled up in the cobblestone drive of the Richmont Mansion, an exclusive members-only club, directed by a cadre of valets and greeters. A uniformed valet opened Laura's door and extended his gloved hand.

Laura had perfected the red-carpet car exit. She put one sexy stiletto out of the car, resting her foot on the ground, getting her balance, while inspiring those outside to wonder who would follow the leg out. Next, she extended her hand to the waiting gentleman and stepped the other foot out of the car. Then she emerged slowly, nonchalantly to the wondering eyes of the people outside. Laura generally felt dismayed for the women who galloped out of the car, head first like a racehorse, leaning on the valet. Or those who shot both feet out of the car, then slid out, as if going down an emergency chute. Laura often thought she should hold classes on being sexy, yet classy, but figured those who needed it most wouldn't show up.

Michael waited on the other side of the valet, with his arm extended, elbow bent. In the bright lights of the mansion entrance, Laura could sense his proud peacock strut of having a beautiful woman on his arm. This was why they hired her.

A string quartet in the marble-floored foyer greeted the guests. Laura and Michael by-passed the coat valet, then were escorted to the main ballroom by another greeter.

There was a live band playing jazz and soul in the corner near the dance floor. The band's soloist wore a multi-hued headwrap around her puffy Afro and a long silver dress. As they entered the room, the singer was bargaining with an unseen nemesis, begging her not to mess with her man, offering her husband instead.

An army of waiters covered the floor, carrying trays of beef tartare, cubes of seared tuna, tasting spoons of caviar, stuffed mushrooms and glasses of wine and champagne. Along one long wall was a full bar attended by a trio of bartenders, shaking, mixing and pouring constantly.

Michael immediately started talking to the other guests. He seemed to know everyone in the room, or at least everyone seemed to know him. Moving through the crowd, he kept Laura close by, holding her hand, hugging her around the waist, or letting her hold his arm. He introduced Laura as his friend to each person he met. When the roving waiters paused near them, Michael picked up a glass of wine for her and one for himself. When the food trays passed by, Michael offered to hold Laura's glass while she enjoyed the hors d'eouvres.

Michael greeted a rookie football player who had his arm wrapped around a pretty young woman. "Congratulations! I heard it was a beautiful wedding."

Laura tried not to act too surprised by the bride who barely looked like she was out of high school. She marveled that this couple who was at least a dozen years younger than her had already checked off marriage on their life to-do list. She smiled and congratulated the couple, too.

"I'd never let one of my players get married without a pre-nup," Michael said as they walked away. He shook his head and grunted. "Do you know what that kid makes? And he married that girl after knowing her less than a year."

"But you don't know they're going to get divorced," Laura said.

"He doesn't know that they won't. That's the point of a pre-nup."

"What about love? Maybe they're really committed to each other," Laura offered.

Michael made the same face as when Laura said she preferred ballet over sports. "Love? We're not talking about love, here. We're talking about millions of dollars. Millions. Stacey, you're a businesswoman, I'm sure you can understand. Love's got nothing to do with it. When you're dealing with someone who has a contract like his, it's all business." He laughed as they continued making their way around the room.

Laura sipped at her wine as she thought over Michael's last statement. Rule Number 5. She wondered if she would sign a pre-nup if ever asked.

While Michael talked to another basketball player, Laura couldn't take her eyes away from the athlete's girlfriend. She was amazed the woman's over-sized breasts didn't float out of her low-cut dress like the helium-filled balloons they resembled.

In a break in the conversation, Michael turned and whispered in Laura's ear. "It's almost impossible not to look, right? It's like not noticing an elephant sitting in your car."

Laura sheepishly smiled, embarrassed she had been so obvious. She tried to keep a straight face and her eyes on the woman's face while they all continued their conversation.

Michael and Laura burst out in laughter as the couple wandered towards the dance floor.

"He bought them for her birthday," Michael said.

"Really?" Laura asked.

"Like I said before, it's all business. I'm sure he gets things from her, she got new breasts from him. Everyone's happy."

After each person he talked to, Michael told Laura an interesting morsel about them, alternately private, embarrassing or humorous. The tragic drug addiction of a couple's son. The extravagance of a couple's South Asian vacation home. A sports star's new yacht. Michael and Laura shared knowing smiles when an acquaintance of his who had recently been arrested for drunk driving waved off the waiter with the tray of wine.

When the band played a great dance song, Michael placed their glasses on the nearest table and pulled Laura onto the dance floor. In his black tuxedo and her figure-hugging black dress, they commanded everyone's attention as they swirled across the empty floor. They jokingly bowed to the crowd's applause after their dance.

"Michael. Over there, is he Warren Johnson?" Laura nervously asked when she saw the handsome, 7'2" brown frame stroll across the room.

"I thought you said you didn't follow sports?"

"I don't. I am probably his biggest fan who doesn't watch him play."

"Ahh, it's the underwear commercials, right?" Michael smirked at his star-struck date, playfully shaking an accusing finger at her. As she started to blush, he took her hand. "Come on, I'll introduce you."

Laura straightened her dress and followed Michael. Surely, he must think this was either a silly crush or a gold digger attraction. She hoped it was the former.

"Hey, Warren, how're you doin'?" The two men shook hands and exchanged greetings. "Let me introduce you to my date. This is Stacey Tavarez, one of your biggest fans." He winked at Laura. "Stacey, this is Warren Johnson, basketball all-star."

Her alias was like a hypnotist's bell to remind Laura she was working, she wasn't enjoying a real date. Throughout the night, she heard the bell constantly as Michael repeatedly introduced her as "Stacey". Not for the first time, Laura wished for the guy who would use her real name.

"And I think I could become one of your biggest fans," the basketball player said to Laura.

"How did you end up with the finest lady in the room?" He said to Michael.

"It's either my good looks or my good luck."

"Well, then you must be a damn lucky guy," Warren replied. "Maybe I need to get you as my agent after all." He laughed, then turned to Laura. "Stacey, I've heard Michael can be pretty greedy, but I hope he'll let me steal you for a dance before the night is over."

Laura grinned and mumbled an agreement before Warren excused himself to catch up with another player across the room.

"Michael, thank you. You were so sweet to introduce me to him."

"He likes you. You better save a few of those dance steps for him."

"Oh, please. I'm sure he just said that. Probably has said it a hundred times tonight."

"He probably has. But he meant it for you." He stopped another waiter for two more glasses of wine and passed one to Laura.

Laura wondered if Michael would in fact, not mind if she danced with him during the evening. Probably not, she thought. He obviously was pretty good at keeping his personal feelings and business activities separate.

After countless glasses of wine, twentieth introduction and fourth dance, Laura almost forgot Michael Stone was paying for her to be by his side. The band singer repeated Aretha Franklin's realization that the nightlife may not be a good life, but it was her life. Laura wrapped her hand around Michael's arm and raised a silent toast to the singer and Aretha.

Define "Fine"

The DJ blared the latest hip-hop songs through the speakers suspended above the crowded dance floor. Squeezing through the crush of people relieved to be released from their nine-to-fives, Sherry and Cookie made their way to the bar.

"Are these seats taken?" Sherry asked two men sitting next to a couple of empty barstools.

"Nah, you can sit there," one said.

"How you doin'?" the other asked, looking directly at Cookie.

Cookie smiled wanly. "Fine," she said. She moved to sit down on the stool furthest from him.

Sherry sat quickly in the seat, as if they were playing a game of musical chairs, forcing Cookie to sit next to him.

"Can I get you a drink?" the man asked.

"Oh, that's okay. I'm just going to have water. But thank you."

The man shrugged and returned to his conversation.

"Really? You're really going to drink a glass of water?" Sherry said, almost loud enough for the man to hear her.

"I don't want him to buy me a drink. Then he'll try to talk to me all night," Cookie whispered back.

"And that would be a bad thing?"

"I don't feel like being stuck with him all night," Cookie said.

80

"He didn't ask you to marry him! He offered to buy you a drink." Sherry shook her head. She waved over the bartender and ordered a martini. "And a glass of water for my friend."

"With lemon," Cookie said.

"Let me tell you what happened after my settlement today," Sherry said after they got their drinks.

"You had a settlement? Good for you."

"Yes, thank God because they have been far and few. But that's not my point. Let me tell you what happened. After we're done, the other broker comes over to me, chattin' me up and all, then asks me out!"

"Really? What'd you say?" Cookie sipped her water. She watched the man next to her out of the corner of eye, hoping he would leave so she could order a mojito.

"I said I wasn't interested. He's white. And he isn't cute."

"Sherry. You're not going out with the man because he's white?"

"No. I'm not going out with him because he isn't cute."

On the other side of the room, they saw Gina's head poking above the crowd as she stood on the landing at the doorway. When she spotted them at the bar, she waved then disappeared into the crowd as she descended the few steps.

"Well, you said 'white' first."

Sherry rolled her eyes. "If I was to go there, he would have to be attractive. Undeniable, no questions of what you see in this man, kind of fine. People Magazine's 50 Finest Men fine."

"Maybe he's nice, would treat you well. Maybe he has a great sense of humor. What about that?"

They watched Gina wedging her way through the dancing people.

"Okay, yeah, maybe he is, but I could get that in a black guy."

When Gina finally reached the bar, she gave Sherry and Cookie each a quick hug. "Laura should be here in a few minutes."

"Then I need to find a guy in here before she shows up. She always gets the good ones," Sherry said.

"Please, Sherry, you look great," Cookie said. "Me on the other hand? We look like Ginger and Mary Ann standing next to each other."

Gina and Sherry tried to cover a chuckle in agreement to Cookie's comparison. Cookie was still dressed in the jeans she wore in the bakery, although she had exchanged her everyday white shirt for a red blouse and her sneakers for black kitten heels. Laura would no doubt make her entrance in a figure-fitted dress, cut low enough to show off her cleavage and high enough to flaunt her toned legs, with heels adding at least three to four inches to her height.

"Well, some people think Mary Ann's cute, too." Sherry grinned, nodding at the men next to them.

"That's because they haven't seen Ginger," Cookie said. "Anyway, you've got a man asking you out and you turned him down."

"Oh, really, now. And who is that?" Gina asked with mock surprise.

"The broker from her settlement today," Cookie said. "He's white," she stage-whispered.

Gina raised her eyebrows at Sherry with real surprise.

"He's not cute," Sherry added. "All I'm saying is - if you're going to date an unattractive guy, you don't have to go outside your own people."

"Sherry! That's so not right," Gina said.

"Says the woman with a cute, white boyfriend."

"I'm not going out with him just because he's cute," Gina said defensively.

Sherry cut her eyes at Gina and twisted her lips. "Maybe not, but you would not be going out with him if he was ugly." She put her hand up to say "stop" before Gina could form a response. "Don't even try to put your lips together to tell a lie Evangeline." She laughed, knowing Gina hated being called by her full name.

"You're still wrong. What if a white person said that? You would be all offended," Cookie said.

"Well, I wouldn't go out with a black guy who wasn't nice looking, either. So, I'm universally shallow." Sherry took a sip of her drink as her friends shook their heads.

"Come on, now, you know when you see a white girl with a not-cute black guy you think 'girl, for all that you could've stayed with white guys.' But at least she didn't take one of our good ones!" She laughed again and, inspite of herself, Cookie did, too.

"Can I get a glass of sauvignon blanc, please?" Gina said to the bartender as he paused in front of them. "And no more for her," she said, nodding towards Sherry. Gina often got sensitive around the subject of interracial dating, she always felt they were talking about her and Alex.

"Oh, Gina, don't get mad. You did it right, you got yourself a nice white guy," Sherry said.

"Are you drinking water?" Gina asked Cookie, staring into her glass. "Why?"

"So she wouldn't have to talk to that guy behind you," Sherry said.

"Shh," Cookie whispered and swatted at Sherry. "He'll hear you."

"Oh, now you're worried about hurting his feelings," Sherry said.

"Hello, girls," Laura cooed as she stepped up to the bar. The men next to Cookie grinned at her, looking up and down her frame, pausing for a moment at the most curviest parts. She ignored them as she greeted her friends.

"And now that you're here," Sherry said, turning to the bartender. "Shots for all of us."

"Thanks. What's the occasion?" Gina asked.

"My two-year anniversary." Legally, Sherry had only been divorced a year, but she considered the day her husband was sentenced as the end of their marriage. After his trial was over, she went straight to the other side of the courthouse with her divorce papers in hand. She spent the evening crying in Cookie's living room, eating too many cupcakes and drinking too much liquor.

"Already?"

"Did he call?"

"Nah, he doesn't call anymore, thank God. He sent me another letter the other day though." Sherry thought about the envelope stamped with the prison's emblem. She had tossed it, unopened, into her desk drawer, along with the other dozen letters her ex-husband had sent since his imprisonment.

The bartender returned with four shot glasses of vodka.

"Okay, so somebody make a toast, drink up and we're gonna be done talking about Mr. Everett."

"To your singleness." Cookie raised her glass.

"To your independence," Laura said.

"Men, beware!" Gina toasted.

"Cheers!" They tapped their shot glasses together and emptied them in unison. They blinked as they set the glasses back on the bar.

"Now, back to Sherry's dating or not," Gina said, still not sure if she should be offended by Sherry's thoughts on dating white men.

"I'm just sayin', if I was to date a white guy, you better believe he'd be a fine ass, out of the movies, blond-headed, white man. Like the one who's always getting arrested for running around naked? And the one with all those kids? That's what I'm talking about."

"So what, would you date a black guy who isn't fine? Is that what you're saying?" Laura asked.

"Nope. If I date anybody – black, white, Asian, Mexican, British, Aborigine – he's got to be good looking. Life's too short to waste on ugly men." Sherry finished the last swallow of her drink and set her glass on the bar.

Gina thought for a moment while sipping at her wine. "Do you think there are different qualifications to be fine depending on whether you're black or white?"

"The actual appearance would be different, but the basic physiological structure would be the same," Cookie replied.

"I was going to say 'no', but what does that mean?" Sherry asked.

"I was watching this documentary the other night…"

"Oh, not another documentary!" Gina said.

"We've got to get you a man, Cookie," Laura said.

Sherry looked over her shoulder for the man who had offered Cookie a drink, but he was gone. "Oh, well, we missed our chance."

Cookie continued as her friends laughed. "So, they said a key part of being attractive is having a symmetrical face. They showed pictures of people who would be considered handsome or pretty and went through all these measurements to show how their face was symmetrical." Cookie patted her cheeks as she talked. "Then they changed their face, you know, photo computer manipulation, so they would be un-symmetrical."

"Asymmetrical," Gina corrected.

"And you could see how the un-symmetrical face was not as pretty as the symmetrical face." Cookie took another sip of her water. "But being symmetrical wasn't enough. There were one or two people they showed who were symmetrical, but they were not pretty."

Sherry felt Cookie gearing up for an explanation of the theory. She picked her glass back up and waved it at the bartender, indicating she needed another martini. Laura quickly held up two fingers.

"And a mojito," Cookie called to the bartender, then returned to her explanation. "It didn't have anything to do with race, although the people in the study were white. They didn't show any black people, but I don't think it would matter."

"What does all this have to do with people being fine or not, Cookie?" Sherry asked.

"Okay, I'm getting to that. There's also other basic human face structure things. Like eyes, should be bright and straight, right across the middle of your face."

"What about Asian people, their eyes aren't straight and there are pretty Asian people," Laura said.

"Straight across their face, I mean. Even with each other."

Sherry glanced around the room as Cookie explained her theory on attractiveness. She nodded to Laura as she spotted handsome men scattered around the room.

"There's all kinds of things to consider. How your face lines up, how it's centered."

"You got all this from your documentary?" Gina asked, not believing her.

"No; seventh grade art class facial drawing. You see, getting to fine is very hard, because you've got to have all the basics covered to just be regular."

"Cookie, you aren't making any sense. Doesn't everybody have a regular face?" Gina knew this was going to be a dissertation.

"Not really," Cookie said.

"You mean regular as in okay looking?" Sherry asked.

"Right; take a look around. It's not as easy as you'd think. Like the girl over there, her eyes are too big for her face." Cookie subtly pointed at a woman sitting at a nearby table.

Sherry found the woman. "Hmm. You're right."

"And the guy over there, at the end of the bar. His lips fall within the width of the space between his eyes, his mouth is too small." Cookie drew imaginary lines down from her eyes to the corners of her mouth.

"Okay, but he isn't ugly." Gina said as she tried to peek at the guy without him noticing.

"I didn't say he was ugly, I'm saying he doesn't have the basic facial structure to even hope to be fine. Now that guy over there."

Cookie nodded across the room. Sherry followed her eyes and spotted a guy talking to a woman in a mini-dress on the edge of the dance floor. He was tall enough, just over six feet tall and had neat, shoulder-length black dreadlocks; very easy to spot. Sherry watched him until she caught his eye.

"Very nice facial structure, good start. Then the other fine-ness requirements."

"Yes, I definitely agree. He's got all the other requirements, too," Sherry said.

"Like what?" Gina asked.

"Like, go back to eyes. They should be dark. Dark brown or black, dark," Cookie said.

Gina tried not to spit out her drink. "Okay, but what about what Sherry just said about the fifty sexiest men? They have blue eyes!"

"Really?" Cookie looked at Sherry for confirmation, then nudged her when she didn't answer. "Sherry."

Sherry kept an eye on tall-dreadlock-guy on the dance floor as she answered. "What? Yes. Dude with the kids, his eyes might be green or gray."

"And the naked one, definitely blue," Laura said.

"Okay, well they're the exception to the rule." Cookie paused in thought. "Really, are you sure? Okay, how about the other guy, the one from *Titanic*?"

"Yes, his eyes are blue, maybe gray. All of the sexiest men alive have not-brown/black eyes except Denzel," Gina informed her.

Cookie considered this unexpected information. "Hmmm, interesting. I'll have to check, but okay for now."

"Hey, maybe it's the blue-eyes thing," Sherry said to Gina.

"What?" Gina asked suspiciously.

"Maybe your mom doesn't like Alex or any other white man because the blue eyes freak her out. Some times they're so light they are kinda spooky," Sherry suggested.

Gina wrinkled her brow at the latest bit of nonsense from her friends. "No. My mother is not spooked out by blue eyes. I told you, she's got a list of all the wrong done to our family by white folks." Gina sighed, exasperated.

"Okay, then. Its not the blue eyes, so let's get back to fine men, shall we?" Cookie said, bringing them back to their lighter conversation before they got derailed into something more serious.

"We shall," Sherry said. She noticed tall-dreadlock-guy staring at her. He was wearing a button down shirt, but in a casual way, not faking as if he were coming from a very important job.

"All right, hair," Cookie continued, encouraged.

"Oh, God. Are we going to go through every bodily feature?" Gina asked.

"I hope so," Sherry said, still smiling at tall-dreadlock-guy.

"Now, hair." Cookie cleared her throat and continued, as if giving a lecture. "Depending on the face and who the person is, it could be long, short, but its got to be neat and it can't be in cornrows. Dreads are fine, very neat braids are maybe, but cornrows, no. And that's only black guys; white guys should not have any type of dread, braid, cornrow, nothing."

"Or, bald can be nice, too." Despite herself, Sherry briefly reflected on rubbing her hand over her ex-husband's smooth head.

"Why can't white guys have braids? You don't think Alex would look nice with cornrows?" Gina laughed at herself as she started to feel the affects of the wine.

"Is she drunk?" Laura asked Sherry.

"She must be. Continue," Sherry said, taking a swallow of her own drink.

"As I was saying, hair is variable, as long as it's neat."

Tall-dreadlock guy and mini-dress girl were dancing, but he kept his eyes on Sherry. He winked at her over his dance partner.

"But dreads are definitely a possibility," Sherry said, smiling, shaking the image of her ex out of her mind.

Cookie glanced again at Sherry's new-found prey and laughed.

"What?" Gina looked around the room, following Sherry's eyes to the guy on the dance floor. "Ohmigosh, Sherry. How old is that boy? He probably had to have his momma drop him off tonight."

"He ain't that young, but he's young enough," Sherry said.

"His girl's going to come over here and slap the both of you."

"Oh, please. She can't handle me. Let her come on over."

"Why's it have to be so violent?" Cookie giggled.

Laura nudged Sherry. "You see how his jaw – ooh – just so? That looks pretty symmetrical to me."

"Right, right. Do white guys' jaws do that?" Sherry asked, directed at Gina.

"Yes, the fine ones. And if they're good, they can get the goatee thing going and not look raggedy." Gina stroked her chin slowly, as if she, too, had a goatee.

"Yeah, that's kinda tricky for guys, black or white, to get right," Cookie said.

"Oh, wait, he's leaving. Is he leaving?" Sherry said.

They watched tall-dreadlock-guy and his dance partner head towards the front door.

"Oh, well. Lost one. Who else is in here?" Sherry said, surveying the room.

"A couple other guys who just turned 21 are dancing around," Laura teased. "I'll keep my eyes out for you."

"You need to be keeping your eyes out for yourself," Sherry said.

"Who? Not me. Men don't like women who date other men for a living. You must be talking to Cookie."

Cookie made a face as if she was confused, but she knew where the conversaton was headed.

"Cookie, you know what she's saying. You talk about what's fine and what's not, but what does it all matter?" Gina said.

"True. You didn't even want to talk to that guy and he was kinda nice looking," Sherry said.

Again, the conversation made its way back to Cookie's dating life.

"Well, well." Cookie stumbled, thinking of a response. "I don't feel like being bothered, that's all."

"But what's the bother? We're having fun. No one's taking anything serious here. A drink, a dance, enjoy yourself," Gina said.

"I don't have to go out with everyone who asks me." Cookie pulled a lipgloss out of her purse and applied it, pouting and blowing an air-kiss at Gina.

Laura pinched Sherry on the arm and nodded towards the door. Tall-dreadlock-guy was walking back in, alone, and straight towards her, grinning. Sherry returned his smile.

"Where's that bartender? I need a drink," Gina said.

Gina

"Babe, you ready to run?" Alex asked.

"Are you asking me because I now have a choice? Because if I do, I choose not to run and to go to the diner for breakfast. Or we could stay in bed this morning," Gina purred. She was sure she could lure him back into the coziness of the comforter and get him to cancel this crazy idea of training for a marathon, at least for today.

"Get up." Alex coaxed Gina out of the bed and prodded her towards the bathroom.

Gina pulled her hair back in a ponytail, dressed in a pair of black running pants and a red designer athletic top she had bought from a sportswear boutique downtown with hopes not to ruin it with any actual sweat. She threw a towel around her neck.

Now that she looked like a runner, Gina decided that she would try to have a better attitude. Maybe she could actually learn to like running; Alex certainly did.

"Ready?" Alex asked, handing her a water bottle.

"Yeah, sure." Gina grabbed her iPod from the shelf near the door and followed Alex to the elevator.

"I think we can maybe get in a short run, five to eight miles," Alex said as he pushed the elevator button for the ground floor. "Depending on how you feel. Let's see how we do for half an hour."

"Sounds good to me," Gina agreed, determined to be positive.

Out on the sidewalk, Alex led Gina through a few stretches before they started running.

"Are we done, now? Can we go get some breakfast?" Gina asked jokingly and began to strap the iPod onto her arm.

"You know, you really shouldn't run with those in your ears. You might not hear car horns or a police siren coming by."

"Alex. I've survived wearing earbuds while walking down the street thus far, I'm sure I'll be fine."

"It would be good practice not to wear them, you can't wear them in the real run."

Gina ignored him and placed the earbuds in her ears then searched her hips and hands trying to figure out how she was going to carry the water bottle. Alex gestured for her to give him the bottle. She heard him faintly through her headphones.

"Give it to me, then I'll be balanced carrying mine. Maybe I'll get you a CamelBak before our next run."

Gina had no clue what a CamelBak was but it didn't sound very attractive. She handed him the water bottle, then jogged along-side him. By the third block, he picked up his pace.

Come on, girl. It's really not so bad, just a little bit faster, Gina thought. She quickened her steps. In the background of her own thoughts and her music, she faintly heard Alex talking.

"We'll build up our speed over the next few blocks, then settle in at a pace that we can still maintain a conversation."

She wasn't sure how they were going to run and talk at the same time.

Gina concentrated on keeping up with his lead. She reached out and took the water bottle from him, tried to take a sip, spilled water all over the front of her shirt, then passed the bottle back to him.

With this method, we might as well sign up for a relay, too, she thought.

Twenty minutes in, Gina had had enough. Her sides hurt and she was thirsty because she had gotten tired of passing the water back and forth.

"Alex. Can. We. Take. A. Break? I. Don't. Think. That. This. Is a. Pace. To keep. Up. A. Con. Ver. Sation." Gina fell a few steps behind and had to raise her voice for Alex to hear her.

"Come on, Gina. You can keep up. You're doing great." Alex was breathing hard, but he could at least get out an entire sentence. Gina found herself jealous of Alex's superior lung capacity.

"I. Think. We. Should. Slow. Down. I'm. Tired. And I'm. Thirsty."

"Babe, we've got to keep on moving. If you stop it's going to be hard to get going again. You've got to build up your endurance."

I'm going to build up my endurance by kicking your butt after I get my breath back, Gina thought, too tired to even talk to herself.

She gritted her teeth, which she hoped would be mistaken for a loving smiling. She was, after all, working on her positive attitude. She appreciated Alex's efforts to make a good impression on her mother. She was touched that he even cared what her mother thought. But she was exhausted.

Alex handed Gina the water bottle and slowed his pace by a few strides.

Again, Gina tried to drink, run, and breathe all at the same time.

This is not sexy at all, Gina thought as she dribbled water out of her mouth like a two-year old. Running could be detrimental to their relationship. Her sweating and dribbling could change the way Alex viewed her, especially when she fell out on the sidewalk, he might not think she was so pretty and sexy and graceful.

Gina slowed to a fast walk. The problem with running out on the streets was that there's no way to just quit and be done. There's no STOP button.

Alex had told her to bring her ID. Gina realized she also should have brought money for a cab-ride home when she had had enough of this foolishness. She promised herself that the next time, she was going to slip her debit card into her shoe along with her driver's license. That was a lesson Gina's mother had taught her almost twenty years ago.

"Don't go out with no man with no money, at least a quarter to call home for someone to come get you. Even better if you take money enough to get yourself home," her mother always had reminded her.

And here she was, a grown-ass woman, having forgotten her mother's words of wisdom from high school.

"Yes, this is why Momma doesn't approve of him. He's the type of white man that makes me forget my good sense," she mumbled.

"How're you doing back there, babe?" Alex turned around and gave Gina the thumbs-up sign, waiting for her to do the same.

Gina threw her thumb up quickly before he ran into a light pole. When they got back and she could speak in complete sentences again, she would warn him about running and turning around to look at her. After she finished kicking his butt.

When she couldn't stand the cramp in her side anymore, Gina finally slowed to a walk and Alex ran ahead. About a mile later, she could see him at the end of the block, running in place waiting for the light to change.

He must be waiting for me, she thought. She smiled and quickened her pace to catch up to him.

"You ready to run the last part? We only have half a mile to go," Alex said as Gina got closer.

Gina took a deep breath and reluctantly nodded her head.

Alex grinned and nodded towards the street as the walk sign began to blink on the opposite corner. "Let's go."

Gina ran slightly behind him, noticing that he was running slower than his usual pace. They approached a blonde woman running in the opposite direction. She smiled at Alex and opened her mouth as if to say something, then quickly closed her mouth and dropped her smile as she glanced at Gina. The woman almost imperceptibly sneered at them, then continued to run past them.

Gina pursed her lips. She briefly wondered if the woman's reaction was because she was disappointed that Alex wasn't alone or because Alex was white and Gina was black. She never had to consider the options when she was with Jason, or any of her previous boyfriends, who all had been black. Having to think about race was one of things that had gone through her mind when Alex first asked her out six months ago.

"Gina. Are you free for dinner tonight?" Alex asked, standing in the doorway of her cubicle.

"Who wants us to go?" Gina asked, not looking up from her computer. She wondered if their director was sending them out or the restaurateur had invited them in order to get on their list of recommended restaurants.

"I do," Alex said.

Gina looked at him quizzically. "You do? Why?"

"Because, I would like to take you to dinner," he said, stepping toward her desk and lowering his voice.

She was sure he was joking. "For real. What's the deal?" This time she turned and gave him her full attention.

"For real, I want to take you to dinner. Is that allowed?" When he smiled, parentheses appeared to highlight his straight nose and thin lips.

"You mean, like, you and me? No work assignment?" Gina searched his sometimes gray-sometimes blue eyes for any hint of a joke. She was not about to fall into an office prank and be embarrassed.

"Yes."

"As in, we don't have a per diem, no reimbursement? You're paying?" She glanced over his low-cut brown hair.

He laughed as she emphasized "you". "Yes."

"Meaning, you are going to pick me up and escort me to a restaurant with cloth napkins?" She considered, not for the first time, the shape of his shoulders in his blue button-down shirt. And what he would look like without it.

"Yes. Yes, yes, yes. Whatever you want – yes," Alex said, at the same time joking and pleading, and waited for more questions.

"So, are we going?" He asked when she didn't say anything.

"Let me think about it," she said, already having made up her mind. She grinned flirtatiously at him. "I'll stop by your office in a bit." She still had to play hard to get.

"Well, okay." He shook his head. "But I'm not waiting forever," he said as he walked back out of her space.

Gina watched the top of his head slide past her cubicle partition, then inhaled deeply and slowly let all the air out while having her own private debate and run of questions in her head. She tried to reason with herself that though she was inclined to say "yes", she should give it some more consideration.

They went to work events all the time and they enjoyed each other's company. But, a date? Would this be a date? It sounded like it. What if it didn't work out, wouldn't work be awkward? Or, what if it did? *And oh, yeah — he's white!* She'd never been asked out by a white guy before. Was it racist to think about it? No, she concluded, it wasn't racist, it was a fact. He was white, she was black, and they would be an interracial couple. Had he thought about it? Did she want to be an interracial couple? Was she thinking too much into this? It was just dinner. It was an interracial date, but that didn't make them a couple. And so what, should it even matter? *Hell, yeah, it mattered.* Her mother would have a fit if she brought home a white man. She was supposed to bring home a guy who looked like her father: tall, dark, handsome, preferably from the south, or at least his people were from the south. But what if she didn't? What if the person meant for her didn't look like her father at all? She had never given that possibility any consideration.

All the guys she had ever dated were black. But obviously, none of them had worked out too well or she wouldn't be single, getting asked out by a guy from work. She had gone out with a couple of guys since her last boyfriend packed up and moved across the ocean. One, who her mother would've liked was handsome, a lawyer, with a nice place in the right part of the city and family that was from North Carolina. And he was a total jerk.

On their last date, he went on and on about his current case. Blah blah blah, all he could do for his client, how he would defend him so excellently and get him off, blah blah blah. Finally, when he took her home, she told him she didn't think she was the right girl for him. She gave him the "it's not you, it's me" line, and given his ego, he went for it. There had been another guy who didn't want to go out to dinner; he insisted that she cook. After ordering in a few times, she couldn't fake it anymore and finally admitted she didn't know how to boil an egg.

Now, here is a really nice, cute guy --- true, a bit melanin challenged -- asking me out for dinner and damn it, I'm going, she thought.

Gina got up from her desk and went to look for him in his office. Instead, she found him standing at the receptionist's desk. She pointed back to her office and he nodded. A few minutes later he was standing at her doorway again.

"What time are you picking me up?"

"I made reservations for seven. I can come and get you about six. If we're early, we can check out the bar."

"Sounds good." She wiggled her toes as best as she could in her gray stilettos and tried to keep her voice business-like, not letting any girlish giggle of excitement about this surprise date slip out. "Now, are you ready for our 3 o'clock to talk about the grand opening reception at the new Hyatt?"

Gina realized that living in a cosmopolitan city like D.C., they were part of the diverse background of characters in the city landscape, but she still wasn't convinced that race wasn't an issue in dating. At least her friends didn't treat her any different or have any negative comments about their dating, although they had plenty of jokes. Now, she only had to convince her mother that, despite their family experiences, all interracial relationships and interactions weren't bad.

They reached the end of their morning run in front of Alex's apartment building. He stretched and pulled off his sweaty shirt.

Gina shook her head. Although, his body still bore the proof of his years on the college swim team and summers as a lifeguard, she wasn't really keen on the idea of him stripping on the sidewalk, but he did it every time they ran.

Yeah, that right there just may be worth Momma's disapproval, she thought, following him into the building.

Laura

Laura wheeled her suitcase to her apartment, home from another client trip. The client was a local businessman who had been honored in his small hometown for donating money to renovate the downtown theatre. He hired Laura because he didn't want to return home and attend the dinner and first performance at the theatre alone.

She went back down the hall to Gina's apartment to pick up her dog. She could hear classic Motown coming from inside the apartment as she waited for Gina to answer the door.

"Welcome home. How was your trip?" Gina stepped aside to let Laura in the door. "You look nice." Gina glanced over Laura's blue wrap-dress and matching heels.

"Thanks. It was good. Nothing exciting, but interesting enough. It was a small town, so I stayed at this quaint little bed and breakfast instead of a hotel. You don't get too many chances to stay at a good country B & B." Laura told Gina about the chicken-and-dumplings and sweet tea at the little mom-and-pop restaurant.

"Thankfully, between dinner and all the festivities, we didn't have to go to a family meal or anything like that."

Laura's dog, Lady, lay under the window in the rectangle of sunlight seeping through the blinds. She lifted her head as soon as Laura spoke and trotted over to her. Lady never ran, apropos to her name, but stepped a bit quicker whenever Laura came to retrieve her. The dog nudged her head against Laura's leg.

"Hey, little Lady. How you doin'? Did you miss me? Of course you did." Laura cooed and rubbed Lady's head and under her neck.

"Let me get her things," Gina said, heading to the kitchen.

Laura hummed along with the Sam Cooke song on the radio, then started to pay attention to the words.

"Do you think he's right, Gina?" She frowned at the stereo as if upset with the singer.

"Who? About what?" Gina returned from the kitchen with the dog's bowls, food, and leash and looked around her living room.

Laura nodded her chin towards the speakers to the singer's voice crooning, "you may be king, you may possess the world and it's gold; but gold won't bring you happiness when you're growing old."

"Like he said, that you're nobody 'til somebody loves you."

Gina listened to the song for a moment. "Well, yeah, kinda. I mean, if no one loves you, who are you? But luckily, everyone is loved by somebody."

"Everybody? You think everybody is loved by somebody?"

"Sure they are: their momma and daddy, their boyfriend, husband, wife, their kids, their friends, their crazy stalker. Then, depending on who loves you, that kind of love is going to be different for each person. Your momma's not going to love you like your man, but each person's love is going to shape who you are."

"So, if no one loves you, you aren't anybody. Like he said."

"But everyone is loved by somebody."

"Really? Then, who loves us?" Laura challenged. She put her hand on her hip while waiting for an answer.

"Us? Oh, lots of people love us," Gina said, clasping her hands to her shoulders in a dramatic self-hug.

"Name one. Name one person who loves you."

Gina playfully started singing a classic Sunday School song. "Jesus loves me, this I know."

"Oh, Jesus loves everybody. He doesn't count." Laura sucked her teeth and waved off Gina's song.

"My mother loves me. My daddy loved me."

"Then who loves me?" Laura asked. "My parents are sittin' in heaven."

"Laura, your friends love you."

"Well, I guess that'll have to do for now, huh?" Laura attempted a laugh.

"You okay? Anything happen on your trip you want to talk about?"

Laura had tried to explain her business to Gina a number of times. When she first told her she was a personal escort, like most people, Gina had assumed she meant there was a sexual component to her work. She had emphasized that she was strictly an escort, only meeting her clients in public venues. Gina was impressed by Laura's ability to manage her own business, with herself as the sole product, making a profit on the genetic luck that she was a very attractive female. But Laura didn't think any of her friends understood the personal cost of always being a date for hire. Especially the loneliness.

"Nothing really. You know, I go to all these great events. Most of the times, my clients are the guys who know everyone and everyone wants to know. The single women, even some of the married ones, are ready to break my leg to get me out of the way."

Laura patted Lady on the back, watching the dog wag her tail.

"But, it's not like there's any point bothering to get to know the guys. It's like any other business relationship. And I don't really feel excited about the events. The dinners and conventions get kinda boring after awhile."

"What about the comic convention?" Gina asked.

"Okay, maybe that one was interesting," Laura said, laughing. "And my new client, he's nice, too."

"The one from this weekend?"

"No, this other one." Laura paused to think back to her appointment with Michael. "We went to a birthday party, of all things, and I actually enjoyed myself."

"A birthday party?"

"Yeah, this rich guy's birthday. But there was great food and drinks. And we danced." Laura smiled as she reflected on sweeping across the dance floor. "No one ever takes me dancing."

The doorbell rang.

"Who is it?" Gina asked.

A male voice called through the door just as she opened it.

"Hey. What're you doing here?" Gina's smile softened her words.

"And hello to you, too," Alex said as he walked in. He wore loose fitting jeans, a graphic tee, a UConn baseball cap, and sandals and carried a restaurant carry-out bag.

Laura watched the comfortable interaction between him and Gina with a little bit of jealousy.

"I brought you dinner." The smell of fried fish accompanied him into the apartment.

"Dinner?" Gina asked.

"I figured you've probably worked up an appetite between our run this morning and your housecleaning this afternoon. I stopped by that fish and ribs place you like." He suddenly noticed Laura standing by the couch. "Oh, hey, Laura," he said.

"Did you bring enough for everybody?" Laura asked.

Alex shook his head. "If I had known you'd be here, but I'm sure Gina will share."

Laura laughed. "Thanks, but I should get going. You two enjoy your dinner." She gathered Lady's tote bag and bed. "Come on, baby. Thanks, Gina, for watching her for me."

"You're welcome. Get some rest, you seem like you had a rough trip." Gina gave Laura a hug.

"He's cute and he feeds you? He got a brother, cousin, friend, something to bring with him next time?" Laura joked as she walked out the door.

Sherry

"No running for you this morning, huh?" Sherry whispered, sliding over to make space for Gina and Laura.

"Girl, I did a raindance last night. The marathon-gods must've taken pity on me so I could get out of training." Gina shimmied out of her black, ruffle-collared trench coat, damp from the morning drizzle, folded it neatly inside out and laid it on the back of her seat. She pulled off the scarf tied loosely over her hair and ran her fingers quickly through her hair.

Laura rubbed her arms, trying to whisk away the chill from the spring rain. "I wish they served coffee," she whispered.

"Where?" Sherry asked.

"Here," Laura said. She had taken her hat off when they entered to shake the rain off and was now readjusting it on her head.

"In church?" Sherry asked.

"They serve wine, they could serve coffee," Laura replied.

"I don't think they actually 'serve' wine," Cookie said.

"It would be nice if we could have little bites of cheese to go along with the crackers, though," Gina said to Sherry.

"I don't think we're getting the wine and crackers service today, anyway," Sherry said.

"They're serving hor d'eourves afterwards, they could've easily put a table in the back for us to enjoy before they got started," Laura said.

Gina glanced at her watch. "What time does this start anyway?"

"Four o'clock," Cookie said.

"I don't know why I thought it might start on time," Gina said, shaking her head.

"Me neither. Monica's not been on time a day in her life," Sherry said.

Sherry and Gina had known Monica since college, and the others had become friends when she moved to D.C. last year to be closer to her fiancée. This was the first wedding that Sherry had been to since her divorce. Sherry had cried when the wedding invitation first arrived. Several times she had suggested the date for an open house, but Corey checked her calendar and reminded her about the wedding. As she sat, waiting for the ceremony to begin, Sherry wondered if she might now be an embittered divorcee.

"Your hair looks nice. When'd you get it done?" Cookie asked Gina.

"Yesterday. And why did I have to get it done in between my regular appointments?" Gina dramatically framed her hands around her head. "Because I'm running every other day training for a marathon! This is why I need to listen to my mother and leave this white man alone."

"Yeah, right. You're not leaving him," Sherry said, snickering. "I'm surprised you even got an appointment."

"Well, I didn't. Not with Nadine, anyway. I had to ask Janelle, the receptionist at work, for her stylist's number because Nadine can't get me in for another two weeks. It's a conspiracy."

"Between who, Alex and the hairdresser?" Sherry asked, amused by her friend's outrageous conclusion.

"Yes, my man and my hairdresser are in cahoots against me," Gina said. "What other explanation is there as to why I can't get an appointment for two weeks?"

"I keep telling you to go natural."

"What's the difference? You have to go get your hair touched up, conditioned, cut, whatever it is you do."

"Yeah, but a week or two doesn't make a big difference to me. I don't have to rush off to the hair dresser just because I've got a bit of new growth or a bead of sweat touched my head."

"Whatever. We have this reception to go to this week and all this running's got my hair lookin' a hot mess, so I went and let Janelle's hairdresser condition it, blow it out, flat iron it real good until I can get it done. And I'm not running or sweating or moving or nothing until then." Gina patted down her shiny, straight hair.

"Sure. See what Alex has to say about that," Laura said.

Sherry noticed Cookie already fluttering her eyelids as if she was going to fall asleep and gently elbowed her in the side.

"Sorry. I had a big order yesterday. Someone was having a huge Sweet Sixteen last night and ordered 100 cupcakes. The baking wasn't so bad, it was decorating all those things. And then I opened this morning. I'm exhausted," Cookie said, yawning. She pulled a fan from the shelf on the back of the pew in front of her and fanned herself.

"Where was Sarah?" Sherry asked.

"Yesterday, she was taking care of customers in the front during my normal hours, but then she had to leave. She was filming another video for somebody. She was there for a little bit this morning."

"Are you there by yourself a lot? I never thought about it, but is it really safe for you to be in there by yourself?" Gina asked.

"Sarah and I manage pretty well and I can't really afford another person." Cookie.

"Maybe you need more than one day a week off." Gina said. "Let Sarah run the bakery one day. She's dependable, you trust her."

"I don't think so. Sarah's only kinda dependable; I know she'll show up, but I know she's going to be late. And as far as being in charge of all the baking and planning and stuff, that would be a lot more than she does now. She can't manage the place on her own."

"So close up two days. Put up a sign, 'Sleeping, be back on Tuesday.'"

"I wish, but I can't close for a couple days. I've got to work," Cookie said. "When you take a few days off, you get vacation pay or sick pay or whatever. Me, I don't have sick days and vacation days. When the bakery's closed, there's no money coming in."

"Well, I think you should think about training Sarah how to run the place so you can take a break," Gina said.

The pianist and violinist began playing a Pachelbel's *Canon in D Minor* as musical instruction for the guests to take their seats and quiet.

"That's not so bad, only fifteen minutes late," Gina said, checking her watch again.

"Hey, have you told your mother about this marathon running?" Laura whispered to Gina.

"I told her about it last week. We've decided to do the Sugar Run, to raise money for diabetes awareness, instead of the DC Parks one. I thought maybe doing something for a good cause would make the training not seem so terrible."

"What'd she say?"

"She's a little bit impressed about the diabetes part."

"Now you really do have to do it!" Laura said, laughing. "You should be glad you have a guy who cares about what your mother thinks. That's nice," Laura said. "Then that could be you up there one day." Laura nodded to the front of the church.

"Girl, please. That's not going to happen," Gina said profusely shaking her head.

"Why not?" Laura asked.

"It's one thing for my mother to like him as my boyfriend, but I don't think she'd go for having a white guy for a son-in-law."

"I didn't know you all were serious enough to be talking about being in-laws," Sherry said.

"We're definitely not, but my mom thinks we're on the road to marriage. I keep telling her we're not anywhere near talking about getting married, but she feels like if I don't think I'm going to marry him, then why am I wasting my time. She says I'm too old to be dating for fun."

"So why are you with him if you don't think you might possibly want to marry him, or even consider it?" Cookie asked, leaning over Sherry's lap.

"Why is anybody with anybody? I like being with him, I like talking to him, he makes me laugh," Gina said. "He's a cool guy to hang out with. I'm sometimes surprised how much fun I have with him because we do things I've never done on a date. Did I tell you he finally got me into a cooking class? I can make spaghetti and clam sauce and garlic bread, now. And even pair it with a great wine."

Sherry laughed at her friend's excitement about her new culinary skills. She hadn't cooked a meal for more than one in years now. She hadn't wanted to cook for any of the guys she had dated. It required too much work and felt like too much of a personal commitment.

"Your mom's got a point. Most people in their thirties are at least trying to consider if the person they're dating is marriage material, right? I'm not saying you have to know right now if you'll marry him, but if you feel like you definitely won't, why bother?" Sherry asked.

"How about you and that young boy from the club? You gonna marry him?" Gina asked although she knew Sherry had no intention of marrying her newest guy.

"Girl, please. He ain't nothin' but a good time for right now and he better know it. Let me tell you, he might be the prettiest crayon in the box, but he definitely ain't the sharpest," Sherry laughed.

The woman in front of them turned around again, scowling at the row of chatting women.

"Yes?" Laura whispered to the woman, who then rolled her eyes and sharply turned back toward the front.

"Why do I have to be looking for marriage material and you get to hang around with these pretty boys?" Gina whispered.

"Because, I been married already, so I'm done," Sherry said.

"You don't think you'll get married again?" Cookie asked.

Sherry peered at the woman in front of her, then turned to Cookie and whispered. "H-E-L-L no. Once is enough for me, thanks."

"But what if you find the love of your life? Wouldn't you marry him?" Laura asked.

Sherry bit her lip a second to keep herself from tearing before she spoke. "I found the love of my life and I married him. Then he broke my heart. So. I'm done."

The judge at her husband's trial might as well have slammed his gavel into Sherry's heart because that was the moment it irreparably broke apart. Up until that point, she had tried to forgive her husband. She had tried to understand the need for his greed and unlawfulness. She had tried to reconcile the lost trust and faith between them. But she refused to be punished for his crimes, although some days, she felt like she had been.

As the violinist finished playing and took her seat, the pianist played *Ode to Joy* by Beethoven to signal the beginning of the processional. The preacher stepped into the middle aisle and marched to the pulpit. In turn, the paired groomsmen and bridesmaids followed.

"Everybody can't wear pink," Laura muttered. Gina snickered in agreement. The woman in front of them turned around and pursed her lips, looking at them like they were a bunch of noisy teenagers. Laura smiled back.

Sherry watched the half dozen women dressed in bubblegum colored satin float down the aisle. Monica had asked her to be in the wedding and Sherry struggled to come up with a good reason why she couldn't. She had no desire to walk down the center aisle in a wedding processional ever again. Fortunately, Monica had decided to cut the wedding party from ten to six escorts and Sherry gracefully bowed out of the duty.

As the flower girl and ring bearer stepped into the aisle, the pianist changed songs again.

Laura, Gina, and Cookie gaily hummed and swayed side to side as Monica and her father began their walk towards the front of the church. "Dum dum de dum, here comes the bride."

Sherry watched as they moved forward, then dropped her eyes to the floor after her friend passed their aisle. She tried to wipe the few tears forming without attracting any attention.

"Dearly beloved...," the preacher began. "If there is anyone with any reason as to why these two should not be joined as husband and wife, let him speak now or forever hold their peace."

Sherry folded her hands together to keep from raising her hand like a schoolgirl and screaming, "Don't do it, Monica! He's going to promise to love you, but then he's going to renege. He's going to do something stupid and have all your business and dignity paraded on the news and in the courts and end up in jail leaving you all by yourself with nothing! Run, girl, run!"

She saw Cookie peer at her from the corner of her eye as if she could hear Sherry's thoughts. Sherry stared straight ahead.

No one in the church suggested a reason why the couple in front of them should not be married, so Monica's father passed her hand over to her fiancé and took his seat on the front pew. Everyone else sat back down.

"Do you have the rings?" The preacher asked Monica and her husband-to-be.

The young boy serving as the ring bearer stepped up next to the couple and presented the preacher with his little pillow. The preacher carefully untied the rings, held them in his hand, and raised his hand.

"These rings represent the unbreakable, unending bond between you. You will always be connected, now and forever more."

For better or for worse, til death do you part, Sherry thought. Amen.

Cookie

The cellphone buzzed on the shelf. Cookie zipped the bank bag, filled with the day's cash from the register, and locked the top. She retrieved her phone from its basket, safe from the flour and sugar dust all over the tables, and read the message from Gina.

C – r we still on 4 dinner 2nite?

Yes! can't wait. Sherry coming? Cookie typed.

probably not. Going to settlement

Laura?

Working, but should be there by dessert

OK

See you @ 6

Cookie dropped the phone and the bank bag into her red leather tote. It was almost closing time and Cookie was ready to lock the doors for the day. She pulled out the bowls and spatulas for the next morning and set them up on the worktables.

"Cookie, you're okay with me leaving a bit early?" Sarah called from the front of the bakery.

"Sure. I'll be right behind you. Where are you going again?" Cookie glanced through the doorway at Sarah. Her last customer stood at the front counter, contemplating the remaining cupcakes.

"To interview with the production company that's gonna be filming that reality show here. Remember I told you about it?"

"What're you going to do in this show?" Cookie asked. She remembered Sarah coming in last week excited about a new reality show, but she thought the show was about families who needed nannies for their bad kids, not twenty-year old bakery assistants trying to figure out what they wanted to do with their lives.

"Gimme the chocolate one, please," the teen asked, his voice midway between puberty and manhood.

Cookie noticed that he was the size of a grown man, but still had the tastebuds of a kid. The young at heart always pick the chocolate, she thought.

"Cookie! Don't you pay attention? I'm trying to be one of the cameramen," Sarah replied.

Cookie was surprised that Sarah had stuck with the idea of being a cameraman for so many months now. Her plans to be a make-up artist or a drummer hadn't last that long.

"Do you want it boxed or you gonna eat it now?" Sarah asked her customer.

"I'll take it to eat later," he said.

"Make sure you straighten up the front real quick before you go," Cookie called through the doorway.

"Of course, I will," Sarah said.

Cookie heard the ring of the cash register, then Sarah talking to the boy again. "There you go. And you're our last customer for the day. Have a good evening!"

"Thanks," he mumbled. The cowbells on the door clanged as he left.

"Cookie, I'm so nervous. This could be it, my big break," Sarah said.

Cookie heard Sarah's voice in rising and falling volumes as she went about closing the front and talking about the new show and how many cameramen it would need for all the families involved. Cookie tried to listen as she set up the kitchen for the next day.

When she was finished her work, Sarah grabbed her backpack and went into the bathroom.

"How do I look?" She asked, emerging with a fresh coat of lipstick and her golden orange afro released from its hairnet.

"I'd hire you," Cookie replied. "Good luck."

"Thanks! See you tomorrow, unless they send me directly to Hollywood," Sarah sang on her way out the back door.

Cookie swept up the last bit of crumbs and dumped them in the trash. As she untied her apron, she headed to the front of the shop to check the lock on the front door. She was startled to see a young man standing inside the front door. She didn't recall hearing the clanging of the cowbells.

"Sorry, we're closed. I forgot to lock the front door...Oh, I guess you liked the chocolate cupcake, huh?" He had a blue knit cap pulled low on his brow, but Cookie recognized him as the teen who was there a few moments before.

"You're welcome to come back tomorrow for another one, but I'm closed for the day," she said, walking towards the boy.

"I don't want another cupcake, just gimme the money in the drawer," he said, his voice artificially lower than when he ordered the cupcake.

Cookie froze in the middle of the floor as her heart started to race. Her eyes jumped from him to the window. Sarah had pulled the shades and now no one could see inside. Cookie started wringing her hands together, not sure of what to say. There was less than $100 in the cash drawer, change for the next day. Should she explain this to him, just give him the money in the drawer or offer him the bank bag? Cookie tried to think quickly what would be the smartest and safest choice.

"Hurry up, gimme the money," he said again, his voice gaining another octave.

"Well, I..." Cookie put her hand to her chest as if to conceal her audible heartbeat. She glanced back at the counter, trying to think what to do. She wondered if giving him the money in the drawer would be enough to make him go away.

As Cookie turned back to the boy, she saw him take his hand out of his pocket, holding a dark object. He quickly stretched out his arm and Cookie found a gun being pointed at her. She felt a trickle of sweat slide down her back.

"Look, I..." Cookie's voice was shaking. She raised her hands to reassure the boy that she was not only defenseless, but truly not a threat to him. "Let me get..."

"Come on, lady! Hurry up!" He held the gun turned to the side like the gangsters on TV and in music videos.

"Okay, okay, okay," Cookie repeated, feeling the tears fill her eyes. "You don't need the gun, I'm gonna get you the money."

"A'right then, hurry up!" The boy waved the gun at her despite his words.

"Just let me..." Cookie started while trying to tell her feet to get moving.

She heard a pop crossing paths with her words, then felt a sharp push in her left shoulder. Gasping, she lost her balance and stumbled backwards. She reached behind her to try to take hold of the counter. Misjudging the distance, she fell backward against it. She slid down to the floor. She opened her mouth to scream when her brain registered that she was in pain. No sound came out.

The boy stared at the gun, then at Cookie, as if he, too, was in shock that she had been shot. It took a few seconds for him to recover from his surprise, then he jumped over her legs as he raced behind the counter. Cookie heard him banging on the register and wanted to tell him he only needed to hit the Change button for the drawer to slide open. She wanted him to hurry up and leave her alone.

She reached for her left shoulder with her opposite hand. Blood squeezed through her fingers, spreading across her white shirt and pink and brown polka dotted apron. She laid her head back against the base of the counter and tears slid past her closed eyelids. She heard the boy continue to bang on the register, pushing buttons at random, until the cash drawer finally sprang open with a *ding*. Dollar bills rustled and crinkled as he grabbed them from the drawer. Coins rolled across the counter and jangled as they hit the floor. Cookie felt his sneakers brush over her legs as he leapt back over her. The bells on the front door clanged.

At the sound of the bells, Cookie opened her eyes. For a moment, she and the boy caught each other's eyes as he turned back quickly on his way out. His eyes said, "I'm sorry" before he ran off down the sidewalk. Hers slowly slid back closed, grateful he was gone.

Gina

Alex pulled up in front of the restaurant and turned to Gina. "I can still get you a ticket to the hockey game if you change your mind," he teased.

"Thanks, I'm good," Gina said. "I don't see Cookie's motorcycle." She searched along the curb. "But she should be here any minute. See you later?" She asked as she unlocked the door.

"If the game doesn't run late," he said. "I'll call, see if you're still up."

"Sure. Have fun." She gathered up her purse and gave him a quick kiss before climbing out of the car.

Gina found a seat at the bar and ordered a glass of wine. She played a word game on her phone until she realized that her glass was empty and Cookie still wasn't there. She clicked the game off and sent Cookie a text message.

At the rest. Where r u?

Gina considered that if she was on her way, Cookie not only wouldn't be able to check her text, but also wouldn't be able to respond. She called the bakery only to get Cookie's answering service message telling her the bakery was now closed. Gina guessed that was a sign she had left the bakery and anticipated Cookie should be there in less than ten minutes. Gina absentmindedly watched the TV above the bar, tuned to the pre-game show for the hockey game on the sports channel.

Yeah, Alex wouldn't have gotten me there. She shook her head at the thought.

By the commercial, Cookie still hadn't shown up. Gina tried calling her, but again, she received a voicemail message. It wasn't like Cookie to be late or not to answer her phone.

Gina started to get worried. "I bet she's distracted with some new recipe," she said to herself as she paid her bar tab and caught a cab for the short ride to the bakery.

"Ah, looks like a accident or somethin' up ahead," the cabdriver mumbled, slowing the car down in view of the flashing red and blue lights beyond the next corner. As they slowly approached, Gina noticed that the commotion was near Cookie's bakery.

"What's going on?" Gina asked the cabdriver. "Can you see?"

"Can't tell. Looks like some cops, a ambulance. Bunch-a folks standin' around. But whatever it is, I think it was over in those shops, don't look like it's a car accident," he said, pointing towards the strip of stores which encompassed the bakery.

"Oh, shit! Are they at Cookie's?" Gina threw the cab driver a $20 bill, the smallest bill she had, and jumped out of the cab.

Gina ran towards the bakery, her heels threatening to tip her over into the street and her heart racing as if she had indeed run a marathon.

A couple of men in blue uniforms pushed a gurney into the ambulance. Gina shielded her eyes from the emergency lights, but still couldn't see the face of the patient. She gasped sharply when she noticed a police officer putting a familiar red tote bag in the ambulance.

She tried to convince herself that that didn't mean anything. Plenty of people have red Coach bags. Cookie wasn't the only one with that bag.

The EMTs jumped into the ambulance with their patient and the scream of the ambulance siren filled the air as it raced down the street. Gina stared after the blue and red lights, not wanting to believe Cookie was inside.

Gina turned to the bakery for a clue among the cacophony of store-owners, passersby and police. One of the police officers was asking questions of the people gathered in front of the shop. Another officer was taking pictures. A couple of others were walking around inside the bakery. She slowly walked towards the bakery, hoping that as she got closer, Cookie would appear from inside or among the crowd. Cookie would explain the whole thing. Some minor incident, a kid threw a ball through her window, a customer slipped on a cupcake. Silly little things, nothing to worry about. Then she would lock up and they would head to dinner as planned. Gina thought through the options for simple, non-threatening scenarios.

As she reached the police officers holding back the crowd, Gina could see into Cookie's open door. A splatter of red marked the front of the counter and ran onto the floor. Gina squinted, wondering if she could trust her eyes. Her mind slowly began to comprehend that the red mark was blood.

"Breathe," Gina said out loud and forced a deep breath.

The voices of the people in front of the bakery started sounding like the buzz of a thousand bees and Gina stared at them in confusion, trying to figure out what they were saying.

"Ma'am, are you all right?" One of the police officer asked her.

Gina looked at the officer. She started to nod "yes", an unconscious response to the everyday question. But, staring at Cookie's open door, Gina began shaking her head instead.

"No. No. I don't think so. What's going on here? Where's Cookie?"

"I'm Officer Scott and we're here investigating an incident at this bakery. Do you know the woman in the bakery, Ms. Carter? The neighbors said she's the owner."

Gina nodded again, biting her lip and wrapping her arms around herself. "Yes, Cookie, Amanda…Amanda Carter. She's the owner. Did something happen to her?" Gina realized she was starting to ramble but couldn't stop herself. "She's my best friend, I'm Gina Morrison. We were supposed to meet for dinner and I was waiting for her and when she didn't show up, and she didn't answer my text or my call, I came over. Is she all right? What happened? She's all right, right?"

"I'm sorry, ma'am. There was apparently a robbery this evening. Ms. Carter's been shot and is being taken to University Hospital as we speak."

Gina stared at the officer as he continued talking. She watched his mouth move and heard the sound of words come out, but wasn't comprehending what he was telling her. She imagined this is what it was like to have a conversation under water. When the Officer's mouth stopped moving, Gina took it as her cue to start crying.

Officer Scott led Gina to a police car and ushered her into the back seat. He spoke to the younger officer standing near the car then leaned into the back door.

"Ma'am. This is Officer Bynum. He's going to take you to the hospital. Your friend is in surgery, so she probably won't be able to have visitors yet. I'll be over to check on her and will see you there."

Gina nodded automatically.

At the hospital, Officer Bynum helped her find a seat in the emergency waiting room then went over to speak to the nurse at the receiving desk.

"The nurse isn't sure how long the surgery will take. You can wait here, if you'd like, but you may not be able to go in to see her. Immediate family only, you understand. But you were the closest relation we had at the moment."

Gina nodded, the best response she could manage this evening.

"Do you know if she has any immediate family we should call?"

"Her sister and her father, they live outside of Richmond."

"Do you have their numbers?"

Gina scrolled through the saved numbers on her phone. Finally, she found a number and showed it the officer. "Her sister, Elizabeth. Call her; her father will be too upset, and he can't travel anyway."

Officer Bynum copied the number down in his notepad. "Thank you. I'll give her a call."

Alone, Gina surveyed the room. A young woman held a baby on the far side of the room. She seemed frustrated as she rocked the crying baby, wrapped in a light blanket. Initially distracted by the crying baby, Gina noticed the blue black circle around the mother's eye and the redness of her lips, startlingly bright on her café colored face. When their eyes met, the girl turned her brown eyes down to her baby. Gina turned away, too, somehow embarrassed for seeing the girl's pain. Her gaze floated to the ceiling, letting her eyes travel along the straight paths of the ceiling panel frames.

She wondered if the robbery had happened before she got to the restaurant. Did Cookie ever receive her text? Did she try to call for help? Should she have gone to the bakery first?

Gina was full of questions for the police when they came back.

Who was the shooter? Did they have any idea? What did they take? Gina assumed they only took money, what else would they want from a bakery?

Who would do this to Cookie?

Gina pulled out her phone to call Sherry, then remembered that she was supposed to be in a settlement, and instead hit the speed dial for Alex. He answered after the fifth ring.

"Hey, babe," Alex shouted with the noisiness of the crowded stadium filling the background. "What's up?"

As soon as she heard his voice, she started crying again.

"Gina? What's the matter? What's going on?"

"I'm at University Hospital," she whimpered between tears.

"What happened?"

"No, I'm fine, it's Cookie. There was a robbery at the bakery, Cookie was shot."

"Oh, shit. Okay. I'm on my way. Just sit tight. See you in a bit."

Gina wiggled, trying to get settled in the uncomfortable plastic chair. In the opposite corner, an old man slumped in his wheelchair, a worn jacket thrown over his legs. His head hung down to his chest. Gina worried that he was dead, until he reached up and scratched his gray beard and murmured a string of gibberish without opening his eyes.

Gina turned from the people stationed around the room, she had too much of her own misery to worry about theirs. She went back to tracing the ceiling panels. She had circled around the path of the tracks at least twice and started counting the holes in the panels when, peripherally, she saw a blue uniform coming towards her.

"Ma'am?"

She rolled her eyes toward the voice without moving her head. She recognized him as the police officer who had met her at the bakery. She knew he had told her his name, but at the moment, she couldn't remember it.

Gina wiped her face, sat up straight, and turned towards the officer.

"Officer Scott," he said as a greeting.

"Right. You find out anything else?"

Officer Scott shook his head. "No, not yet. We've fingerprinted and talked to the witnesses, putting the case together. It'll take a bit of time, it's not like on TV."

"Yeah, I guess not. Well, could you find out how she's doing? The nurse over there hasn't said anything to me yet."

"I checked in with her when I came in. Ms. Carter's still in surgery; it's going well."

Gina blew out another deep breath. "I can't imagine, who would do this to her?"

"May I?" Officer Scott asked, indicating the seat next to her. He sat down as he summarized what they knew so far. Cookie had been shot once in the left shoulder. No one had any idea who the shooter was. Mrs. Parish, the owner of the neighboring office supply store, heard the loud bang from the direction of the bakery and saw a male in a knit cap and dark coat running down the sidewalk. She came out of her store and went next door to the bakery to see if Cookie had heard the sound, too. Mr. Archer came out after the man in the knit cap ran past his liquor store and saw Mrs. Parish standing in front of the bakery, staring at the door, which had been inadvertently propped open by a fallen chair. He ran up to the bakery and rushed inside to find Cookie lying there on the floor.

Cookie was gasping for breath and could barely talk. Mr. Archer tried to talk to Cookie and Mrs. Parish called 911. The operator said they had already received an alarm from the bakery and emergency vehicles were on the way. The shop owners waited there with Cookie until the police and ambulance showed up.

"But why shoot her? You think he was trying to kill her?"

"I doubt it, it looks pretty amateurish. She probably got in the way of a kid who thought this would be an easy robbery."

The cash register had been broken into but the police weren't sure how much there had been in the cash drawer. They had found Cookie's tote bag in the back with a locked bank bag in it. Nothing else seemed to have been disturbed in the bakery. Other than the gunshot wound, she didn't seem to have been injured or touched.

"I need to go take care of some paperwork," Officer Scott said. He rose from the chair, keeping his eyes on Gina. "I'll be back as soon as they tell me she's out of surgery. Can I get you anything in the meantime?"

"No, thank you."

The police officer nodded then headed down the hallway in the same direction as the other officer.

Gina's head was starting to hurt, a dull ache from crying. She laid her head back on the chair and hugged her arms around herself again. Sitting there alone, she remembered that she still hadn't talked to Sherry. Instead, she sent both Sherry and Laura a text message.

Call me ASAP – emergency.

Two minutes later, Gina's phone rang. She began to sob as soon as she saw Sherry's name on the caller ID. After Gina told her briefly what happened, Sherry said she would be over as soon as she could get her clients out of her office.

On the other side of the room, Gina heard the hospital doors slide open and voices outside. She was disappointed that Alex didn't walk in, but instead a pregnant woman waddled into the emergency room with a man supporting her. The woman was breathing heavily and holding her belly, walking slowly. The man was sweating and looking nervous. Gina winced at the woman's obvious pain.

A nurse came from behind the desk with a wheelchair and the woman collapsed into it, screaming as she held her stomach.

The couple's drama was a welcome distraction for Gina.

"My wife is having a baby," the man explained.

"Yeah, that's what I thought," the nurse said. "Where's your car?"

He stared blankly at the nurse.

"Your car? The thing you drove here. Did you leave it in the driveway or park it in the lot?"

After checking his pockets and not finding what he was looking for, he ran back out the door. The nurse shook her head, then pushed the woman to the desk, wrote on a clipboard hanging nearby, and picked up the phone. Another nurse in cartoon-covered scrubs walked off the elevator as the husband came running back in the door carrying an overnight bag.

Gina watched the cartoon-covered nurse usher the wheel-chaired mother-to-be and her husband onto the waiting elevator for their ascent to parenthood. She sighed as the elevator doors closed, plunged back into her own worries.

As she slumped in the plastic seat, the emergency door slid open again. Gina watched to see who would be next in the cast of emergency room occupants. A tall, white man dressed in jeans, a red hockey jersey and baseball cap walked in. Gina jumped when she realized it was Alex and called to him. He rushed over and collected her in his arms, holding her tight.

"G, what happened?"

"Oh, God, Alex. She's in surgery. I don't know anything, the police don't know anything." This time when Gina began to cry, she felt like she could empty all of her tears.

She was startled by a vibration in her hand, having forgotten she was still holding her phone. A few minutes later, Sherry and Laura swept into the waiting room, walking as fast as they could, their heels click-clacking across the tile floor.

As they hugged Gina, Sherry explained that she had called Laura and her client had offered to bring her to the hospital.

All cried out and emotionally exhausted, Gina told Alex, Sherry, and Laura everything Officer Scott had said.

When she was done relaying the information, there was nothing to do but wait. Alex left the women in the waiting room while he went off to find them coffee.

The women sat next to each other, neither knowing what else to say. At the same time, they each reached for the other's hand and held on tight, closing their eyes and laid their heads against one another, waiting for Alex, or a doctor, or a policeman to come back to them. Just waiting.

Cookie

Cookie lay in the bed, an IV in the back of her hand, her arms crossed over her chest and blankets. All morning, she had faced a new visitor each time she woke up.

First, there was Elizabeth in the middle of the night. Cookie remembered waking up and barely recognizing her sister or comprehending why she was there. She was crying and pacing the room, not realizing that Cookie was awake. When she woke again, Elizabeth was gone.

Later, Gina had come by the hospital on her way to work.

"Did you see Sugar?" Cookie asked, wondering if she had only dreamed of seeing her sister.

"Yeah, she got here late last night. She was pretty upset so we took her back to your place. She'll be back."

Cookie felt calmer, knowing her sister was nearby.

Sherry stopped by soon after, sitting with Cookie as they watched the morning news. When a news reporter appeared in front of the bakery, Sherry braced herself for Cookie's response. Cookie quietly asked her to turn the TV off then laid her head on the pillow and went back to sleep.

This time when she woke up, she was greeted by the nurse.

"One of your friends came by while you were sleep. She left this for you," the nurse tapped a gift bag on the nightstand.

"Who? What's in it?" Cookie asked groggily. She lifted her left arm to rub her eyes, forgetting it was bandaged and in a sling. She winced in pain and rested her arm again.

The nurse laid the bag on the bed so that Cookie could reach it. There was a note from Laura scribbled on a piece of hospital stationary. Laura had been by and didn't want to wake her; she was leaving her some items to help her fight the boredom of being stuck in the bed. Cookie smiled as she slowly went through the bag, flipping through a few magazines, a sleeve of gourmet cookies, and a new tube of lip gloss.

"All right, now let's put this back over here, Ms. Carter," the nurse said, finished with the tests and updates to Cookie's chart. "You have another visitor. Let's make sure you're presentable." Like a caring grandmother, the nurse straightened out Cookie's hospital gown, pulled up her blanket and patted down her hair. She left without giving a clue about her visitor.

As she waited, Cookie noticed a bouquet of flowers with a note from Sarah on her nightstand.

She heard the nurse talking in the hallway. A male voice replied. She could hear their voices but not distinguish what they were saying. The male voice was familiar, but sounded out of place in the halls of the hospital, like a flower in the middle of a snowstorm.

"Come in," Cookie responded to the knock on the door.

The door crept open and David stood in its space.

"David?" For a second, Cookie wondered if it actually was him or a hallucination from the drugs the nurses kept pumping into her.

He stepped forward awkwardly. "Hi, Cookie." He was dressed in his blue delivery uniform, holding a vase of flowers.

She made a small wave with her good hand. "Come on in."

"I, um, just stopped by to see how you were doing."

Cookie made a non-committal groan, indicating nothing and closed her eyes to stop herself from crying. Her emotions were confused, ranging from surprised by his visit to physical pain.

"They're taking care of me. I'll have to be sure to send them some cupcakes when I get out of here," she said.

David stood at her side watching her sad smile. He offered the vase of pink and white tulips. "I brought these for you."

"Thank you," she said, touched by his thoughtfulness.

"You're welcome. The nurse told me to put the flowers over here..." he walked towards the nightstand on the opposite side of her bed. "I noticed you have tulips sometimes at the bakery," he said, placing the vase next to the bouquet of roses and carnations already there.

"They're my favorite." Cookie thought how sweet it was for him to notice. It was mid-afternoon and she wondered if he was on his lunch break. "Are you going to stay a minute or do you have to go?" she asked. Even if he was imagined, she enjoyed him being there.

"No, I can stay, if you don't mind my company."

Cookie nodded at a chair on the other side of the room. David pulled it up next to her bed.

"How'd you know I was here?"

"I saw it on the news this morning." David told Cookie how he heard the name of her bakery on TV while he was getting dressed. "I turned to the TV and there was the news reporter standing in front of your shop. I could see the yellow police tape covering your door and thought, what the hell is going on? The reporter said that last night, someone came in your bakery and shot Miss Amanda Carter. I didn't know that was your full name so it took me a minute to realize he was talking about you. He said the robber stole money from the cash register. Then she said you were brought here and in stable condition."

"And here you are. You found me." Cookie felt tears forming again.

"And here I am. I found you," he repeated.

They nodded their heads self-consciously. Cookie studied the tube going into her veins. David peered at the partition hanging in the middle of the room as if he might be able to see if there was anyone on the other side.

"So, 'Amanda', huh?" David finally said.

"I was named after my great-aunt. Me, my sister, and my cousins were all named after women in our family -- grandmothers, aunts, you know how that goes." Cookie paused to catch her breath. This was the most she had talked all morning. "To avoid confusion, my grandfather called us all his sweet little girls -- 'Candy', 'Sugar', 'Cupcake', 'Peaches', and 'Cookie'."

"Everyone else still goes by their nicknames, too?"

"Candy and Peaches, my cousins, they do. But not my other cousin and my sister. They've grown up into 'Delilah' and 'Elizabeth'. My sister gets such an attitude if you call her 'Sugar' outside my father's house."

"You never grew into 'Amanda'?" David leaned back in the chair and crossed his arms across his barrel chest.

"I always thought it seemed like an old woman name. I use it when I need a more adult name, which in a bakery is hardly ever."

David squinted at her with one eye almost closed, his thoughts almost obvious to Cookie.

"I know, I don't look like an Amanda, but it'll grow on you."

He smiled. "Interesting. Then, I should call you…?"

"Cookie is fine," she said.

Cookie's sad smile returned as she thought of her mother, the only person who called her Amanda. And, then, Dexter, who used to sing her nickname Mandy. She started to wonder if the nurse had slipped her a pill that had turned her emotions to "high."

"Am I your only delivery today?" Cookie asked to change the subject.

"No. Well, you're the only delivery here, at the hospital. I wanted to come see you, to make sure you were okay."

"They've got me on so much stuff, I don't really know how I am doing. I feel like I've been asleep for about a week. My shoulder feels weird, but it doesn't really hurt. And my face feels funny. Do I look terrible?"

David tried not to make a face that would mirror the bruises and swelling on the side of hers.

"You can tell me. How bad do I look?" Cookie half-joked.

"You're beautiful." David leaned forward and put his hand gently on top of hers.

Cookie looked down at their hands, with only a partial memory of the reason she was there. She only remembered a boy in the bakery.

"Were you there? With me?" Of course he wasn't. He never comes in the night, only in the morning. Only at the bakery. But yet, he was here now, in the hospital.

"No, I wasn't there. I wish I was, though."

He saw it on the news, she remembered.

Cookie could feel the tears behind her eyes. She thought that if she didn't blink, maybe they wouldn't fall.

"What about Sarah? Where was she?"

"I don't know, the news said you were there by yourself." He started to lift his hand. "Maybe the nurse knows. I can go ask her."

Her empty hand reached for his and pulled it back down.

He sat still. "Or we can wait to find out later what happened, exactly. I'm sure Sarah's fine."

"What does my place look like? Have you been by there?"

"No," he shook his head, then added, "but I can go by there this evening, to check on it if you want me to."

She slowly nodded, still trying not to blink. Out of the corner of her eye, she noticed the white tape on her shoulder. She noticed the hospital gown and the hospital covers. She felt like she was seeing the entire picture of her lying in the hospital bed, IV in her hand and medical tape holding the gauze on her arm. And then she started to silently weep, without even trying to stop the inevitable tears.

She lifted her head and lay back on the pillow.

"I'm so sorry this happened to you. But you're gonna be fine." He reached with his free hand to stroke her hair, stopping to pull a knot of dried blood off a few strands.

Cookie cried with her eyes closed, squeezing his hand as he continued to whisper his encouragement.

Finally, she opened her eyes and asked, "What am I going to do?"

"You're going to get better. The doctors and nurses are going to take really good care of you and you're going to get better. And then you can do whatever you want to do."

"Should I go back to the bakery?"

"I think so."

"Will you come to see me again?"

"Yes. I will be anywhere you want me to be."

Cookie closed her eyes. Almost ten minutes passed before her eyes fluttered open again. David sat patiently by the bed, watching her.

"The nurse said you might fall asleep for a few minutes or a few hours. I thought I'd wait to see which it would be."

Cookie managed a tired smile. She wanted to say "thank you" but couldn't get her brain to tell her mouth to say the words. She blinked and hoped that conveyed the same message. Her eyes slowly blinked a few more times then stayed closed.

She dreamed of David lightly kissing her bruised cheek and holding her hand. When she woke, Elizabeth was sitting in the visitor's chair, winding a ball of yarn. She looked up and smiled at her sister. "Hey, sleeping beauty. That prince charming said he had to go."

Cookie looked around, surprised, and disappointed, that David wasn't there.

Memorial Flowers

Gina, Sherry, and Laura stood with Sarah in front of the bakery, staring down at the pile of flowers and cards by the front door.

"Who the hell put all these flowers out here!" Gina said to no one in particular, more of a statement than a question. She was still incensed from the ordeal of convincing the police to give them the key to the new lock on Cookie's door. The visits to the station and to the hospital were more than she thought were required. They were grateful that the officer who helped Gina get to the hospital the night of the robbery helped move the process along.

As Sarah began gathering the envelopes, Gina pushed the bouquets lying by the door aside with her foot, unlocked the door and went inside, followed by the other women.

"Gina, people brought them here with thoughts of Cookie," Laura said as she picked up a few bouquets near the door. She knew her words were useless in calming Gina, but said them anyway to fill the still air.

"Well, she's not dead," Gina snapped. "And anyway, she still can't see them, laid up in the hospital. It's so stupid. All those memorials are stupid. I hate those flowers on the side of the road and I hate those teddy bears tied to chain link fences."

"Don't be ridiculous. Who hates memorials?" Sherry said, starting to get frustrated by Gina's bad attitude.

"I do. They're depressing. And people who bring all that crap don't even know the person who it's for, so what's the point? If they care so much about the kid killed by a random drive-by, why don't they help clean up their neighborhood, offer to watch a kid while the mom's at work, tell the kids to go home instead of runnin' up and down the street at 11 o'clock. What the hell is a raggedy teddy bear supposed to do for a dead child? I hate those things."

Sarah stood near the door, surveying the bakery while the women continued their manic yet calm conversation.

Gina raged, arms flailing. "What's next? We're going to stand out here lighting a bunch of damn candles talking about how terrible crime and gun violence is, and an old lady will cry and someone will say how nice Cookie was and she didn't deserve this. A news camera will come and we'll all sing *Kum Ba Yah*. And then you know what will happen? Absolutely nothing! After these flowers are gone and we blow out the candles, one of these knuckleheads will go shoot another kid for a pair of sneakers or rob another store for a hundred bucks or snatch an old grandmother's purse."

Laura understood how deeply she was hurting. She reached out and massaged Gina's shoulder. They eventually dropped from their hunched up position, but her face remained stressed.

"Sarah, what do we need to do?" Sherry asked. They needed to be productive before they all had a meltdown.

Sarah walked behind the counter, on the opposite end from the register. In front of the counter, there was a faint circle, slightly brighter than the floor surrounding it, where the police had mopped up Cookie's blood. The bakery was eerily clean, although it was in the same condition Sarah had last seen it.

"Well, I was thinkin' we should clean out the kitchen. Who knows how long the bakery'll be closed, but it probably would be nice if we didn't have to deal with spoiled milk and dried out cupcakes whenever we reopen."

There was a knock on the glass window and the women jumped. Sarah ducked behind the front counter. Sherry went to the door and cautiously opened it.

"May I help you?"

"Hi. I'm Karen, from the Neighborhood Watch a few blocks over, in the apartment complex there, and heard about the shooting here. How terrible for the young lady, the owner wasn't it?"

Karen continued talking as Sherry gave a quick nod, anxious for her to leave, so the women could be alone again.

"Well, we're really sorry about what happened and want to talk to the police about stepping up security around here. It's ridiculous something like this could've happened in our neighborhood."

"Really? Why is it ridiculous? Because you live in a pretty condo high-rise in your quasi-urban neighborhood, you shouldn't be touched at all by any violence? There should be an invisible force field around this place because there's a nice fountain in the middle of the square?" Gina was in tears before she even realized she had raised her voice.

Sherry caught Laura's eyes and nodded towards the kitchen as she pushed Gina back towards her.

"I'm really sorry," Sherry said to the Neighborhood Watch woman, keeping her out on the sidewalk. "This has been quite traumatic for all of us. We're still not really sure how to handle it. Still trying to sort out our emotions and reactions. But we'd be happy to help with whatever you have planned." She looked back toward Laura and Gina, then faced the woman again. "Well, as long as you aren't planning a candlelight vigil."

Sherry smiled weakly at this request, which she knew sounded bizarre. She understood Gina's anguish, but also realized they had to represent

Cookie. It was her neighborhood and she would participate in the neighbor's plan if she were here. Cookie would even bring cupcakes.

"But anything else, just stop by and let us know. Or leave a note, there's a little mail slot right there in the door, I almost forgot it was there. Leave us a note and we'll be happy to help. Well, not happy given the circumstances, but we'll help. Thanks for stopping by."

Sherry stepped back to gently close the door, not feeling as comforted by the woman's visit as she probably was supposed to be. She locked the door behind her and waved through the window, then took a deep breath and headed toward the kitchen. She wasn't sure how they were going to make it.

"What're you doing?" Sherry said, placing her hands on her hips and watching the women covering the bins of sugar and flour in plastic wrap.

"So bugs don't get in it," Laura said, nodding at Sarah.

"And we wanted some coffee," Gina said. "But Cookie only has the 500 gallon, industrial-size coffee maker, so we're having tea."

Under Sarah's direction, the women put away the baking pans and display trays, all the things that Cookie usually sets up for her baking the next day.

Sherry tapped the floor-model mixer. "How does she run this place by herself?"

"What do you mean, by herself? What am I, invisible or something?" Sarah asked, pulling out boxes of tea.

"Sorry," Sherry said. "How do you two run this place?"

Sarah shrugged. "I don't know how she does it. It's a lot of work, I know that." She took some mugs off the shelf above the stainless steel sink. "She comes in real early and bakes a lot of this stuff before I even get here. Then she's on the move most of the day, baking even more." She disappeared into the walk-in refrigerator at the back of the kitchen and emerged with a tray of muffins. "She doesn't like serving day old muffins to the customers, but we can eat 'em." Sarah put four muffins on a small baking pan and put them in the oven. "I don't know what she's going to do when she gets back."

"Maybe, you can help a bit more with the baking?" Laura asked.

"Who me?" Sarah asked. She prepared four cups of tea and distributed them to the women as she continued to talk. "Nah, not me. Cookie doesn't let me near anything until it comes out of the oven. I can frost a cupcake to beautiful perfection, but I can't bake worth a dime. Put me back here and this place will be shut down so fast, Cookie'll have to start selling cupcakes out there on the street." Sarah emptied a few sugar packets into her mug and threw out the tea bag.

"What about us?" Laura suggested. "Maybe we could help her out."

Gina and Sherry considered her question.

"What are we going to do? Y'all can't cook. And we all have our own jobs to go, too," Sherry said.

"I'm kinda free in the day," Laura said.

"But you don't know how to bake?" Sarah asked.

"I'm sure I could learn. How hard can it be?"

"I've tried to learn and it is hard," Gina said. "I can imagine baking at this scale is really hard." She looked around the kitchen, for the first time really considering how much work her friend must do in her bakery.

Sherry sighed and swished the tea bag in her mug. "How's she going to run this place and make any money?"

"Does she have any money saved up?" Laura asked.

The women looked at Sarah.

"You asking me? All that's above my pay grade, ladies. I know what comes in and I know what goes in my pocket. Other than that, I don't know nothing about Cookie's money," Sarah said.

"I think Elizabeth handles all of that for her," Gina said.

"I can't imagine how scared she is. About the business, but of course, mainly about being shot and almost dying."

"I don't think people usually die from gunshots to the shoulder. She might take a while to be able to use her arm, though," Laura said. "I have a lot of free time in the day to catch up on all the cop shows," she said when Sarah looked at her quizzically.

"Dead or not, I can't imagine being shot anywhere," Gina said, wincing at the thought of the pain. The other women all cringed simultaneously as if they were all thinking and feeling the same thing. "Do you think she has a will?"

Laura looked at Sherry, who shrugged.

Sarah pulled the warmed muffins out of the oven and again, doled them out to each woman. "I told y'all, I don't know nothing about Cookie's money."

"I don't mean to be morbid or nothing, I was wondering. I need to write one myself." When the other women turned back to her, Gina continued. "You never know. Don't you want to have some say in who gets all your stuff?"

"Who do we have to leave our stuff to?" Laura said. "You all can split up my stuff if you want it. Gina, you can take care of my dog."

"I don't know. I guess Viv and Jordan would get all my stuff. They could sell the house," Sherry said.

"Oh, I can I have your house? I mean, I'd pay Viv for it," Laura said.

"Really? You want my house?" Sherry asked, surprised they were even having this discussion.

"Yeah, it's nice. It's the kind of place to settle down. Raise a family."

Sherry nodded. "It is," she said simply.

Sarah started putting the mixing bowls away. "Well, I'm using all my stuff. I'm wearing all my good clothes and eating the best food I can afford. I'd eat it on some good china if I had some. I'm hanging out with my brother whenever I can. All this makes you think, right, about living for today everyday. Don't leave nothing on the table."

Cookie

A knock on the door woke Cookie from her nap. Wearily, she mumbled, "Come in." Her friends and David had already taken their turns visiting, Elizabeth had gone to the cafeteria. Who else did she know?

A policeman stepped into her room. "Good afternoon. I'm Officer Scott. I've been assigned to your case."

Cookie greeted him and felt safer finally seeing a police officer.

The policeman had a gentle look, not really a smile, but his face was sympathetic. "How are you feeling?"

"I think I need more drugs." She reached for the blanket and pulled it up as much as the IV tubes would allow, rethinking her words. "Is that okay to say to a cop?"

He laughed softly. "Yes, ma'am, that's fine. Do you want me to get a nurse for you?"

"No, thanks. One should be here eventually. We'll see if I last 'til then." Cookie adjusted the blanket again. "In the meantime, go ahead. I don't imagine the police department is paying you to just stand around and look at me. You can tell me whatever you're supposed to tell me or ask me whatever your supposed to ask me."

"You're right, I do need to get some information from you. Your neighbors, Mrs. Parish and Mr. Archer, gave us a description of a young man they saw running down the sidewalk after the shooting. However, neither actually saw him shoot or even rob you, they just saw him running away. And they didn't get enough of a good look at him to draw a sketch. Maybe you have more details to add?"

Cookie was usually good at remembering people, but she didn't get a good look at the boy. She had only seen him for a few seconds when he came in for the cupcake. And she was too scared when he came back to pay attention to what he looked like.

"I don't know. A black guy, a teenager. Medium height, slim. My assistant would probably be more helpful, she waited on him. Did you talk to Sarah?"

"Someone spoke to her at the station."

Cookie paused a moment. "Do you get tired of hearing that description of suspects? 'Young, black male'."

"Yes, I do. It's even worse having to chase them down and lock them up. Then they look at me like I'm betraying them. But when they go and shoot someone's child, or mother, or father, I've got no sympathy for them. I don't care what color their skin, their background or their reason. Doesn't even matter."

"It's sad though, isn't it? So many kids, getting in trouble. Going to jail. So many young, black kids."

"It is. But the families who lost their loved ones or even their property, that's even sadder."

Cookie stared out the window, thinking about what the policeman said. Was it odd giving her shooter any thought, feeling bad for him? She knew she was supposed to be angry, lying in the hospital with a torn-up shoulder. She didn't even know how or when she was going to get back in the bakery.

"So, if you find this kid, what happens to him?" Cookie turned back to the officer.

"He's arrested, charged with armed robbery, assault, maybe attempted murder. Probably as an adult, since from the descriptions, it seems like he's at least an older teen. After we find him, the court takes it from there."

Thinking of the boy's wasted young life, Cookie's eyes began to fill with tears. She tilted her head back and sniffed to try to contain the tears.

"Ms. Carter, it's not your fault, don't upset yourself. He made this choice, those are the consequences."

"Yeah, I know. But still. It's sad."

"I do have another question for you. How much money do you think he took?"

It was the first time she thought about the financial loss of the robbery and started to panic.

"Did you all find my purse? My bank bag? I think I had taken the money out of the cash register and put it in my deposit bag. But I don't remember if I put it in my purse, or maybe I left it on my desk? Should've been almost $1000 around the place, that's about my usual. Then I usually leave about $100 in cash in the drawer for change." Cookie thought back, remembering the noise of the boy banging on the register. "I think he took that," she said softly.

Officer Scott searched the small room. "May I?" The policeman asked, stepping towards the closet in the corner.

Cookie nodded. Inside, he found the tote bag in a plastic, hospital-issued plastic bag labeled Personal Items and brought it to her bedside. She patted the space next to her on the bed, indicating for him to give her the bag.

"We found this purse in the back of the bakery. We didn't open the locked bank deposit bag in it. The cash register was empty."

With her good arm, she started rummaging through the bag. Keys jingled inside. Cookie's face relaxed as she sighed with relief. Almost immediately, her eyes reversed their calmness and widened in panic.

"Did you lock my shop? How are you keeping people out of there?"

"We've had it locked by a locksmith, we didn't know if he had taken any keys. We gave the new keys to Sarah. Remember, we spoke about this earlier."

Cookie didn't remember.

"He took the money from the register? I used to keep more change, but everyone uses their debit card now -- swipe for their coffee and muffin -- no cash needed." She motioned as if running a charge card through a machine. "Don't tell me I've almost been killed over $100."

Officer Cole's silence was his only answer.

"I guess the other option would be that he got everything. I don't think I'd feel any better if I was almost killed for $1000, either."

What is a sufficient amount to be killed for, she asked herself.

After the officer left, Cookie lay back on the pillow, staring at the ceiling and letting her mind wander. She thought about almost dying. Then she thought of Dexter.

After Dexter died, she felt compelled to read the obituaries in the newspaper every day. All those people had lived a life, one important enough for their families to tell the world about. Cookie felt obligated to acknowledge those lives by reading their obituaries. And when she opened her bakery, it was almost an automatic reaction to participate in their funerals by sending cupcakes.

Each morning, Cookie read through the obituaries. She picked someone who had died young or somehow stood out amongst all the listings, then packed a dozen cupcakes and said a prayer for the family left behind. Then she stacked them up, waiting for David to deliver them.

Sometimes, she would get a thank you card, addressed to "whom it may concern" or "Cookie's Oven"; usually she didn't. But she didn't mind since she never signed the cards. She didn't want the family to feel obligated to respond. She only wanted to let them know someone else shared their grief.

Elizabeth thought it odd but attributed it to her mourning process. Neither imagined the habit would last for so many years.

Gina

Gina tried to keep up with Alex as they ran along the trail through Rock Creek Park. He had already gone five miles on his own, she was joining him for the second half of the run.

The aching in her legs didn't even register anymore, but it was hard to ignore the sharpness in her side. She raised her arms over her head and tried to breathe deeply to make the cramp go away.

There were so many other things she could be doing with her Sunday morning. Even cleaning her apartment would be better than all this sweating and foolishness. Besides, she thought she should be at the hospital checking on Cookie, not running through the park

A vision of Cookie lying in the hospital bed flashed in Gina's mind. Cookie's face was still swollen but the bruising was going away. She hadn't stayed long; Cookie was still on a lot of pain medication and was pretty groggy. She was awake and coherent maybe 30 minutes then she started rambling nonsense, crying for more pain medication and when she finally got it, she fell asleep. Gina planned on going to the hospital again today.

"Great, babe. You're doing great! We're almost done. About another mile to go."

He is too excited about all this running, she thought. Though Gina was in good shape, she was questioning whether running for 26 miles was worth it, even if it was for diabetes awareness. For the first time since they came up with the idea, she calculated how long it would take to run a marathon. At thirteen to fourteen minutes a mile, at a minimum -- because there was no way she was getting up to a eight-minute mile like Alex was talking about -- it would take her at least five hours to complete the race. No way was she running for five hours.

This is it, after this run, she thought. I am absolutely done. He can run if he wants to, but I'm not doing it. I quit!

Alex and Gina came to the end of the trail, back where they had started. Alex kept running in place, slowing down slightly and checking his wrist pedometer. Gina stopped running, grabbed the water bottle from the holder on her hip and sat on the ground.

"Babe, we did great. We've moved our time up. Between both of our runs, we're up to 10 miles in a little over an hour and a half."

"You know, Alex, I've been thinking."

Gina drank more water, catching her breath and trying to make sure she got the words right. She didn't want to hurt his feelings, but she wanted to make sure her message was clear. How should she say this?

"I don't want to do this anymore," she blurted.

"What? What do you mean?" Alex asked, drinking from his own water bottle.

"I mean this race. This training. I don't want to do it. I don't want to run 26 miles. I don't want to run a marathon." Gina handed him the towel hanging around her neck.

"Thanks," Alex said, swiping at the sweat dripping down his face and around his neck. "You're only saying that because you're tired. But you're doing great, you…"

"No, Alex. I am not tired. Well, yes, I am tired, but that's not why I don't want to do this. I just don't want to do it. I don't want to run this damn race."

"But, G, this is for us, to prove to your mom…" He stood up straight from his hamstring stretch.

"Alex, this is not going to do anything for my mother. We could run from here to Africa and back, she wouldn't care. It's not going to erase the 60, 70, I don't know, 100 years of black-white family history. Running around a city, passing out in the streets is definitely not going to convince my mother that you're a great guy and we're a great couple."

Alex sighed deeply and raked his fingers through his hair. "I think it's worth a try, but okay, if you say so. But you said you wanted to do the run for diabetes. What about that?"

"I'll write a check. Cut back on sugar, whatever. I'm not running."

"So, then what? What do we do?"

"You know what we do? We keep on doing what we're doing. My mom'll come around or she won't. But running a race is not going to make my mother get over missing her mother for every holiday family dinner because she was cooking and serving for the white family she worked for."

"Is that the issue? Your mother's upset that your grandmother was a maid?"

Gina snorted. Oh, if it could be summed up so simply.

"Forget it, don't even think about it. You don't get it. Look, I've had boyfriends before she didn't like, so it's not such a big deal. Unless we're getting married, it doesn't even matter."

"I didn't know you wanted to get married," Alex said, dropping his hands to his side.

"What? I didn't say I wanted to get married. I said if we're not getting married –– and I'm not even saying I want to get married, at all or to you –– we're just going out so it doesn't matter whether she likes you or not. She doesn't have to like everyone I date."

"So, you don't want to marry me?"

"Marry you? Alex, what are you talking about? We've never even talked about getting married."

"But I'm asking. You brought it up." Alex completely gave up his stretching to concentrate on Gina's explanation.

"I didn't bring it up. My point was that it doesn't matter whether my mother approves of my boyfriend."

"Unless you were going to marry him," Alex completed.

Gina sighed in exhaustion and frustration.

"You've already decided you don't want to marry me?" Alex asked.

"Are you kidding me? Are you actually asking me whether I want to marry you or not? We've never even talked about marriage, never even talked about anything beyond next week and you want to get all, all, whatever, about getting married? Really?"

"Is it because I'm white?"

"What the hell? I'm not even having this damn conversation with you, Alex! All I said is I'm not running this damn race and you're out here making this into a civil rights case for white men. What the hell? Where's my car? I'm outta here."

Gina fumbled getting up from the ground, her legs achingly protesting her quick rise. She patted her pants searching for her keys and wallet.

Alex stared intently at her, obviously hurt.

"I drove. Let's go," he said. He turned brusquely away from her and walked to the car, pushing the key fob to unlock the car on the other side of the parking lot.

"I don't need you to take me nowhere. Give me my wallet, I can find my own way home."

Gina tried to march to the car, full of indignation, but it came out more as a weak-kneed hobble. She still held her head high, lips pursed in disgust.

"Gina, get in the car. What do you think, cabs wander through the park? Are you going to stand here waiting for a bus? Or are you going to hitch-hike out of here? Get in the car." He opened her door then walked around to the driver's side where he settled behind the steering wheel while she continued to fuss.

"Don't freakin' tell me what to do! I don't need you to tell me what to do. Think I'm not marrying you because you're white. What the hell."

Gina leaned into the passenger door and opened the armrest between the two front seats. "Exactly, what my mother's talking about. White men are always trying to run your life, tell you what to do," she mumbled as she fished out her wallet and keys.

Alex took hold of her wrist before she could retreat from the seat. "Gina, get in the car. I'm not leaving you out here. I don't care if you don't say anything 'til I drop you off, but I'm not leaving you out here."

She didn't want to admit it, but Gina didn't want to be left out in the woods. If someone, or something, came chasing her, she would definitely be caught because her legs were not going to carry her anywhere fast. Compared to the risk of being mauled by a lion escaped from the zoo or thrown into a ravine by a crazed serial killer, she figured riding home with Alex was probably the better option. Gina rolled her eyes and got into the car. She buckled her seatbelt with as much attitude as possible for such a simple action and kept her eyes forward, staring out the windshield.

As they drove out of the park, Gina noticed him stealing glances at her. She wondered what he was thinking and waited for his apology.

She replayed the argument in her head, still wondering how they went from quitting a 26-mile run to breaking up. Had they broken up? Were they done?

Her mind spun frantically trying to settle on one emotion. One moment, she was annoyed that he was offended that she didn't want to marry him. The next moment, she regretted saying that she didn't. Perhaps, one day she would want to marry him, she honestly hadn't given it any thought, but she did enjoy spending time with him now and didn't want that to end. She realized that he probably wouldn't be coming by to bring her dinner later. Already, she missed their Sunday nights eating carry-out dinner and watching movies.

She wondered if she should ask him to be sure. But then, what if he said yes, they were through, and no, he wasn't picking her up for dinner, ever again. This was another outburst gone too far. The same temperament that had gotten her sent to the Principal's office in school was still getting her in trouble.

This time, it was her turn to steal a glance at him. Just in case they had broken up, she didn't want him to have the satisfaction of her checking him for a reaction. He was watching the traffic, with both hands on the wheel -- a sure sign he was mad. He only drove in proper driver's ed mode when he was upset.

Gina picked up her phone and went to her Facebook page to update her status: *Gina is dealing with race relations.*

Alex drove the entire way to Gina's apartment building without speaking. He finally spoke when they reached her apartment building.

"Bye," he said, not bothering to look at her. He didn't even put the car in "Park".

Gina didn't know what to say other than, "Bye", and got out of the car. Before the door was fully shut, he pulled away from the curb. Gina stood on the sidewalk, looking after the blue convertible floating away.

♠ ♥ ♣ ♦

After washing away the sweat and park dirt, Gina invited Sherry over for drinks and dinner. She needed to talk to about the confusion with Alex.

"Explain this to me again. You're runnin' along in the park," Sherry said while running in place, "and you get to the end of your run." She continued her charade of stretching and drinking water.

"Then you say 'I don't want to run no damn 26 miles' and he says 'then you must not love me because I'm white' and y'all drive off into the sunset, broken up?"

"Not exactly how it happened, but yeah, that's the gist of it."

"And you haven't talked to him anymore since he dropped you off this morning? No email? No text message? No hung up phone call?"

She glanced at the phone on the charger, in case she had missed his call while in the shower. Gina shook her head.

"Facebook?"

"Alex is finished with this race."

"Huh?"

"That's what his status says."

"Really? Like, he's done with…what 'race'? What's that mean?"

Gina shrugged

"This doesn't even make sense. More had to happen. I mean, did you curse him out? Did you trip him while you were running? Oh! He didn't call you a n-, right?"

Gina rolled her eyes and sighed. "No. To tell you the truth, I'm not even sure how we got from 'I don't want to run a damn marathon' to 'then you must not love me 'cause I'm white.' I really don't know."

Gina fought back the tears she had been resisting since their ruined run. She refused to cry over a break-up, as if she was a heart-sick teenager. She was a grown-ass woman and she would handle this like one.

On the refrigerator, Gina spotted Alex's training chart, mapping out their weekly mile targets to get to 26 miles. There was an ad clipped to the chart for a CamelBak water bag.

"That damn Alex and his stupid race!" she muttered as she ripped the papers off the fridge and threw them in the trash.

She took a lime from the fruit bowl and rolled it around on the counter.

"So. Maybe he was also a little hurt that I said I didn't want to marry him," Gina said pensively.

"What? He asked you to marry him?" Sherry asked.

"No, no he didn't. But, somehow, the topic came up." She continued to roll the lime under her hand. "I don't think I've ever dated anyone who would've been upset that I said I didn't want to get married."

She sliced the lime in half, then squeezed the juice into a glass half filled with ice, topping it off with liquor from Alex's bottle of Bombay Sapphire.

"What if he's the only person that cares if I want to marry him? What if he was 'the one' and I messed it up?"

"Then you need to fix it. Apologize."

Gina's eyes widened not only at the idea of taking the blame for their break-up, but also for the notion that she should apologize. "But I didn't do anything. I just didn't want to run anymore."

Sherry shrugged. "Well, if you want him back, you're going to have to work it out, somehow. Do you want him back?"

Gina frowned. Did she want him back or did she just not want to be alone?

She tasted her drink. She winced at the liquor burning her throat as she emptied the glass.

Laura

Laura sat in the backseat of the town car staring out of the window at Michael Stone's office building. She was getting annoyed that her client was running late. She drummed her fingers on her leg, trying to recall the driver's name. Simon? Seymour? No, the name of a city. Sidney.

"Excuse me, Sidney? Are you sure everything's okay?"

He glanced up in the rearview mirror and started to answer when his phone beeped. The driver turned his head towards Laura. "I'm sorry, but Michael just sent me a text. He's still held up in his meeting, he should be done soon."

Laura squinted and pursed her lips; she was skeptical. When the driver picked her up at her apartment, he said they were going to return for Michael at his office because he was stuck in a meeting. They seemed like respectable men, but she wasn't sure if they were up to something, or what it could be.

"Excuse me, this is him again," the driver said as the phone rang. He looked apologetic as he answered. "Yes? Yes. Okay." He kept his eyes on Laura, then handed her the phone. "He wants to talk to you."

"Stacey, I'm sorry. I'm running a bit late. These negotiations are taking much longer than I planned. But I'm going to put these guys out of my office as soon as I can. If you don't mind his company, I'd like Sid to take you for a drink instead of sitting in the car."

Going off schedule pushed Laura out of her comfort zone. "I don't usually work..." she began.

"I am sure you have your own standards of work and I don't mean to contradict them. I only suggest it as an option more comfortable for you than waiting in the car. If you want him to take you somewhere else, the mall, bookstore, a bar, and leave you alone, he can do that, too."

She remained silent while he paused a second before going on.

"But I do hope you'll wait and join me for the party. I'll compensate you for the change in plans."

Laura thought over his suggestion, eyeing the driver. It's a little odd, but what could be the harm? He seemed like a nice guy.

"All right. I'll work it out with Sid."

"Again, I'm really sorry. I promise it will be a fun event, worth the wait."

Laura said good-bye and handed the phone back to Sid.

"Any preference?" Sid asked.

"I'm sure wherever you choose will be fine." Laura smoothed her hand over her red silk dress hoping he would pick a restaurant appropriate for her appearance. She leaned back in the seat and sighed.

After a short ride, Sid pulled the car into the valet lane of a popular steak restaurant.

"I eat here all the time, one of my favorites," he said as he opened Laura's door.

"Good evening, Mr. Stone." The hostess greeted Sid and Laura as they entered the busy restaurant. "I'm sorry we didn't know you were coming. I don't have a table available right now, but there are a few seats at the bar."

"The bar is fine, thank you, Yvonne," Sid said.

Laura wrinkled her eyebrows, wondering why the hostess called him by Michael's name, especially if he ate here as much as he said. Surely, it wasn't mistaken identity; other than their height, the two looked nothing alike.

Yvonne lead them across the atrium and indicated two open seats in the middle of the long bar. The bartender greeted and shook hands with Sid, then turned to Laura.

"Hello, beautiful, how're you? Sid, what'd you do, kidnap yourself a date?"

Sid laughed off the bartender's joke and introduced Laura without explaining their relationship.

"Nice to meet you, Stacey. What can I get you this evening?"

"If you like French martinis, he makes the best," Sid suggested.

She would have preferred her regular lime martini, but agreed so as not to appear too picky.

"You don't drink?" Laura asked Sid after the bartender walked away.

"I'm the designated driver, remember?"

This was Laura's first chance to really look at Sid. He had sharp features set in a brown face, framed by a close shaved beard and mustache. Sid had taken off his hat when they entered the restaurant. He was not bald as Laura had assumed, but had a close cut of wavy black hair. She thought he was handsome.

"How's your friend? The one in the hospital," Sid asked.

Laura had been at dinner with Michael when Sherry had called to tell her about Cookie. After she returned to the table, obviously distraught, Michael and Sid drove her to the hospital.

"She's recovering pretty well, slowly. The doctor's say it'll be awhile before she has full use of her arm, though. I don't know how she's going to get back to work," Laura said.

"What does she do?"

"She has a cupcake bakery."

Sid nodded. "Yeah. I don't even know how to cook, but I can't imagine how you would do that with one arm."

The bartender returned and poured the martini into a frosted glass. "I hope you like it," he said to Laura. He placed a club soda with a slice of lime in front of Sid.

Laura tasted the martini and was impressed with such a good drink suggestion. Sid and the bartender talked about the basketball game from the night before, giving Laura the chance to think about this new situation. She wasn't sure how they were supposed to relate while waiting for Michael. What were they supposed to talk about?

"Aren't we going to dinner?" Laura asked, hearing Sid ordering food from the bartender.

"You're supposed to be, but with Michael running late, I'm not sure. It'll depend on how soon he wants to get to the party. I figure, better safe and have a full stomach so you aren't hungry. Believe me, you're barely going to eat at the party. Between Michael moving around the room and talking to everyone and the little bit of food they pass out at those things, your stomach'll be grumbling like crazy."

Laura appreciated his thoughtfulness.

"How long have you been driving for Michael?"

He stirred the ice in his glass, as if the action helped him remember the answer. "Maybe ten years, now? I've lost count."

"Did you drive for anyone else before then?"

"No. Before I drove for him, I was hoping to be an NBA superstar," Sid pantomimed shooting a basketball over the bar. He told Laura that he had played basketball in college, then in Europe when he didn't get picked up in the NBA draft. After a few seasons, he damaged the rotator cuff in his shoulder and returned home for surgery and rehabilitation.

"While I was rehabbing my shoulder, hoping to still be able to try out for other teams, Mike was starting his agency. I worked with him to get new clients and when we had meetings, I would drive. He's a terrible driver, he's colorblind and nearsighted." Sid grinned and said, "Don't ever tell him I said that."

Laura laughed at this small betrayal of confidence. She noticed he referred to his boss as "Mike" not "Michael" or "Mr. Stone" as he previously had done.

"After a while, I went back and played another season in Europe, but the pain in my shoulder and the cocktail of prescription meds I needed to get through a game was too much. I cut my losses, retired from basketball and came back to work with Mike again." Sid shrugged and scooped up a handful of peanuts from the bowl in front of him.

"He was still growing, but didn't really have much of a staff. I took on a few clients and still, I always drove. And it's been like that ever since. Maybe one day we'll need to hire a real driver. But until then, I don't mind."

"He went from being your agent to your employer? He's a good agent."

"He's a pretty good agent." Sid took a sip of his soda. "He's also my cousin."

"Really?" She was surprised at their family connection, but now the hostess calling him "Mr. Stone" made sense.

"Yeah. Our fathers are brothers. We grew up together. I was the athlete, he was the bookworm. It's worked out well for us."

The bartender brought a plate piled high with calamari and hot peppers, a basket of sourdough bread, and a spinach salad for Laura.

Sid thanked the bartender, then waited as Laura bowed her head quietly over her plate. He spoke again when she opened her eyes.

"So, what about you? How did you come into your, umm, line of work?"

Laura finished chewing a mouthful of salad. She couldn't recall a client ever asking how she got started as an escort. Usually, the primary question was if she included sex in the contract.

She told Sid about the grad school professor who asked her to go to a family event with him, offering to pay for her travel expenses and time.

"At first, I was so offended! I told him I didn't come to grad school to be his floozy. Then he explained that he was gay and was tired of his family always asking him about a girlfriend and when was he going to get married. I guess he wasn't ready to come out. He figured it was mean to ask a woman to pretend to be his girlfriend with nothing in it for her, so he wanted to hire someone to be his date. And he asked me."

Sid was amused and laughed while munching on a calamari ring.

"Well, we had such a good time. He didn't have to try to change the subject about a girlfriend and I answered everything about our 'relationship' -- when we met, how long we'd been together, you know, all the stuff your nosy aunt asks you when you take a friend home. We had a good time." Laura took another sip of her martini.

"I went with him to a few other functions, then he referred me to a couple of his friends who also needed a cover. At the same time, I was busy interviewing with different hospitals and services for a steady job after graduation. Then, one day I realized I was making a decent amount being the fake date so I stuck with it and the rest as they say, is history."

"So what were you in grad school for? What were you going to be before you found your calling as the fake date?"

"Psychology. I wanted to be a therapist." She wondered how much she should tell Sid. "Here's a confession -- I never told my mother what I actually do. I could never tell her *this* is what I was doing with my life.

But, I guess in a way, I am like a therapist. Rich men pay me to listen to their issues or at least pretend they don't have any, but instead of a therapy couch, I have a backseat of a car, driven around by handsome chaffeurs."

"So your mother, she thinks you're a psychologist?"

"Thought. She passed away a few years ago."

"Oh, sorry to hear that."

Laura shrugged off the comment with a smile and returned to her story. "But not just a psychologist, a doctor. It didn't matter that I only had a Master's degree, which I explained to her a million times. When I would go home, she would still introduce me to her friends and the ladies at church as Dr. Laura. 'She's a psychologist -- works with people who, you know, ain't right up here'." Laura tapped her forefinger on the side of her head then chuckled, thinking of her mother.

"Laura? Is that what your family calls you?" Sid asked.

While she berated herself for the slip and debated how to answer, Sid's phone beeped. She wondered if he would tell Michael and if he would be upset about this deception. She watched him read and reply to the text message and hoped he would forget that she hadn't answered his question.

"So, your mother called you 'Laura'?" He asked, finishing his drink and wiping his mouth with his napkin.

"Yeah, well, 'Laura' is my real name. I go by Stacey, uhh, professionally, to keep a division between my working self and my real self."

"Putting that psychology degree to work, huh?" Sid held up his phone and said, "He's ready. You want to finish your drink?" He waved over the bartender to get the bill.

When they got in the car, Laura nervously leaned forward and spoke over the seat.

"Are you going to tell him my real name?"

"Are you going to tell him I said he can't drive?" He turned and winked at her then started the car.

Spades Night

"You're sure we can't bring liquor into the hospital?" Laura asked.

Gina rolled her eyes at Laura.

"Absolutely sure," Sherry said, shaking her head.

The trio stood waiting for the elevator, looking more like they were on their way to a formal picnic than visiting a hospital. Laura had been home all day and was dressed in what she deemed casual, an abstract printed mini-dress and heeled sandals, with her make-up expertly applied. She held on to a tote bag originally designed for a day of yachting. Sherry wore an outfit appropriate for a day of getting in and out of the car, going up and down steps, showing houses all day: brown slacks, a beige blouse, and low-heeled shoes. Gina tiptoed along in a pair of flower-print peep-toe stilettos and a black wrap dress, carrying dinner in a red and white gingham print insulated container.

"Mmm, I really could've gone for jerk chicken," Gina said. Her friends had vetoed her choice, suggesting the Caribbean smell would infuse the room and linger in the hallways.

"Or ribs," Laura replied. They had thought two-handed and messy foods were not a good option for Cookie and nixed that idea, too.

"Y'all can have jerk chicken and ribs tomorrow. Tonight, enjoy your pizza," Sherry said. No offensive smell, no mess, no silverware. Pepperonis, green peppers, olives, and mushrooms, divided in various halves and quarters to match each woman's preference.

The elevator chimed and the door slid open to reveal a teenage boy with a cast on his leg sitting in a wheelchair. A middle-aged, tired looking woman stood behind him with a soccer jersey thrown over her shoulder.

"I hope you won," Sherry said to the boy.

"We did! Three to two," the boy said proudly.

His mother rolled her eyes and snorted, pushing him off the elevator.

The women stepped quickly onto the elevator for the ride up to the fifth floor.

Gina knocked on the slightly opened door and peeked in. "Can we come in?"

Cookie sat up in her bed, surprised by her evening visitors. "What are you all doing here? I wasn't expecting anyone tonight."

"It's second Tuesday, did you forget?" The women rushed into the room and surrounded Cookie's bed.

Spades night, Cookie remembered.

They immediately started a litany of questions in a jumble of restrained excitement, as if at least one of them hadn't been by to see her in the past day.

"How're you feeling?"

"Are the nurses treating you good?"

"Did the police tell you anything new?"

"How's your arm? Can you move it around, yet?"

"Where's Elizabeth?"

"When can you go home?"

Cookie tried to keep up with all of the questions. The answer she was most excited about was that she was going home the next day.

When they were ready to eat, Sherry spread a square tablecloth over Cookie's tray table.

"Do you have a room-mate, now?" Laura stood by the bed on the other half of the room. A rumpled blanket and a half-done knitting project laid on the bed.

"Not officially. That's my sister's stuff. She went to go get herself some dinner," Cookie said.

Laura pushed the extra bed tray over to Cookie's side to hold the pizza box. Gina cut the slice into smaller slivers, making it easier for Cookie to handle.

And despite Sherry's warnings, Laura pulled out a bottle of wine from her tote bag.

"Oh come on, it's not really Spades night without a drink." Laura gave Sherry a hug. Turning to Cookie she said, "Don't worry, I brought something for you, too."

Laura reached into her bag for a small bottle of sparkling cider. She poured wine and sparkling cider into plastic wine glasses.

Cookie smiled, glad to be included.

"Salud," they toasted, touching their plastic cups together.

The nurse on duty stepped into the room. The women turned towards the door, looking like kids caught with their hands in the cookie jar. They munched on their slices of pizza and held their cups as far from the nurse's eyes as possible, down by their sides, behind their back. The nurse walked over to Cookie's bedside with her clipboard, wheeling a small cart.

"Excuse me ladies, this will only take a minute." The nurse began her routine procedure, putting a blood pressure cuff around her healthy arm. She pumped up the bulb connected to the cuff and watched the pressure reading. She glanced at the wine bottle and the cider bottle on the bedside table.

"Shall I do a blood test, too?" The nurse asked as she made a note in her chart.

"I'm clean, apple juice," Cookie said before the nurse stuck a thermometer under her tongue.

The nurse eyed the three other women, sliding her eyes up and down each one slowly for a full minute. She pulled the thermometer out of Cookie's moth, checked it, and made another note on her clipboard. "Enjoy your pizza," she said, then wheeled her cart out of the door, letting the door shut behind her.

The women grimaced at each other, paused, and laughed all at once, then toasted their plastic cups again. They continued to enjoy their dinner while Cookie gave them updates on her health, the case, and her plans to get home.

"The police officer came by. He's actually kinda cute," Cookie said, raising an eyebrow at Sherry. "But maybe a bit too old for you, I guess police have to be out of college."

"Did he have anything new to tell you?" Sherry asked, laughing.

"No. No fingerprint match, no good description. He said it's probably a kid who thought robbing a little shop would be an easy way to get a few bucks. Too bad he shot me." Cookie dropped her eyes and her voice. "If they catch him, he's going to be in a lot of trouble."

"Cookie, please don't start getting soft and feeling bad for this poor kid," Gina said.

"Well, no, I don't feel bad for him. I feel bad for me. Do you know how much he got? Maybe, *maybe*, $100! For a hundred bucks, here I am, shot up, face all messed up. Who knows when I'll get back in my bakery?" Her good hand started to shake. She put down her cup and wiped the tears starting to fill her eyes.

"Okay, okay, don't get all upset," Laura soothed.

"She's right, Cookie. Let's not talk about him right now. Let's let the police worry about him," Gina agreed.

"Hey, I heard there was a party in here!" Elizabeth said as she pushed through the door, carrying a tray from the cafeteria.

The women greeted Cookie's sister and made room on one of the bed trays for her dinner.

"You want a drink?" Laura asked, lifting her own cup.

"Sure, don't leave me out. You got something that goes with cafeteria club sandwich?" Elizabeth said. "What's going on? Well, other than this one getting shot?" She squeezed her sister's leg playfully.

"She was telling me about this cute police officer who's been coming by," Sherry said.

"You didn't meet him that first night? Oh, yeah, Sherry, he's cute," Elizabeth confirmed.

The women continued their jovial conversation until they finished up the pizza and sandwich.

"Now, time to get going." Sherry clapped her hands and rubbed them together. She pulled a fresh deck of cards out of her bag and slid off the plastic wrap.

After picking cards to determine partners, Gina and Laura pulled up chairs to arrange themselves around Cookie's bed.

"You couldn't get the deluxe room?" Laura joked, trying to get comfortable in the wood frame chair for visitors.

"She'd probably have to get shot in both shoulders for that," Gina said, settling into her own chair on the opposite side of the bed.

"Elizabeth you want to play?" Laura asked.

"I'll take Cookie's turn when she falls asleep," Elizabeth said. She climbed up on the empty bed and picked up her knitting.

Sherry sat at the foot of the bed as Cookie's partner. She tried to unwrinkle the bedsheet as much as possible with Cookie under them while Gina shuffled the cards and dealt the first hand.

"I think we should get credit for an extra book for having the leg of this table in my face." Laura said.

"You know they're gonna try to come up with an excuse for Cookie's arm, right?" Gina responded.

"How's Jordan?" Cookie asked Sherry, ignoring Gina's remark.

"She's all right I guess, considering. Her and Viv are arguing a bit. They're both so stressed out." Sherry threw out the ten of clubs.

Gina peered at it and glanced at Laura. Either Sherry had all the face cards or was distracted and she wondered what Laura would play. With her game face set, Laura threw out the Jack. Gina guessed Sherry was distracted thinking about her niece.

"Right now, she's just trying to finish school and confirm her admission somewhere."

The women allowed Cookie a little extra time as she looked over her cards, laid them face down in her lap, picked up the King and threw it on the pile -- all with one hand. She kept her injured left arm close to her body.

"And her mother is just as confused. One day, Viv is saying she should leave the baby with her, then the next day, she's talking about she's not raising any baby. But she knows good and well, she will if she has to. And she has to, who else is going to do it?"

"But doesn't your sister have to work?" Laura asked.

Sherry waited for Gina to play her card then scooped up the book. She threw out her next card.

Gina sucked her teeth, upset about the lost book, then returned to the conversation. "But she's got to help her daughter and grandbaby".

"What about you? I still think you could take care of the baby," Cookie said.

"What kind of drugs do they have you on? I don't need a baby," Sherry said. She furrowed her brows as if she had no interest in raising a baby. As if she hadn't thought about it since her sister told her about Jordan's pregnancy. "I'm not raising Jordan's baby."

"Then what about the boy and his family?" Cookie asked.

"Oh, hell, if I know. I told Jordan she needs to figure out what *she's* going to do about school and her baby and her life. She can't depend on him. No matter what he does, she's going to have this baby and it's going to be with her. Then she got mad at me for implying he's not gonna be around and Viv got mad at me for upsetting Jordan," Sherry said.

"Family. All I've got is my mom and she is more than enough for me," Gina responded. She threw out the queen of hearts.

"Speaking of. How's Alex and your marathon?" Cookie asked.

"We broke up," Gina said bluntly. She continued to look at her cards, not making eye contact with any of her friends.

Cookie's eyes widened in surprise.

Sherry shook her head lazily, the only one who knew about the dissolved relationship.

"When? You didn't tell me that!" Laura said. Her feelings were hurt that Gina hadn't told her.

"The other day. We went running, I said I didn't want to run anymore, we got into an argument right in the middle of the park, blah blah blah... We broke up." Gina threw up her hands mimicking an explosion.

"Because you didn't want to run in the marathon?" Cookie asked.

"Because, because I don't even know why. My mother is stuck in her ways, all old people are. She's not going to change her mind, no matter how far I run or why so what's the point? He doesn't get it, he thinks it'll be as easy as convincing her that turkey bacon tastes as good as regular bacon. And we know she's never going to believe that." Gina looked at her cards. "I mean, how much am I supposed to weigh my mother's feelings and prejudices in my own personal decisions?"

"When it comes down to it, family's all you got," Sherry said.

"You think what your family wants should supersede what you want?" Laura asked.

"Yeah, hell yeah. Family should come first. People need to think about how what they do affects the people that love them. How their stupid actions can mess up their whole family. Yes, I think what your family wants supersedes what you want." Sherry blinked quickly, fending off tears, no longer talking about Gina and her boyfriend. Her ex-husband's imprisonment wasn't just a shock and an embarrassment, it was the dissolution of everything she had hoped for.

Cookie filled in the silence before Sherry could allow herself to think too long about her ex-husband. "Gina's mom's not going anywhere. She might be mad for a while, but she'll still be there for her."

"Yeah, she'll be there. Talking about my grandmother and great-grandmother rolling over in their graves because I've taken up with a white man. After all these years, Martin Luther King and Rosa Parks, and I'm taking the whole race back to slave times."

The women laughed at Gina's impression of her mother.

"But seriously, you broke up? You're not trying to get back with him?" Laura asked. She thought Alex was a nice guy and made Gina happy. It seemed worth it to reconcile.

Gina pursed her lips. "I don't think so."

"Really? I mean, I thought you really liked him? I don't know you to go running through the streets for just anybody," Cookie said.

"I did like him, but what am I supposed to do? My mother won't accept him and he's stuck on running this damn marathon."

Sherry sighed heavily. "He's stuck on trying to change your mother's mind so he can freely be a part of your life. I doubt he really cares about the marathon. He's a good guy." Cookie and Laura nodded in agreement.

"Right. His attempt to change her mind is the one thing he can control. If he gives it his best shot, then he at least has no regrets about trying to make it work. So your complaining and not wanting to run, to him, probably is like you not giving your relationship your best effort," Laura said.

"I don't need to be psychoanalyzed, Laura. It was just a break up. It didn't work. It happens," Gina said, trying to cover any hint of interest in her analysis.

"I think Laura might be right; sounds good to me," Cookie said.

"Anyway, it doesn't matter. Maybe I should go back to black men. Things were easier." Gina returned to studying her cards, her signal that she was done with the discussion.

Cookie and Sherry picked up their cards, too, aware that Gina wasn't going to say anything else. Laura glanced at her cards, then let her hand fall in her lap again.

"Well, I have some black man news," Laura cautiously.

Over the few years the women had known her, Laura had rarely volunteered any personal information about a man. All of their interest fell away from their cards again.

"Really?" Cookie asked.

"Do tell." Sherry said.

"A new client?" Gina asked.

"Kinda." Laura betrayed her game face and smiled widely. "Actually, its two men."

The women gasped in greater surprise.

"No, no, no. Not like that. There's just two men who I've met recently, and, well, I kinda like them both."

At her friends' encouraging stares, Laura continued.

"Okay, it's a bit confusing because they're my clients. Well one is, the other is his driver."

"Driver?" Gina asked.

"What kind of guy has a damn *driver*?" Sherry followed.

"He, um, well, he does pretty well for himself," Laura stumbled, wanting to keep both Michael and Sid's identities vague. "And he, the client, he is fine. And he's so nice. You'd think he would be an ass because he has money and is kinda high-profile, but he's not. He's polite, gentleman like, classy. He's very business-like, but we still have real conversations and he talks to me like he really wants me around. I know I'm working, but it doesn't feel like it."

Her friends were curious, trying to think who the client could be.

"And the driver?" Sherry asked.

"Oh, he's a great guy. He's funny and sweet, real laid-back. He's cute too, not like the client guy. He's actually the better looking one. But he's cute. The driver, I mean. He's taller, darker, more muscular. And he wears these glasses, you know, those dark framed glasses like Clark Kent. He's traveled a lot and he actually likes going to the theatre, as in live stage, ballets, operas and all, can you imagine? We end up talking a lot when Mi- when my client is running late." Laura inhaled to catch her breath.

"You can't tell us their names?" Gina prodded.

Laura hesitated, looking at each woman in turn. Then shook her head. "No, not yet."

"Oh, come on. Who are we going to tell?" Gina asked.

"Especially me. Other than the nurses?" Cookie added.

"It's not that you'll tell anyone, I know you won't. It's just, it's not like I actually have a relationship with either of them. You know, I purposely keep an emotional distance between me and my clients."

Gina and Cookie made faces at each other, trying to telepathically come up with a plan B to figure out Laura's men of interest.

"And you like them both?" Sherry asked.

"I know. Sounds bad, right? But they are both nice, handsome. But different. One's formal, the other's laid-back. If you could mush them into one," Laura formed her hands around an imaginary ball, "—they'd be the perfect guy."

"But if you had to pick one?" Cookie asked.

"It would be the driver."

Gina smiled and took a sip of her wine, still surprised at Laura's revelation. She always wondered how Laura worked with these men and never fell for any of them.

"What about the Rules? None of them apply?" Gina wondered specifically if Laura would break her rule against getting romantically involved with her clients again.

"Rule Number Five." Laura held up five fingers. "Bit me in the ass last time I broke it, so yeah, it's something to think about."

"What's Rule Number Five?" Cookie asked.

"Don't mix business with pleasure," Gina and Laura said simultaneously.

The nurse came in again carrying a small cup. She stood at Cookie's shoulder and watched Cookie play with one hand for a few books. When it was Cookie's turn again, the nurse turned to her. "May I?" she asked.

Cookie nodded.

The nurse pulled out a card and placed it on the pile. Cookie and Sherry laughed as they won the book and thanked the nurse. She smiled and gave Cookie her pills and a cup of water, then walked out and closed the door.

Sherry smirked at Laura. "So, when you figure out rule number whatever, how 'bout you take one and introduce me to the other?" She threw out the king of diamonds to win the next book.

Sherry

Sherry pulled her red silk robe closed, tying the belt as she walked into the kitchen. With well-practiced movements, she took the vodka from the freezer, simple syrup from the fridge, and two martini glasses from the cupboard. She sliced a lemon and squeezed the juice into the martini shaker with the other ingredients. She turned around at the sound of footsteps coming down the stairs.

Chase stood in the kitchen doorway wearing only his black boxers, no shirt. His dreadlocks drifted over his shoulders. When they met a few weeks ago at the club, Gina and Cookie had teased her about how young he was; they'd be surprised to find out they had overestimated his age. As he kissed her, she handed him the shaker then leaned back against the counter. She was entertained by watching the small muscle movements of his chest and biceps as he shook their martinis.

"That's good," she said, reaching out for the shaker. She turned to the counter to pour their drinks into the glasses.

He held on to her waist and she felt his kisses alight on the back of her neck, like small wet butterflies making her neck and shoulders tingle. She slowly turned to hand him his glass.

"Hungry?" she asked.

"I could go for a little snack, I guess, to get ready for round three."

As she reached into the refrigerator again to get a wedge of cheese, Sherry thought she heard a bell.

"Are you expecting guests?" Chase asked.

"Was that my doorbell?"

"It sounded like a doorbell."

It rang again. Sherry looked toward the door, wondering who could be on her porch. Her friends rarely stopped by without at least calling first. She went over to peer out the peep-hole.

"Oh, shit! Get upstairs!" she hissed at Chase.

"What the fu… Who is it? Damn. If you got a husband or crazy boyfriend, I…"

"Hush and get upstairs!" Sherry turned the doorknob as Chase leapt up the steps. "Hey, Jordan!" Her eyes scanned her niece from her face to her belly and back up again.

"Aunt Sherry." The girl glanced at her aunt's silk robe and the martini glass in her hand. "May I come in?"

"Of course, baby. I'm sorry. Come in, come in." As Sherry took Jordan's suitcase and ushered her in the door, she saw Marta, the woman who rented her basement apartment, waving from the bottom of the steps. With both hands now full, Sherry raised her glass and grinned.

"Thank you, Miss Marta," Jordan called to the neighbor.

Sherry closed the front door and hugged Jordan, trying not to spill the martini on her. "What are you doing here? Come on, sit down. Let me get you something to drink. Are you hungry?" Sherry shook her head. She was having a weird déjà vu moment, having asked a half-naked man the same question a few moments prior.

"No, I'm fine. Your neighbor made me dinner, really good pasta and a salad."

"She's a great cook, huh? How long have you been here?"

"I knocked on the door earlier, but you weren't home." Jordan raised her eyebrow, glancing again at the martini glass, as if she was now suspicious as to why her aunt didn't answer the knock. "She saw me sitting out on your porch and invited me over to wait for you there. She offered to call you at work, but I told her I already had."

"You called me? I didn't hear..." Sherry was feeling increasingly guilty. She and Chase had been home for almost two hours.

Jordan was shaking her head. "I didn't. But I didn't want her to call you. I didn't want you to come home and be mad already."

Sherry adjusted herself, making sure she was as modestly covered as possible in the ass-skimming robe. "Okay. So, I'm going to assume your mother doesn't know you're here since she hasn't called me."

"Um, no, she doesn't. She's called me like nine times, though."

Sherry sighed and stared at her niece. She didn't like the attitude in Jordan's voice and wondered how long she should wait before calling her sister. "Well, yeah, Jordan. I'm sure she's worried sick! How'd you get all the way up here?"

The sound of a toilet flushing came from upstairs. Jordan looked at her aunt, eyes wide.

Sherry held her head up high and took a sip from her drink. She debated whether to say anything about the man hidden in her room. She shouldn't have to hide the fact she's dating. But then Jordan would figure out she actually was home when she was ringing the doorbell. That was more than the girl needed to know.

"So, go on," Sherry said, as if they hadn't heard anything.

Jordan smirked and continued. "I packed my bags while Momma was at work last night. When she got home and went to bed, I took - I borrowed her VISA and some cash."

Sherry stared, stunned, at her niece.

"I was all ready to leave, like I was going to school. Then she woke up and asked why I was leaving so early. I told her I needed to make up work at school. She said okay, kissed me good-bye and went back to bed." Instead of the school bus, Jordan had caught the bus to the Amtrak station.

After more than six hours on the train, Jordan took a cab to Sherry's doorstep, arriving there about an hour ago. Marta noticed her on the porch on her way home and invited her to stay at her apartment until Sherry got back. When they saw a light come on in Sherry's kitchen, they figured she must be home. Or, as it was, out of the bed.

"Jordan, have you lost your mind! Your mother's got to be worried sick about you, girl!"

"You don't know what it's like Aunt Sherry. All my friends are leaving me behind. I can't be on the lacrosse team. Last week, Brandon had a track meet and I was too tired to go. Plus, how stupid do I look -- all pregnant, jumpin' up and down at a track meet. So, after the meet, he went and hung out with his friends. He didn't even call me. Then he went to a party last weekend without me." Jordan started crying as she told her aunt about the argument she and Brandon had about his life remaining unchanged since her pregnancy.

"Okay, but that's no reason to runaway. How could you? And you haven't called her yet?" Sherry stood up from the couch, again fixed her robe, and finished her drink.

"But, she was on his side! She said what did I expect he was gonna do, sit home with me for nine months? She said I shoulda known better."

Sherry passed her niece a few tissues while retrieving her purse from the floor where she dropped it coming in to the house. She rustled through it searching for her cell phone.

"Jordan, you've got to call your mother."

"But, she's supposed to be on my side!" Jordan blew her nose in the tissue. "Did you know, the pregnant girls in public high school get to stay in school? Some of 'em even offer childcare, nobody cares. But my teachers all look at me side-eyed like I'm a two-headed cow."

Sherry stood with her cell phone in her hand, still incredulous her niece had run away from home.

"Are you going to call your mother?"

Jordan pouted, staring down at her feet. Sherry remembered this face from when Jordan was five years old and wrote on the living room wall.

"But Aunt Sherry, can I go to the bathroom first?" Jordan got up from the couch.

"Good Lord, girl, go." She couldn't stop a pregnant girl from going to the bathroom. As Jordan shuffled to the powder room, Sherry sighed and called her sister.

"Vivian. Where's your child." It wasn't a question. Sherry expected that her sister would tell from her voice that she already knew the answer.

"Sherry, I don't know! I've been calling her and calling her. They said she didn't come to school today, but she... Did she call you?"

"No, she didn't call me. She's here in my damn bathroom!" Sherry said. She was caught between being upset her sister had lost track of her own daughter and being sympathetic to Jordan's confusion.

"What? What is she doing there? Did you tell her to come up there?"

"Why? Why would I tell her to come here, Vivian?" Sherry spoke between clenched teeth. "I had a date, he is upstairs. I've had a very good evening enjoying being a single woman! Why would I call your daughter up here?"

"Well, then what's she doing there? How'd she get there? And what man do you have in your house with my daughter?"

"She took the train. After she stole your credit card." Sherry ignored her sister's last question and regretted even mentioning Chase.

"She did what?"

From the sound of keys jangling on her sister's end of the phone, Sherry assumed she was going through her purse.

"Oh my God, Sherry. She did take my credit card!"

"Yeah. So, now what are you going to do? When are you coming to get her?"

Vivian sucked her teeth before answering. "I'm not coming up there. She can bring herself back home the same way she got up there."

"Vivian. You cannot leave her here. You better come get your child and your grandbaby!"

"See, I told you she wouldn't care. She's probably glad I left."

Sherry turned around to see Jordan standing behind her.

"Is that her? What'd she say?" Vivian said, her voice now sounded both hopeful and worried.

"She said she's sorry that she worried you by running away and wants you to come get her," Sherry lied.

"No, I didn't! I'm staying here! Don't bother coming up here!" Jordan yelled loud enough for her mother to hear.

"Oh, really? She really thinks she's grown now, huh? Okay. Fine. Tell her little fast behind to stay there!" Vivian's voice broke behind her tears.

"Viv. You don't mean that. And even if you do, too damn bad! Come get your child!" Sherry paused, listening to her sister's sobs. "Okay, sorry I yelled at you. Look, I'll give you two the week to cool down and get yourselves together. But by the time Sunday rolls around, you need to be up here to get your family."

"She don't want to come home. She had an argument with Brandon, then she comes yellin' at me about how I'm not being supportive…"

"She told me all about it. And really, that doesn't even matter. You're the mom, you're the grown-up. Get over it. Get over your hurt feelings, get over being mad she stole your card. Y'all need to work it out because you have a pregnant daughter who needs to finish school and needs to get ready to have this baby."

"I'm not coming up there. Put her back on the train and send her home," her sister said stubbornly.

"Vivian, you better be here Sunday. Bye." Sherry hung up the phone, frustrated, upset, and tired. She went into the kitchen and was glad to find she had left the drink ingredients on the counter. She made herself another martini, skipping the shaker this time, before joining her niece at the table.

Jordan sat at the table, folding and unfolding a napkin. "Aunt Sherry, I'm not going home," she said, staring at the napkin. "And if you don't want me here, I understand."

"Jordan, I know you and your mom aren't getting along right now, but really, you have to work it out with her. Despite what I said to your mom about coming to get you, I'm glad you felt safe enough to come to me. And you are welcome to stay here 'til y'all work it out. But you can't just runaway. Your mother's worried about you. And you are in a pretty special situation."

Sherry wrapped her arms around Jordan while she cried and fussed about what she was going to do with her life.

"Sorry for messin' up your date," Jordan said quietly.

Sherry smiled, trying to dismiss the immodest fact and acknowledge her niece's apology at the same time. "Come on, sweetie. It's been a long day. Let me go get the guestroom together. You can go take a shower and wash all that Amtrak dust off."

Sherry picked up her niece's bags and led her upstairs to the other bedroom. Once she got Jordan settled in her new home away from home, she pulled herself to her own room. Inside, it sounded like a small bear had taken up residence.

Chase lay on his back, his hands folded across his stomach. He snored softly, peacefully. Sherry sat on the edge of the bed and put her hand gently on Chase's now shirted chest.

"Chase. Chase," she called.

He grumbled awake, peering at her with one eye, then both. "Hey."

"Hey."

"Sounds like you got family issues goin' on," he said.

"Yeah, a little bit."

"I should go." He sat up and finished buttoning his shirt.

Sherry wasn't sure if it was a statement or a question, but agreed either way. She followed him down the stairs to the front door.

"I'll call you later." Sherry gave him a quick kiss.

"Make sure you do," he winked on his way out and Sherry shut the door behind him.

How much had her cards shifted in one evening?

Cookie

A few days after Cookie returned home from the hospital, Gina came bearing lunch, dessert, and a bottle of wine.

"How are you doing? How's your arm?"

"What's my bakery look like? Has Sarah been over there?"

"Did you forget that Cookie can't have wine? She's on drugs?" Elizabeth took the bottle from Gina and followed her into the kitchen.

"Was that on my instruction list?" Cookie called, staying seated on the couch. She set aside her cookbook and notes waiting for them to return. She heard the clank of plates and silverware as they transferred the food from the carryout containers to her tableware.

"It definitely was, and we can check with David if you don't remember," Elizabeth teased. She placed Cookie's chicken salad and pita bread on the folding tray next to her.

"David? The delivery guy who's always at the bakery?" Gina asked.

Cookie grinned, but before she could answer, her sister and Gina continued the conversation without her.

"Yes, and the guy who was stopping by her hospital room almost every other hour."

"Are you for real? I don't even remember seeing him," Gina said.

"He came several times, either during his run in the morning, while he was in the neighborhood at lunch, or after dinner. I don't know how you could've missed him," Elizabeth said.

"Cookie, are you blushing? Are you actually admitting you like someone?"

"It's nothing." Cookie tried to laugh off the question, still reluctant to admit her feelings. As excited as she wanted to be about him, Cookie felt a little bit confused. After constantly visiting while she was in the hospital, she hadn't heard from him at all since they waved good-bye in the driveway. It was probably better this way, she had resigned herself to thinking. There was no telling how it would all end up anyway.

"Ha! Coming to see you in the hospital? Come on, Cookie. Even you know that means he likes you." Gina took a bite of her chicken salad.

"Okay, so yeah, he came to visit me in the hospital. But…well, it doesn't mean anything."

"Oh, please! What are we? In the sixth grade? Like hell it doesn't mean anything. Why won't you admit it? This guy likes you and you like him? When're you gonna go out with him?"

"He hasn't asked me out, Gina."

"So? Then you ask him out."

Cookie spoke quietly. "He hasn't called me since I've been home."

Gina started to speak, then paused. She looked at Elizabeth who nodded in confirmation. "It's only been a couple of days. Maybe he's letting you get settled now that you're home. Why don't you call him?"

"I'm not doing that."

"Why not? I'm sure he'd be glad to hear from you. Any man who comes to see you in a hospital is surely interested in you."

"I'm just not…"

"What? Ready? That into him? Sure he likes you? Come on, Cookie. You're not what? What excuse do you have this time?"

"What do you mean, 'what excuse'?" Cookie put down her fork and forced a smile to hide being offended.

"You always have an excuse why you won't go out with a guy." Gina took a bite of her bread and waved the rest at Cookie while she talked. "He's too tall. He's too short. He talks too much. He doesn't have good grammar. He doesn't like sweets. His face isn't symmetrical. It's always something. When are you going to go out and enjoy yourself?" She took another bite, chewing while waiting for an answer. Gina had started her questioning as a joke, but as she went on, it took a more serious tone.

Cookie blinked away the tears forming. Between the pain medication and Gina's sudden pushing, she was getting a headache.

"Gina, that's enough." Elizabeth looked at her sister's friend with a warning. Gina was Cookie's best friend, but she could be a bit over-bearing at times.

"Come on, Elizabeth, you know I'm right. She hasn't dated anyone in years. There's always this wrong with the guy or that's not quite right. Something."

"Gina. Leave it," Elizabeth said.

"So, you've got it all figured out, huh, Gina? You're the expert now on love and relationships? Oh, wait, where's Alex?" Cookie spat.

"No, I don't have it all figured out. But you know what? I'm trying. I'm putting myself out there and trying. Where's Alex? I don't know, but I could call him. I could find out where he is. I could go see him if I wanted to. What about you, who you gonna call? Cookie, don't you want someone to be able to call?"

"Gina, stop," Elizabeth warned again.

"He's gone. Dexter is not coming back," Gina almost whispered. "You've got to move on."

Cookie's head started pounding stronger. She screamed, clenching her eyes closed.

"Shut up, Gina! Why are you doing this to me!" Cookie yelled. Her eyes sprung open and she glared at her friend, letting the tears roll.

Gina put her half-bitten bread back on the plate and swallowed. She reached out to touch Cookie's leg. "I'm sayin', you've got to move on. You've been so lonely all these years, waiting for him to come back and we all know, you know, he's not." Gina's voice softened in contrast to her words. "Dexter drowned in the ocean that day and you let your heart go with him. He would not want you, 10, 15 years later, still waiting for him to come out of the water. He would want you to keep going, to live, to be happy. He would want you to have the life you dreamed of."

"What the hell do you know about what Dexter would want? What the hell do you know about anything, about love, about losing someone? How am I supposed to live the life I dreamed of when he was part of that dream?" Cookie sputtered through her tears and runny nose.

"I think you should leave now," Elizabeth said and got up to open the door.

"I'm, I'm just saying...we all want you to be happy." Gina looked to Elizabeth, eyes pleading for agreement. Elizabeth glanced at her sister.

Gina turned back to Cookie. "You know it's true. You're scared, you're lonely. But you can't live like this forever."

Cookie hugged her knees close to her chest and laid her head back on the couch.

"Come on, Gina," Elizabeth hissed. "Do you really think she needs this now?" She handed Gina her purse. "Did you forget she almost died last week? What, you don't think she's under enough stress right now without you sending her into this psychotic spin?"

"But Elizabeth..."

Elizabeth unlocked the door. "She doesn't need this right now."

Gina huffed and spoke on her way out. "I'm sorry to upset her. I'll call her later."

"Don't." Elizabeth closed the door.

♠ ♥ ♣ ♦

"Ugh, who is it now?" Elizabeth moaned as she dragged herself to respond to the doorbell. She wasn't too surprised to find Sherry on the other side of the door.

"Hey, Elizabeth. How're you doing?"

"I'm fine, thanks. It's my patient that's not so happy."

"Hey, sweetie. How you feeling?" Sherry asked, leaning over the back of the couch.

Cookie heard Sherry's voice above her as she watched the classic movie channel on TV. "Mm," she responded without looking up. Instead, she re-shifted her blanket, pulling it up further on her shoulders, and kept her gaze on the TV.

"She and Gina had a fight," Elizabeth answered for Cookie.

"Gina told me. Still pretty upset, huh?" Sherry tapped Cookie's hip.

Cookie groaned, her only response.

"That and she just popped another Percocet." Elizabeth strolled across the living room and fell back into her chair. She picked up her knitting needles and the sweater-in-progress.

Cookie pulled in her legs and feet to give Sherry space at the opposite end of the couch.

"Jordan's here. She ran away from home," Sherry reported.

"Hmm, that's nice," Cookie said.

"I told you she was all drugged up," Elizabeth said.

The three focused on watching *Carmen Jones* without saying a word.

"Why do we watch sad movies when we're in a bad mood?" Sherry said. She continued when neither of the other women answered.

"Shouldn't we watch funny stuff? Like Chris Rock or Kevin Hart or something? Shit, some old Richard Pryor would be better than a sad movie."

Dorothy Dandridge sang and danced across the TV screen, happily, as if refuting Sherry's claim about the movie.

"You know how this ends, though, right?" Sherry finally asked Cookie.

Cookie looked at her, then back to the screen, grabbing up another handful of popcorn. Elizabeth looked up from her knitting and shrugged. Sherry sighed and went back to watching the movie.

Cookie's phone rang. Gina's picture popped up on the screen.

"You gonna answer it?" Sherry asked.

Cookie kept her eyes on Dorothy Dandridge as she tried to seduce Harry Belafonte, to initiate their ill-fated and short-lived romance.

A minute later, the phone beeped. Cookie picked up the phone to check the text message and Sherry peeked over at the screen.

I'm sorry. Please call me.

Cookie dropped the phone back on the couch and scooped up another handful of popcorn.

"You gonna call her?" Sherry asked.

Again, Cookie ignored her question.

"She said she's sorry. What more do you want from her?"

Elizabeth intensified her stare at the stitches in her sweater and her needles moved quicker.

Cookie turned to Sherry. "I want her to leave me the hell alone."

"But she said she's sorry."

"She says she's sorry? So what? Everyone says they're sorry. What does that mean?" Cookie turned back to the television. "I don't have anything to say to her."

"No, Cookie, everyone doesn't say they're sorry. A lot of times, when people have a fight, one of the people says 'forget you, I'm right, you're wrong, we're done' and the fight ends and the people never speak to each other again. It doesn't end up with one person calling and texting the other ten times a day to say 'I'm sorry'."

"Great. Then let me be the one who says 'forget you, you're wrong, we're done'."

"But why? Because she said something you didn't want to hear? All she wants is for you to be happy. That's what friends do; they tell you the shit you don't want to hear. Yeah, she coulda let you continue on, waiting on Dexter, putting your life on hold, but she knows, and you know, he's gone. You needed to hear it, you needed her to kick you in your ass to get moving."

"I didn't ask her! And I didn't ask you, either." Cookie yelled through tears. "Do I tell her what to do about Alex and her mother? No, I don't. And no one asked her about David or Dexter or anybody else. She's such a damn busy-body as if she's got everything together."

Cookie continued to cry while Carmen sang in the background.

"Sherry, please," Elizabeth peered over her partially stitched sweater.

"I'm not trying to upset you and I'm not taking Gina's side. Maybe she was butting in where you didn't want her to, and maybe she said shit you didn't want to hear or admit. But she's only looking out for you. She's only trying to push you along." Sherry paused.

Cookie wanted to move on, she wanted to be happy with someone. She had felt David might be that guy, but his sudden silence made her question what she thought was going on between them. She was too tired to explain this all to her friends and wished they would let her figure it out at her own pace.

Sherry took Cookie's silence as permission to keep going. "You deserve to be happy, you deserve to have someone in your life. I mean, if your best friend can't butt in to your business, what the hell are we here for?"

Cookie knew they were all right. But she was so used to holding everybody at arm's distance, she was used to not having to deal with her emotions. She saw the people who came into her bakery in love, broken-hearted, happy, sad. If there was one thing she was sure of, it was that she didn't want to be one of those broken-hearted people, not again.

Cookie leaned back into the couch cushions and stared at the TV. She thought about the tragic ending to the movie, one lover dead, one's life over.

Poor Carmen, she thought. Don't you know how this ends?

Gina

Tyrone. He was one of Gina's colleague's roommate's brother's friend. They had met last week at a happy hour when Sonya spotted her roommate's brother and talked him into buying her and Gina drinks. After a couple Long Island Teas and staring into his pretty brown eyes, Gina had given Tyrone her number.

They applauded as the last comedian ended his set and ran off stage. Gina hoped the heat in the comedy club hadn't made her sweat enough to mess up her hair. As the lights started to come up, she quickly dabbed at her hairline with a handkerchief then stuffed it back in her purse.

"What a great show," Tyrone said. He held Gina's waist as they bumped along with the exiting audience until they finally made it out onto the street.

Tyrone suggested that they go to a bar down the block. "We can walk."

Gina looked down at her high-heeled shoes and wanted to suggest driving.

"Come on, it's not too far." Tyrone grabbed her hand and started down the sidewalk.

Gina pulled her hand free, then tipped along slowly, getting more annoyed with each step as her shoes pinched her toes. "How much further is this place?"

"Just another block or so," he said. As they continued walking, Tyrone rambled on about the new technology that sped up the decomposition of waste and increased the amount of landfill gas.

Really? Is this what you do with your day, Gina wondered. She wasn't really sure what a landfill was and, as it seemed they were never going to get to their destination, didn't care.

Tyrone stopped at a glass door, guarded by a sleepy looking giant of a man. The door had been blackened with paint that was now chipped, letting glints of red light shine through. The muted beat of go-go music seeped through the door. Without saying a word, Tyrone took out his wallet and showed the man his driver's license.

The bouncer glared hungrily at Gina, raising one eyebrow as he slid his eyes from her head to her feet, then back to her face. He nodded at her. "ID?"

Gina rolled her eyes and pulled out her wallet to prove she was over twenty-one. She couldn't remember the last time she was carded to get into a club.

Satisfied they were old enough to enter, the bouncer pulled open the door and the music rushed out. Gina's heart raced in time to the loud music. Tyrone took her hand and pulled her into the dark entryway.

Inside, they were met by another bouncer, almost as large as the first one. Tyrone gave him two bills and then shoved his wallet back in his pocket. He raised his arms and waited for the bouncer to run a metal detector over his sides and legs. When the detector remained silent, he nodded and waved them on down the corridor towards the music. Tyrone took hold of Gina's hand again.

She followed him along the perimeter of a crowded dance floor until they finally reached a bar on the opposite side of the entrance. Gina grabbed the single seat available and Tyrone squeezed in next to her. He leaned over the bar and shouted at the bartender. She couldn't hear what he said, but Gina hoped it was a drink order. She was ready for a glass of wine.

He stood next to her, dancing in place and grinning at her. They tried to have a conversation over the blaring dance music.

"….work….Sonya?" Tyrone yelled.

"Yeah, I do the event planning for our clients," Gina yelled back.

This is ridiculous, she thought. How were they supposed to have any kind of conversation like that?

Tyrone picked up their drinks off the bar. He handed her a glass of blue liquid.

"What is this?" She asked.

"….good….taste it…," she heard him say in between beats.

She sipped at the sweet blue liquid, some type of liqueur drink. She managed a fake smile, so as not to hurt his feelings. She wondered how she could distract him enough to get rid of the drink. She took another sip to convince him she liked it, then sat it on the bar behind her.

She ignored the drink and hoped he wouldn't notice.

He continued to dance next to her as he emptied his glass.

"…dance?" He asked. He reached behind her and picked up her glass still full of the blue liqueur.

"Oh, I thought I finished that," Gina said, feigning surprise. She took it from him, sipped a little bit, then agreed to dance as an excuse not to finish the drink.

"Go ahead, finish," he insisted.

Gina finished the drink, hoping she wouldn't be sick in the morning. He pulled her onto the dance floor where they were immediately crushed by the other dancers. She knew her hair was going to look like hell.

"Wow, that was great. I need a break," Gina exclaimed at the first break in the music, which didn't come until after about twenty minutes. Her feet ached and she felt like she was in a sauna. Hanging out at a cool ice hockey rink seemed like a welcome alternative.

Tyrone pulled her off the floor, past the bar, towards a flight of steps. A couple of guys were stationed at the base of the staircase, leaning against the wall. A woman stood on the bottom step, her arm wrapped around the shoulders of one of the men. They watched Gina and Tyrone ascend the narrow steps.

It was a bit cooler upstairs, not as crowded, and the music was muted as it came through the floor. She fell onto an empty couch near the windows.

"Oh, my feet!" Gina said, relieved to finally be off her feet.

Tyrone glanced down at her shoes and smirked. "I don't really get why women wear such uncomfortable shoes."

They're only uncomfortable when someone makes you walk ten damn blocks and then jump around in a crowded-ass club, she wanted to say. But, instead of answering him out loud, she merely smiled and shrugged as if it was such a silly thing to do.

"You want another drink?"

"No, no. I'm good," Gina waved off his offer. She wasn't sure that she could handle another neon colored drink. While Tyrone went to the bar for himself, she debated taking off her shoes. Concerned her feet would swell like balloons if released, she rubbed the top of her feet gently until he came back.

Plopping into the space next to her, he studied the plastic cup from the bar. "I wonder if they recycle these?"

Gina furrowed her eyes at him. Was he for real?

"You know, most people don't really know all the materials that actually are recyclable. People throw away so much stuff," he continued.

He was for real. Gina took a break from rubbing her feet and settled back into the sofa.

"So much ends up in the landfill which could be recycled."

She remembered him telling her the first night they met that he was a manager at a landfill. Whatever Gina didn't know about trash, she was sure he was going to tell her by the end of the night.

"But on a small scale, individuals can do a lot to reduce garbage in their own homes, too. For instance, having composting bins in their backyards."

"Yeah, I don't have a backyard," Gina said, attempting, unsuccessfully, to end the conversation. She longed for a wine and cheese tasting with a discussion about a new artsy film. She missed Alex, she realized.

By the time he was explaining how landfill gas was an excellent alternative energy source, her feet had gone completely numb and her stomach was starting to grumble. She checked the time on her phone. It was past midnight and they hadn't eaten all evening.

"Aren't you hungry?" she asked. Perhaps the lure of food would end his monologue on trash and they could get something to eat.

"Now that you mention it, I could go for something to eat," he said. "You want to eat here or go somewhere else?"

"Let's eat here." Gina wasn't sure of the extent of the menu. She had only seen people eating chicken wings, but she didn't want to endure walking anywhere other than to Tyrone's car for the ride home.

He waved the waitress over and asked for a menu. The waitress reached into her apron pocket and handed them a small, laminated card, then walked away. Gina looked over Tyrone's shoulder at the bar menu:

chicken wings, chicken fingers, smoked sausage, burgers, cheese sticks, onion rings, french fries.

"You ready?" The waitress asked when she passed by them again. They ordered the wings, smoked sausage, and an order of onion rings with a couple of sodas.

Tyrone noticed the waitress bring an order out to another couple sitting at a nearby table. "Humph. Paper plates."

Oh, shit, not more trash talk, she thought.

"Such a waste. They're thrown away after only one use."

Gina shook her head. Obviously, you didn't grow up washing dishes every day.

The waitress eventually brought their food and he continued theorizing how restaurants and business could do a better job in being environmentally responsible.

Gina ate, ignoring Tyrone's dissertation. Gina laughed to herself and couldn't wait to tell Cookie about her awful date with this waste-management guy. Then she remembered Cookie still wasn't talking to her or answering her calls.

She had been trying to call and text Cookie to apologize about what she had said about Dexter. She began to think that maybe Elizabeth was right. In Cookie's first few days home from the hospital after getting shot and robbed probably wasn't the best time to bring up getting over Dexter and finding a new boyfriend. But Cookie seemed to really like David, even if she wouldn't admit it, Gina reasoned.

Gina found a big, juicy onion ring and dipped it in ketchup. She was disappointed to find it soggy and greasy, not like the crunchy ones that were a staple at the sports bars Alex hung out in. She never really cared for onion rings until she started dating him.

She chewed on the greasy onion ring, considering whether she regretted having gone out with Alex in the first place. Gina thought about the time they had spent together, outside of the office, over the past few months. The dinners, movies, dancing. Waking up snuggled next to him. Maybe the running wasn't even as bad as she made it seem. No, she didn't regret any of it.

Seeing him at work had become awkward. Not because he was distant, as she expected, but because he wasn't. He still offered to pick up her lunch when he was making a run to the sandwich shop. And he didn't mind if she hung around his office after a meeting to chit-chat. However, he didn't invite her to happy hour or to play darts anymore. It was almost like before they were dating, but worse.

Dating wasn't, of course, one hundred percent perfect. There was the obvious issue of race. But other than trying to convince her mother otherwise, it didn't seem to be a major factor. Until the blow-up in the park. Until then, they were a boy and a girl having a good time with each other. She wondered how she messed that up and how she could fix it.

She definitely was not going to approach him first. Not only would doing so be a bit too forward, it would be akin to actually admitting their break-up was her fault. And what if he didn't want to get back together with her? She couldn't risk the embarrassment of being rejected. She decided to wait and see if he ever ask her out again.

"How's the sausage?"

Tyrone's voice startled her back into the present. She looked down at her plate to realize that she had indeed eaten all of her food, leaving only a few crumbs of the roll.

"It was good," she lied. "You come here a lot?"

"Yeah. Probably every Saturday night. You like it?"

Gina smiled. "Good music." She couldn't, however, imagine coming to the bar every weekend.

"You want to go back downstairs and dance?"

Her toes throbbed, begging her not to move and willing her to shake her head. "My feet are killing me. You mind if we get ready to go?"

"Sure. Maybe, I could massage them for you when we get back to your place," he said, winking at her.

Gina was annoyed that he assumed he would be invited into her home on their first date. If for no other reason than the fact that she couldn't take hearing anymore about landfills, she didn't want him to come in.

Tyrone waved the waitress over for the check as Gina finished the last of her soda.

"Yours'll be $83," Tyrone said looking up from the bill.

Gina sputtered out her drink, covering her mouth quickly with a napkin. "Excuse me?"

"Your half – it'll be $83, including the comedy show ticket and the cover here. You want to see the bill and check for yourself?" Tyrone offered her the check.

"Oh, no, no, that won't be necessary. I didn't realize we were splitting it, that's all," Gina said in her fake happy voice, setting the plastic cup down. "So, my half is what, $83, you said?"

"Well, I had a little bit more to drink, but I did pay for parking, so it evened out," Tyrone said.

Gina sat motionless, except for her eyes which darted around the table, then the restaurant, while she tried to decide if this man was for real. Since he continued to sit there earnestly while waiting for her half, she decided, he was. Gina fake-smiled and pulled money from her wallet.

"I don't have any ones," Gina said. "And I'll have to stop at the ATM for the rest. I didn't think to bring cash."

"Okay," Tyrone pulled one of the five dollar bills off the tray. "I'll just take this back and we can call it even for dinner." He put the bill back in his wallet as he stood. "Ready?"

Outside, Gina debated tipping painfully back to the car in her shoes or walking shoe-less. Spotting a few beer bottles thrown up against the side of the building and unidentified puddles, she decided to go with the painful walk. She winced all the way back to the car.

Perhaps there was something to Laura's application process for her clients. Gina considered that maybe she should have a more selective process of picking dates other than going out with a colleague's room-mate's brother's friend. She needed to play her hand more skillfully.

Cookie

Cookie had grown restless staying at home, being away from the bakery. The highlights of her days were visits from Sherry and her niece and Laura, and watching Elizabeth's balls of yarn turn into a sweater.

"I think I should get out," Cookie said one afternoon to her sister. They were sitting at the dining table, figuring out how she would recover from being closed for weeks. They considered her electric, cable, and phone bills, her mortgage payment, the rent on the bakery and were calculating how long her savings would last.

"Out where?" Elizabeth asked, looking up from her laptop.

Cookie shrugged with her good shoulder. "I don't know. Somewhere." She slowly rose from the chair. "Maybe a walk around the block. I need some fresh air."

Elizabeth finished typing in a number. "Okay, I'll come with you. Let me finish figuring out how much you owe your suppliers."

"No, I'm all right. I won't be gone long."

Cookie went out her door for the first time in weeks. Out on the sidewalk, she looked up and down the street, almost surprised that, despite her own personal trauma, the neighborhood looked exactly as it did on the last morning she rode away on her motorcycle.

She noticed the birds in the tree that reached up past her living room window. She absentmindedly wondered what would happen to a bird with one wing. How would it get from one branch to another? How would it build its nest? Would any other bird want to mate with a one-winged bird? How long could a bird survive with only one wing?

As the birds continued to flit in the branches, Cookie turned right and began her journey around the block. She passed the café that she and Gina liked for their Sunday brunch.

Gina hadn't called in a few days. Cookie wondered whether she should set aside her pride and call her back. She wasn't mad at Gina for telling her what she didn't want to hear.

All these years, Cookie carried around this irrational hope that Dexter would resurface. In her dreams, she waited for Dexter. She was not a grieving, heart-broken, thirty-something who was scared to risk love again. She was a fiancée, waiting for her college boyfriend to come back into her life so they could live happily ever after. And each time Dexter emerged from the ocean and started walking across the beach, she would awaken as soon as she started running toward him. She would quickly close her eyes and try to return to the dream, but it would be gone, replaced by darkness and red squiggly lines flashing across her eyelids.

Cookie was mad at Gina for reminding her that her dream was just that and neither she nor Dexter would ever cross the beach.

Her walk around the block tired Cookie more than she expected. She turned into her building without noticing the delivery van parked next to the curb.

"Whew. I think they made the block longer while I've been stuck in the house," Cookie said falling through her front door.

"Hey, Cookie."

Cookie was surprised to find David standing in the middle of her living room. Elizabeth stood next to him, grinning.

"Hey, David," she said slowly. "What're you doing here?" She wasn't sure if she sounded rude, but she was confused by his presence. She missed his visits while she recuperated at home and was hurt that he hadn't come.

"He called right after you left and asked if he could come by," Elizabeth said.

"I was in the neighborhood. I hope you don't mind."

Cookie eased herself onto the couch. "I don't mind. I'm a bit surprised that's all. I haven't heard from you since I left the hospital."

Cookie knew she should offer him a seat, ask him if he wanted something to drink. Instead, she leaned back and watched him. She didn't want to put too much meaning in him standing in her living room.

"Sit, sit, David," Elizabeth said. She waved towards a chair and pursed her lips at her sister. "That walk must've taken a lot out of Cookie. She's taking a while to recover."

David glanced at Cookie and when she didn't oppose him sitting down, he sat in the chair across from her.

"You know, you're hard to find," he said.

"What do you mean? I've been right here up until half an hour ago."

"Yes, but I didn't know where 'here' was. After you left the hospital, I realized I didn't have your number or know where you lived. I only had the number and the address at the bakery," David said.

Cookie furrowed her eyebrows, looking at him suspiciously. "Then, how…"

"Let's say, those nurses require a steep bribe. I'm going to be baking my own boxes of cupcakes to deliver for quite a while," he said smiling. "But, at least I don't have to stalk the bakery every day waiting for you to re-open."

"He found you again!" Elizabeth said, clasping her hands together and making a wistful face, as if she was watching a romantic movie.

Cookie glanced from her sister back to David. "Hmph," she grunted softly, nodding her head. "So he has."

David grinned. "You're not even listed in the phone book."

"No, I'm not," Cookie admitted. "I don't have a phone here. I only have a cell number." She winced as she moved positions.

"Well, now you know where I live and have my number, you can find me anytime, anywhere."

"I promise not to lose you again."

Cookie smiled, almost imperceptibly. She wasn't sure how to respond. She liked the idea of not being lost. Elizabeth excused herself to the kitchen. To Cookie, it looked like her sister was skipping.

"So, how've you been?" David asked.

"Alright, I guess. I've been here, watching Discovery Channel, cooking shows, reruns of Good Times and the Cosby Show." She nodded at the TV.

"And your arm?"

"Um." Cookie did her one-shoulder shrug. "Being new to this getting shot thing, I can definitely, expertly, say, it's awful." She exhaled a laugh and smiled. "I would not recommend it for anyone."

They returned to the ease of conversation they enjoyed in the hospital. Seeing him again, Cookie realized how much she had missed him, despite trying to put him out her mind. She had always been tentative about her feelings for David. She knew she felt an attraction for him, but she wasn't sure if he was casually flirting when he came to the bakery or whether it was an earnest expression of his true feelings.

"I went by the bakery. Looks fine. It's still locked up. The yellow tape is gone. Someone moved the flowers that were piled at the door."

"Sherry. She took them all to the maternity floor at the hospital."

"Other than that, then, everything looks the same."

"So what do you do when not delivering cupcakes and food or tending to injured bakers?" Cookie asked.

"I play the sax. My band plays at different clubs and events in the area." He smiled at Cookie's surprised look. "What, I don't seem the jazz band type?"

"It's not that. I had no idea you played the sax at all."

"In high school, I played the trumpet. Then I was in the marching band at Howard."

Cookie imagined David in a tall hat with a plume sticking out the side.

"I learned the sax in college. Every now and then, I got the chance to play background for a solo singer or sit in with a band at one of the clubs near campus."

"I can't wait to hear you all play."

"As soon as you're ready to dance, I'll take you along to one of our gigs"

"I would like that," Cookie agreed.

"And maybe we can go out for dinner when you're feeling better," David said.

"Definitely." Cookie grinned, excited. She cataloged this as a request for a real date.

Cookie felt herself getting tired. She heard David talking, but she couldn't really focus on his voice. She started blinking, longer and longer.

When she managed to open her eyes again, the room was dark and the nightly news was on, quietly reviewing the scores of the night's basketball games.

"He waited a while, but then went home when you were clearly out," Elizabeth said.

Contrary to what her friends thought, she did want to have a relationship. She missed Dexter, but she did want to move on. She just didn't know how.

Sherry

Sherry usually slept late on Sunday mornings. But since she hung out watching movies on demand with her niece instead of going out, she was up early. After repeatedly trying to fall back asleep, only to have her mind racing around what she was going to do about her niece, she got up to make breakfast. She decided that her sister should be up early, too and dialed her sister's number.

"It's Sunday. Where you at?"

"How's she doing?" Vivian asked.

"She's fine, she's sleep. When're you coming?"

"I can't. I can't right now. Can't she stay with you for a little while? I think we need the break."

"What...what about school?"

"I'll have the school send her work. I'm sure they'll understand. In fact, they might even be happy about it."

Sherry heard the stuffiness in her sister's voice, she must've been crying all morning.

"What about...what about school activities? Prom, end of year whatever? Graduation?" Sherry was sure there had to be a reason for Jordan to go home.

"She doesn't want to go to the prom. We'll see about graduation."

"What about her doctor's appointments?"

"She's not due to go back for another few weeks."

"Okay." Sherry knew when she was beat. Whether it was holding their breath underwater as kids or arguments as adults, Vivian could always beat Sherry by pure stubbornness. "But, you've got to talk to her. She really needs to know that you aren't abandoning her like all her friends. She needs you to be with her in this one hundred percent."

"Yeah, I know. I know. I'll call her later. And I'll call the school tomorrow."

"All right."

"Tell her I love her. Bye. And, Sherry, thanks." Vivian hung up the phone leaving Sherry to return to cooking her omelets and pancakes.

Sherry heard a familiar contemporary gospel song coming from upstairs.

Jordan must be up, she thought. She pushed herself from the table to go talk to her niece. As she climbed the stairs, she heard singing. Sherry called to her niece and knocked on the closed door. When Jordan didn't answer, Sherry gently opened the door and peeked in. Her niece was sitting on the bed, leaning back on the headboard with her eyes closed. She was singing with the headphones on, in her own state of rapture. Jordan was proud to be on the church choir, often getting the solo. Sherry stood still, enjoying the sound of her niece's voice. When the song ended, Jordan opened her eyes and was startled by her aunt standing near the foot of the bed. She took the headphones off.

"Hey, Aunt Sherry. Was I bothering you?"

"No, no. I came up to tell you I spoke with your mother."

"I guess she's not coming, huh?"

"She thought you both needed more time to sort out your feelings. She's going to call the school about your work. And she said to tell you she loved you."

Jordan nodded, wrinkling her nose to keep from crying. Sherry had almost forgotten this little gesture from when she was a child. It hardly ever worked so Sherry tried to change the subject real quick.

"It's been so long since I've heard you sing, I almost forgot how beautiful your voice was. You're still singing at church, right?"

"For now. I'm sure I'll be kicked off the choir by the time I get back home."

"Why would they do that?" Sherry sat at the foot of the bed, pulling one leg underneath of her.

Jordan looked at her aunt with a mischievous smile. "Well, I was also on the dance ministry, until the leader told Momma that given my 'condition' she didn't think I was a good example for the other dancers or for the church in general and Momma should consider taking me out of the ministry."

Sherry rolled her eyes and braced herself to hear her sister's reaction.

"And my darling sister said?"

"Momma told the woman to go to hell."

Sherry screamed, knowing her sister well enough to not be totally surprised. Sherry recovered from laughing long enough to ask her niece how that was related to being kicked off the choir, too.

"She's the choir director's sister."

Sherry and Jordan fell on the bed, rolling in laughter.

Cookie

After Elizabeth left, with the promise to come back if Cookie needed her, Cookie roamed aimlessly through her apartment and took walks around the neighborhood, waiting for David or one of her friends to stop by and visit. By the third week of walking in circles, Cookie finally decided to go back to work.

The first task was getting to the bakery. After constant debates with herself about being able to maneuver her motorcycle in traffic, Cookie reluctantly admitted she had to give up the bike. She pouted as she slid into a cab for the ride to the bakery, wistfully glancing at her bike parked on the street, covered from the weather.

The cab stopped in the spot behind the bakery usually reserved for Cookie's motorcycle. She got out of the yellow car, still standing there as the cab driver pulled off. Cookie stared at the bakery door, mentally preparing to go in.

She unlocked the door, slowly stepped into the kitchen and switched on the light. She hung her poncho and new green tote bag in her locker. She stepped into the middle of the kitchen, getting reacquainted with the space. With her arm still in a sling, she wasn't really sure how she would bake anything, but she was determined to get in there and do something. Sarah and her friends had left the place so clean and orderly, Cookie didn't have any straightening up to do. Maybe she'd just sell coffee today.

The doctor thought it was too early for her to get back to work, but she kept asking herself what else she was going to do. She couldn't take off for six weeks, like the doctor said. She and Elizabeth had run the financials and it wasn't possible. Maybe if she had some more employees she could manage, but then she'd hardly be making any money. She walked around the kitchen, looking into the empty fridge, checking the bins of flour and sugar.

"Okay, God, I get it. This is your way to make me admit I need some more help. Maybe a front counter person or a prep person to crack eggs, mix frosting, pour batter? I hear you and will try to pay attention to your subtle hints before I get shot in the other arm," Cookie said aloud, in the direction of heaven.

Cookie started a pot of coffee, thankful for the water faucet installed over the coffee pot so she wouldn't have to lift water into the brewer. In a few moments, the warm smell of coffee filled the kitchen. Cookie started feeling comfortable in her space again and wandered to the front of the bakery.

She walked around the front of the counter to open the blinds of the storefront. She unlocked the door and stepped out, looking up and down the shopping strip. She realized how much she missed being at work and acknowledged that being back was going to be good for her.

When she turned to get back inside, Cookie was struck by an image of herself lying against the counter. Blood pouring out of her shoulder. The memory of how she had gotten there played like a movie in her head, as if it wasn't about her at all.

She had put the money and charge receipts from the register into the bank bag and thrown it in her tote to drop off at the bank. Sarah waited on her last customer for the day, a boy getting a chocolate cupcake, while Cookie cleaned the kitchen. Sarah left for her interview and Cookie went to lock the front door, where the boy was waiting. Then there was a blast. The boy rummaged through the cash register as he cussed and banged on the keys. He ran out of the bakery, leaving her lying on the floor.

She remembered moving onto all fours, trying to crawl after the boy left. The injured arm had shuddered and collapsed. Cookie reached up to the left side of her face and could still feel the swelling where her face had hit the floor. Her hand shook. Goosebumps sprouted across her arms and her knees felt like they would fold. She pulled out a stool and sat down at the counter. Maybe she wasn't ready for this after all.

What seemed like an hour passed before Cookie wiped away her tears and got up from the barstool.

"Come on, girl, pull yourself together," she said out loud. "We can't operate a bakery crying and carryin' on like this. Run or get back up on the porch," she told herself, invoking her father's age-old advice.

Concentrating on putting one foot in front of the other, she followed the smell. The promise of coffee beckoned her into the kitchen. She picked out the "Don't frazzle the animals" mug from one of Gina's zoo events. Sipping her coffee, she tried to figure out what she should do next. She noticed the empty shelves and decided to order supplies and ingredients.

She turned on the computer and waited patiently as it began to hum and the bakery logo and little icons populated the screen. With only one good arm, she resolved to keep it simple this week.

When Sarah came in, she could do the mixing and baking if she picked the basic cupcakes. Cookie could do the frosting, nothing fancy, maybe dusting with confectioner's sugar.

The memory of her mother's chocolate cake, with a lacey design on top from sifting the sugar through a doily, made Cookie smile for the first time that morning. Her mother had been Cookie's inspiration to be a baker.

Her mother, however, was not pleased with Cookie's plans to go to pastry school.

"All the years out of slavery, people marched and died so we could have an equal chance to go to college, to make something of ourselves and you want to be a cook? You could be a doctor, a lawyer, a teacher, anything, and you're throwing it all away to be a cook." Cookie could hear her mother's voice as if she was standing right beside her.

Cookie had tried to explain that this wasn't frying fast food burgers, it was cooking school to become a pastry chef and manage restaurant kitchens. It didn't matter. As far as her mother was concerned, Cookie was single-handedly reversing the civil rights movement to become a domestic, an educated one from an expensive school, but a cook, nonetheless. What did the Little Rock Nine brave their way into high school for if all she wanted to do was be a cook, her mother bemoaned. No wonder her mother and Gina's had gotten along so well.

Maybe she had been right. Maybe if she had become a doctor, she would be patching up a busted shoulder rather than suffering from one herself.

Cookie was glad her mother wasn't alive to see her now. She would be crying as she went through her litany of "I told you so's." Her father, fussing from afar about the disrespect and lack of discipline of young kids and uselessness of the city police, was enough.

But at the same time, she did wish her mother were alive. When Cookie was four years old and fell off the porch steps, her mother was there to wipe off her elbow and assure her it wasn't broken. When Dexter disappeared, her mother held her and told her she would heal and be strong again. And she needed her mother now, to tell her that she wouldn't be scared and nervous forever. Cookie needed her mother to kiss her right on the top of her head and pour a glass of milk.

"Oh, Momma."

Again, Cookie started crying. But this time, she wasn't so silent. This time, it was the snotty-nose wailing of a little girl who missed her dead mother so desperately. She put down the coffee cup, laid her head back and cried. She held her bad shoulder, scared she would shake it loose. Cookie wept until she was empty, her face even more swollen.

She went into the bathroom to splash cold water on her face.

"Wow. Now that's a mess," she said to her reflection. She tried to pull her hair back into a neater twist and replaced the hair pin with one hand. A tube of lipgloss sat on the edge of the sink, a reminder from Gina to fix herself up before going out to serve customers. It had been about two weeks since their argument. All logic, as well as Elizabeth and Sherry, told Cookie she should return Gina's calls and accept her apology. But her hurt feelings wouldn't let her pick up the phone.

Cookie swiped the gloss across her lips and stepped back into the kitchen.

The cowbell on the front door rang. Cookie jumped at the sound and stared towards the doorway.

There were footsteps, then an unfamiliar voice called out, "Hello?"

Immediately, Cookie's hands started shaking as she remembered that she had poked her head out the front door, then never re-locked it. She was trapped.

"Hello?" the voice called again. It was a woman's voice.

Cookie shook her head at her own senselessness. "Okay, now, get out there," she whispered.

She cautiously walked to the front of the store.

"Yes? Good morning."

A middle-aged, woman stood in front of the counter. "There you are. I wasn't certain you were open. I'd like to get a muffin and a cup of coffee, but...?" The woman glanced down at the empty display case, then back up at Cookie. Her eyes moved back and forth between Cookie's swollen, bruised face and arm in a sling.

"Yeah. We aren't really open yet. Well, I mean I do have coffee, if you'd like a cup? Freshly brewed. But I don't have any muffins." Cookie tried to smile as if it was normal to be in a bakery without any baked goods.

"Well, that's okay then," the woman said, turning to leave.

"Sorry, maybe tomorrow." Cookie followed her to the door and locked it. She put her hand over her wildly beating heart, knowing she wouldn't make it through the day.

Cookie went back to the kitchen and picked up her purse. When she got out onto the front sidewalk, she remembered to lock the door.

She walked to the liquor store and was relieved it was open. Cookie wondered what kind of people bought liquor so early in the day, as she roamed around the store, picking up bottles of rum and vodka.

"Hey, how you doing? You back to work already?" Mr. Archer asked.

"Opened today. Trying out new recipes," Cookie said, trying to casually explain why she was buying liquor at 9:30 in the morning.

"Cupcakes with rum? I'm gonna have to come get one. Hey, you should try Kahlua, that would be good."

She picked up a brown bottle of the liqueur as she wandered down the aisles.

"Can you handle this?" The cashier asked, putting the bottles into a shopping bag.

"I can have him carry it back for you," the manager said, tapping the cashier on the shoulder.

"No, no, I'm fine. I can manage." Cookie thanked them both and took the bag of liquor, cradling it in her good arm.

When she was safely back inside her bakery, Cookie made sure to relock the door again.

She selected a small measuring cup from the shelf and poured a shot of rum. It was actually too early for vodka she had reasoned. In a long swallow, she finished off the rum, as tears started to well up in her eyes again. She was done crying for the day.

She poured another shot and swallowed that, too.

She sat back down at her desk to order more eggs, milk, and butter.

"Lord, let's get through this day," she prayed out loud. "Amen."

After an hour of staring at the computer screen, Cookie gave up and called a cab.

When she arrived home, she immediately resumed her spot on the couch. She cried from the pain in her shoulder because she had forgotten to take her medication. That in turn, gave her a headache, making her even more miserable. When she finally couldn't take the pain any longer, she dismissed her fear of mixing drugs and alcohol and took a few painkillers and climbed in the bed.

Laura

The bakery looked dark, but Sherry had said Cookie was supposed to be open again. Laura pulled the door, unsuccessfully. She knocked on the glass of the bakery door and waited for Cookie to answer. She looked around and noted that there wasn't a bell anywhere, which after she thought about it, made sense. She knocked harder, nervous she might crack the glass.

The curtain moved aside and Cookie peeked out the window. Laura wiggled her fingers "hi" through the window. Cookie opened the door and stepped back to let Sherry in the bakery.

Laura looked quizzically at Cookie and nodded her chin at the whisk her friend held like a bat.

"What were you going to do with that?"

"You never know when you might need to defend yourself. I could beat someone with it." Cookie laughed at her joke. When Laura didn't respond, Cookie shrugged and said, "I guess you got to be a baker to get it." She dropped the whisk to her side. "What're you doing here?"

"Sherry said you were open. I thought I'd stop by. See how you were doing." Laura listened carefully. It sounded like Cookie's words were slurring together and she wondered if it was the effect of the medication she was taking.

"That's nice of you, thanks. You want some coffee? Come on in the back. I haven't really opened, yet." Cookie turned and led the way to the kitchen. "I was here yesterday, but not for long. I was a little nervous and tired and realized I didn't feel up to staying around all day."

"The coffee's there on the counter," Cookie said pointing to a small coffee maker and handing Laura a mug.

"Is that new?"

"Yeah, I brought it this morning. It's too much work making a big pot of coffee if I'm not opening."

"You should take it slow. Could you change up your schedule to make the baking easier?" Laura poured herself a cup of coffee from the carafe.

"I don't know. I had a routine that worked: come in early, bake, set-up for the day, get deliveries ready. But, yeah, I don't know if I can do it that way now. I used to do a lot of the morning work by myself." Cookie reached up to rub her shoulder.

"What're you doing with those?" Laura asked, pointing at the half empty bottles of rum and vodka on Cookie's desk.

"Oh, those? They, I, I was thinking of working on some new recipes," Cookie stuttered.

"Really? I didn't know there were any muffins made with rum and vodka."

"Rum cake. Bread pudding," Cookie said.

Laura thought she spoke a bit too nonchalantly. Generally when Cookie was working on a new recipe, she excitedly explained her idea. Laura suspected she was trying to hide something.

"Those should sell well. For a crazy second there, I was thinking you were drinking them, but then I remembered that you were probably on a bunch of pain killers and antibiotics and who knows whatever else and surely you wouldn't be drinking while taking a bunch of medication." Laura looked Cookie squarely in the eyes. "Right?"

Cookie blinked and laughed lightly. An obvious nervous, fake laugh. "Of course. Right. No, those are, like I said, for a recipe."

"Good. So, other than that, what else are you up to around here? When do you think you'll reopen?"

Cookie waved at the computer. "Hopefully, in a couple days. I was sitting down to order a few things. I'm out of milk, eggs." She sighed and sat at the desk. "I guess I'll start small, simple."

Laura took a seat at the same worktable she had a few weeks prior. "You know. Maybe I could help out a little bit."

Cookie laughed, a true laugh this time.

Laura returned the laughter. "Come on, I can't cook, but I can do something." She pointed at the computer. "I can order stuff. I can follow directions. Surely, I can mix some stuff together if you tell me what to do."

"Then we better start right now if I've got to tell you everything."

"Okay. Well, don't say I didn't offer."

"Anyway, surely you're too busy to be hanging out here with me," Cookie said. She leaned back in the seat and sipped at her coffee.

Laura noticed that Cookie made a face as if she remembered something and peered into the cup.

"Nope. My days are actually pretty quiet. I'm busy most nights, but usually in the day, I'm just wandering around by myself. I was thinking about getting a part-time job."

"A part-time job doing what?"

"Well, I thought my friend would hire me in her bakery," Laura said. "Now, I'll have to see what else is out there." She of course, did not want, nor need, another job. But she did feel like she wanted something to fill her days and occupy her mind.

"Maybe I could be a librarian," Laura said.

"Really, a librarian?"

"That would be kind of a cool job, don't you think? You get to sit at a big ole' desk and tell people where to find their books. And you could always be the first person to get a book."

Cookie laughed. "You'd have to start wearing glasses."

"I do wear glasses."

"You do? I've never seen you in glasses."

"That's because you've never been in my house late at night or early on Saturday when I'm too lazy to put in my contacts."

"Huh. Learn something new every day."

"See? Maybe I could learn to make cupcakes."

Cookie looked around the kitchen. "Okay, let's see what you can do."

Laura happily tied on a pink and brown polka-dotted apron and gathered the ingredients as Cookie called them out. With some embarrassing difficulty, she measured out flour and sugar and vanilla. She had to retrieve a few broken egg shells from her bowl. An hour later, she slid a tray of cupcakes into the oven.

"Oh, my gosh. Mixing cupcakes is a lot more work than I imagined," she gulped down a full mug of water.

"You all thought it was easy, huh?"

"I didn't think it was easy, but I didn't think it was *that* hard. You're definitely going to need some help."

"I thought you were going to be my help?" Cookie joked.

Laura glanced at the clock. "It took me an hour to make a dozen cupcakes! You really will be out of business with me doing the baking."

She poured more water into her mug. "Maybe I should stick to my night job."

"Speaking of which. How's the new client, the one with the driver?"

"He's good. We're supposed to be going to San Diego later this week. He's a really nice guy. And quite honestly, being with him is what's making me feel like, maybe I want to do something else."

"How so?"

"Since taking him on as a client, I've just started thinking about how I've gotten to where I am. I mean, I have a college degree and I'm working as an escort. Really, if it weren't for my Rules, I'd be totally in another lady profession, right?"

Laura didn't wait for Cookie to come up with the right answer.

"But, it's really the driver that's got me thinking. I had convinced myself that it's got to be 'get a normal job and have a boyfriend' or 'be an escort and be lonely.' And I had chosen the latter. Until I met him, I didn't realized that that's not really what I want to choose."

She anticipated her scheduled meetings with Michael, because it meant seeing Sid. For other clients, she selected outfits that would make her standout in the crowd, in order to make him look good. When preparing for an event with Michael, Laura picked outfits she hoped Sid would like, making conscious decisions to impress him.

Although it was his job to drive her and Michael around, Sid seemed to genuinely enjoy their few minutes alone. When she was in the car alone or he waited with her for Michael to wrap up a meeting, they talked about their personal life, their hobbies, their likes and dislikes. She knew oatmeal raisin with walnut cookies was his favorite, the scar on his arm was inflicted during an ill-fated game of cowboys and Indians with neighbor boys when he and Michael were ten years old, and he never went to bed before midnight. For the little time each evening they were together, it felt like an all-night affair.

But when he dropped her off at home at the end of the evening, she felt like Cinderella at the end of the ball. In an instant, the fantasy was over. Sid would walk her to the empty lobby and then Michael, Sid, and their black carriage would disappear until the next time.

Cookie checked on the cupcakes, poking one with her forefinger. The smell of vanilla wafted from the hot oven.

"Maybe you could come work for me after all," Cookie said as she pulled the tray out of the oven.

As the cupcakes cooled, Cookie gave Laura instructions for making frosting. They carefully measured out the confectioner's sugar, butter, and vanilla.

"Who knew frosting was this easy? I could be making frosting at home all the time," Laura said, enjoying her baking lesson and imagining working in a bakery.

Laura knew it wasn't real. But it all reminded her that she wanted something that was.

Sherry

Sherry wandered through the aisles of maternity-wear. In her fifth month, Jordan still wore her regular clothes, using the excuse that she was small. Now that she wasn't in school or around her friends, she wore sweatpants and a tee shirt on most days. With an eye to her stretched out teenage wardrobe, Sherry had finally convinced her niece she needed to wear clothes more appropriate for a mother-to-be.

"Aunt Sherry, these are all old lady clothes," Jordan said, holding up a smocked-front, empire waist maternity top.

"What did you expect, the Junior Maternity line?"

"Ugh. I can't walk around in this stuff. I'll look all pregnant!" Jordan flipped through the hangers of flowing tops on the rack.

"Well, my dear, you *are* all pregnant. And fashion is about your least worries right now."

Sherry searched through the dresses. She held one up in front of her and glanced in the mirror. Before she let herself imagine the dress being for her, she held it out to her niece. "Here's a nice dress."

Jordan twisted her mouth at the pale, floral print wrap dress. She held her hand out and took it from her aunt.

"Maybe, I could go to my regular stores and buy larger sizes."

"That might work for tops for a little while, but I'm not sure your butt and belly are going to continue to fit in those skinny-minny sweatpants."

Jordan sighed and trudged over to the next rack. She searched through the pants until she found a couple pairs of jeans without a wide maternity belly band.

"I'm gonna try these on."

Sherry took a seat by the door of the dressing room. She ignored the maternity magazines and pulled out her phone to check her messages. There were four: one from Vivian, one from a potential client who wanted her to list their home, and two from Chase. She had hardly spoken to him since Jordan arrived.

"Your mother called and asked how you were doing," Sherry called across the dressing room door.

"Tell her I'm fine," Jordan shouted back.

Sherry texted her sister, telling her that they were maternity shopping.

"Well, what do you think?" Jordan asked. She turned in front of the three-way mirror, her eyes sliding up and down her reflection. She practiced holding her hands on the mound over her stomach and twisting side to side, taking in her new profile.

Sherry stared at her niece's instantly bigger belly.

"Prego-pillow," Jordan announced, reaching into the jeans' waistband and pulling out a pillow. "It was in there so you could see how the clothes would fit in a few months." She turned back to her reflection to see how her butt filled in the jeans. "These aren't so bad, right?"

"What is it about us women that we have to check our butt when we try anything on?"

"You think these make my butt look big?" Jordan laughed at herself.

"I don't think it's the jeans. But, I do think they look nice."

Jordan went back into the dressing room to try on the dress Sherry had picked out.

"Oh, I like that. Should I take a picture for your mom?"

Jordan shook her head, glanced in the mirror, then quickly went back into the dressing room. She came back out with the clothes and carried them to the register.

"Pizza? Chinese?" Sherry asked as they left the store, heading towards the food court.

Jordan and Sherry scanned the assortment of food vendors and settled on a full-service restaurant in the corner of the mall. Inside, the waitress seated them at a booth in the middle of the room.

"You talked to your boyfriend lately?" Sherry asked. She peeked over her menu to watch for Jordan's reaction.

"His name is Brandon. And no, I haven't talked to him. I don't even think he knows I've left. If he has, he's probably happy I'm gone."

Sherry noticed Laura standing at the hostess stand and excused herself to go invite her to join them at their table.

"Jordan, this is my friend, Laura. Laura, Jordan, my niece."

"Hey, Jordan. I've heard a bit about you."

"Hi, Miss Laura. I can imagine what you've heard." Jordan blushed.

"Oh, not just about the pregnancy," Laura reassured. "Miss Lacrosse MVP, AP student. Your aunt always talks about the daughter she wishes she had."

"What're you doing out here today? What're you buyin'?" Sherry interrupted her friend before she revealed how much she didn't mind her niece staying with her.

"Oh! I found the most fabulous, sexy, wonderful dress at the boutique across the street. So I went to get it just in case I get invited to a fancy dinner and need a new dress. And I made sure she hadn't sold one to anyone else." She turned to Jordan and continued. "That's important when you are going to a fancy dinner so no one else waltzes in there in your dress."

Laura paused to allow the waiter to tell them the lunch specials. Sherry and Laura ordered wine. Jordan asked for a glass of water and an order of fried cheese sticks.

"Well, the dress was a bit big in the waist but the seamstress is on site today and said she could fix it real quick. So I came over here to wander while I waited. What about you two? Momma-to-be shopping?" Laura nodded at the maternity store bag at Jordan's feet.

"Yeah, little lady is starting to grow out of her regular clothes. But she says the maternity clothes are 'old-lady clothes', go figure."

"Why don't you buy larger sizes of clothes you like?" Laura asked.

"That's what I said," Jordan sing-songed, rolling her eyes at her aunt.

"Because pregnancy clothes fit a bit different. You know, bigger in the belly, fitted everywhere else," Sherry explained.

"So get them altered," Laura replied.

"Laura, no one's buying and altering clothes for a couple months, not when there are maternity shops. Plus, she needs to save any money she has for alterations to take care of this baby."

"Hey, if she needs a job, I think Cookie's hiring. She needs someone to help her out in that bakery."

"I thought you were going to work there?" Sherry laughed.

"I did, too. But, it's a lot of work."

"Anyway, Jordan can't cook."

"Cookie can teach her." Laura started to tell Sherry about her day in the bakery when they noticed Jordan crying all of a sudden.

"Jordan, baby, what's the matter?" Sherry asked.

Jordan sniffled back her tears then replied, "I was thinkin', a few months ago, I was sittin' in a food court booth with my own friends, fussin' where we should shop next for the cutest clothes and now here I am, trying to find cute *maternity* clothes."

"Oh, sweetheart. Oh. I know, life is funny that way," Sherry said.

"You know, I just wanna be like a regular girl again. I wanna go back to school and be getting ready for the prom, for graduation. I wanna walk down the hall with Brandon and have everyone smile at us because they know we're going to be prom king and queen. I wanna hang out with my girls." Jordan took a deep breath and bit into another cheese stick. "I just wanna be happy."

"You know, happiness is over-rated. 'Happy' ain't everything," Laura advised.

"Laura," Sherry said to her friend.

"Really. Everyone is always 'oh, I want to be happy.' Jordan, I am sure that right now, you don't feel happy. But you are healthy, your baby is healthy, you are safe, you have people who love and care for you so much. Even now, after you've stolen your mother's credit card, wandered across state lines, and run away from home, you don't have to worry about what you're going to eat today or tomorrow or where you're going to lay down your head. You have your whole life in front of you to be happy."

"This isn't the life I planned," Jordan quietly replied.

"Daggone it, what is it with you and your mother about this life you planned!" Sherry said.

"Okay, so this isn't the life you imagined for yourself, but it is *your* life." Laura said more calmly. "No one's living the life they imagined for themselves. I'm sure as hell not." She shook her head. "Neither is your aunt, nor your momma. Even the President of the United States didn't really think he'd ever be the President of the United States. Good or bad, no one's living the life they planned. That's God's way of laughing at us, thinking we actually have any control by making plans. But what are you going to do? You can't exchange your life for another one."

"But can't I at least be happy?" Jordan asked.

"Oh, baby, don't worry. You'll be happy again, before you think you will. Then you can move on to other things, something more important. But happy will come and go, don't sit here pouting because at this moment, you aren't happy," Laura said. She sipped her drink while looking at the young girl who sat there breathing deeply, trying not to cry even more.

Sherry didn't know what to say to her friend or her niece. Did Laura give her too much real world, hard life lessons or was it the smack of reality that she needed, that Sherry and her sister were too scared to give her?

"Are you happy? Don't you want to be happy?" Jordan finally asked Laura.

Laura tossed her head back and forth. "Sometimes I am, sometimes I'm not. Right now, I am because I'm waiting on a beautiful dress to be altered for me so I can be the most beautiful woman at the fancy dinner I'm going to be invited to. But if I some heifer's got on my dress, no, then I will not be happy, and neither will she when I rip it off of her."

"Aunt Sherry, what about you?"

Sherry thought about the question. She nodded and said, "Sure I am." But, she wouldn't bet on it.

Cookie

The bakery had been re-opened a week and Cookie was getting used to her new normal. She was resigned to taking a cab instead of riding her motorcycle. She wore a light poncho because it was easier than a jacket. Her hair was braided so she wouldn't have to pin it up each morning. Instead of coming in early to bake muffins and cupcakes for the day, Cookie and Sarah baked everything the night before.

By the time Cookie wheeled out the baking carts from the refrigerator with the selection of coffee cakes and pound cakes in the morning, the coffee was ready. She poured a shot of rum in her mug and topped it off with cream and coffee.

Singing along with the morning gospel program, Cookie sliced the cakes and arranged them neatly on the display trays. She transferred the trays to another cart, then slowly wheeled them out to the front of the bakery.

Under the "Closed" sign, a "Help Wanted" sign leaned against the window. She had finally posted the sign the day before with Laura's insistence, Cookie's silent admission that she could use more assistance.

David walked up the sidewalk and stopped in front of the bakery. He read the new sign while waiting for Cookie to unlock the door. She hadn't made any deliveries since she had been back in the bakery, but David came by each day anyway once he realized how much physical work Cookie put into the bakery.

"Good morning," he said, kissing Cookie on the cheek.

This was a new part of her morning prep that she enjoyed. "Good morning. You're here early," she said as she returned behind the counter.

"I've got a lot of deliveries on the other side of town and wasn't sure I could get back over here during lunch." David followed her behind the counter to help put the trays in their place.

"Anyone apply for the job?" David asked.

"A few. I've got to call them back." Cookie was busy during the day and exhausted by the end of it; she hadn't called any of the five people who inquired about the job.

"I think I'm starting to get pretty good at this," he said, standing back and looking at the arrangement of trays. "Maybe I could apply for the job." David headed towards the kitchen without waiting for directions from Cookie.

"Yeah, I might have to keep you around," Cookie said.

He took a case of cupcake boxes and customer bags to the front, placing them under the counter where Sarah could reach them easily. Returning to the kitchen, he dragged bags of trash out the back door.

"Thank you," she said and handed him a cup of coffee.

"Where is Sarah, anyway? Isn't she usually here by now?"

"She's running a little late this morning."

Sarah had called to say she would be late because she worked in the studio all night. Cookie told her to stay home and get some rest, but she didn't want to tell David she'd be alone all day.

"I don't know Cookie. You being here by yourself still makes me a little nervous."

"Oh, don't worry. Sarah'll be here any minute, now. Anyway, that's all I've got today."

"All right. What about tonight? Are you still going to make it to see me and my boys play at the club?"

"Definitely."

As David opened the door, Cookie spotted Officer Scott walking down the sidewalk.

"I'll see you this evening," David said. He nodded to the officer as they passed outside the bakery door.

"How are you doing this morning?" Officer Scott asked.

Cookie glanced at her arm and slightly raised it. "Livin'," she responded with a shrug of the other shoulder. "So what do I owe the honor of this visit? You have any more information for me?"

Cookie stepped back into the bakery. "You want a cup of coffee?"

"Sorry, no new information yet. Unfortunately, the description we have isn't detailed enough to really identify anyone." He searched the ceiling and corners of the bakery. "You don't have a security camera in here?"

"No, I don't. You think I should? I do have security alarms on the back door and the silent alarm on the cash register."

Cookie's hand started to shake. She still had David's empty cup in her hand and looked around for her own. She remembered her rum-laced coffee was on the back worktable.

"A camera would be good. Sometimes it's a deterrent. At the least, it would at least provide more information in such a case as this." Again, he looked around the bakery, then through the doorway leading to the kitchen. "You might also think about not being in here alone. You don't have anyone else to help you?"

"I do have help, but she's not here yet. She does other freelance work, so her hours are pretty flexible."

"I understand with a small business it's hard to afford help on a full-time basis, but you really should consider having someone else who can be here with you," he advised.

"I put up a 'Help Wanted' sign," she nodded towards the sign in the window. "And I also have my girlfriends, I think you met them at the hospital, right? They'll come around, too."

This last part was a hopeful lie, seeing as she had cursed out her two best friends and wasn't sure when they would show up again.

"Right, I did drive one of your friends to the hospital," Officer Scott said. "She was pretty upset, showing up here in the middle of all that commotion. I thought we would have to get an ambulance for her, too. You all must be pretty close."

It had only been a couple of weeks and Cookie missed her friend. "Yeah, we were, I mean, are. We've been friends a long time, went to high school together."

"Really? That's nice." He scanned the cakes in the glass case. "Now then, let me get on to work. Can I get a slice of almond pound cake to go?"

Cookie wrapped up the cake as he promised to come around regularly to check on her. After he left, she retreated to the kitchen.

She sat at the desk and took a few more pain pills. David had become even more of a constant, comforting presence since she returned to the bakery. On the other hand, the police officer's visit reminded her of the attack and made her feel nervous again.

Cookie poured another cup of coffee with a shot of rum. Since coming back to the bakery, she had experimented and settled on rum and liqueurs for her coffee. Although these weren't the strongest liquors, nor the least pungent, they were enough to calm her nerves and she could make plausible explanations of why they were in the bakery: new recipes for rumballs, liqueur-infused cakes and frostings. So far, she hadn't figured out what baked good she could soak with vodka or gin.

Over the next hour, she served her customers and finished her cup of coffee. After the morning rush, she started gathering her ingredients for the next day's baking. She knew it would take her longer since Sarah wasn't coming. Her rum, coffee, and Percocet cocktail made her preparations and baking go even slower.

♠ ♥ ♣ ♦

Through a sleepy haze, Cookie heard someone calling her name.

"Miss Cookie?"

She heard light, cautious footsteps coming towards the kitchen doorway and lifted her head from the desk.

"Are you here?" the voice called. "Hello?"

Cookie realized it was Jordan standing in the middle of the kitchen.

"Oh, hey, Jordan. What are you doing here?" She spoke slowly; her voice was hoarse and her head ached.

An empty coffee mug sat on Cookie's desk. She clutched a photo of herself and Dexter at a football game in her hand.

"I, uh, came down here to…I was kinda bored sittin' at the house all day by myself." Jordan scratched at her belly.

The kitchen was filled with the smell of sugar and butter. And burnt bread. There was a large pile of flour spilled on the worktable next to a mound of softening butter, as if Cookie had been in the middle of a recipe then quit to take her coffee break. More flour laid on the floor, a trail from the flour bin near the wall.

"Yeah, your aunt's a busy lady. I guess she doesn't stay home too much. You can have a seat." She nodded towards a stool at the worktable. "You want something to eat?"

Jordan surveyed the options on the worktable. Two dozen clumsily frosted cupcakes were arranged haphazardly on a display case tray. A row of burnt loaves of bread sat on a baking rack.

"Um, no, I'm fine." She sat on the stool, holding her small belly, balancing carefully. "How're you doin'?"

Cookie leaned back in her chair. A few braids fell from the scarf tied around her hair. Her pink and brown polka dotted apron was covered in splotches of flour and frosting. She brought her cup to her lips for a drink then peered into it, remembering that she had already emptied it. "I'm here. How about you?"

"Yeah, me too." Jordan pushed a pile of flour aside and rested her arm on the table. "I was thinkin', maybe I could come work for you? Miss Laura said Sarah was getting busy with her film stuff and you needed some help."

"Of course she did. Everybody thinks I need help." Cookie's words lazily slurred together. She turned from her empty coffee mug to Jordan. "You know how to bake?"

Jordan twisted her lips. "Okay, so no, I don't know how to cook."

Cookie raised one eyebrow, silently asking, "Then what will you do?"

"But maybe I can work at the counter, ringin' up customers or cleanin' up. Then you would only have to worry about bakin'."

"Baby, I don't even know if I can do that anymore." Cookie scanned the cupcakes and bread she had already ruined. She leaned her head back and closed her eyes to hold the tears back.

After a few minutes, Cookie opened her eyes again. Finding Jordan still sitting at the table, she spoke.

"What are you gonna do about that baby?" Cookie pointed the empty coffee cup at Jordan's belly, mounded under a green maternity t-shirt.

"What do you mean? I'ma keep my baby." Jordan wrapped her arms protectively over her stomach.

Cookie nodded. "What are you gonna do about school?"

"Mm-hmm." Jordan shrugged. "Momma had the school send my work up here, so I've been keepin' up. I don't know if I'ma go home for graduation, though."

"What about college?"

"I don't know." Jordan wiped at the flour on her forearm, avoiding Cookie's eyes and possibly anymore questions about her uncertain plans.

"What about your boyfriend?"

"Ex-boyfriend," Jordan corrected, stressing the "ex". "I ain't heard…"

"I haven't heard," Cookie corrected. "'Ain't' ain't a word. Surely they taught you that in school."

"I haven't heard from him since I been here," Jordan repeated. "He doesn't even answer my emails, my texts, nothin'." She wiped at her eyes although there were no tears there. Instead, she left a streak of flour across her cheek.

"Don't wait for him," Cookie said.

"Huh?"

"If he's smart enough, he'll come back for you. Then you can decide if you want him back. Which you will, 'cause he's your baby daddy. That's good. In the meantime, don't waste your time waiting. Next thing you know, your whole life has passed you by."

Cookie waved the picture of Dexter at Jordan. "See this guy? I was supposed to marry him. We were young, a little bit older than you and we were so in love." Cookie smiled for the first time since Jordan had come in, but it was a sad smile. "We had our whole entire life planned, we were going to be together forever."

Jordan reached to take the picture. "So, what happened?"

Cookie rolled her chair over to the worktable, then handed the frame to Jordan. "He died." She took a deep breath, then started again.

"He died and I kept on waitin' for him to come back. And I've waited and waited. And he's not coming back, is he?" She looked at Jordan as if she had a better answer than the one she already knew.

Cookie took another breath, then broke down and cried. She laid her head down on the table and wept quietly. She felt a gentle pat on her back as she cried into her good arm, making a muffled sound.

Cookie weakly raised her head. She pushed herself up from the table and placed the photo back on her desk. Patches of wet flour clung to her face.

"Could you get my purse out of that locker for me?" Cookie pointed to the set of lockers by the backdoor.

Jordan checked the first two lockers and found them empty. In the third one, she found a green tote bag. Jordan helped Cookie pull it over her arm, then gently wiped at Cookie's face, clearing the flour.

"Thanks, sweetie." Cookie started walking towards the front of the store and waved to Jordan to follow. She was still crying, still not making any noise.

When Cookie reached the front door, she flipped over the "Closed" sign and took the "Help Wanted" sign out the window, tucking it under her good arm. Jordan walked out onto the sidewalk and Cookie locked the door behind them.

Cookie reached to hug the girl.

"You start tomorrow. See you at nine."

Cookie walked down the sidewalk towards the street, leaving Jordan standing alone in front of the bakery.

Gina

Gina tapped the phone screen. She scrolled through her contact list to Cookie's name. She did this although Cookie was on speed-dial; Gina only had to hit the number "25" to dial Cookie's number. She peeked across the room, where Laura sat in the big easy chair with her legs curled underneath of her, flipping through the latest *Washingtonian* magazine. Gina sighed, then tapped more buttons on her phone.

"I don't know what you're waiting for. Call her already," Laura said from behind her magazine.

"I am, I am," Gina said. "I just…"

"You just what? What's the big deal?"

"I…What am I supposed to say?"

"What, you've never apologized before?"

"Yes," Gina said, but then paused to think. "Of course I've apologized before. I just don't know what to say. Sorry you still miss your old boyfriend?"

"Uh, no. Sorry you upset her while she was recovering from getting shot. Sorry you were being all nosy and telling her what to do. Sorry you won't leave her alone about dating. Sorry…"

"Okay, okay, okay. I get it. Damn." Gina dropped the phone on to her lap. "I wasn't that bad," she mumbled.

"Yeah, you were," Laura responded, returning to her article about the best of everything in Washington.

"So, let me ask you," Laura said after a few minutes. "Cookie's never dated anyone since her fiancé died?"

"Nope. Not really. I mean, she's gone out with guys. But she's never stayed in any relationship for any time. She always finds a reason why she doesn't want to see them, or acts so not interested, the guy eventually stops calling her."

"Why do you think she hasn't see anyone else? Obviously she misses him. But is she scared?"

"Scared?"

"I don't know. That maybe if she goes out with someone else, something will happen to him to? Or, maybe she feels guilty that she's still living and he's not?"

Gina sighed and ran her hands over her face. "Yeah, I guess I could see that."

As much as Gina tried to push Cookie to get past Dexter's death, she did sympathize with her. She had watched her change from a young woman full of dreams of marriage and a family with the love of her life, to a depressed not-really-a-widow fiancée college student. Cookie had done well for herself professionally, but there was always a shadow of sadness following her in the shape of Dexter.

"They had talked about going away together for spring break. But since it was our last one, they decided to do trips with their friends, a girls' trip and a guys' trip, because they were supposed to have the rest of their lives together. Almost like early bachelor and bachelorette parties. I think she's always regretted not going with him. That maybe, had they done their own trip, he'd still be alive."

"Cookie thinks he was her one true love?"

"Cookie definitely thinks he was her true love."

"So what about this David guy? You think she'll give him a chance?"

"I do. I really do think she likes him. And I guess I said what I did because I also think Cookie needs permission to move on, someone to say 'hey, you don't have to be in mourning your whole life'. I think she's lonely and would love to be in a relationship. And she's so sweet, she deserves it. I mean, it's been over ten years now."

"How about you, you've never mentioned a true love," Laura said.

"No I haven't. I don't think I've found him yet."

"Not Jason? Not Alex?"

Gina thought about her previous boyfriend. She slowly shook her head. "No, not Jason. I liked him a lot and would've stayed with him if he hadn't moved. But I don't think he was my true love. And Alex?" Gina pursed her lips. "Well, I've made a mess of that haven't I? Anyway, I don't think we had even gotten close to the love stage at all."

Laura fanned the magazine pages like a flip-book.

"What about you? You've never mentioned a true love," Gina said.

"Nah, I definitely haven't found him either. It's kinda hard when you're working as an escort to find Mr. Right. But maybe, one day. Maybe when I'm wandering the aisles at Whole Foods, he'll come around the corner and our eyes will meet over a pile of organic limes."

"Limes?" Gina asked, laughing.

"Yeah, limes. Because of course he'll like martinis with lime, too," Laura smiled. "That's how I'll know I've found him."

"What's my sign? He won't be in running sneakers?"

"Maybe Alex was the man for you, he just had a bad plan."

"I don't know. Alex is sweet and yeah, I have a good time with him. But. I don't even want to talk about it. I'm over him." Gina hadn't convinced herself that was true, but thought if she said it enough times she could make it so.

Gina played with her phone, sliding the menu up and down making the little icons float across the screen.

"Go ahead, call her." Laura picked up the magazine again and hid behind the open pages.

Gina sighed and hit the "2" and "5" buttons. The phone rang.

Cookie answered on the third ring.

"Hey, Cookie." Gina tried to sound like everything was good between them. She wanted to judge Cookie's response before wasting an apology.

"Hi, Gina. What do you need?" Cookie answered. She sounded as if she had been asleep, but Gina swore she could hear her eyes roll.

"I was just calling to see how you were doing. Um…the other day, um…we…" Gina paused, not sure what to say next. She half hoped Cookie would fill in the blank for her.

"Uh huh," was all Cookie said.

"Well, I know you still miss…"

Gina was interrupted by Laura clearing her throat and fluttering her magazine.

"I mean, I'm sorry. Yeah, I'm sorry." She looked over at Laura who was revolving her hand in a gesture that said keep going.

"For making you upset."

Laura continued to twirl her hand.

"And telling you what to do."

As Laura continued egging her on, Gina shrugged to indicate she didn't know what else to say.

"Really. Thanks. And who helped you come up with that? Laura? Sherry?"

"What do you mean? I am sorry."

"Gina, you have never apologized to anyone in your life."

"I have so."

"Really? When, to whom? It wasn't to me when you told me it didn't matter where Dexter was, he was probably going to die anyway. It wasn't to me when I cried on his twenty-fifth birthday and you told me to get over it. It wasn't to me when you said I was never going to find another man after getting a 'D' tattooed on my chest."

Gina slapped her face into her free hand while Cookie ran down her list of sins against friendship. She winced each time Cookie ticked off another bad deed she had said or done.

Laura watched Gina with concern.

"Okay, okay, Cookie." Gina continued to hold her head with her eyes closed as she re-launched her apology. "Okay, I get it. Maybe I didn't apologize all those times, but I was sorry. And I'm sorry now. I'm sorry I upset you. I'm sorry you still miss him and can't…"

Laura threw the magazine at Gina, hitting her on the top of the head.

"Ouch, shit!" Gina sat up straight and glared at Laura.

With eyes wide open to emphasize her words, Laura stage whispered, "Stop putting it on her. This is about you!"

"I'm not, I know," Gina hissed back.

"What's the matter?" Cookie asked.

Gina rubbed her head, "Nothing. What was I saying?"

"You were telling me how I still miss Dexter."

"Right. Well, that's not my business if you miss him, it's what's in your heart, you have the right to feel however you want."

"Well, thanks, Gina. Glad I have your permission now."

"I mean. Look, Cookie. You know I'm bad at apologies, obviously you know that better than I do. So let me say this. I'm sorry I made you cry. I never want to do make you cry, I don't want to make you sad. I want you to be happy. I'm sorry."

Gina listened to Cookie breathe on the other end, but she didn't say anything. Again, she laid her head against the chair, closing her eyes. Several minutes passed before Cookie spoke.

"Thanks, Gina. I know you were only trying to help."

Gina let her shoulders down with a release of her breath. When she opened her eyes, Laura was still watching her. Gina noticed another magazine rolled up in Laura's hand, as if it were a missile waiting for her to go off script again.

"I need to go now, I think my drugs are wearing off and I need to take a nap."

"All right. So, maybe I'll come by and visit tomorrow?"

"Yeah, well, give me a call. I'll let you know if I'm up for company or not."

Company, Gina thought. Since when am I company?

"And tell Laura 'hello' for me. I'll talk to you later."

Gina heard silence, then a ring tone. She turned her phone off and shrugged at Laura. "I guess she accepted my apology."

"That was one weak-ass apology. I wouldn't have accepted it. I would need you to beg me, get down on your knees and plead."

"Would you charge me extra?"

The next magazine sailed across the room and hit Gina dead center in the chest.

Cookie

Cookie was on the computer, finishing a supply order for more sugar and flour when she heard the front door open.

"Cookie! I'm here! Let's sell some cupcakes," Sarah yelled, coming into the kitchen jangling her keyring. Since she never knew what time Sarah would actually show up and she didn't want to leave the front door open, Cookie had given Sarah her own key.

"What are you doing just sitting there? We've got work to do. Why were closed yesterday anyway?"

After the mess of spilling flour and burning bread the day Jordan came by, Cookie had gone home, made a nasty concoction of her pain medication, rum, and coffee, and lay on the couch. She slept until the next morning. She didn't open the bakery, but had come in for a couple hours once her headache had passed to clean up her mess and tell Jordan to come the next day instead. Then she went home and back to bed.

But she didn't tell Sarah any of that. Instead, Cookie rose from her desk and grabbed two clean aprons from the laundry basket. Sarah helped her tie the strings behind her back, then put on her own. They pulled out the trays filled with baked goods from the refrigerator. Sarah took her position at the front counter and Cookie started slicing coffee cakes.

"You said a new girl starts today?" Sarah called.

"Yes. Jordan. She's my friend Sherry's niece."

"The pregnant girl?"

"Yes. I want you to teach her how to take care of the front counter so you can help me more back here."

"Cool. I always wanted to do more of the baking."

Since when, Cookie thought. What about her career as a cameraman?

As she arranged the cakes on a display tray, Cookie heard her favorite combination of sounds. The cowbells hanging on the door clanged, followed by a whistling tune. She didn't even have to look up to know that David was walking through the kitchen doorway. She was excited he was there, but also nervous that she had missed his band playing at the club.

"You're back. What happened to you? You didn't make it to the club, you didn't answer the phone, you were closed yesterday. I was getting worried."

She scratched her head. "Yeah, sorry. I guess the other day I was more tired than I thought. I went home to change for the club and fell asleep. And then I had a splitting headache yesterday, I couldn't even move."

"Well, glad you're okay. You should at least let someone know what's up with you."

Cookie felt bad for making him worry.

"You need me to do anything today?"

"Actually, I have a delivery. I know it's late, I should've got these out earlier, but better late than never, right?" Cookie picked up a box from the worktable.

He took the box and read the label, *University Hospital, 5th floor Nurses station.* "For the nurses who took care of you?"

She shrugged when he raised his head from reading the label. "It's the least I could do."

"I'm sure they'll appreciate it."

Cookie handed him a cup of coffee. "Think you'll make it back this evening?" Cookie didn't want David to feel obligated to pitch in, but did appreciate his help. She wouldn't admit to him the great deal of pain she still felt. She didn't tell anyone about the nagging nervousness that was only temporarily relieved by the extra shot in her coffee.

David closed one eye, twisted his mouth as if in deep thought, then answered. "Yes."

"Good," Cookie nodded.

"Hey, maybe when I come by this evening, we could get a bite to eat. You know, if you're hungry."

Cookie couldn't believe it had taken him so long to ask her out. "I'm sure I'll be hungry."

A steady flow of customers, Sarah's random shouts through the doorway, and the slow pace of frosting cupcakes blurred the hours of the day. Jordan had been in for a few hours and worked with Sarah in the front. They had sent her home after the lunch rush to do her homework.

"Cookie, we're done!" Sarah called.

Maybe instead of a camera, I should get an intercom system, Cookie thought as she dropped the cleaning towel on the worktable and went to the kitchen doorway, checking the wall clock.

"Already? It's only four o'clock."

Sarah locked the front door. "Just sold the last cupcakes." She gestured at the empty display case.

Since they didn't bake during the day anymore, Cookie and Sarah agreed that there was no use in staying open after the last cupcakes were sold. This new rule resulted in them sometimes closing at five, at the latest, or as early as three o'clock on a busy day.

Sarah turned over the "Open" sign to the side that now read "Closed – out of cupcakes 'til tomorrow" and hung it back in the window.

They finished the baking for the next day and lined all the muffins, cupcakes, and cakes in the refrigerator. Sarah cleaned up the kitchen while Cookie counted the money and credit receipts from the cash register.

"Ready to go?" Sarah asked, pulling her backpack over her shoulder.

Cookie checked the wall clock again. "Not yet. You can go ahead." She fished distractedly through her tote bag.

"And what are you waiting for, or should I say 'who', as if that's a mystery?" Sarah asked.

Without answering, Cookie opened a small bottle and shook two round pills into her palm. She gulped them down with a cup of water.

"Do you have a date? And are you not telling me about it?" Sarah teased. "Oh, okay. That's how we're playing this." Sarah laughed, wrapping a tie-dye scarf around her neck. "Well, mystery man better come on, because I've got to get to the studio and I'm not leaving you here by yourself. New rule, right?"

There were a lot of new rules in the bakery and not leaving each other at the end of the evening was one of them. Cookie realized there was no way she could keep her date with David from Sarah. She had been reluctant to mention it all day, not wanting to jinx herself on their first date, but was excited to finally tell someone.

"Okay, nosy. Yes, I'm going out with David. He's supposed to be here at six."

Sarah squealed in excitement. "Yay! Where you goin'?"

"I don't know. We're getting dinner. You know, real casual."

"Were you going to go like that or were you going to change after I left?" Sarah pointed at Cookie's hair and face, then her outfit. Cookie was dressed, as usual, in her jeans and white button-down shirt.

"I didn't expect to be going out, so this is all I have. Do I look bad?"

Sarah tilted her head. "I wouldn't say you looked bad, I mean, the man has seen you laid up in that hospital bed so you don't look like that, but you could maybe fix yourself up a little bit, you know what I mean? Let the man see how pretty you are," she said, while rummaging through her backpack and finally pulling out a red scarf and a jumble of beads. Without bothering to ask, Sarah unpinned Cookie's braids, letting them fall down her back, then wrapped the scarf like a headband around her head. She shook out the beads, which turned out to be a necklace and placed them around Cookie's neck. She unfastened the top button of her shirt.

"You do have some lipstick in that bag, right?" Sarah asked.

Sarah looked disapprovingly at the worn tube of brown lipstick Cookie found in her purse and shook her head. "Now that you have a boyfriend, you're gonna have to do better." She applied the lipstick to Cookie's mouth, stood back and appraised her work. "But that'll have to do for now."

Boyfriend. Cookie recalled her and David's conversation about the proper title for a significant other. *Lover.*

Sarah and Cookie walked out of the door when they saw David walking toward the bakery a few minutes before six o'clock.

"Hi, David. Bye, David. Bye, Cookie. Have fun," Sarah called as she hurried away towards the Metro.

"Where should we go? What do you have a taste for?" he asked.

"How about The Grille, right down the street?" Cookie suggested.

David wore a light blue checked shirt and jeans instead of his regular uniform. It didn't bother her so much when Sarah had mentioned it, but now Cookie wished she had had a fresh shirt to change into, too. If she had spoken to Gina today, she probably would've brought her one. At least Sarah fixed her hair and applied a fresh coat of lipstick before David got there.

At the restaurant, they sat at the bar while waiting for a table.

"You want something?" David offered.

Cookie automatically began to order a mojito, but remembered the pills she had taken only an hour before. "I'll just have a soda."

"How'd it go today? Feeling better?"

"Yeah, I'm feeling much better. We're getting there, day by day. Thanks for all your help. Without you and Sarah, this would've been tough. I couldn't have reopened by myself."

"What? You had to reopen. What else would you have done with yourself?"

Cookie thought, rolling her head back and forth. "I don't know. At one time, I wanted to be a teacher. Maybe I could've done that. Taught in a culinary school."

"Hmm. That would've been a good second career. But I couldn't come by your classroom every day for coffee, so I'm glad you stuck with the bakery."

Despite the past few weeks, Cookie enjoyed her bakery. She loved seeing the happy children when they got a cupcake on a day that wasn't their birthday. She enjoyed the sweet couples who came in for their morning coffee and muffins. The office workers who needed the chocolate on chocolate to help them forget the stress of their demanding bosses, unsatisfied clients, and uncompromising co-workers.

"What about you? Would you play in your band full-time if you weren't delivering cupcakes and flowers and food?" Cookie asked.

David stared at Cookie's image in the mirror over the bar. "Definitely."

"Why aren't you doing that then? How'd you get into the delivery business, anyway?"

David shook his head. "When I was going to school, my father said my music was useful for getting a scholarship and admitted playing in clubs could be fun, but the life of a musician wasn't stable and I should pursue something more dependable. So, I majored in business management, specifically in entertainment."

"Totally understand. My mother cried when I said I was going to culinary school. I took some business classes to assure her that I wasn't going to become a house slave."

"Exactly! My father pictured my life playing the trumpet on the street corner with my case laying on the sidewalk, waiting for people to throw in some nickels and quarters."

David and Cookie laughed, considering each other's dreams and their parents' fears.

"How'd you go from sax player to delivery guy?"

"When we graduated, a couple friends and I came up with this courier business idea. We started with one used truck and it grew from there."

"I didn't know you owned the business."

"Yup. Now it's me, a friend, and another friend and his wife. It works great because I drive all day and am finished in time to get to the club at night. Everybody's happy." David said.

The hostess moved them from the bar to a table for two near the window. Cookie loved window seats because she could pursue one of her favorite hobbies: people watching.

They shared tastes of her chicken and mushroom alfredo and his filet mignon with straw onions. They talked like they had been having dinner and hanging out for years. They skipped dessert, then walked hand in hand back to his car.

David opened the passenger door for her. "You're still taking a cab to the bakery?"

"Yeah. I'm still nervous about trying to ride my motorcycle." Cookie slid into the seat, tickled that he was offering her a ride home.

In the car, they continued their dinner conversation and she interjected with directions to her home. Once there, they stood in front of her building where he lightly kissed her goodnight. Cookie wondered if she should invite him inside. He kissed her on the lips once again, just a little bit longer, after she unlocked the front door.

"I'll see you in the morning," he said, answering the question in Cookie's mind.

Laura

To anyone who noticed them, Laura and Michael appeared to be like any other couple arriving home from a weekend excursion.

In fact, before they left, they had had a meeting about the terms of their contract. He asked her to escort him exclusively. She agreed and would be paid quite well to do so. Although he had agreed to let her keep a couple long-time clients who she didn't want to drop so suddenly; her part of the deal was not to accept any new contracts. He wanted her to always be available to him, whether for a formal dinner or a basketball game. It was a business arrangement she had never gone through, but made her realize why he was such a good negotiator.

They walked through the airport terminal, his hand resting lightly on her back, talking about their trip to San Diego where he had client meetings and they attended a party and a Clippers game. While Michael was in his scheduled meetings, Laura had time to wander though La Jolla, go shopping, and get a massage. When he was free, they walked along the beach, watched sea lions on the rocks, and had dinner by the marina. She hadn't broken her rule about separate rooms, but ignored the one about one-on-one "dates". Their red-eye arrived at Dulles airport in time for breakfast on Monday morning.

"You're okay with Sid taking you home?" In agreeing to their new contract, she knew she would see Sid more. And possibly, as in this case, more by himself.

"Yes, that's fine."

"I'm real sorry I can't go along with you. But, I got that call right before we got on the plane and I need to get up to New York."

"I know, I know. Really, it's fine." Laura wasn't used to a client trying to make any accommodations for her, it was usually strictly by the contract: what time she got picked up, when she was dropped off, where they were going. He had business to take care of and when she was honest about the facts, she was only another part of his business.

Besides, it gave her an opportunity to talk to Sid.

"There he is," Michael said and waved to Sid, who was waiting for them beyond the security terminals.

Laura unconsciously grinned at the sight of him. Whenever she saw Sid, she had to make a conscious effort to control her giddiness. Although the attraction may not have been sensible, she really wanted to run into his arms. She wondered if either man noticed her reserve.

"So, how long will you be gone?" Laura asked, trying to sound casual.

"Should only be a few days. I've got a meeting down here at the end of the week that I don't want to change. Can I say good-bye here?" Michael asked. There was a long line of passengers queued for their morning flights, waiting to get through security.

"Of course, there's no point in you walking me ten feet then having to stand in line to get back in. Thanks for a great weekend."

"Thank you. It wouldn't have been half as fun without you."

Laura walked past the "No return from this point" sign. She took a deep breath and relaxed before she reached Sid.

He greeted Laura with a cup of coffee and took her overnight bag. Laura turned to wave to Michael, then followed Sid out of the airport. They talked about the trip to San Diego on the way out to the garage.

Laura was amazed by his sense of humility. She imagined that if she had to wait around and drive for any of her cousins, she would have more attitude and be more resentful than Sid ever appeared to be. It was another trait that made him attractive.

She constantly had to remind herself that it was all business whenever she felt her heart quicken as his hand brushed her or she started to giggle at one of his jokes. "Rule Number Five, Rule Number Five," she repeated when she imagined the cut of his shoulders underneath this suit jacket or the feel of his lips on hers. Her feelings were further complicated by the circumstances of their relationship.

But, she was running a business, engaged in contractual partnerships. When the contract term was over, the partnership was over. Even more complicated, her contract wasn't even with Sid. She didn't really have a rule for this situation. Did Rule Number 5 still apply?

"Home, I presume?" Sid said, imitating his best valet voice on their way to the garage.

As they settled into the car, Sid asked if she was hungry. "We can stop and get something to eat, if you'd like."

Laura had taken her usual seat in the back. "I am so tired, I don't know if I could make it through breakfast." Laura watched an airplane take off. "Oh! But I know the perfect place to stop real quick for the best muffins!"

"Tell me where you want to go."

Laura told Sid the street for Cookie's bakery then leaned back. Within a few minutes, she had fallen asleep. She awoke when Sid gently shook her leg as he leaned in the passenger door.

"Cookie's Oven? We're here."

Laura shook her head to wake herself up. She checked inside her purse, looking for the mints from the hotel. Coffee and sleep breath, how attractive, she thought.

She gracefully climbed out of the car to walk with Sid to the bakery.

A line of people were waiting for their morning muffin and coffee. Others were scattered at the few tables, checking their phones or typing on their laptops. Watching all the people, Laura realized this was the earliest she had ever been in the bakery.

"Hey, Jordan! How's it going?" Laura asked, delighted to see the girl at the front counter.

"I'm becoming quite the bakery assistant." Jordan proudly patted the pink and brown apron covering her growing belly. She turned back to the man at the counter to give him his change. "Miss Laura's here," she called through the kitchen doorway, pausing between her customers.

"What kind of muffins do you like?" Laura asked Sid. "Cookie has all kinds and they're all delicious."

Sid read the labels propped next to trays of muffins in the display case. "Blueberry, Apple Cinnamon, Mocha. Caribbean Sunshine?"

"She uses coconut milk, adds in pureed mango and banana," Jordan explained while ringing up another customer.

"Sold. Give me two." Sid turned to Laura, "Oh, yeah, you want something, too?" he joked.

Laura playfully waved off his question. "Actually, I want the apple crumble."

Cookie came from the kitchen, wiping her hands on a towel hanging from her apron.

"Hey, lady," Cookie greeted Laura.

"I see you gave Jordan my job," Laura said.

Cookie smiled as her eyes shifted to the man in a suit standing next to Laura. "Yes, well, you seem like you found a way to occupy your day."

"Cookie, this is Sid. Sid, Cookie. She's the owner and baker of all these fine muffins and cupcakes."

"Nice to meet you Sid. Where y'all going?"

Laura could hear the "this time of morning" implicit in the question. "I just got back from San Diego on the red eye. Sid was taking me home from the airport and I thought we should stop for a quick breakfast."

"Oh, right, the San Diego trip. How was it?" Cookie asked.

"It was good. You know, any chance I get to walk on the beach, it's a good time for me," Laura said.

"And what about you; you like digging your toes in the sand, too?" Cookie asked Sid.

Laura's eyes widened as Cookie spoke to Sid. She wondered how he would answer, if he would admit that he didn't go and was only driving her home. And would Cookie take the hint that he was not the client, but the driver, the one that she liked.

Sid's lips curved into a lop-sided grin. "Nah, I didn't get to the beach this trip. Maybe next time," he said.

"Too bad. So what can I get you two this morning?" Cookie asked.

"Caribbean Sunshine and Apple Crumble," Jordan said, setting the box of muffins on the counter. There was a slot for one more muffin.

"I have peanut butter and jelly. You want one?" Cookie asked Laura.

"Yes! Pack one of those, too. I'll have it for lunch," Laura said.

Cookie placed the last muffin in the box and poured two cups of coffee. Laura reached in her purse for her wallet, but Sid got to his first.

"Thank you, young lady. Keep the change," he said to Jordan as he handed her a few $10 bills.

Jordan thanked him, giggling as she put most of the money in the register. She put the change in a jar on the back counter with a hand written sign that read "baby $$."

"Bye, Laura. Nice to meet you, Sid," Cookie waved to them as they walked out.

Laura knew from Cookie's face that there would be more questions to answer the next time the women got together.

Sid took a bite of his muffin once they were back in the car. "You're right, these muffins are good."

"We, I mean, you, should come back when the cupcakes are ready, they're delicious." Laura bit into the muffin, trying not to drop crumbs all over her skirt and wondered if he heard her mistake.

"So, Sid, what do you do when Michael's out of town?"

"Whatever I want to. I'm free as a bird." He smiled at her in the rear-view mirror.

Like me. She smiled back at him and thought about how both she and Sid were tied to Michael's calendar.

"Is there anywhere else you want to go?"

Laura wondered if Gina had taken Lady to the dog sitting service. Gina didn't like leaving Lady or the having the dog walker in her apartment. Laura sent Gina to ask her where she left the dog.

"Actually, I think I'll need to stop and pick up my dog if that's not too much out of your way?"

"I am here to serve you, my lady," Sid said, returning to his faux English valet accent.

Laura gave him directions to Doggie Daycare. She ran in to pick up Lady and came out ten minutes later carrying her in a purple, quilted dog carrier.

"Okay. That's the last stop, for real." Laura unzipped the carrier and petted the dog as they drove home.

Sid parked in one of the three parking spots in front of the building reserved for car services, taxis, and delivery vehicles. Laura felt like she had been gone for a week rather than just a few days as they juggled her overnight bag, Lady in her carrier, coffee, muffins, and her purse.

"I can help you to your apartment. If you'd like," Sid offered.

"Thank you. That would be helpful." Laura led the way to the front door where they were greeted by the day shift doorman.

"Good morning, Mr. Porter. Sid, Mr. Stone, has parked his car outside to help me take these things upstairs." Laura nodded back towards the parking spaces.

On the elevator ride up to the fifth floor, Laura took the dog out of the carrier. When the elevator doors open, Lady trotted down the hall towards Laura's apartment.

"She knows her way home?" Sid and Laura followed the dog home.

She unlocked the door and glanced around the apartment quickly to make sure everything was in order. She generally left her apartment neat, but she was still nervous about how her home would appear to Sid. Surely, Michael lived in a beautiful home and her place would be like a dollhouse in comparison. She wondered what Sid's home might be like.

"You can leave those right by the door." Laura turned on the lights in the living room on her way to the kitchen while Lady took her own tour of home.

Sid set the overnight bag and the dog carrier down by the door.

"Do you want anything to drink? Water, anything?" Laura called.

"No. I'm good."

"I feel so dehydrated. I guess it was that long flight," Laura said, returning to the living room with a glass of water. She picked up the remote and turned on the TV, collapsing onto the couch. "So, no big plans while Michael's gone?"

Sid remained standing by the door. "I actually do work in the office when we're not out. When he's away, it's the best time for me to get what I need to get done, undistracted by his calendar."

Laura felt a little embarrassed. She wondered if she had hurt his feelings, assuming and implying that he sat around twiddling his thumbs when he wasn't driving. She also felt a tad jealous that he did have something else to do.

"Really? I didn't know you..." Laura started, then didn't know how to finish the sentence. "Well, I was going to say you were welcome to stay if you weren't busy, but if you need to leave..." She got up from the couch to let him out.

"I've got all day. I can spare a little time." He smiled at her invitation. He walked over to her and gently put his hand on the side of her face. "I'd love to stay for a bit."

"Oh. Okay." She stood still, not wanting to displace his hand. She stared at him and wondered, now what?

He answered by leaning down and gently kissing her on the lips. Laura was surprised, but responded in kind, returning his kiss and putting her arms around his waist. She felt him walking her backwards, back towards the couch. They fell onto the couch, still passionately kissing each other, their tongues twisted together and their hands grasping for each other, wanting to touch every part of each other's body. He slowly started pulling on her blouse. They broke away from each other's lips briefly while she raised her arms to let him lift it over her head. His lips trailed down her neck to her breasts. She helped him unbuckle his belt.

Lady barked at the confusion on the couch. For a second, Laura was distracted enough to wish she had left her in the carrier. She quickly shook thoughts of the dog from her head and refocused on the man in her arms. She inhaled as he slid into her and wrapped her arms tightly around him.

Finally, in a groan of mutual satisfaction, they relaxed into the couch cushions. Sid rolled to the side with Laura tucked in his arm, safe from rolling off the couch. He kissed her eyes and nose. She smiled, keeping her eyes closed. She wasn't sure how they ended up naked on her couch and wasn't sure if she should question it. But she did wonder if it would happen again.

"That was nice," he whispered.

"Very."

"So. You need to get ready for your day?"

"Nope. I'm good. How about you?"

"I'm fine right here." He kissed her hair.

"Me too." Laura fell asleep and dreamt of walking arm in arm with a man on a sidewalk that lit up like the one in Michael Jackson's "Billie Jean" video.

Sherry

"Wishin' I was still sleep, dreamin' instead of talkin' to you." Sherry sat up in bed, agitated by her sister's phone call so early in the morning. "Don't you worry about who I'm dreamin' about, what do you want?"

This was not going to be a short conversation, calls early in the morning rarely were. Sherry climbed out of bed and pulled on a robe over her nightgown. She went downstairs to the kitchen to start a pot of coffee while Vivian rambled on about Jordan.

"She's doing fine. She's eating, resting, growing. In fact, we're going to the doctor's today." Sherry took the leftover biscuits and strawberry jam out of the refrigerator. "But, more importantly, why can't the girl cook?"

Sherry, surprised by Jordan's lack of cooking skills, had her in the kitchen as often as she had time. Last night, they cooked fried catfish and greens, along with the biscuits she was warming up in the toaster oven.

"What do you mean? She can cook," Vivian said.

"She couldn't figure out how to batter the fish for dinner. Then was making faces about having to touch the fish and get her fingers messy. What's she going to do when she has to change a diaper? You need to stop spoiling her. It's time for her to grow up, real quick, now."

Sherry heard her sister sigh on the other end of the phone. She remembered when Vivian was so energetic and positive, but that light seemed to have waned as Jordan got older. Sherry wondered if single mothers tired out faster than married ones.

"Why're you going to the doctor?" Vivian asked, obviously ignoring Sherry's attempt to give advice.

"Jordan's been up here over a month, she needs a check-up. I'm taking her to the OB I saw last year, the one in my GYN's office." Sherry was proud of herself for being a good aunt and knowing Jordan needed a monthly check-up from reading her niece's copy of *What to Expect When You're Expecting.*

"Okay. You'll tell me if anything's wrong? Call me afterwards, either way."

"Of course, I would tell you if there was a problem. Everything's gonna be fine, but I'll tell her to call you as soon we're done." Sherry spread jam on the warm biscuit. She was calming herself before her next sentence, hoping not to upset her sister.

"There is one thing, though. Jordan sure does miss her momma."

"She said that?" Vivian asked.

"She doesn't really say it, but she asks if I've talked to you, what I think you think about her and her baby. Whether I think you are mad at her. Will you let her come home, will you let her and the baby live at home. Then she gets real quiet." Sherry stopped talking and listened for her sister's response. All she heard was her breathing deeply on the other end and guessed she was crying, or trying not to.

"Don't go and get yourself all upset, I didn't say all that to make you feel bad. I just figured you should know how she's feeling."

"Thanks," Vivian said, between sniffles.

"What are you doing today, anyway? Why are you calling me so early in the morning?" Sherry asked.

"I worked night shift and I'm off today. I'm getting ready for bed."

"Okay, well, I'll tell Jordan you called. And I'll let you know how the doctor's appointment went. Bye. Love you."

Sherry finished her coffee and biscuits. She contemplated what, exactly, were they going to do once the baby came.

"Jordan! Wake up!" Sherry knocked on the bedroom door on her way to the shower. An hour later, they were on their way to the doctor's.

It was debatable who was more nervous when they got to the office, Jordan or Sherry. They checked in with the receptionist and then sat, waiting nervously for Jordan's name to be called. After filling out all the new patient forms, they each picked up one of the baby magazines on the side tables. Jordan read an article about baby products, what were the perfect toys for your newborn that would make them the smartest in their pre-school class. Sherry read about pre-natal care, how much folic acid and calcium a pregnant woman should have and then how much as a nursing mother.

"Jordan Goodman," the nurse called reading her name from a clipboard.

As Jordan stood up, she looked at Sherry, her eyes asking her aunt to come along.

Sherry kept her magazine and followed her niece. She concentrated on staying calm as the nurse weighed Jordan, took her blood pressure and measured her belly circumference. Sherry held her breath each time the nurse stopped to write a number in her chart, waiting to hear a nervous mutter or see a worried look flash across her face. But none came. Eventually, the nurse gave Jordan a paper robe to put on, then indicated for Sherry to follow her out of the room.

Sherry sat outside of the room, waiting for the nurse to return with the doctor.

"Have we met before? Have you had an appointment with me?" A voice asked Sherry.

Sherry looked up to see Dr. Lee. The doctor looked exactly as she had the last time Sherry had seen her. She was dressed in her white doctor's jacket and black pants, and had her gray hair pulled up into a bun with her brown framed glasses pushed up close to her eyes. She was impressed the doctor remembered her.

"Yes, about a year ago. I saw you about options to get pregnant."

If she were going to have her own baby, Sherry would need to have a sperm donor; she wasn't going to leave her baby's genes to chance by sleeping with someone she met at a club. The doctor had explained insemination, in vitro, and the costs and risks of both options. The cost would be a challenge, but she was confident she could handle it.

The doctor nodded. "Right, right. So, I guess you decided against it?"

"I'm still thinking about it, but I'm also considering adoption." Sherry surprised herself by answering in the present tense. She hadn't looked at the adoption applications in months.

"Adoption is an excellent option; there are a lot of children out there who need a good home. Now, let's go check on this baby."

Dr. Lee knocked gently on the door, listening for Jordan's response before she and the nurse went into the exam room. In the split second of hesitation, while Sherry wondered if she should continue to wait outside or join her niece, the nurse shut the door. She retook her seat in the hall and continued to flip through the baby magazine.

Sherry thought about soon being a "grand-aunt" and whether it was too late for her to have a baby. Would it be ridiculous to have a grand-niece or nephew older than her own baby?

Sherry and her ex-husband had planned on having a couple of kids to fill their home. But after their divorce, Sherry had initially given up on the image of a happy home with a yard full of children.

Whenever Sherry saw a woman about her age pushing a stroller, she reconsidered the possibility of her being a mother. She had a nice house, earned a dependable income, was in good health. She'd be a good mother. Then she would think about the other side. The debates about single women purposely having a baby on their own, cheating the child out of the opportunity to have a father. But there were plenty of women who were single mothers by life circumstance -- divorce, death, bad choice of fathers. Was purposely being a single mother any worse?

The nurse touched Sherry on the shoulder, startling her out of her thoughts. "Your niece would like you to come in," she said. "The doctor's getting ready to do the ultrasound."

Sherry quickly got up from the chair, dropping the magazine on the floor. She fumbled to pick it up and laid it back on the seat, then rushed in after the nurse into the darkened room.

"It's easier to see the image with the lights off," the nurse explained. She squirted a clear gel onto Jordan's exposed belly. Jordan turned to her aunt and held her hand out. Sherry stepped over and took her niece's hand, in complete wonder.

The doctor flicked on a TV monitor and held what looked like a mini-vacuum nozzle to Jordan's stomach. In a few seconds, distorted white shapes and shaky lines showed up on the screen and when the doctor turned a knob on the console, a swishy-swashy sound of ocean waves filled the room. The doctor moved the vacuum nozzle contraption around until the waves gave way to a distinct pattern and the shapes on the screen became more solid, though still unidentifiable.

"There you are," the doctor cooed to the screen and smiled. She turned to Jordan. "You've got a beautiful baby in there, missy."

Jordan gasped and clenched her aunt's hand. Sherry squeezed back. She concentrated on everything happening so she could relay it all to Vivian exactly.

"That sound is the baby's heartbeat amidst the amniotic fluid. It's a good heartbeat, steady, strong." Dr. Lee pointed out the white shapes on the screen. "See here? That's her head. Her heart. Looks good. Her feet. Two of them."

The nurse stood near the screen, watching and taking notes as the doctor spoke.

"Her?" Sherry asked. Vivian didn't want to know the sex and Jordan didn't trust herself not to tell her mother if she knew, so they had agreed not to find out.

"Means nothing. I prefer a personal pronoun over 'it' and since mom's a 'she,' seems good enough for the baby," Dr. Lee explained.

Jordan stared at the black and white screen. When she reached to touch her stomach, she knocked the transducer off its position on her belly and the baby disappeared from the screen

"Ah, she's gone!" Jordan whined.

The doctor reassured her and put the instrument back, finding the baby again. She pushed a key on the console and a shiny, fax-paper series of images slid out of the machine. The nurse took the papers out and handed them to Jordan.

"There's your baby. You can show your mom."

Jordan and Sherry had given the doctors a brief history to explain their situation. They understood that her mother was still in North Carolina while Jordan stayed here with her aunt and sorted herself out. Dr. Lee was very understanding of the situation. Surely this was not the first teen-pregnancy to cause family upheaval.

"Thank you," Jordan said in a whisper, staring at the printed image of her baby while the nurse wiped the gel off her stomach and cover her back up with the paper robe. The doctor turned off the ultrasound machine. Jordan and Sherry were startled when the nurse flicked the lights back on.

"You and baby are fine, miss. Keep listening to your aunt. You can get dressed then make your next appointment with the receptionist. And you can go to the bathroom." Dr. Lee now turned to Sherry, "Aunty, she needs to stay on her pre-natal vitamins and drink plenty of water. Her weight is good, but don't let her get carried away with over-eating."

Sherry kissed her niece on the forehead before following the doctor and nurse out of the room, leaving Jordan to get dressed.

"Feel free to make another appointment with me, for yourself, if you need to further discuss your options," Dr. Lee said to Sherry when they were alone in the hallway.

Sherry nodded. Maybe she was qualified to be a mother.

Gina

Gina pushed through the bakery door. "Mornin', Sarah. Mornin', Jordan. Cookie's in the back?"

The girls waved and nodded while continuing to wait on their customers. Gina rounded the counter and slipped behind them to the kitchen. She found Cookie sprinkling a mixture of cinnamon and sugar across a tray of hot muffins.

"I think I'm taking a break from dating," Gina announced.

"Good morning. What're you doing here this time of morning?"

"I don't have any meetings this morning, so I'm running a few errands before going in. Ooh, are these hot?" Gina reached for a freshly sugared apple cinnamon muffin.

Cookie sighed heavily, pretending annoyance, and replaced the muffin with a new one. "Here, go put these in the case out front."

Gina took the tray to the front counter and passed them off to Sarah, then returned to the kitchen. She bit into her stolen breakfast and poured herself a cup of coffee.

"So, why are you not dating?" Cookie continued to arrange the muffins as she talked.

"I'm tired of going out with these random guys." She sipped at her coffee. "Maybe I need a break."

Cookie peered at her friend. "What about Alex? Any chance of you two getting back together?"

Gina shook her head. "I don't know about that. I mean, sometimes I think he's flirting with me, subtly. He stops by to drop stuff off he could've left with Janelle to give to me. He brings me coffee when we have a morning meeting." Gina took another bite of her muffin. "But, he was like that before, so I don't know if it means anything."

"So, let's say he does want you back. What about your mother?"

"I don't know what I'd do about her. After going out with these guys who my mother would think are great husband material, I'm thinking, I may not find someone who makes us both happy. Maybe I don't care what she thinks." Gina replayed the last statement in her mind, listening to how it sounded.

Instead of answering, Cookie followed with another question. "How was your date the other night? How'd you meet him?"

Gina rolled her eyes in disgust. "This last one was Laura's friend. It was almost as bad as the one before that."

"Who was that with?"

"I didn't tell you about that one? I went out with this woman in my office's brother's roommate. He made me pay for my own food and comedy show ticket. A show he picked out! Old cheap-ass."

Cookie grabbed a napkin just quick enough with her good arm to cover her mouth and keep from spitting out her coffee.

"And this one was as bad at that?"

"Almost. But I'm still going to wring Laura's neck when I see her."

Cookie continued to laugh as she wiped a few drops of coffee slipping down her chin.

"We had decided to go to lunch. You know, lunch is supposed to be the 'safe' date, limited time, no going home afterwards, no weird awkwardness. He picked me up from work and I asked him to stop at the zoo, I needed to drop off paperwork from the event a couple weeks ago. He starts about how terrible a place the zoo is. It's so cruel and un-natural for the animals. But I didn't really say anything, I was like 'okay, everybody doesn't like zoos, that's fine.' Then, we go to lunch at Southern Table; I figured, if nothing else, I knew I'd at least get a good meal. And I brought cash, in case I ended up paying for it myself."

Gina paused and broke off a piece of the muffin.

"Cookie. The man was a vegan!" She popped the piece of bread in her mouth, letting the information sink in with Cookie. "What are there, like five black vegans in the world and I go out on a date with one of them? I thought I would slap him if he said another word about my sausage and shrimp gumbo. First the zoo, then my lunch, talking about animal cruelty and ocean bottom feeders and shit. Wait 'til I get a hold of that Laura."

They laughed together over Gina's dating ordeal.

"I mean, come on. An environmentalist and a vegan-animal-lover. What the hell? Since when did black men become so earth-conscious? I could've gone out with another white guy for that non-sense."

Gina enjoyed seeing her friend laugh, and didn't mind it being at her expense. It had been so long since she had seen Cookie in a good mood.

"So, you're adjusting pretty well? Getting around and all in here?" Gina asked when they finally recovered from laughing. She scanned the kitchen.

Cookie started wiping up the remnants of frosting, sugar and cinnamon from the morning's set-up. "Yeah. We've changed our baking routine. I'm closing up a little bit earlier. Jordan's working for me now. So it's all working out fine."

"Wow. You have made a few changes around here, huh?"

Cookie nodded. Gina sipped her coffee and Cookie continued wiping the table, both silently acknowledging that Gina would have known about the changes had they not had the argument.

Sarah's orange afro poked over the swinging kitchen doors. "Cookie, Officer Scott is here."

Cookie hung up the dishtowel and wiped her hands on her apron on the way to the front counter.

"I guess I'll be going anyway. I need to make another stop before going to work," Gina said, grabbing her purse and half-eaten muffin. She stopped mid-step when she noticed the police officer standing on the other side of the display counter.

While one part of Gina's brain was trying to figure out if the officer looked familiar, the other part was noticing his brown eyes and super long eye-ashes.

"Good morning, Officer Scott. This is my girlfriend, Gina, the one you took to the hospital."

"Right. Good to see you again. How're you doing?" He reached over the counter to shake Gina's hand.

"Hi. I'm fine. Good to see you, too," Gina answered staring at the officer's eyes.

A-ha! Gina thought. How could she have forgotten those eyes?

"So, what's up?" Cookie asked after an awkward few seconds of Gina and the policeman grinning at each other flashed by.

"Just checking in on my favorite bakery." He looked over the display of baked goods and asked Sarah for one of the banana nut muffins.

Before she could reach the muffin, Gina stepped up to the counter.

"Sarah, here, let me help you. You're so busy with your other customers."

Sarah shifted her eyes to the only customers in the bakery at the moment, a pair of old women sitting at a table, sipping their tea, then slid her eyes back to Gina. "Sure, go ahead." She stepped aside and leaned against the back counter.

Gina, uncertain as to the protocol for getting food from the case, searched the counter for some kind of hint of what to do first. Sarah pulled a piece of wax paper from a box and handed it to her. Gina smiled and slid open the case.

"I checked on the security camera, like you told me. I'm not convinced. They're expensive," Cookie said to the officer.

"What do you mean? Cookie, your place was robbed, you were shot, you could've been killed!" Gina said. She didn't know Cookie was considering a security camera but in that instant was sure she should get one.

"Gina, having a security camera would not have prevented anything. Everything would've still happened, the only difference would be that there would be video footage." Cookie wiped her hands on her apron again. "And I'm not so sure I'd want to see that anyway," she said softly, directed at the floor.

Gina opened her mouth to speak then closed it and pouted. She wanted to console her friend and make her laugh again, but she didn't know what to say. She was sufficiently distracted when Officer Scott cleared his throat and handed Gina a $5 bill in exchange for the muffin.

Gina pushed the CASH button on the register and the drawer slid open. She proudly placed the bill in the designated slot and closed the drawer. She smirked at Sarah to say, "see, I do know what I'm doing."

Sarah subtly shook her head before taking the few steps over to the register. She hit the CASH button, counted out a few coins and a $1 bill and handed it all to the policeman.

"Thank you," Sarah said. She rolled her eyes, making Jordan laugh.

Cookie continued her discussion with Officer Scott about the merits of security cameras and options she had considered. Gina watched his eyelashes as he looked across the papers Cookie showed him. She watched his brown hands as he pointed to the places in the ceiling where the cameras should go. She remembered the first time when she was struck by the contrast in holding hands with Alex, her brown hand next to his white one. She wondered if maybe she should give a few more black guys a chance. Maybe it was less disruptive to the natural order.

"Well, I need to get back to work. Let me get another one of these," the policeman said, raising his bag and holding another $5 over the counter towards Gina.

Gina moved quickly to bag the extra muffin and waved off the money. "My treat."

"No, no. This isn't for me, it's for my partner. I wouldn't have a woman paying for my food, I'm definitely not going to let you pay for his." He winked at Gina, then turned to the others. "Thanks. I'll see you ladies later," he said as he walked out the door.

"Bye, nice to meet you. Thanks for coming by," Gina called after him. As soon as he was out of eyesight, Gina playfully swung at her friend and slapped her good arm. "Cookie! How many times has he been here and you have not said one word about a sexy police officer coming to check on you?"

"I guess I forgot to mention it." Cookie shrugged, then winced from the pain. "Sarah, I'm done in the back, could you finish cleaning up?"

"How could you forget a fine man coming here?" Gina asked.

"He comes by almost every morning," Sarah said in a dreamy voice, dramatically batting her eyelashes.

"What difference does it make? You're done dating, remember?" Cookie asked.

"Maybe I'm reconsidering," Gina said.

"He even comes in on his day off. In his running shorts." Sarah sang as she started towards the kitchen.

Gina grabbed two $10 bills out of her purse and pushed one into each of Jordan and Sarah's polka-dotted apron pocket. "If that man comes in here, in shorts, one of you better call me. Bye." Gina said, grinning on her way out the door.

After waiting in her office for Alex to pick her up to go the museum, Gina walked down the hall to the receptionist's desk.

"Janelle, have you seen Alex? We're going to be late for our meeting."

"Umm… I don't think he's here." Janelle clicked her mouse and the computer screen flipped to a calendar. She clicked on Alex's name. "Yeah, he left a while ago. He had an appointment for lunch and said he was going straight to the museum from there. He hasn't been here all morning."

"Really? Hmm. I thought he…I could have sworn he said he wanted a ride over to the meeting." Gina tried not to look surprised or flustered while wondering who he met for lunch. "Maybe he said he wanted a ride back. I guess I got it confused."

"Umm…no, I don't think so. He's got a…" Janelle stuttered, "a, uh, another appointment after your meeting. I don't think he's coming back to the office."

"Well, good then. I don't have to worry about getting him back here. I had made plans for after the meeting, too. Great." Gina said in a faux casual tone as she wondered where Alex could be going.

Gina went back to her office to gather the materials for the Smithsonian, as well as her laptop and files she could work on at home. She didn't want Alex to think since they had broken up, she had nothing to do but stay at work all night while he went out carousing around the city.

She drove over to the museum mulling over her short conversation with Janelle, still wondering where Alex had gone for lunch and where he was going this evening.

The museum receptionist walked Gina down the hall to a large meeting room. "Carolyn, the promotional manager for the event, was just in here a few minutes ago talking to the other guy from your office. But she had to make a quick call, she'll be back in about ten minutes."

"Well, we're on a pretty tight schedule," Gina said sharply. They really weren't, but Gina always wanted to give clients the appearance that she was so they wouldn't squander her time.

"Oh. He said it was okay," the receptionist said. She pointed at Alex sitting in the conference room.

Gina sighed and rolled her eyes. She waved off the receptionist and stepped through the glass-framed door. Alex sat with his back to the conference table, facing the window.

"Yeah, I don't think this meeting should take too long. We've got a pretty thorough presentation, so it should be cut and dry. I should make it over there no later than like five or so," Alex said.

Gina noticed the phone earpiece flashing in his ear and dropped the presentation materials on the table, making a loud thud. Alex spun the chair around and grinned at her, waved, then spun the chair back around.

"Hey, look, she's here," Alex paused for a quick laugh. "Yeah, I've gotta get to work, now. Yeah. See you there," Alex said.

Gina wondered what about "she's here" was so funny. Automatically, her head cocked to the side and her hand went to her hip as Alex spun around and stood up.

"Hey, you made it."

"I was waiting for you at the office, you didn't tell me you were coming over early. By yourself."

"Oh, sorry. A friend called about getting lunch, so I figured why bother go back to the office, I could just come straight on over. I guess I forgot to tell you." He reached for a presentation board to set up on the end of the table.

"That's fine. You don't have to report to me." Gina started arranging their presentation materials, while Alex cued the video on the computer.

"So, I see you had a date the other night," Alex said after a few minutes of working quietly.

Gina stopped reading over her script to wonder how he knew.

"You had it on your Facebook status," he answered her silent question. "Your status still pops up on my page. I happened to see it the other day."

Gina thought back to her status a few days ago. "Sushi and bowling. What a night."

"Yeah, went to Tokyo Table." She hoped she sounded pretty casual, but was thinking, yeah, went to your restaurant, how you like that? She peeked at him out of the corner of her eye. He was making the mean eyes face he did when he was upset but trying to hide it.

"Hmm. What'd you get?" He spun his pen between his fingers. He fumbled it and ended up dropping it on the floor.

"A tuna roll and spider roll." She said in response to his smirk. He always said she ordered the same thing whenever they went out. "One day, I'm going to surprise you and get a totally different order."

"I would probably keel over in shock if you ordered anything different. Name the restaurant and I will name your order." They laughed lightly at their ongoing joke of her predictability.

"So, you're going out after the meeting?" Gina wondered if she could get him to say where he was going without coming out and asking him.

"Yeah, meeting up with a couple friends for drinks at Posh."

Gina tilted her head and tried to not let her disappointment show. Gina had no idea he was going to check out the new bar. They always checked out the new happy hour spots together, even before they were dating. She wondered if this was how it was going to be now and who were the couple of friends who were taking her place.

"I was going to ask you, but, well, I wasn't sure if you were busy," he added.

"Well, yeah. I have work to get done. I have a meeting tomorrow about the arts festival next spring. I'll send you the notes, I'm sure it'll come up on your calendar eventually."

Gina picked up her paper and pretended to go back to reading over her script. In her mind, she was fuming over his plans to go out and her plans to go home with her work.

Alex leaned down to pick up his pen and found it near Gina's feet.

"Boyfriend's Favorite Red?" He asked, referring to the nail-polish color she was wearing the last time they had been together. Then, they were lying on his couch watching AtRequest movies.

Equally embarrassed and emboldened by the name of the new shade, she answered.

"One Night Stand."

Spades Night

Cheese and jalapenos topped the nachos, hot out of the oven. Laura picked out one of the cheesiest and finished mixing the margaritas. She tasted her first sip as the doorbell rang.

Gina and Cookie tumbled into the door.

"Laura, did Gina thank you for setting her up on that *wonderful* date?" Cookie teased.

"I don't know why she's complaining. Okay, the man didn't eat meat but he's very nice," Laura said.

Gina rolled her eyes at the mention of her vegan date.

"How're things at the bakery?" Laura asked, handing Cookie a margarita, then one to Gina.

Cookie wanted to ask Laura about the man who she came in with her to get muffins, but Gina spoke first.

"Speaking of the bakery, has your police officer been by lately?"

"Actually…" The doorbell rang as Cookie began to speak.

"Must be Sherry," Laura said, opening the door.

Sherry blew into the apartment, rambling about the home theatre in a newly listed million-dollar home. Jordan followed, her steps still steady and light, despite her growing belly. The women became a jumble of excitement, chattering about baby shopping, changes at the bakery, and bad dates while munching on the buffet of nachos, quesadillas, and mini tacos.

Gina pulled four bright blue rubber bracelets from her purse.

"Before I forget, here's your passes for the Potomac Music Festival next weekend. You can come through the VIP gate."

"I think I might be coming with my client," Laura said.

"Is he one of my sponsors?"

"I don't know, he didn't say. He just mentioned going."

"The important question is: Is he bringing any friends?" Sherry said.

Laura refilled everyone's glasses and poured a soda for Jordan as they took their plates to their seats around the card table. She sat the pitcher on the edge of the table then opened a new deck of cards. She fanned out the cards in her hand and held them out for everyone to draw one.

Cookie and Sherry sat across from each other, Laura and Gina took the other two seats. Jordan pulled up a seat between her aunt and Laura.

"Jordan, don't go and tell your aunt what cards I've got," Laura said.

Jordan smiled and reassured her she wouldn't. "I don't even know how to play Spades so I wouldn't know which cards to tell her about anyway."

"What do you mean you don't know how to play Spades? What's your momma been teaching you?" Cookie asked. She handed her partner the deck of cards to shuffle for her.

"Well, we can teach you before you head home," Gina offered. "You need to know how to play cards before you go to college."

"Gina, I don't think kids play cards in college anymore," Laura said. "How much longer are you staying up here, Jordan?"

"Her momma should be coming up for her soon so she can get back to school. And don't even roll your eyes Jordan," Sherry said.

Jordan rolled her eyes anyway.

"I hope not too soon. I don't feel like actually interviewing anybody to work at the bakery," Cookie said.

"The point of the game is to play the highest card and collect 'books.' You have to play a card in the suit that leads off. If you don't have that suit, then you can cut it by playing a spade. A spade trumps everything else," Laura said.

"Or you can throw off and play another suit, maybe to save your spade or if you don't have one. You won't win the book, though," Sherry said, shuffling the cards.

"But, you've got to play fair. Be sure you don't have the leading suit before cutting it. If you play that suit later, that's reneging and you lose three books," Cookie said.

"And your partner will kick your ass," Gina warned.

"You bet how many books you think you will get each hand. You get points for each book you collect, you lose points if you don't make your bet. We bet as partners," Laura continued, pointing to herself and Gina.

"There's thirteen books per hand, so you want to get enough that your opponents can't make their bet," Sherry interjected.

"Now, cutting the deck, that's important. That's the dealer's way of saying 'see, I'm not playing any tricks, you can move the cards all around if you want'," Cookie said as Sherry set the deck in front of Gina.

"And it's the other player's way of saying 'that might be so, but just in case you're cheating, let me reshuffle a bit'," Gina said, restacking the cards and sliding them to Cookie.

Cookie laughed. She maneuvered the deck into her hand in the sling and dealt with the other like she had been doing this every day of her life.

Sherry cursed her cards under her breathe.

"And that's your aunt's way of saying she ain't got nothing!" Laura continued.

"Cookie, next time deal with your bad arm, 'cause this shit is a mess," Sherry teased.

"I got you, partner, don't worry," Cookie said.

"Stop talking across the table, you two," Laura scolded. "See Jordan, you've got to watch out for sneaky stuff."

"Whatever. No bid. Go Laura," Sherry said.

"'No bid' means she ain't got nothing, like I said. It's up to her partner to make a bid."

Laura lead off with the ace of diamonds. She played the highest card in the suit, confident she'd win the first book.

"'Diamonds are a girl's best friend', my ass," Sherry said, throwing in one of the only two diamonds in her hand.

"So you see, Spades is a lot like life. Sometimes you get a great hand, it's clear you've got a bunch of high cards, a good number of spades. You're sure in your bet," Laura said. As her eyes flitted over her cards, her expression didn't change.

Gina laid the two of diamonds on the pile, followed by Cookie's five. Laura swept up the pile, tapping the cards on the table and laying them next to her. She played the ace of clubs, drawing Sherry's jack and rolled eyes. After Gina and Cookie played their cards, Laura again swept them up and set them on top of the first book.

"But you've still got to be smart and careful. Things look great and easy, but the wrong move. Boom, you could lose it all," Laura said contemplating the cards in her hand. Before choosing her card, Laura turned to Gina. "Do you have anything to do with the boat show?"

"No, that's a private event. Are you going?" Gina said.

Laura nodded. "I think they're shopping."

"Ooh, fancy."

"Wait, wait. Who's boat shopping? The guy who you came into the bakery with?" Cookie asked Laura.

Gina turned to Laura in surprise. "What, Cookie got to meet Mr. Bigbucks?"

"Oh, yeah, she came in with a *fine* man. Tall, tall, dark. Nice jaw, sexy smile. *Early* in the morning," Cookie said. She left a question mark hanging over the "early" part of her response allowing for Laura to fill in more information.

Laura tried not to grin too hard thinking about Sid, but her response came out nervous and jumbled. "He's th...he works with...he's the driver for my new client." She paused and sighed. "That was Sid. Yes, he and my client are going to the boat show."

"Sid? He's got a name?" Cookie teased.

"He's finally got a name!" Gina said.

"But is he symmetrical?" Sherry asked, laughing already at her sarcastic joke.

Laura turned to Sherry. "Yes, he's symmetrical." She felt her cheeks flush and was sure they were bright red.

Sherry's laughter escalated and she slammed her cards on the table to keep from dropping them.

"So, was it a date or was it work?" Gina asked.

"It was, umm, it was work." Laura hadn't spoken to Michael or Sid since and wondered, what, if anything, her tryst with Sid meant. She kept telling herself it was nothing more than a one-time spontaneous, sleep-deprived, sexual-tension energized fling. Sid and Michael, surrounded by the groupies following their sports clients, probably did it all the time without a second thought. She was surely just another checkmark on Sid's calendar. Despite trying to reason this all in her head, there was a part of her hoping it did mean something more.

"You should work on making it a date," Cookie said.

"I don't really like to mix the two," Laura said. She knew standing by this important rule of escorting was imperative to her success, regardless of what her hormones or her heart wanted.

"Yeah, I could see where that would get kinda sticky," Sherry said.

Laura redirected the conversation from her own situation back to Gina. "Anyway, Gina. My friend's a nice guy, you should give him another chance. Go to a salad-y place or a nature preserve, instead, not the zoo. What's your other option?"

"Well, I was kinda thinking about maybe getting back with Alex, but I don't know. It's hard to read him," Gina replied. She quietly played her next card.

"What? Alex is back?" Sherry asked.

"I can't figure him out. We're still doing stuff for work. We go out, have a good time, like we did before, but then at the end of the night, when we used to get in the same cab, or walk together to the garage, we go our separate ways. I guess that's what it was like *before* before. But he confuses me by flirting with me one minute, then, I hear him on the phone making plans to go out with someone."

"Like a woman?" Sherry asked.

Gina shrugged. "I don't know, but he did get quiet when he realized I was standing there like he didn't want me to hear him. So I'm thinking it was a woman. If it was one of his boys, he wouldn't do that, right?"

Laura and Sherry shifted their eyes to each other, not answering. Cookie looked at Gina without saying a word, waiting for her to answer herself.

"But, I guess I can only be so mad. Us breaking up was partly my fault," Gina said.

"Partly?" Sherry and Laura asked at the same time.

"Whatever. Yeah, 'partly'," Gina said, throwing a tortilla chip in their direction.

All the women laughed at their friend. They all thought it was wholly her fault, she was the one who had made the wild jump to break up and none of them could really recall what had instigated her move.

"And what about Officer Scott?" Cookie cooed.

"Officer who?" Sherry asked.

"The police who came to the bakery that night." Cookie paused. She still got frazzled putting the incident into words.

"Apparently, Cookie's got this sexy police officer hanging around the bakery she's trying to keep a secret," Gina finished.

"And him and Gina were in there making googly-eyes at each other like they were 15 years old." Cookie and Jordan batted their eyes at each other, mocking Gina.

"Trying something new, huh? Adding another card in the deck of 'Gina's dates'?" Sherry asked.

Gina rolled her eyes. "Nothing has happened. I saw the man in the bakery. Met him the other day, that's all."

While talking, Sherry missed the count of cards and mistakenly played her jack of hearts. She held her breath for a short moment before Gina slapped down the queen, grinned at Laura, and reached across the table for a high-five. Cookie threw in a low heart.

"What's the matter partner? Don't tell me you've lost it?" Cookie said to Sherry as Laura played her card and pulled in their won book.

"Don't worry, baby, I ain't lost nothing. Come on Gina, what you got?" Sherry replied.

Gina threw out the ace of hearts, pulling Cookie's last heart, a high card from her partner, and a low one from Sherry. Laura piled the cards in front of her.

"Since we're on a roll with these hearts," Gina began, "let's talk about a certain delivery truck driver who has been hanging around Cookie's Oven." She threw out the nine.

Cookie placed a spade on top of the card. "You mean David?"

"Yeah we mean David." Laura said. "You have another delivery man in love with you?"

"This bakery seems to be the spot to find a man to fall in love with. Maybe I need to come get a muffin," Sherry said.

"Oh, please, like you don't find a new man-of-the-month every time we go out," Gina said.

"Hush, there's children here," Sherry said, tapping her niece on the knee.

Jordan covered her mouth and snickered, peering at her aunt as if she was in on a secret.

Laura didn't have any hearts left either, but there were still a lot of cards to play before she had planned on pulling out her spades. She pursed her lips and tossed a black-suited card on the table.

Sherry threw in her one and only spade, trying to save her partner. Cookie scooped up the pile, relieved that they had finally got one book.

"Then other times, you get a bunch of nothing and you don't think you're going to make any books at all. But you've got to make those cards work," Laura said to Jordan, returning to her tutorial.

"Okay, David," Sherry said, taking a sip of her margarita. "What's up? When y'all gonna go out?"

"Actually…" Cookie started, then paused. She looked around the table at her friends. "We went out for dinner the other night."

The other women screamed in surprise.

"He came by after work and we just went for dinner. Nothing fancy, just down the street. Had a drink, ate, chatted. It was nice." Cookie smiled, thinking about their first date.

"Aww. Cookie, that's so nice," Gina said.

"And then, after dinner?" Sherry asked.

"Then, he took me home."

"No glass of wine, no cup of coffee?" Laura asked.

"Nope. He just dropped me off and left. But that's okay. It was – good." Cookie nodded her head, reassuring her friends she was happy with the pace of this new relationship.

Gina smiled. She knew it was a big step for Cookie to allow herself to feel a romantic attraction.

Cookie looked over her hand and in her head tried to count the cards already played. She held three spades and one diamond but still would have to play them strategically to ensure she got all four remaining books. She quickly pulled in the first three books with her spades. She threw the last card, a remaining diamond. Laura threw a club on the table, as did Sherry.

Gina tossed a club on the table and got up from her chair.

"Now Jordan, were you watching? That's how you win a game," Cookie said. Now it was her and Sherry's turn to slap high-fives over the table.

Sherry cheered and refilled Laura and Gina's cups. "Drink up. Better luck next game."

Laura emptied the glass in one long swallow then took the pitcher into the kitchen, shaking her head.

"Cookie, that was too sweet! See, that's why you can be my partner, you don't get all rattled when you bring up a man like some people." Sherry glanced at Gina to make sure she heard her, then almost fell out the chair ducking the nacho chip Gina threw at her in response. "You better stop throwing those chips all over Laura's floor. See what I mean? Folks nerves get so rattled," she joked.

Laura came back to the table with the refilled margarita pitcher and passed Jordan a glass of iced tea.

"Come on, Laura, finish bartending, then get these cards back out. And make them good ones," Gina said to her partner as she piled up the cards and set them at Laura's spot.

Laura shuffled the cards and passed them to Cookie. She made a grand display of cutting the deck, replacing the top half with the bottom half and gently pushed them back.

"Shit, it's like the Red Sea over here." Sherry was looking over her cards, frowning at the array of hearts and diamonds in her hand.

"Hey, no talking across the table!" Laura scolded again, still dealing cards.

"Ain't nobody cheating. Talking about geography, that's all."

"Okay, Jordan. So you see, no matter what happens, no matter what cards you get, no matter what luck you think you have, good or bad, eventually, you'll work through that hand. And there will be another and you get to start all over again. It's like a new day," Laura said.

They all nodded, thinking about the cards they had been dealt in their lives. The aces they were sure would bring a win, but ended up getting cut. The fives that seemed a lost cause, but ended up being a surprise win. The High Jokers they were absolutely sure of and could always count on.

Cookie

Cookie leaned in the kitchen doorway, watching the bakery return to its normal buzz. Behind her, Gina sat at the kitchen worktable eating her breakfast. She talked to herself, going through a checklist before she headed to the waterfront to prepare for the seafood festival. Jordan sat on a stool at the front counter ringing up a customer. Sarah took coffee to a couple sitting at the table by the window.

A young man was glancing over the counter, ready to order.

There was nothing about the boy at the counter that resembled the one who shot Cookie, other than being black. Yet, Cookie had to remind herself not to be nervous, not to shake when any young guy came into the bakery. With people around, she felt safer. She knew it was an irrational fear, maybe even a kind of racism, if that was possible against your own race, but she couldn't control it.

The young man politely asked for a carrot muffin with cream cheese glaze and a bottle of milk. He paid for his order and left. Cookie unwittingly released a deep sigh.

"Don't worry. It'll get better," someone said to her.

Cookie jumped and was surprised to see Officer Scott. She hadn't noticed him come in. As he nodded toward the boy leaving, she realized he must have noticed her tense reaction.

"Oh, man, am I that obvious?"

"That's why I get paid the big bucks, to notice these things."

Cookie felt a mix of embarrassment over still being scared and fear from thinking about the shooting. She took a deep breath to swallow the tears forming. She was really getting tired of always being on the verge of tears and wondered if there was medication for the condition. Since the day Jordan found her in a mess of burnt food and sugar, Cookie had started to taper the rum in her coffee and constantly felt on edge.

"Okay. So what can I get you?" She tried to smile. "Your regular?"

He returned her smile. Cookie felt reassured she would, one day, be fine.

"I've always wanted a place I can walk in and just say 'give me my regular,' you know, like in the old movies. They weren't talking about cupcakes, but it's all the same."

Cookie spotted Sarah standing by the front window staring at the officer. Until then, she hadn't noticed that he wasn't dressed in his uniform. Instead, he stood there in a sweatshirt with a wet mark down the center of the chest. Sarah raised her eyebrows, then scanned her eyes downward, subtly nodding towards him. Cookie slowly tilted her head to the side to try to peek through the display case. On the other side, his very muscular, brown legs extended from blue running shorts.

"You know what, Cookie, a fresh tray just came out the oven a few minutes ago," Sarah said. She approached the case and stood next to the policeman. "Gina, could you bring Cookie that tray of banana nut muffins we just took out, please?" Sarah yelled into the kitchen.

"Busy!" Gina hollered from the kitchen.

"It'll only take you a minute." Sarah called back.

Cookie wondered how obvious Sarah's ruse was. The officer's grin told her "very".

Gina came from the kitchen, wearing a pair of white and pink polka dot oven mitts, carrying the tray of muffins above her head like a waiter.

"Madame," she said in a terrible French accent, bowing her head and presenting the tray to Cookie.

Cookie smirked. "Thanks. Officer Scott is here and he wanted a muffin."

"It's my day off. You can call me Glynn," the policeman said.

"Oh, hey!" Gina said, hearing his voice before noticing him standing on the other side of the counter. She glanced around at Cookie and Sarah, then decided to set the tray down and quickly pulled off the oven mitts. "What're you doing here?"

"Came for the best banana nut muffin in town and a chocolate milk."

Cookie put his muffin on a plate and poured a bottle of milk into a glass -- an invitation to stay. She placed the plate and glass at a seat at the counter.

"No coffee?" Gina asked.

"This is better for post-workout muscle recovery. I just finished my morning run."

"Oh, really? Where do you run?" Gina asked.

Cookie and Sarah tried not to laugh, wondering whether Gina had any idea what "post-workout muscle recovery" meant. Then Cookie shooed Sarah back to work.

"Through the city, through the park. Do you run?"

Cookie covered her laugh with an oven mitt.

"Umm, yeah, well, I used to. It wasn't for me I guess." Gina said.

"Maybe you want to start again, come run with me?"

"I'm sure you're a much better runner than me. You'd leave me in the dust."

"Nah, I wouldn't do that. What kind of man would leave you behind?"

Cookie went to stand behind the cash register, pretending she wasn't listening.

Jordan was waiting, wax paper in hand, to get a muffin for a mother trying to explain to her toddler son he could not have a cupcake this time of morning.

"Want the choc-lit one!" The boy screamed, kicking the footrest on his stroller.

"How about the carrot or raisin bran muffin? Don't they look yummy?" The mother suggested pointing to the alternative muffins, unsuccessful in convincing him that they were a better option.

"I make a yummy chocolate chip oatmeal muffin. And for this time of morning, they are much better than cupcakes," Cookie offered. Maybe the mother didn't want her son to have chocolate in the morning, but the boy obviously was not going to trade in his demands for a bran muffin.

The boy stopped screaming, watching Cookie and his mother.

The mother sighed. "Okay," she surrendered.

"Right here," Cookie pointed out the muffins on the lower rack. "Would you like one of those?"

The little boy nodded. Cookie handed the muffin, smaller than the usual size, to his mother. She poured the mother a cup of coffee without waiting for her to ask, she knew that 'I need caffeine' look.

Cookie turned back to Gina and the policeman.

"Okay, so I'll go ahead and get tickets?" he was asking Gina.

"That sounds good. And I'll bring dinner."

He put the empty glass on top of the plate. "Great. Cookie, thanks for the muffin and milk. See you."

"See you." Cookie put her hand on top of her friend's hand. As soon as he walked out the door, she turned to Gina.

"Did I hear you offer to make him dinner?"

"No, please. I offered to *bring* dinner. Big difference."

"Bring dinner where? And where are you going to get this dinner?"

"We are going to the blues concert out at Wolf Trap next week. And I'm going to call Gourmet-to-Go."

Cookie laughed at her kitchen-impaired friend. "But, what about Alex? What about not dating?"

Gina shrugged. "There's always a trump."

Sherry

Sherry glanced at the ultrasound image of the baby as she entered listings for houses into the realtors' database. Jordan had been so excited about her ultrasound, she had taken the print-outs to the bakery and shown them to Cookie and Sarah. She emailed a photo of them to her mother. She had left a copy on Sherry's desk in her office.

Her thoughts returned to Dr. Lee's invitation to come see her again.

"Don't forget you're supposed to be meeting Mr. Clark in an hour at the store on 16th Street," Corey said, dropping a pile of mail on her desk.

"I'm on my way, now." Sherry slid her feet back into her shoes and grabbed her purse and briefcase. "And I'm not coming back; I've got to get Jordan."

Sherry picked Jordan up from the bakery late in the afternoon, in time to go home and fix dinner. As part of their now regular cooking routine, Sherry poured herself a glass of wine and a glass of milk for Jordan. They sipped their drinks while they prepared chicken parmesan with angel hair pasta and broccoli.

"Do the chicken like we did the fried fish, but we're going to add cheese and put it in the oven," Sherry instructed as she pulled out the ingredients for dinner. "Did you get any school work done today?"

"A little bit, it was kinda slow after lunch. I had Calc and World History, so I need some quiet to concentrate."

Sherry laughed. "The bakery's not quiet enough?"

"Even when it's empty, it's not quiet. Sarah talks non-stop. But she's so funny and the reality show she's working on is hil-a-rious!" Jordan laughed along with her aunt. "I'll finish after dinner, then email my work to my teachers."

"Did you talk to your mother today?" Sherry dipped another chicken breast in the egg and breading mix and placed it in the baking dish.

"Yeah, she's still amazed by the ultrasound. I think she was crying."

"Your mother's always crying."

Over dinner, they talked about when Jordan would be ready to go home. Jordan hadn't decided yet if she would go back for graduation, but was sure she wanted to miss the prom.

"Brandon emailed me a few days ago asking when I was coming back"

"What'd you say?"

"I didn't answer him, yet," Jordan said.

Sherry half hoped Jordan would stay until the baby was born but knew that was selfish. She didn't push her one way or another as they continued cooking, then ate their dinner.

After their meal, Sherry sat on the sofa and watched a show about women convicted for killing their husbands while Jordan went upstairs to finish her homework.

At the commercial break, Sherry went into the kitchen to scoop herself a bowl of strawberry ice cream. She went to the steps to offer Jordan a bowl when she heard the sound of a doorbell.

She peeked at the TV, suspecting the sound might've been a part of the commercial, but the woman on the screen was in her garden trying to sell the virtues of a new device that would help pull all those pesky weeds. There was no doorbell in her pitch, so Sherry went to the door, then peered through the peep-hole. She stepped back to open the door.

"Jordan," she called up the steps, while still looking at the couple on her doorstep. "There's an old black lady and a handsome young man at the door. Which one do you want?"

Jordan and Brandon sat on the couch, their knees carefully not touching each other, their eyes carelessly staring at each other. Vivian sat in the chair recently vacated by her sister. Sherry sat across from her in the other easy chair.

"Brandon was wondering how you were doing, Jordan," Vivian said to her daughter.

Brandon smiled at Jordan, in the way a 6-year old would stare at the pretty teenaged babysitter, his infatuation all over his face. But no words came out of his mouth.

"I don't work tomorrow and his parents said he could come up and see you," Vivian continued.

"You're only staying until tomorrow?" Sherry asked. Although surprised by the visit, Sherry hoped her sister would stay longer.

"I'm gonna put him back on the train tomorrow evening. I can take a few more days off of work." Vivian glanced at her daughter, who was still staring and smiling at her baby's father.

"I hope that's okay, Miss Sherry? My mother said to make sure I ask you if it's all right for me to stay here tonight. If not, she gave me money to stay at a hotel," Brandon said.

"That's fine, Brandon. Thanks for asking," Sherry said. "You'll have to sleep here on the couch, though. I don't have anymore bedrooms." Despite them getting ready to be parents, Sherry didn't think she was supposed to let them sleep together in the guest room. It didn't seem right, even with this circumstance. Noticing her sister nodding her head, Sherry trusted that she had made the correct decision.

"Why don't you two go ahead in the kitchen and talk. Jordan, get the boy some dinner," Sherry instructed. She waved the young couple off toward the other side of the house. When they had left the room, she turned to her sister. Her raised eyebrows were enough to ask the question, "What's going on?"

"Jordan sent him the ultrasound picture and he showed it to his parents. I guess that snapped them into reality. They called me the other night. Said they've talked to him about the situation and he admits that this is his baby."

"Was there any doubt?" Sherry said, instantly offended.

Vivian put her hand up to stop her sister. "Apparently, only in their mind, but don't even get me started. I had to hold my tongue not to curse his mother out as soon as she said it. But anyway, his parents feel like they should share some of the responsibility. They are offering to help support the baby."

"Support as in send Jordan a check every month or actually raise the baby and be her family?"

"They said they want to be involved with the baby, it is his child and their grandchild, afterall. We haven't worked out all the plans, yet, but yeah, we'll do visiting and holidays and all that, along with the financial support. Lord knows, they've got more money than me, so I have no shame in accepting their help."

Sherry felt like she was going to cry but wasn't certain about what. "What about school?" she asked, while trying to arrange her emotions.

"He's still going to go to college. He got accepted to a few out-of-state schools, but also to UNC and Duke, so they're going to encourage him to stay in state, if that's what Jordan does."

Vivian played with her fingers, taking turns gently wiping one hand across the back of the other.

"What if they decide to go out of state?"

"Then we, me and his parents, will take care of the baby. His mother doesn't work, so she's available. We'll come up with a plan. It's only four years and they'll be back for holidays and summer. Then, I guess they'll have to decide what to do from there."

"Is he staying with Jordan? Or he's just supporting the baby?"

Vivan vaguely shook her head. "I'm not really sure. That's why he wanted to come to talk to her and work it out. He said he didn't think it all would go well in an email conversation." Vivian looked across the hall, although there was no way to see the kitchen from where she sat.

Sherry realized her newest emotion was almost like mourning. A few brain cells had imagined adopting Jordan's baby, or at least keeping her until she finished school. Now, with Brandon and his parents coming to their senses, that notion was instantly gone. She was missing the baby already, and not only was it not here, it wasn't even hers.

Sherry and Vivian continued talking about all the possible options for taking care of the baby and who was going to be responsible for what. Every now and then, they would hear sounds coming from the kitchen. Jordan or Brandon's voice, footsteps, a chair scraping. After about an hour, the two sisters headed into the kitchen.

"Anyone want ice cream?" Sherry asked, pouring out her melted bowl of strawberry. She retrieved the box from the freezer and started pulling dessert bowls from the cabinet.

"Got everything figured out?" Vivian asked.

Jordan dropped her head and shyly glanced at Brandon before answering. "Yes," she said, then poked him in the side.

Brandon smiled at Jordan then turned to Vivian. "Ma'am. I really do like your daughter. In fact, I do believe I love her. And I will with all my heart, love our baby. And we think that we want our baby to have a whole family." Brandon stood up and looked straight into Vivian's eyes.

"May I marry your daughter?"

"Shit!" Sherry whispered as she almost dropped a bowl. At this rate, she wasn't going to have any dishes left by the time this baby was born. She set it down on the counter and turned to her sister. "Sorry."

Vivian stood blinking, her eyes gliding back and forth from her daughter to her want-to-be son-in-law. Jordan was grinning like a kid with a new box of candy.

"Brandon? I thought we were just trying to get Jordan to come home?" Vivian used a gentle, happy voice that belied the confusion going on in her head.

"Yes, ma'am, that's what we talked about," Brandon said, wagging a finger between himself and Vivian. "But now that I'm here and have been talking to Jordan, I realize how much I want us to be a family. I don't want my baby to be without me. I want her, or him, to have me, their father, around." He put his arm around her shoulder. Jordan smiled up at him with puppy-dog eyes and grinned.

Sherry watched her sister. She stood ready to grab her sister or hold her up, whichever became necessary.

"Jordan?" Vivian asked.

Jordan shifted her gaze from Brandon to her mother. "I want to marry him, Momma. I want us to be together."

Vivian turned to Sherry, with the same "what's going on?" look her sister flashed just over an hour ago. There were tears in her eyes and she started sighing.

"Well, that's a really big move, kids," Sherry said, realizing her sister was finished talking. "It's good that you all are thinking about the baby and how you want to be a family. But marriage is an important decision and you should truly understand what you are getting into, it's not something to be taken lightly. Brandon, you should probably talk this over with your parents, as well, before we make any final decisions."

"But, isn't it our decision, Aunt Sherry?" Jordan asked.

"Yes, I guess in a few months when you turn 18, it will be. But, I think these things work out best when everyone agrees and is on the same page. You will need all the family support you can get." She didn't mean for her statement to sound like a threat, but was aware it might.

"Thank you, Miss Sherry, for your advice," Brandon said. He took Jordan's hand and patted it before she started to cry. "I will talk to my parents when I get home tomorrow and I'm sure they will agree that we should get married. Then, can I marry Jordan?" Brandon turned to Vivian for the last question.

Vivian still leaned against the refrigerator, where she had propped herself after the surprise proposal.

"We'll talk about it when we all get home."

Potomac Music Festival

Gina walked alongside the waterfront, checking items off the last minute punch list. The Potomac Music Festival was one of her biggest events of the year, kicking off the summer festival season. Each year, she was meticulous in making sure it went off as perfectly as possible. Stage decorated, sound-check complete. All the musicians had arrived. The cooks were busy in the food booths. She could smell the Old Bay and scent of fried everything floating in the air. The bartenders were setting up thousands of plastic cups and chilling hundreds of bottles of beer and wine. The cashiers were preparing at the entrance gates to exchange money for food and drink tickets. There were of course, the inevitable dropped trays of crab balls, the broken beer bottles, and drunken fights late in the afternoon. She had already planned for these regular bumps in her plans, too, with extra food, extra beer, and extra security.

Gina turned into the walkway to check in with the hostesses for each of the Sponsor tents. Stone Sports' tent, filled with its own dedicated staff of bartenders and foodservers, was first in the row. Courtney, a spirited college student, was the tent hostess.

"Gina, come in, come in. We're almost ready. The bar's set up, they're bringing the food over. And look at the ice sculpture, isn't it the best?" Courtney waved her hand around, pointing out each area as she talked and then finally pulled Gina towards the ice sculpture in the middle of the tent.

A large frozen blue crab served as a dispenser for vodka. The liquor would flow through the crab, dispensing from a spigot in one of the crab's pinchers, delivered ice cold into one of the hundreds of blue shot glasses stacked nearby. Gina hoped she wasn't going to regret approving the unending shots.

Stone had requested 100 entry VIP wristbands for his guests, more than twice as many as she usually included with the tent sponsorship package. They had negotiated a price for the additional wristbands and he had included having the local sports figures sign autographs if she made the space available nearby. Gina jotted a note on her list to make sure to have security check on both the tent and the autograph area regularly to control the crazed fans, male, and especially female.

Gina noticed the line forming outside the gate and checked her watch. Thirty minutes until the gates opened. Satisfied everything was ready to go, she left Courtney with instructions to call her when the sponsor arrived and headed to the next tent.

Cookie strutted down the hallway from her bedroom like it was a fashion show runway.

"So, how do I look?"

"Ni-i-i-ce, Cookie!" Sherry exclaimed.

Cookie wore an orange and yellow ombre maxi dress with a yellow pashmina wrap thrown over her arm. Her hair, still in braids, was neatly twisted on top of her head, with a few braids falling alongside of her face.

"Do you have on make-up?" Sherry leaned close to her friend's face.

"Just a little eyeliner and mascara. Lipstick. Does it look all right or is it too much?"

"No, you look great," Sherry said, smiling. Eyeliner and mascara were a big step for Cookie. "What time's your dude play?"

"He said the first set is around two." David's band was scheduled as part of the seafood and music festival entertainment. Cookie was nervous about seeing him. She had been wondering if this made their relationship real, by seeing each other in public, with their friends.

Cookie turned to the mirror hanging in the hallway. She pulled a braid back behind her ear, turned her head from side to side.

"Well, then let's go before some chick tries to take your man," Sherry said. She picked up the VIP wristbands Gina had given them and hurried Cookie out the door.

Sid winked and smiled at Laura as she approached the car. "Good afternoon. You look beautiful," he said. She smiled back, fighting the urge to hug him.

Michael greeted her as she slid into the back seat next to him.

Laura noticed that neither were in their regular suit and tie. Michael wore khaki's and a blue button-down shirt with the cuffs neatly folded up, revealing a gold watch and toned forearms. Sid had on blue jeans and a green polo shirt with a cream colored Kangol hat.

"This should be fun. Thanks for inviting me along," Laura said, confident in her white skinny pants and orange gauzy top that she was dressed appropriately casual.

Laura wasn't sure which rule applied today. Sid had called to invite her along, instead of Michael's secretary, but it was clear this was Michael's event. He had said they thought she would enjoy the event and just wanted her to come with them for fun. With Michael as her primary client and all of her girlfriends coming, she didn't have anything else to do. Plus, it was another opportunity to see Sid and try to figure out if there was anything to their relationship.

"I'm sure you're going to have a good time. You'll get to meet some of my clients. I know, you don't like sports, but they're good guys. And when you get bored of them, Sid'll walk you around the festival."

Laura tried not to flinch, blink, or smile at this last comment. Was he guessing or had Sid told him about them, she now wondered.

"Sounds good," she said, trying to sound calm, not letting a waver in her voice. For the rest of the ride, they talked about the musicians scheduled to play at the festival and the buffet of food Michael had ordered for his tent.

Sid pulled the car up to the curb and let Michael and Laura out.

"See you inside," he said as he got back in the car.

Laura waved and wondered to which one of them he was directing his comment. They passed long lines of people at the entrance gates and eased through a gate marked "Sponsors" without waiting. They showed their goldenrod yellow rubber bracelets to the man standing inside the entrance who directed them to the Stone Sports tent.

Laura heard the guard announce to someone on the other end of his walkie-talkie, "Stone plus one is on his way in."

Sherry dug the two bright blue VIP rubber bracelets out of her purse and shook them at Cookie. While slipping them onto their wrists, they headed towards the much shorter line.

"It smells so good from here, I can't wait to eat. How come we haven't come in the past couple years? I feel like it's been forever since the last time we came," Cookie said.

Sherry wrinkled her brow trying to remember back a year, then shrugged. "Who knows? You were probably working. I have no idea where I was last year. The year before, I think I was a bit depressed."

Cookie nodded and mumbled an agreement, remembering Sherry's post-divorce moping as she tried to figure out life as a single-again woman.

"He plays at two?" Sherry asked, glancing down at her phone.

"Yeah. And then again later, early evening, like six."

"Are we staying until then?" They took a few steps forward as the line moved closer to the gate.

"I don't know. Maybe?" Cookie wasn't sure Sherry would keep her company that long, but she wanted to hear both of David's band's sets.

"Let's just play it by ear."

Cookie knew this meant, "let's see how many guys I find attractive and how good the bartenders are" and accepted that was the closest answer she'd get to "yes".

"Bracelets?" The young woman sitting at the ticket booth asked.

They raised their arms, showing off the blue bands as if they were sparkling diamond charm bracelets. In exchange, the woman gave them a handful of red and yellow tickets.

"Red tickets are for food, yellow tickets are for drinks. Have fun." She gave Cookie and Sherry a perfunctory smile, then turned to the couple standing behind them. "Bracelets?"

Cookie tilted her chin towards one of the first tents they saw, adorned with a sign: SweetCakes. "His cakes are so dry. I don't even know why people line up outside and pay his outrageous prices for those dry old cupcakes."

"We're here to have fun, not check out the competition." Sherry pulled Cookie away from the bakery stall and led them to the first bar in the walkway. She smiled at the brown-skinned bartender.

"Good afternoon. What can I get for you?" the bartender asked.

"I don't know. What do you do well?" Sherry asked in her flirty voice.

"I do a lot of things well," he answered, licking his lips. "But as far as drinks, we've got a special Potomac Martini."

"What's in it?" Cookie asked.

Sherry waved at Cookie to be quiet. "We'll take two."

The bartender mixed the red drinks and handed them to the women in exchange for the yellow tickets. He threw the tickets in a miniature crab bushel basket on the bar.

"Guaranteed you'll like them. If not, come back and I'll make you something else."

Sherry tasted the martini and smiled. "Mmm. And if I do like it?"

"Come back and it'll be even better the next time."

Sherry smiled over her shoulder as she and Cookie walked away.

"I forget how much a flirt you can be," Cookie said.

"What else have I got to do? You should try it. Oh, but no, you wouldn't now, you've got a ma-a-n," Sherry teased.

"He's not my man, not really."

"What, you waiting for him to ask you to go steady? Come on, Cookie. What're we doing here if he's not your man? You're either a groupie or his girlfriend."

"What about friends? Can we be friends?"

"No, you can't. We're too old to be friends."

"You don't think men and women can be friends?"

"No, I don't. The only reason men want to have anything to do with us is for sex." Sherry took a sip of her martini. "And vice versa."

Cookie didn't respond while she glanced over the line of food tents. "Let's get food. I'm ready for a crabcake."

They followed their noses to the strong scent of Old Bay and a long line of people. After standing in line long enough to finish their drinks, they hungrily traded in two red tickets for platters with coleslaw. They wandered through the tables, searching for the perfect spot to see the stage, as well as to people watch. Cookie finally took a seat at a table a few rows back from the stage.

"I can't sit here without a drink," Sherry said. "I think I'm going to get a beer." She headed back towards the handsome bartender, yellow tickets in hand.

"Get me one, too," Cookie called. She took a bite of her sandwich and surveyed the crowd. She spotted a familiar looking guy at a table on the edge of the seating area. She chewed thoughtfully while trying to place the face and short brown hair. He was sitting with a woman who had long, brown hair with blondish highlights and they were sharing a cup of Boardwalk fries. Cookie felt like she had seen him in her bakery, but didn't recall him as a repeat customer. The man said something only he must have thought funny because while he laughed, the brown-haired woman slapped him on the arm, but obviously not enough to really hurt.

Cookie tasted a forkful of coleslaw then scanned the rest of the crowd. She came back to the couple still eating french fries. Admittedly, she didn't know a lot of white people, outside of bakery customers, but she was sure she knew this guy. It finally occurred to her that the man was Gina's ex-boyfriend.

"Alex!" Cookie said out loud. She wondered if the woman was his new girlfriend.

"Whew! He's a popular bartender, I thought it was going to take me forever to get our drinks." Sherry sat the beers on the table and took the seat next to Cookie.

Cookie pointed towards the couple. "I think that's Alex."

"Where?" Sherry followed Cookie's finger to find him at his table. She remembered him from the night he came to the hospital. "Yeah, that is him. Who's the lady?"

"I don't know."

"She's pretty."

"I noticed."

"Girlfriend?"

"Maybe. They're sharing fries."

"Definitely more than friends," Sherry said in her 'I told you so' voice.

"You think Gina will be upset?"

"She shouldn't be. She broke up with him."

"We're talking about Gina."

"Right. Yeah, she'll be upset."

Cookie and Sherry continued watching Alex and the woman eat, talk, and laugh as they ate and drank their own lunch.

"Hey! I thought you two were going to text me when you got here. You already have food and drinks? How're the crabcakes?"

The women jumped at the sound of Gina's voice and turned to find her standing next to their table.

"Oh, hey, girl. Great festival," Sherry said.

"These are good. You want a taste?" Cookie offered her sandwich.

"No, no. I'll eat later."

"Beer?" Sherry offered.

"Nah, I'm working. Are you having fun?"

"So far. Nice looking bartenders. Did you hire them?"

Gina laughed. "Figured you'd notice. I only hired the bar service. The bartenders were part of the package." She glanced around at the people scattered across the tables listening to the band on stage. "Good crowd."

Sherry and Cookie watched her cautiously.

"Hmm," Gina said quietly.

"What's up?" Sherry asked, as if she didn't already know. Gina's sunglasses covered her eyes, but they knew she had spotted Alex and his woman when her smile fell slightly and she bit her lip.

"Umm. Nothing really. There's a guy over there who looks like Alex," Gina replied.

"Oh, really? Where?" Cookie tried to sound surprised.

"Over there, in the last row of tables. I brought him to the bakery a couple times. See him?"

"Oh, yeah. He does kinda look like Alex."

Gina raised her sunglasses and squinted in his direction. "That is him. I've seen that battered UConn cap enough times to recognize it anywhere." She replaced her sunglasses and crossed her arms. "Interesting. He's supposed to be allergic to shellfish."

Sherry and Cookie grimaced at each other, silently urging the other to distract Gina.

"I wonder who that is with him?" Gina said.

Cookie took a bite of her sandwich and chewed dramatically.

"Hey, this band is really good. Where'd you find them?" Sherry asked.

"I dunno know, they played last year," Gina said absentmindedly, still staring in Alex's direction.

He and the woman had finished their french fries and were watching the band on stage. Alex looked around the crowd. He stopped when he was facing Gina. He said something to the woman as he stood. She nodded in response to whatever he said to her and remained at the table as he started walking through the maze of tables towards Gina.

"All right, well, let me get back to work. I need to check on, umm, the next group, make sure they're ready to go on. I'll get back with you all a little later." Attitude and nervousness were mixed in Gina's voice. She walked quickly away before her friends could respond.

"Gina!" Alex called across the crowd.

"Uh oh," Cookie said.

Gina kept on walking away, maneuvering through the tables.

"Gina!" Alex called again. He dropped his cup into a trash can then jogged towards her, dodging around the chairs and strollers scattered through the aisles. The brown-haired woman watched him run through the table then got up from the table. She started walking towards him, but stopped and turned to watch the band on stage.

"Ooh, he caught up with her," Cookie reported unnecessarily to Sherry. They watched Alex and Gina chatting, wishing they could read lips; Gina had walked so fast, they were out of earshot.

"If she moved that fast while they were training, she wouldn't have any problem with the marathon," Sherry said.

"Hey, Gina," Alex said, as he ran up beside her on the opposite boundary of the table area.

"Alex. What a surprise to see you here." Gina looked back at her friends. Not surprisingly, Cookie was biting her fingernail. Sherry was pursing her lips and Gina imagined her eyes were squinting in suspicion behind her sunglasses.

"I thought I'd come out and see what you've been working so hard on," he said, grinning. He shifted his hat and smoothed his hair underneath.

She ignored the memory of running her fingers through his hair. "Checking up on me?" Annoyance crept into her voice.

"No, not like that. I mean, well, you did win the bet, after all."

Gina recalled their wager over a game of skee-ball. She was so glad that she didn't have to go to a hockey game. It seemed so long ago, she was surprised, and impressed, that he remembered it.

"Anyway, I thought it would be nice to come see your big event."

"I thought you would break out in hives and die if you came?" Gina glanced at his woman companion. She was facing the stage, bobbing her head to the music.

"I took a couple Benadryl before I came," Alex said. "I thought it would be worth the risk to see you in action."

"Well, you've seen me at work before. This is just outside." Gina wasn't sure if he was supposed to be flirting with her or not, especially since he wasn't alone.

"So, you came by yourself?" She asked to hear what he would say.

"No, my sister was in town so I brought her along. She's, uhh..." Alex looked around the tables where he had run off from the woman. "There, that's her, with the ponytail and the blue dress," he said pointing to her back.

"Your sister? You didn't mention she was coming down to visit." Gina was ready to unravel his lie.

"You've hardly been in the office all week and anyway, she just called me last night and said she was coming. She's going to a concert tonight over at the Verizon Center."

Gina still wasn't convinced. It seemed like a long trip from Connecticut for an impromptu, last minute trip for a concert.

"If she could break away from watching the band, I could introduce you. I'm sure she'd like to meet you."

The walkie-talkie on Gina's hip beeped. She had the volume turned down but made out the word "tent" and recognized the gate guard's voice. She unhooked it from the holster and displayed it to Alex.

"Shucks, I guess I won't get to meet her. Duty calls. You know how our clients are. Enjoy the festival." Gina fake-smiled then walked away. She pushed the button on the walkie-talkie. "Dante? Gina. I didn't hear you. Where am I going?"

"Stone plus one is on his way in," the guard responded.

As Gina marched over to the Stone Sports tent, she fumed over Alex showing up at the festival. And he brought a date? Was she really supposed to believe that woman was his sister?

She released a deep sigh, forcing herself to get Alex out of her head. She needed her head clear to get through this festival. This was the first time the Stone Sports Agency was a festival sponsor and based on what he had spent already, she wanted to make sure he returned next year. She touched base with Courtney, who assured her that everything was ready with an excited thumbs-up.

Gina stepped back outside the tent just as Michael Stone and his guest turned onto the walkway. Her eyes opened wide and she gasped as she recognized his "plus one."

"Mr. Stone, welcome. Thank you for supporting our event." Gina reached out to shake Michael's hand.

"Hey, Gina!" Laura said and gave her a quick cheek kiss. "I was wondering if I'd see you today."

Laura turned to Michael, "What a small world. We're neighbors, she lives down the hall from me."

"Is this the one who watches your dog?"

"Right. Dog-watcher, Spades partner."

"And do you not watch sports either Ms. Morrison?"

Gina wasn't sure of the correct answer, whether admitting she only watched Olympic gymnastics would lose her a repeat sponsor. Laura laughed and answered for her.

"Please. Gina's just as non-athletic as I am. Although, she was training for a marathon."

"You're going to run a marathon?" Michael asked.

Gina again shook off thoughts of Alex. "No, I'm not going to run a marathon. Well, I was training for one, but I'm not now. Anyway, it's a long story, and not an interesting one. How about we go on in and check out your space?"

Gina led Michael and Laura into the tent and introduced them to their tent hostess. "Mr. Stone, Courtney will be here throughout the event. If there's anything you need, just let her know. And if you need me, she can always get a hold of me." Almost in unison, the women patted their walkie-talkies.

"It seems some of your guests have already arrived," Gina said. She looked around at the dozen men standing around, enjoying the drinks and food and flanked by a few women dressed in the standard hanger-on-trophy-girlfriend uniform: micro-mini-skirts, halters, and high heels.

"Excuse me ladies, let me say 'hey' real quick." Michael, in his ever-gregarious form, made his rounds, shaking hands and talking to everyone under the tent.

"I started the crab vodka fountain," Courtney squealed in a loud whisper.

"Great, it should be ready by the time we take him over there." Along with the rest of the tent staff, even Gina was most excited about the ice sculpture.

"Wanna drink?" Gina asked, leading Laura towards the bar.

Laura ordered a lime martini and a scotch on the rocks.

"Michael Stone is your client? Why didn't you tell me?" Gina asked.

"I didn't know he had a tent. Plus, I don't like to name names."

"Well, when the name is one of the biggest tents I've got out here, it would be nice to know."

"Anyway, I'm not really working, I'm just hanging out today."

Gina wrinkled her brow. A few weeks ago Laura had explained that he had asked her to have him as her exclusive client. Gina didn't understand that change, nor this new twist of 'just hanging out.'

"I know, confusing."

The bartender placed the drinks on the bar. Laura put a few dollars in the tip glass before picking them both up.

"So, he's a sports agent?"

"Yeah. And he's real sociable. Everywhere we go, he's like this." Laura grinned while watching him wander around the crowd. When he turned and caught her eye, she raised the glass of scotch. He spoke to two more people then made his way back to her.

"Thanks." He tasted the scotch. "Good choice," he said to Gina.

"Glad you like it. Would you like to see the food selection?" Gina led Michael towards the buffet tables where they reunited with Courtney.

Laura wondered if she needed to let Gina know it was okay to call her by her real name. She couldn't recall if she had mentioned that she had broken Rule Number 1 with Michael. In fact, she had pretty much torn up the whole rule book.

After Michael went with Gina for a quick tour, Laura sat at one of the tables and watched the mini-skirted, well-endowed women follow behind their sports guys. She wondered if people looked at her the same way, assuming she was merely the rich guy's sex toy. Another bauble to go along with the Pro-rings and diamond stud earrings.

Sid ducked into the doorway and scanned the tent. Laura waved to get his attention, although with the tent still mostly empty, it wasn't necessary.

"Hey. This is nice. Where's Mike?" Sid stood over the table, surveying the tent.

Laura noticed his eyes rest on one of the women roaming the tent.

"Checking on the food," Laura said, nodding in the direction of the buffet.

"Leave it to him, has to check out every detail. I'm gonna get a drink. You good? Save my seat?"

Laura assured him she would.

"Make sure you eat, everything looks good," Michael said, coming back to the table with Gina.

"I wouldn't expect anything but the best from Gina. What's up there?"

"Mini-crabcake bites, Blue Crab claws, Dungeness crab claws, shrimp cocktail, raw oysters and raw clams, mixed ceviche. Coleslaw, Caesar salad, three-bean salad." Gina ticked the menu off, counting each item on her finger. When she finished the fifteen-item list, she dramatically took a deep breath.

"I didn't forget anything, right?" Michael said to Gina.

"I can't think of anything you could've forgotten," she said laughing.

"You parked that fast?" Michael said as Sid approached the table.

"I didn't have to go far, the lot was right around the corner." Sid placed a martini glass on the table.

"This is Ms. Morrison, sorry, Gina. She's in charge of this whole thing," Michael said, pointing his glass at Gina. "And she's Laura's friend. This is Sidney Stone, my partner."

"Nice to meet you, Mr. Stone." Gina said his name slowly, as if in thought.

Laura giggled, recognizing Gina's thoughtful look and knowing what she was mulling over in her head.

"His *business* partner. Sidney. Nice to meet you, too, Gina," Sid said, reaching out to shake her hand.

"Oh," Gina said, recomposing herself. "How's your drink?"

"Good. Just enough lime."

♠ ♥ ♣ ♦

Cookie drummed on the table and wiggled in her seat as David and his band took their places on stage.

"Just friends, huh," Sherry teased.

"Good afternoon, everybody!" The bandleader said into the mike. "Are you enjoying your time out here on the waterfront?"

The audience greeted him with cheers and catcalls.

"Then let's keep the good times going. Grab your favorite woman and another beer from your bartender and have a great afternoon. We are Soul and Sound." He nodded at the rest of the band and they threw themselves into a song.

Cookie watched David on his saxophone. After a few bars of the song, he raised his head and his eyes drifted over the crowd.

"He's looking for you. Wave," Sherry said. She pushed her friend's arm into the air and waved it back and forth, knowing Cookie would've been too shy and self-conscious to do it herself.

Cookie saw his eyes catch her flailing hand. He raised his eyebrows and held her eyes for a few soulful saxophone notes, then turned his attention back to his band. During each of the following few songs, he found Cookie and played a few notes just for her again. After the third song, David stepped over to the band leader and whispered to him.

"Now, we've got a special song for a young lady sittin' out there, dressed in my sax player's favorite color." The band-leader dramatically looked around the audience, grinning at the various women standing and waving their arms, calling out to him.

"Blue! Is it blue?" yelled a woman in a tie-dye sundress.

"I know it's green, baby. Over here!" The woman whistled and waved a large green sunhat.

"I'm your lady in red," a woman behind Cookie called.

Sherry jostled Cookie, slapping her on the arm and laughing. "Look at all these women after your man."

"Oh, there she is," the bandleader said, eyeing Cookie. He turned around to David. "You're right, she is a mighty pretty lady. Hmm, how 'bout her friend? Is she single?"

David laughed and shrugged, then said something the audience couldn't hear.

"Yes she is!" Sherry stood up and screamed across the audience.

"Hey, there, sugar. We need to talk later," the bandleader grinned at Sherry. "But in the meantime, David's woman, this is for you." He nodded in Cookie's direction as he began the count for the next song.

Sherry pinched her friend, "He's talking to you!"

Cookie grinned, feeling herself blushing. "You think?"

"Shh — so I can hear the song. What is it?" Sherry hummed along until she caught the Shalimar tune then started to sing along. "But you can't keep runnin' away from love. 'Cause the first one let you down."

Cookie looked up at David. She pressed her fingers to her lips then threw him a kiss.

"Who's playing?" Sid asked Courtney.

She checked her schedule. "Soul and Sound, a local band. I think they played last year and Gina liked them, so she asked them back. They sing a lot of old R&B hits, lots of fun."

"Let's go watch the band," Sid said to Laura as a crowd started to fill the tent.

"What about Michael?" Laura asked.

Sid pointed to his cousin talking to a blond woman dressed in the mini-skirt uniform. "He'll be all right." He grabbed a bowl of mini-crabcakes and led her out of the tent.

Sid hummed with the band as the walked along, weaving through the crowd.

"Can I ask you something?" Laura asked.

"Sure."

"He's an attractive guy, with obviously enough money to keep any woman he wants. Why does he need me?" she popped a crabcake in her mouth.

"Simple. As much as he's 'Mr. Social', he doesn't really like people in his personal business. He doesn't want people to know who he's dating, when he's dating someone new, when he's not dating anyone at all. If she's black or white or Filipino or Swedish."

He laughed at Laura's raised eyebrows. "Yeah, he doesn't really discriminate. He figures it would end all the noise by having one person with him all the time."

"Oh. So, he still sees other women?"

"Uh, yeah. He is a man and he knows you're not going to sleep with him. Are you?"

Laura blinked and stuttered before she could answer. "Umm, no, no. That's not what…no, we didn't…"

"Right. So, he has to have someone else."

"And those women, how many, what do they..." Laura wasn't sure what her next question was going to be.

"Actually, to be quite honest with you," Sid twisted his lips and winced, taking a breath. "It's not 'women'. For right now, it's 'woman.' Singular. Olivia."

"Olivia?"

"Yeah, she's his woman. When he first came up with this idea of hiring an escort, it was to keep all the women, plural, in the background. But then he met her at some dinner or something, I forget now, and he ended the other escort's contract. And I'm glad he did. She was pretty, but she was a b-- she was awful."

Laura listened intently. She wondered how she fit into this picture.

"Then, as it turned out, Olivia's kinda quiet and doesn't care much for sports."

"So, she, Olivia, is like, a real girlfriend? Does she know about me?" Laura pointed at herself, shocked by this piece of information.

"Yeah. In fact, hiring you was her idea. She didn't want to go to all of Mike's events, she said she was too busy, plus she gets really anxious in crowded spaces and she knew if he went alone," he nodded back towards the tent, "all those women would be hanging on to him."

"So, she thought he should hire an escort? Again."

"Exactly. He wouldn't be alone, she wouldn't have to tag along. Perfect solution. With her, he enjoys a private, personal relationship. With you, he has a smart woman he can talk to and take out places, someone with manners and who can hold an intelligent conversation with people."

"Yeah, that is what I do. Although, usually my clients don't have another woman at home waiting for them."

Sid's blatant explanation of her role in Michael's life made her wonder what he truly thought of her. Even though they had talked, even laughed, about how she started as an escort, she felt a certain condescending tone in his summary of her job and hoped it was just her own imagination.

"Those women in the tent? Exactly what he's tired of. And Olivia? She's what he needed to calm down. She just doesn't like to go out. Honestly, it's not a fail-safe plan. You could end up with an absolutely gorgeous and wonderful escort and totally forget it's supposed to be a business arrangement."

Gina almost choked on her drink. She tried to cover her coughs.

"But, well, that's what works for them. For Mike, it takes more than one woman to give him everything he needs. You know?"

"Yeah." Laura took a sip of her martini, then turned to Sid. She tried to pretend she was joking when she asked, "What about you? How many women will it take to satisfy all your needs?"

"When I find the right woman, one."

He held onto her eyes a second longer than she expected and Laura's heart quickened by a few beats. She subtly smiled and took a longer sip of her martini. Sid turned to the band on the stage.

"Is this Shalimar? Wow, they're going way back." Sid bopped and sang along. "Jody Watley was my girl."

"Was she your one?" Laura joked.

Sid laughed, then took Laura's hands and danced between the tables.

"And though others try to satisfy you, baby; with me true love can still be found, love can still be found."

Gina

Gina remembered Cookie's tip to take the labels and price tags off the Gourmet-to-Go food containers, but it was still obvious everything was store bought. She considered for a moment pouring it all into her own plastic picnic containers but decided that that was too much work and not necessary. If she and Glynn did go out again, he would find out sooner or later that she couldn't cook, better for him to know up front.

She arranged the containers neatly in the picnic basket, along with tableware and wine glasses. While waiting for the policeman, she sat and watched the news. There was yet another shooting in the city, again more young black boys. The news reporter said police were not sure of a motive, but it appears that they were embroiled in an argument.

"Probably over shoes or a girl," Gina said to the TV.

The station switched to another news reporter in the county explaining a water main break. The resulting flood cascading down New Hampshire Avenue had caused mass confusion during rush hour. The cameraman showed police redirecting traffic as drivers honked and made wide U-turns in the street.

Gina peered closely at the TV, then walked over for a better look. She hit rewind on the remote, then paused it at a shot of the policeman.

Officer Scott. He was never going to make it in time for the concert.

Gina hit the play button on the remote, again listening to the reporter explain about the water and the detours. She pulled out the breadsticks from the picnic basket and poured herself a glass of wine. She carried

319

them back to the couch and took out her work plans for an upcoming women's conference. She reviewed her plans, jotting down notes about things she still needed to do, while keeping an eye out for breaking news about the water main break. The fireman and water company were there trying to turn off the water.

After the news, she switched to Wheel of Fortune and tried to guess the words before the on-TV contestants. She dug into the picnic basket for something else to nibble on.

By the time she watched a couple more shows she had recorded and finished the cole slaw, her phone rang. Gina was surprised that Alex would be calling her in the evening.

"The manager down at Water just texted me, they've got a great band playing tonight. I thought we could go check it out," Alex said.

Water was a recent addition to their list of new bars in the city that might be suitable for events. She had heard that it had a chic modern décor and great small plates menu. She punched the air, upset about missing the chance to go.

"That is, unless you have plans?" Alex asked.

"Actually." She glanced at the TV and her half eaten picnic. "Actually, I do have plans tonight."

"Oh." Alex was silent on the other end. "Well, okay. Hey, um, if I didn't tell you before, the music festival was nice. You did a really good job. And my sister had a really good time, too."

"You're sister, huh? Did she make it to the concert?"

"Yeah. She met up with some people she went to college with and they all went."

"You didn't go?" Gina was starting to believe that the brown-haired girl was his sister, after all.

"No. After hanging out on the water all day, I came home, took some more Benadryl and went to bed," he said. Gina could hear the smile in his voice. She allowed herself to laugh, too.

"Well, I don't want to keep you from whatever you're doing. I saw you put five stars next to Water, so I just thought you might be free and would want to go out."

"Thanks." Gina said.

"I guess I'll see you tomorrow?"

"Yeah. We have that meeting in the morning, at the hotel."

"Right, ten o' clock." Alex paused. "Maybe we could do lunch afterwards. See if we can find a food truck or something."

"What's tomorrow? Is the burger truck on the Mall?" Gina asked excitedly. As much as they ate in sit-down, white linen tableclothed restaurants for work, when they were on their own, they enjoyed tracking down the best food trucks.

"I'll check and let you know in the morning."

"Okay. See you at the hotel," Gina said. As they hung up, Gina sighed. She thought she might really miss him.

She munched on another breadstick and mindlessly stared at the TV. There was a show about little girls entering beauty pageants.

"Poor baby, that shade of lipstick is all wrong for you," Gina said. She was startled by the phone ringing again.

"Hi, Gina. Glynn. I'm really sorry…"

"Hey." Gina sat up and took the half-eaten breadstick out of her mouth. "I saw you on the news. No problem."

"We can't make calls when we're in the middle…"

"That's okay. I understand."

"I'm done, I'm off duty now."

"What about the water?"

"New guys finally came in to relieve us, I don't know what took them so long. The water company and firemen are still over there, too. I think they're getting it under control."

"That's good."

"I'd like to see you tonight, if you still want to go out. Obviously, we missed the concert, sorry about that. And I know it's late now, but, maybe, you'd like to get something to eat?"

Gina laughed. "Well, I've been kinda munching on this picnic food."

"Ah, I forgot about that, you did say you were going to get food. Man, I really messed up the plans."

"I could still go for a dessert and a drink, though."

"Great. I could be there in about half an hour, is that okay?"

Gina cleaned up the used plates and the half-empty food containers. Then she reapplied her lipgloss and waited again, returning to watching TV. Glynn knocked at Gina's door twenty-five minutes later.

"You know, if you're still hungry, there is still food left. I didn't really eat it all," Gina offered.

"That, actually, would be great. I'm exhausted. It'd be great to stay here."

Gina pulled the picnic cloth from out of the basket and spread it on the living room floor. "We could pretend we were there." With his help, she retrieved the picnic basket and spread the food containers on the cloth. He poured their wine and they sat on the blanket.

"Is this is what police life is like?"

"Sometimes." He laughed. "Every now and then, there are some days that are quite calm. Our life is unpredictable."

There's a trump card, Gina thought. And then there's a higher one.

Laura

Balancing her feet on the end of the couch, Laura brushed red nail polish on her toes and sang along with the radio. As she finished her left foot, the phone buzzed on the coffee table and she leaned over to read the caller ID.

STONE SIDNEY.

She smiled and wiggled her toes as she hit the Speaker button on the phone. It was a new thing for him to call rather than Michael's secretary.

"I know it's short notice, but what does your schedule look like on Thursday evening?" he asked.

"This Thursday?" Laura stared out the window, squinting as if her calendar were floating just beyond the glass. Obviously, she didn't have an appointment with Michael if Sid was asking and she couldn't think of anywhere else she needed to be. "Nothing. What's going on?"

"*Porgy & Bess* is opening at the Kennedy Center."

"Ahh, opening night. Had to be a big night for Michael to go to the opera," Laura said, snickering. "Sure I'll go; I love *Porgy & Bess*."

"Well," Sid said then paused. "Well, they aren't Michael's tickets. They're mine."

Laura sat silently trying to fully understand what he was saying.

"I would like you to go with me," he finally said.

"Oh." Laura wasn't sure in which category his request fell. She wanted to be excited that he was asking her on a date. But, is that what he meant or was this a new contract or some kind of side deal he wanted to swing?

"After, after the other morning, when you got back from the West Coast and we went back to your apartment," he paused again. "And after hanging out at the festival, I'd like us to get together, spend some time together on our own terms."

"Oh," Laura breathed. He was calling for a real date. With permission to be excited, she was so busy thinking about walking around the Kennedy Center holding Sid's hand, she forgot to respond. After a beat too long of silence, Sid continued.

"Hey, maybe this is a bit awkward given the circumstances. I don't know what I was thinking. You probably have some kind of rule against dating customers or something. Right? Sorry to bother you."

Laura quickly returned from her imagined walk to the current phone conversation. What did he say? Was he going to renege on the date?

"Hey, no, Sid!" She reached quickly for the phone and her hip slid off the couch. She grasped for the couch back, then the seat cushions as she tumbled to the floor, ending with her leg hitting the edge of the coffee table. "Ouch, shit!" she whispered, rubbing her calf and grabbing the phone.

"Hello?"

"Yeah, sorry. Umm, no, it's not a problem. I mean, it's not for me. I would love to go with you." She rubbed her calf again. "You think we need to mention it to Michael?" she asked cautiously. She wasn't sure what the rule was or should be since she hadn't made one for the driver-asks-you-out situation, but whatever it would've been, she was sure she'd break it for Sid.

"Michael will be fine with it," Sid said.

"Oh, good. I mean, I don't want there to be any problems between you guys," she said, relieved to leave handling Michael to Sid.

"So. Thursday?" Sid asked.

"Yes, yes, Thursday."

"Great. I'll pick you up around six."

"Yes. Six will be perfect."

"Alright, I'll see you then," he said.

"I can't wait," she said softly, wondering if he heard her.

"Me either," he said.

After they hung up, Laura called to her dog, half asleep in her favorite spot under the window. "Lady, I've got a date!" She scrambled up from the floor and did a little hip shaking dance.

"I got a date, I got a date!" she sang to herself. "Oh, gotta tell Gina!" She slipped on a pair of sparkly flip-flops and danced towards the door. Lady jumped up from her bed and ran to follow Laura, just squeezing through the door before it closed.

Down the hall, Laura banged on Gina's door like she was there to collect overdue rent money.

"Gina! Gina!"

She heard footsteps from inside and started bouncing from one foot to the other. She laughed as she spotted the painted the toenails on only one of her feet. She looked up and started talking as soon as she heard the doorknob turn.

"I've got a date!"

"Great," Alex said. "Are you going dancing?"

Laura stopped her two-step, both almost embarrassed by her excitement and surprised to see Alex standing in Gina's doorway. She stepped on flat feet and tried to calm down.

"Oh, hey, Alex. Didn't know you were over. Is Gina here?"

There's some catching up we've got to do, she thought to herself.

He opened the door wide and called back into the apartment. "G, come quick, Laura's got a date!"

Gina rushed in from the kitchen. "Really?" Her voice was an octave higher in surprise. "With who?"

Laura was grinning, waving her hands like she was going to fly away. She let out a breath and answered.

"Sid asked me to go see *Porgy & Bess* on Thursday!"

"Who is Sid?"

"Sid Stone." Laura sighed at Gina's blank stare. "Michael Stone. Stone Sports. Remember? Potomac Music Festival?"

"Oh! Sid, Michael's partner, Sid. Wait, y'all are dating?"

Laura gave Alex a side-eyed look, then cupped her hands around her mouth. In a very bad, loud whisper she said, "We had sex when I came back from San Diego and this is a real date so it makes it not just a one-night stand, or morning, actually, 'one morning stand'. It means he really likes me." She grabbed Gina's hand and returned to her normal voice volume. "He really likes me Gina! He doesn't even pay me and he asked me out!"

Laura knew she didn't have to explain to Gina what it meant to her to be going on a real date. Gina had heard her whining over countless glasses of wine about finally, one day finding someone who truly wanted to be with her.

"What, wait whoa. You did what with who when?" Gina shooed a grinning Alex back towards the kitchen. She and Laura moved towards the couch in tandem, folding their legs under them and sitting onto the seat facing each other.

Laura cast a glance towards the kitchen. "Are you two back together? What happened with the police guy?"

Gina shrugged. "Ah, he was okay. We didn't make it to the concert, but hung out anyway. We might meet up at a happy hour or something. And, yeah, me and Alex are going to try to work things out, too."

"Plan B, huh?"

"Plan A," Gina said thoughtfully.

"Aww, good. Alex's good for you."

"Okay, okay. Go back to this Sid. And you had sex with him when?"

Laura excitedly told Gina about Sid, all her words running into one another as she bounced back and forth between the night they went out for drinks while waiting for Michael, their ride home from the airport and the ensuing romp on her couch, and his call just a few moments before.

"So, not dating a client. That's not a rule anymore?" Gina sipped at her coffee.

"Yeah, that part's a little weird. Because, he is not technically my client. Michael is. He's also Michael's cousin."

Gina raised her eyebrows and opened her mouth as if to say something.

"Yeah, cousins. I know a bit more complicated, but anyway. I don't think the 'don't date clients' rule applies here." She shrugged, not fully sure she was, in fact, comfortable with ignoring this rule.

"It's your rule. You can do with it whatever you want," Gina said. "But what about Michael? Does he have a say or do you have to ask? How does that work?"

"I don't know. He, Sid, said that he, Michael, was fine with it." Laura's eyes popped open as a new thought came to her. "He's an employee of a client. That makes us both his employees. Well, I'm more of an independent contractor, but same difference. That makes us like co-workers. And co-workers are allowed to date, right?" She winked, glancing towards the kitchen.

"Hmmm," Gina said.

"Right?" Laura giggled, feeling more light-hearted than she had in a long time.

"It depends on your employer," Gina said, laughing and sipping her coffee. "You like him, huh?"

"Gina, he's so sweet. When he picks me up, he's always so nice and gentlemanly. He holds the door and carries my bags and all the stuff men are supposed to do. Yeah, maybe because he's a chaffeur, but I can tell, it's just his way, too. And he's funny. And he likes cupcakes. And he's handsome. And he likes *Porgy & Bess*. And well, yeah, the sex was good, too. He's great."

Laura was excited to have someone she was genuinely attracted to, no pretending per the contract.

Gina smiled at her friend. "What you're going to wear?"

By Thursday morning, Laura had narrowed down her choices to two outfits, neither of which she had worn on outings with Michael: a green, sleeveless sheath dress with sheer panels striped around the legs and a black three-quarter sleeve lace cocktail dress. She'd wait until five o'clock to see what kind of mood she was in and then select the dress.

She wasn't sure if it was a bad sign that she hadn't heard from Michael all week or if it simply meant he had a slow social calendar, which she would have found odd given his normal activities. Perhaps, his girlfriend finally decided it wasn't such an imposition for her to go out in public with him after all. Of all the reasons why men hired her as an escort, this was a new one and a reason she couldn't understand. What kind of woman wouldn't get over whatever social anxiety she had to be seen in public with her handsome, rich boyfriend?

By 5:45, Laura was ready. She had selected the black lace dress, done her hair and make-up.

Her heart was racing and her hands were shaking from nervousness, excitement, or a bit of both. She re-checked her make-up to make sure her trembling hands hadn't resulted in a crooked line of lipstick. Satisfied, she went to the kitchen and poured a glass of wine.

The clock seemed to tick slower than usual. She checked her e-mail, scrolled through her friends' status updates, sipped the wine. She checked the clock on the microwave, hoping it was moving faster than the big hand and little hand hanging on the wall. She unconsciously tapped her foot while counting down the minutes.

The phone rang at 5:57 with a call from the front desk.

She punched the speaker button and tried to sound calm. "Hi, Mr. Washington. I'll be right down."

She debated on finishing the wine, but decided gulping half of a glass of wine would do nothing for her nerves. She slid into her black stilettos, picked up her purse, and inhaled deep to check her cleavage at its fullest, then headed out the door.

Sid stood at the front desk, talking amicably with Mr. Washington when Laura stepped off of the elevator. She saw him say something to the doorman, who nodded and smiled as she approached.

A red Mercedes was parked out on the curb.

This must be his date car. Damn, how many cars do these guys have? Laura wondered as Sid ushered her into the front seat.

In the lobby of the theatre, they ordered glasses of wine from the bar before wandering out onto the patio overlooking the Potomac River.

The sun was sliding down past the city with the lights of Georgetown just starting to blink on.

"You've seen this opera before?" Sid asked.

"Yes, I've seen it a couple times," Laura said. She wondered if he would think she wasn't excited about seeing it again. "But, I love the chance to see it again and again. Its one of my favorites."

"Me, too. The first time I saw it was in a production in London while I was playing ball."

"I imagine you were the only one from your team who went?"

Sid laughed easily. "Yeah, not too many opera fans on the basketball team, even if it is a black opera."

"How did you like living in Europe? Did you like being away from home?"

"I was born and raised in Virginia, went to school in Tennessee, and was so ready to get outta that little piece of the south. I was happy to go to Europe. I lived in Spain, Italy, Germany. I loved it."

"Would you go live overseas again?"

"If I had the opportunity, yes. Mike and I have talked about establishing an office somewhere over there to work with guys who are trying to come back to play here. Who knows, maybe I'll be back in Spain one day."

"That would be interesting to live somewhere else for awhile. Venture to somewhere new, maybe even learn a new language. Did you pick up a foreign language?"

"I learned enough to play ball and order food. Let me tell you, Spanish with a southern accent sounds horrible."

"You've lost all your accents. You don't even sound like you ever lived in the south."

"What about you? Where are you from? Where have you lived?"

"I'm from New Jersey, and don't make a face. I've moved around a bit, but nowhere as exciting as Madrid." Laura drank her wine, then continued. "Where do you live now? You know exactly where I live, but I have no idea where you and Michael come from or disappear off to." She winced slightly; she hadn't meant to mention Michael, but so often she thought of the two of them as one entity. Relieved, she noticed that Sid didn't seem bothered.

"We still live in Virginia; we've got a place down there. And then we've got condos up here in the District."

"So you two live together? In Virginia and in DC?"

Sid smirked. "I know it sounds crazy, but trust me, it's not whatever you're thinking. We've got some land in Virginia — long story — that we went in and bought together, so we both live there. But it's not a little cozy, 2-bedroom rancher; it's, well, like I said, it's a long story. Maybe I can explain it better another time." He finished off his wine.

"And here? Do you live together, too?"

"Oh, no." Sid shook his head dramatically. "We have two separate condos; in fact, they aren't even close to each other. It's where we used to live before getting the place in Virginia. We kept them primarily so we could get away from each other sometime, and for when we're out late and don't feel like going all the way home."

Before Laura had a chance to ask anymore about his domestic arrangements, the usher walked past, striking the chimes to signal it was time for everyone to come in and take their seats.

On their way in, Sid stopped to pre-order their drinks for the intermission. As he turned from the bar, a woman in a skin-tight, leopard print dress started walking towards them.

"Sidney?" The short, buxom woman said, peering at Sid. "Sidney Stone?"

"Diamond? How are you?"

"Long time no see, Sidney," the woman whined.

Laura snorted and scowled at the woman.

Diamond lightly touched his arm and stretched up on tip-toes to give him a kiss on the cheek, pressing her breasts against his chest. The entire time, she watched Laura out of the corner of her eye.

Laura noticed another woman standing a few feet away and guessed she must have been Diamond's friend. Laura fake-smiled at the woman, telegraphing the message, "Watch your friend because I will knock her ass out if she tries something with my man." Diamond's friend fake-smiled back, "Go ahead, I've got her back."

"It's been awhile. How have you been?" Sid asked, taking a step back.

Laura recognized the nonchalance in his voice, it was the same tone he used for the women who followed Michael around. Laura wondered if she was one of his or Michael's women.

"I've been fine. But I have wondered why you haven't called. It was an awful cold winter not to have you around," Diamond purred.

"What is he, a damn fur coat?" Laura wanted to blurt out. Laura forced a smile to keep from rolling her eyes. She wouldn't let this woman ruin her perfect date. She looked back over at Diamond's friend, this time her look said, "Time to come get your girl." Her friend simply grinned back.

Sid chuckled and patted her hand, still resting on his arm. "You seemed to have survived quite well."

"I didn't even know you liked plays, Sidney. But I guess, we had more fun things to do to, I mean, with, each other," the woman winked, then turned, smirking at her friend.

Sid coughed, pulling his arm from the woman to pound himself on the chest. He looked relieved as the bells chimed again and the lights dimmed and brightened. He pulled Laura gently towards him and wrapped his arm around her shoulders. "We should be getting to our seat now. You know how annoying it is for people to come in late."

If Laura was six years old, she would've turned to Diamond's friend and stuck her tongue out, but instead she stepped closer to Sid and leaned her head against his chest.

Diamond shot Laura a sharp look and pursed her lips. "Well, where are you sitting? Maybe we're heading the same way."

What the hell is wrong with this heifer? He has obviously upgraded, Laura thought. She narrowed her eyes and tilted her head, exasperated with the woman's denial of the obvious.

"Umm, I don't know," Sid lied, turning to Laura. "She's got the tickets in her purse and I didn't even pay attention to the seats. But she likes the box seats, so I'm sure that's where we are."

Laura again resisted the urge to stick her tongue out, now at Diamond.

"My friend has our tickets, so I'm not actually sure where we are either," Diamond gestured to the other woman. "So, enjoy the play. Maybe we'll see you later."

"Uh, I doubt it," Laura said as Sid simultaneously said his good-bye and steered Laura towards the staircase. She glanced at him, then laughed as he began to explain.

"We went out…"

"It doesn't matter. I is your woman, now," Laura quoted from the opera.

"You is, you is," Sid responded. He wrapped his arm tighter around her shoulders as they were lead to two seats in a box right of the center.

Laura and Sid hummed along as the mother soothed her baby with *Summertime* and Laura watched Sid in amusement as he cheered and cursed along with the male characters playing craps. They held each other's hands when Porgy finally declared his love for Bess, then again when Bess responded in kind. Laura tried to sniffle as quietly as possible while Porgy wheeled himself around the stage calling for Bess after she left town. Despite her efforts to hide her tears, Sid reached over and patted her leg. She managed to wipe her eyes during the audience's turn to applaud, before the lights came up.

As they filed out of the opera house into the lobby, they spotted Diamond waving frantically at Sid. He waved briefly in return then pulled Laura towards the garage elevator. They walked quickly, like two teenagers hiding from chaperones, and jumped onto a waiting elevator just before the doors closed.

They laughed and Laura shook her head at Sid. He leaned down to give her a kiss on the lips and squeezed her hand.

"Are you hungry?" Sid asked.

"Yeah, I am, actually." Laura was excited that he had asked. She was starting to feel a little anxious that the night was ending.

"Good. I'd hate to eat alone."

Sid pulled into a back alley parking lot, apologizing for the lack of valet service, then walked around the car to let Laura out of the car. She glanced around nervously at the relatively dark surroundings. He took her hand and walked back towards the street. At the corner, he stopped under a purple awning and pulled open a heavy door, decorated with a gold fleur de lis.

The smell of cooked peppers and strong coffee floated through the air. They were flooded by the sound of jazz blaring through the wall-mounted speakers.

"I know this isn't what you're used to, but the food here is great," Sid said.

Laura had to agree that this was not of the ritzy caliber she was used to with Michael, but it was also true that she wasn't born with a silver spoon. She assured him that she was not as delicate as he may think.

They walked past the crowded bar and slid into a small booth in the back of the restaurant.

"Everything here is delicious," Sid said. The waitress nodded in agreement and asked for their drink order.

"We'll take two Hurricanes and a plate of fried green tomatoes," Sid said while Laura flipped open the menu. They were ready to order when the waitress returned with their drinks and tomatoes.

"You know, if I was Bess, I would've waited. Every time I see it, I hope that this time, maybe this one time, Bess will wait for Porgy." Laura speared a wedge of the tomato slice and offered it to him. He opened his mouth and she fed it to him before taking a piece for herself. "This is a really good fried tomato."

"I told you," Sid said. "Maybe she thought he wasn't coming back. Or maybe she just wanted to get out of town and take her chances on finding a better life."

"But Porgy loved her. How could she just leave him?"

"A lot of women leave men who love them. They meet some other dude who promises them glitz and glamour, then they forget about the guy who actually cares about them."

Laura watched him, sipping her drink through the straw, wondering if he was speaking from his own experience. She noticed from the first taste that the drinks were as strong as their name suggested.

"Well, she should've known better. You can't leave a good man like that for some 'maybe'. She could've been happy with Porgy. Now what? Off in the city with some no-good-guy."

"But he goes off to find her. Maybe he finds her and they do live happily ever after."

"What? He's going to make it all the way to New York on that little wheelie cart?" Laura swept her arm through the air as if gesturing on a large map of the United States.

"Yes, in Porgy and Bess II." Sid caught the eye of the waitress and raised his empty glass for her to see.

"Maybe he gets a ride. Some sympathetic farmer picks him up and carries him on up the road a piece." Sid let his long-unused southern accent resurface as they imagined what happened after the curtains fell.

The waitress stood at their table and watched the mini-play, holding the pitcher of reddish-orange punch patiently. She refilled their drinks, then went on to her next table, humming their made-up love song.

"And then she sees him pushing himself along and goes running to him and begs for his forgiveness for leaving him in the first place." Laura grabbed Sid's forearms and pulled him close. "I'll never leave you again Porgy," she said, feigning a southern accent, sounding more like someone from the cast of *Gone with the Wind*, than a down-trodden black woman.

"I'm so glad I found you," Sid said then leaned in closer to kiss Laura across the table. They pulled apart when they heard a cautious coughing sound.

"Next time we'll put you two up front so everyone can enjoy your story. We can charge extra for the show," the waitress joked. She put their plates of fried oysters, shrimp etouffe, and sausage gumbo down on the table. She reached into her apron pocket, pulled out two bottles of hot sauce and set them in the middle of the table one at a time.

"Hot. And Hot as Hell. Now, don't get carried way. Enjoy."

Sherry

The house was finally quiet again. Brandon had gone back home. Vivian and Jordan had gone shopping and to dinner. Sherry stood in her kitchen and welcomed being able to hear her dripping faucet again.

She poured a glass of wine and carried it upstairs to the small bedroom at the end of the hall, which served as Sherry's home office. Before the divorce, it was to be the nursery. She had imagined a rocking chair by the window that overlooked the backyard; it would've been her nursing chair and where she rocked her baby to sleep every night. Next to it would've been a table for their bedtime story books. A toybox was to sit in the corner, filled with either dollbabies or trucks.

Instead the room was filled with her desk and files of paperwork.

Now that it was clear that Jordan and Brandon were going to somehow raise their baby on their own, Sherry was forced to put the idea of her as aunt/adoptive mom out of her head. Jordan would stay with her for a few months since she had no desire to go back to school as she got bigger and bigger. She would continue to work for Cookie, a job she enjoyed, and save money. Then, eventually she would go home to have the baby and begin her life with Brandon.

Sherry opened her desk drawer and pushed the folder of letters from her ex-husband aside. She pulled out the thick blue file folder packed with adoption applications.

She had considered options to get pregnant, but selfishly, Sherry thought about the physical aspects of being pregnant. She had worked hard to lose weight after her divorce and exercised regularly to keep her new figure. She moisturized and sun-screened to keep her skin even-toned and soft. Was she really ready to put her body through the nine months of pregnancy? What would she look like, how much weight would she regain? How much of the weight would she lose? How much time would she have to take away from her business due to morning sickness or backaches or whatever else happened to pregnant women? How much time before she was back on her feet after the baby was born? How much would delivery hurt? And were all these logistical questions evidence that she wasn't really ready to be a mother? She was embarrassed to even bring the questions up to the doctor, in case they did indicate she wasn't a good candidate for motherhood.

Alternatively, Sherry considered adoption as her path to motherhood. But even with this option, she had a maternal-ticking-clock. Many agencies said they preferred the adoptive parents, particularly a single parent, to be younger than 45 years old. She had considered international adoption, preferring to adopt from an African or Caribbean country. She didn't want to endure the questioning looks of strangers or invasive questions as she walked along with a Chinese baby. But certain African countries wouldn't allow single mother adoptions. In the countries that did, many of the children were war-orphans or had AIDS. She wondered if she had the personal strength to raise a baby that may be starting out with trauma or illness. Some agencies preferred not to break up families so multiple-sibling adoptions were required. Sherry found adopting an African baby wasn't as easy as Hollywood celebrities made it seem.

Each application in the pile was highlighted and marked with her notes about procedures, requirements, and restrictions. She re-read the explanation of the process and the testimonies from other families who had successfully adopted a child. After considering each organization, she placed the application in the "apply" pile, the "maybe" pile, or in the recycle bin. She ran the three applications in the "apply" pile through the copy machine by her desk. She put the originals in the file, then began to fill out her rough drafts. For the most part, it was a pretty standard application.

Name. Address. Marital status. Age. Race. Children. Employment. Income.

Why do you want to adopt? Sherry paused. She wasn't sure how to put it all into words. She wasn't one of those women who could only be satisfied with the pregnancy and childbirth experience. Yes, she had wanted that when she was still married and she and her husband were imagining a picket fence and a dog for their Christmas cards. But all that had changed. Now, she wanted someone to hold everyday. Someone she was accountable for and to. She wanted someone to share her life, to snuggle and watch movies with on a cold afternoon. Someone to go on vacation with and show the world, to nurture and teach. She wanted someone to watch grow into a beautiful person and to love un-conditionally. She wanted a baby, a family of her own.

It took her all night to complete the application packets. She wrote her rough drafts, made corrections, and typed up ready-to-submit final applications. She felt like she was back in college, writing a term paper about her life. She listed her references and prepared letters to them, letting them know they would be called upon to testify about how good a mother she could be.

As she dropped the file folder, filled with copies of her applications, back into the drawer, her hand rested on the file of letters from her ex-husband. She closed the drawer and leaned back in her chair. She let herself cry, silently admitting to herself that she missed him and mourned the life they were supposed to have. Sherry wiped her eyes, then pulled out a notepad and a pen.

She wrote until the sun broke through the dawn.

Sherry blinked at the faint light squeezing through the window and stretched. She piled the eight neatly addressed envelopes on her desk: three for the adoption agencies, then one each for Ms. Evangeline Morrison, Ms. Laura Truesmith, Ms. Amanda Carter, Ms. Vivian Goodman, and Mr. Malcolm Everett.

Laura

Sid was standing at the front desk talking with Mr. Washington when Laura stepped off the elevator. He played with the car keys in one hand, while the other was shoved down in his pocket.

Laura felt a tingle down her back as she heard the sound of Sid's deep voice and chuckle in response to something Mr. Washington had said.

"Mr. Washington," Laura greeted the doorman.

"Good evening, ma'am," he replied.

Sid reached out for Laura's hand. "You look beautiful."

His hands felt strong and smooth, those of a man who did mindful work, her mother would have said. She recalled her father's hands, tough-skinned because he thought it unmanly to apply too much moisturizing lotion. She glanced at Sid's well-manicured nails and sharp haircut; he was obviously a man who took care of himself.

"George, good night," Sid nodded to the doorman.

George? Mr. Washington? Laura's mouth dropped open and she laughed at the thought that in all these years of living in the building, she hadn't even known his first name. She wondered briefly if Gina did.

"My father was quite the history buff," Mr. Washington said.

Laura was surprised to see Sid's red Mercedes parked by the curb rather than their black car.

"We're going to Michael's house, or your house, tonight, right?" Laura asked, once settled into the frontseat of the car. She recalled his abbreviated explanation of their joint ownership.

"Right." Sid pulled out into traffic, glancing quickly over at Laura.

"He mentioned having a dinner. But he didn't say if there was a special occasion," she said. He also had briefly mentioned re-evaluating her contract again, but she wasn't sure what that meant. Or if that was part of the night's agenda.

"Uh, just, just a small dinner party. Yeah, for an important announcement."

"Interesting." She reached out to touch Sid's hair. However, he already sounded nervous, or bothered, so she thought better of it and pulled her hand back.

"It's going to be a wonderful evening," he said. Laura thought she heard him whisper, "I hope."

Sid drove the car out of the city and maneuvered onto the highway heading south into Virginia. They talked about their most recent date to a wine tasting at a local vineyard and laughed about old TV shows. They realized that they were both Alfred Hitchcock fans.

"I imagine back in the '50's they were quite scary," Sid chuckled.

"They still are in a way. Not bloody-gory-scary, but you never know whose going to knock someone down the steps."

"Yes, you do. Whoever thinks they're going to get the insurance money." Sid said.

Laura's phone beeped.

Where r u? Playing Spades? Read the text from Gina.

Sorry. Dinner plans. Thought I told u. Laura replied.

Maybe I forgot. Anywhere good?

Stone's house.

His house? Another broken rule?

Yeah, I know. LOL.

Have fun. Be safe. C U later.

After about forty-five minutes, Sid left the highway and turned onto a long narrow road. Laura watched the countryside pass by. She wondered how they could stand to live so far away from everything. But, she also considered the peace and quiet. It was starting to get dark, but she could still make out horse barns and jumping fences in the acres of fields.

"Do you know how to ride horses?" she asked.

"No, I'm not that much of a country boy. Do you?"

"No. But I think I'd like to. They're graceful in their own way when they walk along." She patted her legs alternately, mimicking the clip-clop sound of their hooves. "Or, what's it called, 'trot'? And they look so free spirited when they're running."

Sid pointed out the various vineyards and farms as they passed. He rattled off the names of two other high-tech executives as they passed their walled estates. Laura recognized the companies more than the names of the men at the top of them.

Laura's mind started to wander as they drove along the lazy road.

"Sid. How long since my first outing with Michael?"

Sid cleared his throat. "I believe it's been about three months now since we met."

Laura continued staring out of the window and thinking back on that evening. She had been annoyed that Michael was running late and left her to hang out with Sid until he was ready. That night, back at home, she replayed her conversation with Sid over and over in her mind. She had hoped that on their next appointment, Michael would, again, be running late and she would have to wait around with Sid.

He slowed, then paused at an intricately designed wrought iron gate with an ornate, script "S" in the middle. He punched a code into a keypad by the curb and the gates slowly opened. Laura imagined the stone driveway on the other side was a mile long.

"Damn. Taking the trash out must take all day, huh?"

Sid laughed. "Luckily, that's not my job."

He drove a short distance, then turned onto a narrower tree-lined lane. The arching trees formed a tunnel. She peered through the pale pathway lighting and could start to make out a house at the end of the driveway. Sid parked in front of the Georgian style brick mansion. A short staircase led to a columned covered porch and a pair of impressive, wooden double doors.

He held onto her hand as she carefully made her way up the steps in her heels.

"We usually park in the back and use the side entrance, but since this is your first visit, I thought I'd show some home training and bring you through the front door."

When they reached the top, Michael stood smiling in the doorway.

"Laura! Welcome to our home, darling." He embraced her and gave her a light kiss on the cheek.

Michael walked her into the grand foyer where an older woman in a black dress was standing next to a small table holding three glasses.

"Good evening, ma'am," the woman said. Laura detected a slight Caribbean accent in her voice.

Michael handed glasses to Laura and Sid, then took another for himself.

"We thought it would be nice to have a private evening, here, where we could all talk and get to know each other a bit better."

"Oh, okay. That sounds nice." Laura sipped at the glass. She looked around for the other dinner guests. She wondered if Olivia would make an appearance.

Michael and Sid took a few steps away and whispered to each other. Michael patted Sid on the back.

Laura played with the base of the wine glass, wondering what the hushed conversation was about.

"Laura, why don't I show you around the house while Sid takes care of some things?" Michael suggested as Sid left the room with the Caribbean woman.

He led her into a room to the side of the foyer. A white silk brocade sofa faced a massive stone fireplace that was clearly the centerpiece of the room. A dark mahogany coffee table and matching end tables surrounded the sofa. Laura pictured women in frilly, full skirts sipping Mint Juleps waiting for some young Southern gentleman to ask for a dance. A faded property plot map hung on the wall in burnished brass frame. Before she could make out the writing on the bottom, Michael pulled her along.

"Ready to move on?" Michael asked.

"I'm still admiring this beautiful room. I can't imagine what else you've got in here."

"I think you'll find the rest quite to your liking, as well."

They walked through the house and Michael showed her the library, separated by a velvet curtain from the room they just left. The walls were lined with shelves filled with books, trophies, and sports memorabilia. Framed classic R & B record covers hung from the available space on the walls.

Laura paused to admire the afros and the long sheath dresses of the younger Supremes and started humming one of their hit songs.

They went up a curving staircase to the east wing of the house and walked through an upstairs sitting room, then passed the doorways of several bedrooms and ornate bathrooms. All the rooms were furnished with a mix of dark, colonial furniture and modern accents.

No wonder that they both lived here. With all these rooms they could probably avoid each other for weeks, months if they wanted to. She imagined living in one of the ornately furnished rooms, walking down the grand stair case to breakfast every morning.

Laura noticed that Michael didn't indicate which rooms were his or Sid's. She wondered what was behind some of the doors he didn't open.

They stopped to look out a hall window onto a large, patterned garden in the back of the house. Lighted stone paths wound around fountains and green squares, filled with flowers and vegetables.

"It feels like a plantation house," she commented, looking over the acres of land beyond the garden.

"It is," he said, then "or, I should say, it was," in response to her confused look.

They started walking back down the staircase and Laura noticed that he had skipped the hall leading to the west wing of the house.

"It was the home of a prestigious family for a hundred years or something like that, 'til you know, being a plantation owner went out of style. Sharecroppers stayed on to work the land, but there weren't as many folks as when there were slaves. They sold off some of the property; sold some of it to the sharecroppers themselves, actually. Eventually, the owners' family died off or moved away and got out of the agricultural business, and the estate was sold to the historical society. When the upkeep got to be too much, the historical society put it up for sale. And that's when Sid saw it listed in an architecture magazine, showed it to me, and put an offer on it."

"Had he seen it before then?"

"He had visited it a few times when it was owned by the historical society. This was, and remains, Stone Manor. This was our family's home plantation."

Laura considered his light skin and asked, "Which side of your family?"

"The tobacco-pickin' side," he said with a smirk.

"I'm sure your people worked inside."

They laughed as he led her into the dining room where three places were set with gold-rimmed china plates, sparkling silverware, linen napkins, water and wine glasses. Laura wondered why there were so few plates for a dinner party.

"So, what do you think?"

"Of the house? Oh my gosh, it's the most beautiful house I've ever been in. I'm still amazed that this was your family's plantation." And she was now conflicted about them living there. Was it weird to live there, knowing his great-grandfather and great-grandmother were part of the estate property? Or maybe they were proud that they could come back and buy the house.

"Once we knew that, we knew it was fate for us to have this house. I agreed with Sid that we had to buy it. Our mothers cried when they first stepped into the house, praising God and Jesus and everybody else in heaven for the full circle of blessings." He pulled out a chair for her then took the seat across from her, leaving the seat at the head of the table empty. "Then mine called her priest over to bless it."

Laura glanced at the empty chair. Why's he sitting over there?

"I'd think you would get a little lonely though, way out here by yourself. Maybe a little spooked, too." He must not believe in ghosts. She didn't either, but she thought she might if she lived in a hundred-year old house.

"It can be a little spooky, even with the blessing," Michael admitted. "The walls were pretty thin. Any wind that came along, the chandeliers would shake, papers would rustle. And any time someone walked up or down the steps, it would be ten minutes later and the floor boards would still be creaking. We had a construction specialist come out and modernize the place. There was a lot to do. Not being cable-ready was the least of it.

"But, as far as being lonely, we're not out here by ourselves. In fact, your question is related to why we invited you here tonight."

Sid entered the room carrying a martini glass.

"Here he is, the resident of the west wing," Michael said.

Sid caught Laura's eyes as he took the open seat at the head of the table. A few drops of the martini sloshed out of the glass as he set it down on the table. He started fidgeting with the silverware, straightening each piece in its place.

"She asked if we got lonely or scared out here," Michael said.

The woman in the uniform pushed a cart with three salad plates on it and placed one in front of each of them. She spread Laura's napkin across her lap then left with her cart again.

Sid laughed, answering, "Not with the security team of Ike and Tina."

Laura raised her eyebrows to ask the obvious question.

"Michael's dogs -- an English bulldog and a Chihuahua. They are the true masters of the house."

"And Tina is which?" Laura asked.

"The bulldog."

Laura laughed.

"And although, she hasn't spoken much, there's Esma, the cook," he nodded his head at the door through which the uniformed woman entered and exited the dining room.

"She's the best Caribbean cook around. That woman could make scotch bonnet milkshakes and I'd drink them," Sid said. "And there's Flora, her sister, the maid."

"You mean 'housekeeper'," Michael corrected.

"Right, more accurately and her preferred title, the 'housekeeper,' since she's the one that keeps this place together."

Michael took a sip of his wine, then continued. "Then there's Charles, the groundskeeper, and his assistant, Robert. But they don't live here."

"So, you, Sid, the women, Esma and Flora, live here?"

"And Ike and Tina. Right." Michael replied and Sid nodded in agreement.

Laura put a fork full of salad in her mouth while thinking about the house residents, the fact that the two men owned their plantation owners' home and had live-in staff.

Her thoughts were interrupted when Esma entered the room again, her cart laden with serving platters and three dinner plates.

"For dinner, we have prepared curry beef, blackened grouper, steamed asparagus with oranges, braised collard greens, rice, and peas. Are you ready to eat?" She turned to Sid for an answer, who nodded slightly.

Starting with Laura, she fixed each of their plates and put a platter of cornbread in the middle of the table. Michael introduced her to Laura while she was serving and Esma smiled in acknowledgement and said a polite, "Nice to meet you."

Michael cleared his throat as if he needed to get their attention, although they were all sitting within a foot of each other. Once he had Laura and Sid's attention he said, "Laura, Sid has told me about your, uhh…"

Laura raised her eyebrows, wondering what he was going to say. There were so many surprises this evening, she thought her eyebrows may get stuck like she had too much Botox.

"The change in your relationship."

Laura should've known Sid would tell. She wondered whether Sid told Michael man-to-man or employee-to-employer. She started to blush and blink her eyes as she slowly looked from Michael then to Sid, then back to her plate.

Her mind filled with questions. Was he going to cancel their contract? He couldn't fire Sid. What was she supposed to say, was there a reason to deny it? And could she really, with Sid sitting right there? Before she could fully assess the situation and figure out how to respond, Michael continued.

"Given that, we started thinking about some formal changes in our relationship, as well."

Laura put her fork down and looked from one man to the other.

Michael wiped his mouth although he had barely eaten, scooted his chair back and stood. "Sid can fill you in. Please excuse me. Let me go check in with Esma about dessert."

It was an obvious lie. Laura was sure that he didn't need to check on any last-minute meal plans. She looked back and forth at the two men, really confused about what she was about to step into, or had stepped into. Sid mixed his peas and rice. Michael waved and left the room.

Sid quietly continued mixing his food, then placed his fork down in the silence. "With a cook and housekeeper and groundskeeper, this place still needs a woman of the house," Sid began.

Sid stood as he started talking, finally looking straight at her. "Each week when I drop you and Michael off at an event, I miss you until you step back into the car. It was killing me to think of you going out with other men, too until I convinced Mike to ask you to see him only. But now, I don't even want to share you with him." Sid smiled broadly. "I know it's only been a few months, but it doesn't take long to know when you've found the right person.

"Remember the night we went to the bar for drinks? I loved listening to your stories and watching you laugh. I've known since then, that I wanted to spend every day of my life with you."

Sid reached into his inner jacket pocket and retrieved a small blue box. "Laura, if you feel the same way, too, will you marry me?" Inside the blue box was a smaller ring box. Inside that box was a 3-karat, princess cut diamond ring.

"Oh my. Wow! I can't believe this. It's the most beautiful…oh god… it's gorgeous!"

Laura started breathing so heavily, she thought she might hyperventilate. She covered her mouth with both hands, staring at the ring sitting on its tiny white cushion.

Her mind raced towards a decision. Until now, she'd never been with anyone who she felt was "the one." She'd never had anyone who said they wanted to marry her, to spend their life with her. Like a photo flip book, she reflected on the moments that she and Sid had spent together. How well did she know him? What if there were things about him she didn't like? But how long would be long enough to make a decision? She nodded. She knew enough.

Without thinking further, she held her shaking left hand out to Sid. "Yes."

She felt the inevitable tears as he slid the exquisite ring onto her bare ring finger. She jumped up and Sid gathered her in his arms and kissed her full on the lips.

"I love you," Sid whispered.

Laura gulped before saying the words she had longed to say to a man. "I love you, too."

As they stepped apart, she grabbed a napkin off the table and dabbed at her makeup, hoping she didn't look like a melted mess. Sid picked up a bell from the middle of the table and rang it.

Laura's eyes widened and she wondered what else there could be.

Michael poked his head into the dining room doorway. "Did she say yes?"

"Yes, she did," Laura said.

Michael stepped in carrying a small tray with three glasses of champagne. "Good, because that is an ugly man when he cries." He set the tray down then passed a glass to each of them, repeating his actions from when they entered the house. "Congratulations!"

They tapped their glasses then took a sip of their champagne.

"When's the wedding?" Michael asked.

Laura laughed. "We've only been engaged five minutes. It might take us a bit longer to pick a date."

"But not too long. I don't want her to have time to change her mind," Sid said.

"True. You better get her to marry you tomorrow."

"Tomorrow? That's ridiculous. Nobody gets married in a day, Michael," Laura said.

"They do in Vegas," Sid said to her.

"In Vegas? Yeah, too bad we're in Virginia."

"We could be in Vegas by tomorrow," Sid suggested.

Michael flashed a wicked grin at Sid. "Love Vegas. I'm in!"

Laura paused with the glass almost to her lips. "Excuse me?"

"I was joking, Mike," Sid said.

"Why? Why not get married in Vegas? Tomorrow?" Michael asked.

"Because." Laura couldn't think of how to finish.

"You know women. They've got to line up their friends and get a dress and have a bachelorette party," Sid said.

Laura considered all the steps of wedding planning. She thought about the tales of brides and their mothers fussing over the details of dresses, cakes, and flowers. Without her mother or father, she'd have to rely on her friends to plan her wedding. They would have to do it, she had no idea of how to plan a wedding and hated planning any type of large event. Gina, Sherry, and Cookie would have to help her with it all. Unless they went to Vegas.

"Maybe I don't need that much time," Laura said. She reconsidered quickly, trying to think of one good reason why she shouldn't run off to Vegas to marry the man standing in front of her.

Sid turned to her. "What?"

"Umm, maybe we could get married in Vegas?" Laura ventured. She was surprising herself in actually saying it out loud.

"Really? Are you serious?"

"Yes, we're going to Vegas!" Michael exclaimed.

"Yeah, that would be fun," Laura said, emboldened by her own spontaneity. She did think that would be exciting. She didn't have her parents to consider, she would send her aunts an announcement and picture. And her friends definitely wouldn't pass up on an excuse to go to Vegas.

"I guess we're all set then," Sid said turning to Michael.

"Great! We'll leave after dessert." Michael finished his champagne then called for Esma. She came in promptly, as if waiting on the other side of the door. "We're ready for dessert, dear."

"What? Wait. Tonight?" Laura stammered. Her surprise and excitement started to mix with confusion and panic.

Sid spoke first. "Yeah. You just said...?" He paused. His shoulders slumped. "You didn't mean right now, did you? I know, we're bad at coming up with ideas and just doing them." He pushed Michael in the shoulder, a gesture of frustration since they were kids. "I'm sorry. But there's not a doubt in my mind I want you to be my wife. And if you aren't ready to go today, we can, of course, wait. We can wait until you are absolutely sure."

Her eyes rested on the martini glass sitting on the table. She remembered him drinking a lime martini at the music festival.

"No, I'm sure. I mean, yes, I am sure. Yes. This is, its just so...wow." She shook her head then laughed. Why not, she thought. Why not be spontaneous and stop playing by the rules?

"But I'm not packed, obviously. I didn't bring anything with me, certainly not a wedding dress."

Sid wrapped his arms around her. "Flora can get you whatever you need. Tell her your dress size, personal products, female products, whatever. She'll be sure it's all at the hotel by the time we get there."

"And what about my friends? I don't want to get married without them being there."

"Our plane can be ready for us to go in an hour," Michael said tapping on his phone.

"And we'll get tickets for your friends for tomorrow," Sid said. "How many do you want?"

Laura wiggled three fingers at him. "Three?" She could hardly believe this was happening. She couldn't wait to tell her friends.

"Not a problem. Don't worry, babe. We'll talk about all the details on the flight."

Laura slowly sipped her champagne then sat staring at the sparkling diamond on her left hand.

Movie Night

"Hello-o-o?" Cookie called as she and Gina entered Sherry's front door. They were met by the smell of smoke and vinegar and the sound of old Motown.

Jordan walked out of the kitchen and greeted her aunt's friends.

"Hey, little momma," Gina said. "You all must be cooking up a storm in here. No-one can even come answer the door."

"I barely heard the doorbell over the music. And they say I play my music loud," Jordan said.

"Hey, girls." Vivian finished wiping her hands on a kitchen towel and reached out to shake the women's hands. "Cookie, thank you for giving my Jordan a job. Lord knows, she's gonna need the money."

"She's been a great help. It's been nice have an extra pair of hands in the bakery," Cookie said, patting Jordan on the shoulder. "I even had time to make cornbread for tonight," Cookie pointed to the bag Gina was carrying for her.

"Great. The food's just about ready. Let me finish getting it out on the table," Vivian said, returning to the kitchen.

"It smell's delicious in here. Did you cook all of this yourself?" Gina asked, surveying the array of pans across Sherry's kitchen.

"Sherry and I both cooked it. She should be back down in a minute," Vivian said. She carried a pan of bar-be-que to the table and directed Jordan to bring the macaroni and cheese.

Gina was already making drinks when Sherry came downstairs. She was delighted to see that her friends had quickly embraced her sister and the three were chatting like old friends. Jordan was answering questions about the baby's progress and Vivian was beaming, the proud grandmother-to-be.

"So, have you thought of any names, yet?" Gina asked.

"If he's a boy, James."

"That was our father's name," Sherry interjected.

"If she's a girl, Vivian," Vivian smiled.

"You don't know whether the baby's a he or she yet? I thought everyone found that out right after the pregnancy test?" Cookie asked.

"My mother thought we should wait to find out. 'Til the baby's born."

"Bad luck. Counting on the sex of the baby before you even know whether it's good and healthy," Vivian explained.

After they finished eating, Cookie picked up the deck of cards on the table. "How are we supposed to play Spades with only three people?"

"Again, we need an extra. Vivian, can you make it up here once a month for Spades?" Sherry asked.

Vivian laughed at the invitation to join their group.

"It wouldn't be worth it, Viv's terrible at Spades. One of y'all can have her as your partner," Sherry teased.

"Oh hush, woman," Vivian responded.

Jordan laughed, used to her mother and her aunt's teasing. She said good-night to the women and excused herself to the bedroom.

"Where's Laura, anyway?" Sherry asked on her way to the kitchen.

"You know, I really don't know. She was supposed to have a dinner date with Michael Stone, then she left me a message about an urgent trip out of town." Gina shook her head and shrugged.

"Those Stone guys who were at the Potomac Music thing? I'd go anywhere they told me. Talk about fine? Everybody in that tent was beautiful." Sherry said. "Girl, you shoulda went with us," she said to her sister.

"You need help, Sherry," Gina laughed.

"She needs Jesus," Vivian said, rolling her eyes.

Sherry laughed at herself and left to go into the kitchen. Now that she had submitted her adoption applications, she felt a great load off her mind. Her friends had received their reference forms. It was out of her hands. Now it was in the hands of fate.

"See, this is why we need an extra. We can't even play cards when someone goes out of town or has to work late or has a date," Cookie said.

"What would the extra do the other times, when everyone's here?" Gina asked.

"She could serve drinks." Sherry came back in the room with a tray of glasses filled with Gina's spiked iced tea and passed one to each woman.

"Exactly," Cookie raised her glass to Sherry in agreement. "When's she coming back?"

"Laura? She didn't say. But she did say she'd call later and in the meantime, would I make arrangements to get Lady to the vet."

"I guess it's move night, then," Sherry said.

They all grabbed their glasses and migrated to the living room. Sherry scrolled through the atRequest movie menu as her friends and sister vetoed movie after movie and passed around bowls of popcorn and chips.

"Seen it."

"Hated it."

"Too scary."

"Ohh, loved it. But nah, not in the mood."

"Yes!"

"We're not watching that again."

After going through most of the movie listings, they finally settled on *Casablanca*. Having seen it multiple times, they knew the words and mimicked the characters.

"Play it once, Sam," Gina copied in a high pitched voice.

"What you talkin' 'bout, Miss Ilsa," Cookie said in a fake deep voice.

"Play it again, Sam. Play it for me," Gina said.

"That's not how it goes!" Sherry fussed. "Y'all messed up your lines."

The women continued clowning in their roles. Gina's phone beeped.

"Who the heck would call in the middle of *Casablanca*?" Gina scowled at the phone but didn't move to pick it up.

Cookie's phone vibrated on the table and Sherry's light came on.

They looked at each other quizzically.

"What in the heck is going on?" Vivian asked.

"Gina, check your phone," Sherry directed as "Sam" began to sing in the background.

"What the...?"

"Who is it? Is it Laura?" Sherry asked.

"Uh, huh." Gina nodded her head slowly while staring at her phone.

"What'd she say?" Cookie asked.

Gina read the text message on her phone, "Pack your bags, we're going to Vegas!"

"We who?" Sherry asked.

"And for what?" Cookie followed.

"Well if the 'we' is us, I don't really care what for," Sherry said.

"If the 'we' is y'all, can I be part of 'us'? I could use a vacation," Vivian said.

Gina tapped the phone to reveal the first photo their friend sent and turned the phone to Sherry and Cookie. The screen was filled with a picture Laura at the airport. While they were talking, the phone beeped again.

Gina dutifully read the next message. "I'm getting married!"

"Who the hell to?" Sherry screamed

Gina tapped the phone to the next photo. She showed them the photo of Laura and two handsome men with an airplane in the background. "I guess to one of these guys?"

The women huddled around the phone to see the men who stole their friend to Vegas.

"Oh, they are nice looking," Vivian said.

"Are you kidding? They are fine!" Gina said.

"It's the Stone guys! Oh, damn, Laura. She is so lucky," Sherry said.

"I think the taller one is her guy." Cookie said.

"Either one is good. They're both nice," Gina said.

"Well, I hope the other one plays Spades," Cookie joked.

Three Tickets to Vegas

"How's Gina getting here?" David asked, pulling up to the airline curbside check-in.

"Alex is bringing her," Cookie replied.

"I still can't believe he took her back with her crazy self," Sherry said.

"Well, some people are just meant to be together," Cookie said.

David smiled as he pulled the women's suitcases out of the trunk. After he carried them to the check-in line, he waited, leaning up against the car, killing time until the police came along to shoo him out of the off-loading area. He turned his head as a car pulled up behind him and honked.

"What the hell? Is that Gina?" Sherry said, leaning down to peek into the car parked behind David.

"Hey, girls!" Gina screamed from the car window. She waved and a fluff of pink feathers flew out the window. Gina jumped out of the car, wrapped in a pink boa, and ran to hug her friends. "I can't believe she is getting married! Oh my god!"

"What's with the boa?" Cookie asked, laughing and spitting a pink feather out of her mouth.

"It's for the bachelorette party! Oh, don't worry, I've got one for you, too, right in my bag. Oh, my bags!" She spun around and leaned down to peer in the car window. "Alex?"

"Here you go, G," Alex said, coming from behind the car, pulling a zebra print suitcase and matching carry-on tote bag.

Gina unzipped the tote bag and pulled out more pink feathers. "Here's one for you and one for you," she said, wrapping Sherry and Cookie in matching pink fluff. "Yeah! Take our picture, babe?" She said, digging a camera out of her purse and handing it over to Alex.

A man in a suit was standing behind the women in line and waved his hands to fling off a pink feather and string of glitter that had alighted on his suit jacket. He made an effort to give a fake cough and furrow his eyebrows at the women.

"This'll just take a second," Gina said to the man and smiled, patting him on his arm.

David, still at his perch leaned up against the car, laughed at the women, posing and holding up the check-in line. The women ended their quick photo shoot as a police car slowed down in the next lane. Alex and David hurriedly climbed back in their cars while the women waved their boas.

"Don't forget to make dinner reservations for when I get back," Gina called to Alex.

"Where you all going?" Cookie asked.

"We're meeting my mother for dinner," Gina said. She raised her eyebrows and shrugged. "It beats running."

Once through security check in, where they had to disrobe from their boas and have them scanned for any dangerous materials, the women headed through the terminal. Gina and Sherry stopped at the bar closest to their gate.

"Girls, we cannot miss this flight. Maybe we should just go to the gate," Cookie said.

Sherry pointed to the gate, visible from the entrance of the bar. "Cookie, how are we going to miss the flight? We're going to see them lining up right there."

"What if we aren't paying attention? If we miss it, we will be in so much trouble," Cookie said.

Gina marched over to the agent at their designated gate, bobbing her head gaily as she spoke, then pointed back to her friends still waiting at the bar. The gate agent pursed her lips and pointed behind her to the wall behind it. On it were posted the departure information and a clock. Gina nodded and ran back to her friends.

"Let's go. First rounds on me," Gina said.

Sherry found three seats near the terminal walkway and indicated Cookie to sit on one of the stools. "Now we can see when they line-up, okay?"

"Hey ladies. What's the occasion?" The bartender asked, sliding a bowl of popcorn in front of them.

"Bachelorette party," Gina said.

"Really?" the bartender cocked an eyebrow and swung his eyes over all three women. "Which is the lucky one?"

"All of us. We aren't the ones getting married," Sherry said.

Cookie poked Sherry with her elbow, causing Sherry to rock to the side. She caught herself before falling off the barstool and laughed.

"The bride to be is already gone. She's in Las Vegas," Cookie said.

"A Vegas wedding, huh? That should be interesting," the bartender said. "So, what're you all going to have to toast? Champagne?"

"That sounds perfect," Gina said.

The bartender lined up four glasses and filled them each with champagne, a few bubbles spilling over each glass. "One for your friend."

A Toast

The attendant unlocked the door and stood back to let the women enter the suite. As they stepped into the room, the lights began to flicker, revealing a marble floored foyer. Their jaws dropped and they grabbed each other's hands as they scanned the suite.

"Are you sure this our room?" Gina asked.

"Who is paying for this place? My credit ain't this good!" Sherry said.

"I know I definitely can't sell this many cupcakes," Cookie said.

They were facing a living room decorated in modern furnishings with a yellow leather couch at the center. Beyond the couch was a full wall window overlooking the neon lights of the Las Vegas Strip.

The women stepped further into the suite and noticed the staircase.

"What the...?" Sherry said, tilting her head towards the ceiling.

"Ladies?" The attendant said. "Let me show you your suite."

"This is not a 'suite'. This is a condo that would sell for a good penny in DC," Sherry said.

They dutifully followed him as he walked through the living room. He toured them through the suite, showing them the dining room with seating for ten, the kitchen, and the bar area. They crossed the living room and climbed the spiral staircase. Upstairs, the bellman showed them the four bedrooms and the elaborate bathroom with a spa tub and steam shower. The women chattered and "ooh-ed" and "aah-ed" at every button and fixture he demonstrated.

As they descended the staircase, they heard the front door chime.

"Hello?" asked a familiar voice.

"It's the bride!" Sherry, Gina, and Laura ran down the stairs and grabbed Laura into a jumping up and down, squealing group hug. When they finally broke apart, the attendant greeted Laura. "Mr. Stone said your tables would be ready at ten." He turned to the ladies on his way out of the door. "Good evening, ladies. Welcome to Vegas."

"Hey, we didn't tip him. He's going to think we're trifling," Gina said, noticing the attendant leave.

"Sid said we didn't have to worry about it. He's getting paid well," Laura said.

They all shuffled into seats around the room, nesting on the couch and chairs, still excitedly asking and answering questions, not necessarily in any order or in response to a specific prompt.

"How was your flight?"

"Where's the wedding going to be?"

"When do we get to meet him?"

"Is his friend with him?"

They had covered the basics of who and when through a series of text messages and short phone calls while Gina, Cookie, and Sherry were packing and getting ready for their flight and Laura was sitting in her Las Vegas hotel room waiting for their arrival.

"We're going to meet the guys later for cocktails. We'll do the spa in the morning, have brunch, then get dressed. The wedding's in the afternoon." Laura paused as she let the idea of her putting on a sparking white wedding gown flit through her mind again. She grinned as the same thought made its way through her friends and they each in turn smiled in surprise.

"Oh my god! What's your dress look like?" Gina shrieked.

"So you are getting married for real for real?" Cookie asked.

Laura flapped her hands, excited that someone finally asked. She had spent the day wandering the dress boutiques on her own, depending on the commission-bound opinions of the shop attendants. She missed the experience of having her friends help her pick out a dress. She worried that they, and Sid, wouldn't like it.

"Its real simple. It's long, of course, and straight, like a column. And it comes across one shoulder like this, with a sheer scarf-like piece attached here on this shoulder and on the bottom the same sheer material is kinda like a fishtail thing that trails on the floor a little bit." Laura waved her hands around. Pointing to her shoulders and feet and down her waist as she described the gown, to the ooh's and aah's of the other women. She was encouraged by their apparent approval so far.

"You are going to be beautiful," Cookie said.

"I hope so. I wanted something simple since, well, you know, it's so quick and it doesn't really seem like a Cinderella dress type thing. Plus, I wanted something I could dance in and have fun at the reception."

"You still didn't tell us about the engagement. I mean, the details. How'd he ask you?" Gina asked.

Laura leaned back on the couch, tucking her feet under her, and began describing the evening, starting with Sid picking her up from her apartment until they started packing for their flight.

"You're telling me you came out here with nothing. Just your purse. No toothbrush, no clothes, nothing?" Sherry asked. "And then went shopping when you landed?"

"Not exactly. I ran by the apartment, grabbed some clothes, and fed Lady." She turned to Gina. "But it was too late to come by your place."

"Are you kidding? You were running off to Vegas to get married! There is no 'too late to come by!' I don't believe you didn't come over."

Laura shrugged. "Anyway, I thought you might still be at Sherry's."

"How do you just up and leave in the middle of the night?" Cookie asked.

"They have their own plane. They called their pilot, we met him at the airport, and we were off. It was kinda exciting," Laura giggled.

"So, who has the money? Your guy or the other guy?" Sherry said.

"As it turns out, both of them. Sid has quite a number of clients of his own, about a third of their roster, actually."

"Then why the hell is he driving Michael around?" Gina asked.

"He likes to drive," Laura said, laughing. "I know. It's the damnedest thing. I asked him the same thing. He said he hates going to all the glitzy stuff and likes to keep a low profile."

"But what about for his own clients? He doesn't go to their events, parties, or whatever?"

"I don't know." Laura furrowed her brows and shook her head. "I guess I'll be finding out. As his wife instead of a working woman." She waved her hand in the air. "And speaking of his clients, this suite is a gift to you all from one of them."

"A gift? What kind of clients do they have?"

"The kind who spend a lot of money in Vegas."

"What do they look like? If this adoption thing doesn't go through, I might need a baby daddy of my own," Sherry said.

"You are going to adopt?" Laura asked.

Sherry nodded excitedly. "I sent in the applications a few days ago. You should've gotten the reference form in the mail already."

"We're supposed to say we think she'd be a good momma," Cookie instructed.

"Of course we will!" Laura said.

"What are you going to do with all those fine men always following you home?" Gina asked.

"What d'you mean? I can't have fine men follow me home if I'm a momma? Hmm, I might need to rethink this," Sherry joked.

Cookie shook her head. "That poor baby. Good thing she's going to have us around."

Gina stood by the bar inspecting the liquor. "Whose ready for drinks?" She raised bottles of tequila and vodka.

The other women raised their hands and screamed "Me!" like schoolchildren.

Laura went into the kitchen to get ice and glasses. Gina poured four shot glasses of tequila.

"Wow. We're starting out strong, huh?" Cookie said.

"When in Vegas, baby," Gina said, handing her a glass.

"To Laura. And retirement." Cookie raised her glass.

"To fine men who whisk you away to fulfill your dreams," Gina said.

"To love. Forever," Sherry said, obviously holding back tears.

"Thank you," Laura said, almost whispering.

They tapped their glasses in unison and drank their shot in one gulp. They slammed their glasses down and grimaced.

Gina blinked and cast her eyes around at her friends. "Another?"

The women glanced at each other then all eagerly nodded, laughing.

"You have any cards? One last time before you're an old married woman?" Cookie asked as Gina poured the next round.

Laura ran over to the dining table. "I don't think this place is short on cards." She ran back over with a pack of cards with a hole drilled through them.

Sherry grabbed the deck and shuffled. The other women seated themselves around the coffee table.

"We'll give you the honors, Almost-Mrs. Stone," Sherry said, sliding the cards towards Laura.

Laura cut the deck of cards and slid them back. "You guys, it really means a lot to me that you would come all the way out here for me. Thank you."

"Wouldn't miss it for the world, girl," Gina said.

As Sherry dealt the cards, each woman picked them up and started chastising or praising her for their cards.

"Now, I can do something with this," Cookie said.

Gina passed out the shot glasses again.

"To a good hand," Sherry said, raising her shot glass.

"Cheers!"

Music and Movies Enjoyed in Spades

You Can Have My Husband by Irma Morrison

Night Life by Tad Benoit

You're Nobody Til Somebody Loves You, recorded by Sam Cooke

Canon in D, Johan Pachelbel

Bridal Chorus, Richard Wagner

Ode to Joy, Ludwig van Beethoven

Second Time Around, recorded by Shalimar

Carmen Jones, Oscar Hammerstein II, Harry Kleiner, Otto Preminger, 1954

Porgy and Bess, Dubose Heyward and Dorothy Heyward; George Gershwin and Ira Gershwin; 1935

Casablanca, Julius J. Epstein, Philip G. Epstein, Howard Koch; 1942

ACKNOWLEDGMENTS

Life in Spades has been a long journey, one upon which I like to think I've grown and learned. It has been an effort of time and dedication, by not only me, but also my village of friends and family.

Before I can even name names, I must thank God for the blessing of opportunity, desire, and the love of writing.

And in no particular order: Thank you to my Wednesday Writing Group, Beth, Marian, Santi (and in memoriam, Susan), for reading all of these pages over and over - I cannot promise, but I will try to write shorter sentences and think of the character's feelings. To Naomi and the Sunday Writing Group at (the original) Fernhill for their support and sweet desserts whenever I showed up; one day I would love to have a labyrinth in my backyard, too. Thank you to the friends who I let in on my secret project, Renee, Quinetta, Shawn, Tereska, Melinda, and Brenda, for your encouragement, reading early and final drafts, and never asking "are you done yet?" To my editor, Donna, thank you for reading, for commenting, for all the red marks.

To my mother and father who always let me walk to the library and, although they did say, "Are you done yet?", knew I'd finish eventually – I love you. To my brother, thanks for nothing specific, but I couldn't go through this long list of people and leave out my first friend. My kids have endured my late night hours and distraction and have learned to cook their own breakfast, lunch, and dinner and I'm grateful that they have survived to the finish copy. To these four little parts of my heart, I've loved you since before the day you were born. And with unending, immeasurable gratitude - thank you to my Derrick for always believing, fully funding, and constantly caffeinating my efforts; I love you.

And to you dear reader, thank you for turning the first page on my first novel, for trusting me with your time and mind energy, for making my dream come true. Thank you.

Isaiah 40:31

ABOUT THE AUTHOR

Frances Frost is a graduate of the University of Delaware (where she began playing Spades) and Wake Forest University (where she began drinking coffee). She would be quite content living on a sunny beach overlooking the ocean and drinking sweet tea, but until then, she lives in Silver Spring, Maryland with her husband, their four children, and their rescued Lab/Shepherd.

Connect with Frances online at www.francesfrost.com, on Facebook at Frances Frost – Author, and on Twitter @FrancesFrost.

Made in the USA
Charleston, SC
22 February 2014